"Where's your baby?"

"She's with Rae." Laurel poked a thumb over her shoulder. "I, uh, wanted to talk with you alone."

Sucking in a breath, Wes said, "Laurel, about that night—"

"Sarah-Jane is your daughter." Shoulders squared, she looked him in the eye.

As his brain struggled to comprehend what she'd said, he simply stood there for the longest time. He must not have heard her correctly. "I'm sorry. Could you please say that again?"

"No, I'm the one who should be sorry." Shaking her head, she looked suddenly frazzled. "I'm saying this all wrong." She drew in a deep breath and exhaled before tentatively meeting his gaze. "My daughter, Sarah-Jane. She's your daughter, too."

Thoughts of the frightened infant he'd tried to console yesterday sifted through his mind, stealing his own breath. With all the chaos, it wasn't like he'd really gotten a good look at her. And then at the restaurant, he'd been so focused on Laurel. "You mean your—my—" He stared at the woman before him, laboring to comprehend. "We have a daughter?"

It took **Mindy Obenhaus** forty years to figure out what she wanted to do when she grew up. But once God called her to write, she never looked back. She's passionate about touching readers with biblical truths in an entertaining, and sometimes adventurous, manner. Mindy lives in Texas with her husband and kids. When she's not writing, she enjoys cooking and spending time with her grandchildren. Find out more at mindyobenhaus.com.

Margaret Daley, an award-winning author of ninety books (five million sold worldwide), has been married for over forty years and is a firm believer in romance and love. When she isn't traveling, she's writing love stories, often with a suspense thread, and corralling her three cats, who think they rule her household. To find out more about Margaret, visit her website at margaretdaley.com.

A Father's Promise

Mindy Obenhaus

&

A Baby
for the Rancher

USA TODAY Bestselling Author

Margaret Daley

LOVE INSPIRED

INSPIRATIONAL ROMANCE

LOVE INSPIRED®
INSPIRATIONAL ROMANCE

ISBN-13: 978-1-335-46279-4

A Father's Promise and A Baby for the Rancher

Copyright © 2021 by Harlequin Books S.A.

A Father's Promise
First published in 2020. This edition published in 2021.
Copyright © 2020 by Melinda Obenhaus

A Baby for the Rancher
First published in 2016. This edition published in 2021.
Copyright © 2016 by Harlequin Books S.A.

Special thanks and acknowledgment are given to Margaret Daley for their contribution to the Lone Star Cowboy League miniseries.

Recycling programs for this product may not exist in your area.

This edition published by arrangement with Harlequin Books S.A.

For questions and comments about the quality of this book, please contact us at CustomerService@Harlequin.com.

Love Inspired
22 Adelaide St. West, 40th Floor
Toronto, Ontario M5H 4E3, Canada
www.Harlequin.com

Printed in U.S.A.

CONTENTS

A FATHER'S PROMISE

Mindy Obenhaus

For Your glory, Lord.

Acknowledgments

To my husband, Richard, you are the greatest gift
I could have been given. Thank you for loving me
despite my warts, supporting my dreams and
encouraging me to fly. I love you.

To Stacey Collier, thank you for all of your input
and allowing me to utilize both your career
and your house for this story.

Every good gift and every perfect gift is from above, and cometh down from the Father of lights, with whom is no variableness, neither shadow of turning.
—*James* 1:17

Chapter One

Laurel Donovan had no reason to be anxious. After all, she'd been contemplating this day for weeks. Yet as she maneuvered her fourteen-month-old daughter's stroller along the tree-lined streets of Bliss, Texas, Monday morning, she couldn't shake the feeling that something was about to happen. Something big and life altering.

Breathing in the crisp spring air, she cast the ridiculous notion aside and listened to Sarah-Jane's happy babble instead. Laurel had never expected to be a mother, because to do that one typically had a husband, and Laurel wasn't prone to romantic relationships. Matter of fact, they scared her. She'd had enough rejection for one lifetime.

Unfortunately, she was human. And two years ago, the only faith Laurel had was in herself. But Sarah-Jane was a perfect example of what the pastor always said about God turning even our biggest mistakes into our greatest blessings.

Being a single mother wasn't easy, though, especially when you had no family. And while Laurel's grandmama Corwin had cared for her after her mother passed away, Sarah-Jane would have no one if anything happened to Laurel. She'd become a ward of the state, and Laurel couldn't let that happen. She had to do everything in her power to make sure her daughter would be taken care of by people who loved her, whether she was with Laurel or not.

The late-April sun warmed her face as they approached Rae's Fresh Start Café in the heart of Bliss. The breakfast, brunch, lunch and specialty coffee place had become a daily staple for Laurel even before Sarah-Jane was born. No one but Rae could make decaf coffee taste as good as its caffeinated counterpart. And the amazing brew had sustained Laurel throughout her pregnancy.

Her daily visits had also provided her with three of the best friends she'd ever known. Thanks to Bliss's ad campaign to lure younger folks to the aging town, Rae, Laurel, Paisley and Christa had arrived within a year or so of each other, all looking for a new beginning. And not a one of them had ever judged Laurel for being single and pregnant. Instead, they'd embraced her, walking with her through her pregnancy and beyond. Which was why Laurel had insisted on this morning's meeting.

"G'morning, Laurel." Rusty Hoffman paused his sidewalk sweeping in front of the Bliss State Bank building. "And how is Miss Sarah-Jane doing today?" Leaning against his broom, the stocky middle-aged man with brown eyes and black hair peppered with a hint of gray smiled down at her daughter.

"Happy to be outside and on the move." Laurel pulled back the stroller's canopy to reveal a wide-eyed Sarah-Jane staring blankly at the man.

"Well, I can't say as I blame her," Rusty said. "The Lord's given us a fine morning."

"He sure has." Laurel took in the cloudless sky, grateful that God had led her to Bliss, where bankers weren't too pretentious to sweep sidewalks and streets were built around two-hundred-year-old live oaks. Back in Dallas, they would have cut down the trees in the name of progress.

Laurel coaxed Sarah-Jane to wave goodbye before continuing across the street to the courthouse square. Brick buildings dating back to the late 1800s still lined two of the streets surrounding the square. Some had been painted in bright colors indicative of the Victorian era, while others remained in their natural state. Their charm, coupled with the ancient live oaks and magnolia trees that encircled the courthouse, were what had initially drawn Laurel to Bliss nearly two years ago.

After the death of her grandmother, a pregnant Laurel had been eager for a new beginning. Someplace she could call home. And like the town motto said, everyone needed a little Bliss in their life.

Her daughter chattered and clapped her hands as they moved off the curb to cross to the café.

"You know where we're going, don't you, baby?"

Laurel had been pondering her daughter's future almost from the moment she'd discovered she was pregnant. And after a recent bout with the flu had Laurel envisioning all sorts of horrible scenarios, she was determined to take steps to ensure her daughter would be cared for. So today was the day she was finally going to ask her friends, all of whom were single, if they would consent to raise Sarah-Jane in the event anything happened to Laurel.

Halfway across the street, the hairs on the back of her neck suddenly prickled, and a sense of dread had her feeling as though she was moving in slow motion. Then, out of the corner of her eye, she saw a red Crown Victoria rounding the corner. Another glance had her realizing it was coming straight toward her and Sarah-Jane.

She tried to run but couldn't seem to make her feet move.

"Look out!" she heard someone yell.

Fear tried to close in around her, but she couldn't allow that to happen. She had to protect Sarah-Jane.

As the car inched closer, she propelled Sarah-Jane toward the curb. The stroller had barely left her grip when the vehicle struck Laurel. She rolled onto the hood of the car, only to tumble off again when the driver slammed on the brakes a split second later.

Air whooshed out of Laurel's lungs. She lay there, momentarily dazed, the shaded asphalt cool beneath her fingers and cheek. Her breath returning, she mentally evaluated her body parts, then opened her eyes and lifted her head to see people gathering on the sidewalk.

A man with dark hair knelt beside Sarah-Jane's stroller, concern marring his handsome features as he talked to her. And he—looked familiar.

The car door creaked open then, and a woman shrieked. "I killed her! Oh, help me, I killed her!"

Laurel knew that voice just as well as she knew the vehicle that had struck her. She rolled onto her back as the ninety-three-year-old shuffled alongside her in tennis shoes that were whiter than her hair.

"Mildred Godwin!" Laurel ground out the name.

"Ack!" The woman, who was so small she could

barely see over the steering wheel, pressed a hand to her chest. "You're alive! Thank You, Lord! You're alive!"

"Mildred—" Laurel sat up, grateful the nonagenarian had a tendency to drive at a snail's pace. Though in the moment, it had seemed much faster. "—you know you're not supposed to be driving. How on earth did you get your keys? I thought your son locked them up."

"Ladies—" Drenda Kleinschmidt, owner of Bliss Antiques and Gifts and wife of Laurel's pastor, helped Laurel to her feet "—are y'all all right?" Concern filled her blue eyes as they assessed Laurel.

"I'm fine." Laurel continued to wait for Mildred to respond about the keys.

Instead, the older woman pursed her bright red lips together and looked away, suddenly sheepish.

"Mildred…?" Hands on her hips, Laurel was not about to budge until she had an answer. The woman was a hazard to the entire town.

"I—" The woman lifted one slight shoulder. "I had an extra set." She glanced at Laurel. "And my Muffy was hungry for some of that special cat food. You know, the kind they advertise being served in a crystal bowl. Muffy loves it so much, and I was all out."

"That is *no* excuse. You could have killed me *and* my daughter." The mere thought had Laurel pressing a hand to her stomach.

A siren wailed in the distance, and Mildred's hazel eyes went wide. "They're comin' for me." She latched onto Laurel's arm with a death grip. "Please, don't let them take me. I'd never survive in jail. I'm just an old woman. Please."

"Mildred, I highly doubt you're going to jail."

Drenda, the epitome of a sweet spirit, wrapped an arm around the older woman and patted her frail shoulder.

Confident that Drenda could handle things from here, Laurel pried Mildred's surprisingly strong fingers from her forearm and started toward her daughter. Her steps slowed when she, again, laid eyes on the man beside the stroller.

The sun glinted off his dark hair, and when he looked up, his gaze locked with Laurel's.

Her breath caught in her throat. Why would he be in Bliss?

She absently rubbed her left temple. Maybe she'd hit her head, after all, because she was obviously seeing things.

"Laurel!" From out of nowhere, Christa and Paisley rushed toward her.

Behind them, Rae paused beside the guy at the stroller. She said something to him, then proceeded to unhook Sarah-Jane and pick her up.

"We just heard what happened." Christa's hazel eyes surveyed Laurel from head to toe. "Are you all right?"

"Yes, I just—"

Things grew quieter as the police cruiser pulled up and that obnoxious siren finally stopped.

All of this chaos was making Laurel's head swim. "I just want to see my daughter."

Paisley slid an arm around Laurel's waist. "Of course, you do, darlin'. Come on."

Christa took the lead, parting the group of onlookers who'd gathered. Unlike in Dallas, things like this didn't happen in Bliss every day, so, naturally, all of the commotion had garnered quite a crowd. By noon, the entire town would likely know what had happened, and the story would, no doubt, make the county's weekly newspaper.

"Sarah-Jane is perfectly fine." Rae bounced the child in her arms. "All the commotion had her fretting for a little bit, but that's all."

Laurel reached for her daughter and hugged her to her chest. "Thank You, God for protecting my baby." Tears spilled onto her cheeks of their own volition. Burying her face in Sarah-Jane's neck, Laurel breathed in her sweet fragrance. Everything really was all right.

Except…

Lifting her head, she looked at Rae. "Where'd that guy go?"

"What guy?" Rae tucked a strand of brown hair that had escaped her messy-yet-oh-so-cute updo behind her ear.

"The one by Sarah-Jane's stroller. Tall, dark hair. You were talking to him."

"Oh, that was my brother Wesley." She waved a hand. "He went back to the café to keep an eye on things for me. He was actually on his way to the hardware store when he saw you push Sarah-Jane out of harm's way, and, thankfully, stop the stroller before it hit the curb. That was some quick thinking on your part, by the way."

"Wait." Laurel was growing more confused by the second. "That was your brother?"

"Wesley, yes. I told you he was coming to visit." Rae's brow puckered. "Are you sure you're okay, Laurel?"

Wesley was Wes? If that was the case, then, no, she wasn't okay. Because, unbeknownst to him, Wes was Sarah-Jane's father.

* * *

Wes Bishop needed purpose in his life, and since he'd retired from the navy two years ago, that purpose had been lacking. He wanted to help others, to serve—which was why he'd contracted with the Servant's Heart relief organization to manage their shelter construction program in Iraq. From the moment his friend and former master chief, Eddie Perkins, had presented him with the opportunity, Wes had been all in. Yet when he agreed to come to Bliss, Texas, to visit his sister, Rae, before leaving, he never imagined he'd find his past. A past void of any kind of relationship with God. Yet even though they'd known each other for only one fleeting night that never should have happened, Laurel had left an indelible impression on his heart.

He pushed through the door of his sister's café, still not quite believing what he'd just witnessed. Everything had been such a blur out on the street. The stroller, the car, the woman. Yet while he thought he recognized the voice, he hadn't been certain until Laurel's gray-green eyes collided with his. In that moment, his heart stopped as unwanted emotions washed over him. Excitement, regret... Yeah, he had enough regrets to choke a horse.

Giving himself a stern shake, he decided to keep busy by gathering up the half dozen white coffee cups that had been abandoned when the local ranchers got wind of the accident and rushed outside. According to Rae, her Fresh Start Café was their morning gathering place. Check the herd, then head to Rae's for coffee, discussions of the weather and the latest gossip.

Well, they would have had plenty to gossip about if Wes had acted on his instincts. When he realized it had, indeed, been Laurel out there, the urge to protect and comfort her had surged within him. Instead, he tamped it down and forced himself to return to the café.

Thankfully, she was all right. And her spunk was, obviously, still intact. The way she laid into that elderly driver… He couldn't help chuckling. Not that he didn't feel for the old lady, but it sounded like she had it coming.

Moving behind the antique wooden counter, a remnant of the building's former life as a saloon, he set the cups into the gray bin designated for dirty dishes, guilt tightening his gut. He should *not* have been so happy to see Laurel. Not only was he moving overseas in just a little under a month, but the woman had a baby. Something that had initially given him pause. But the little thing couldn't have been more than nine or ten months old. Not that he knew much about babies. Still, there was probably a husband in the mix. Yet that didn't stop Wes's pulse from kicking up a notch when Laurel's gaze met his. The same way it had the first time he'd met the confident—not to mention beautiful—accountant with long, honey-blond hair and eyes that sparkled when she laughed.

He grabbed a rag and returned to the now-empty table to wipe it down. He was glad Laurel had found happiness and no longer had to face the world alone. A husband, family… It fit her. And Wes respected her too much to ever reveal their secret.

Still, it might be best if he steered clear of her to prevent any awkward situations. Besides, he didn't need the onslaught of what-ifs that were bound to invade his thoughts. There were no what-ifs in his world. He'd determined a long time ago that he would never marry, never have a family… Those were things he didn't deserve. Not after what he'd done to his parents.

The café door opened, and Wes jerked his head up to see Rae and two other women bustling Laurel and her baby inside. Just what he didn't need.

"Paisley, pull out that chair for her," Rae instructed the tall redhead. "Laurel, I want you to sit down so we can make sure you truly are all right."

Still holding her child, Laurel complied. "For the thousandth time, I'm fine."

A woman with chin-length brown hair pulled out the industrial-style metal chair beside Laurel and sat down. "You say that now, but sometimes things are delayed."

"Christa is right." The other woman with long red hair and a syrupy southern drawl peered down at Laurel. "Even if there's nothing evident now, don't be surprised if you wake up sore tomorrow."

Smiling, Laurel reached for the redhead's hand. "I appreciate y'all's concern. I don't know what I'd do without you."

"All right, what can I get for everyone?" While Rae awaited orders from her three friends, Wes glanced from the exposed brick wall opposite him to the wooden stairway at the back of the space. If he were quick enough, he might be able to escape to Rae's apartment upstairs.

Just then, Rae turned his way. "Wesley, come over here. I'd like you to meet my friends."

Great.

Rag in hand, he sucked in a breath and forced his feet to move across the old wooden floor to join his sister at the front of the restaurant.

"Ladies." Nodding, he skimmed the three faces

around the square table, trying not to linger on Laurel's. Still, he couldn't help noticing that she did seem a little shaken up, amplifying his concern for her well-being.

"So, Rae's little brother finally comes to Bliss." The cute no-nonsense woman with short brown hair smiled up at him. "Christa Slocum."

"Christa owns Bliss Hardware," Rae added.

"That's good to know." He rocked back on the heels of his cowboy boots. "I'm going to be helping Rae make a few changes to her apartment—painting, removing a wall—so I'll likely be paying you a visit."

"Well, I appreciate the business." Her hazel eyes drifted to Rae. "Almost as much as your sister will appreciate having that kitchen wall gone."

"That's for sure." Rae motioned toward the next woman. "This statuesque redhead is Paisley Wainwright."

More reserved than Christa, the stylishly dressed woman simply smiled. "It's nice to meet you, Wesley."

"You'll find folks lining up down here every day for some of Paisley's decadent desserts," Rae added.

Wes looked from his sister to Paisley. "Sounds like I'm in the right place, then."

"And our heroic Mama Bear—" Rae set her hands atop her friend's shoulders "—is none other than the fabulous Laurel Donovan." His doting sister reached for the baby's cheek. "Along with Sarah-Jane."

Laurel Donovan. At least he got her last name this time. Albeit her married name.

"Laurel." He nodded, not knowing what else to say. He certainly wasn't about to let on that they already knew each other.

She tilted her head, sending her long hair spilling

over one shoulder as she peered up at him curiously. "It really is you." The corners of her mouth lifted ever so slightly. "For a second, I thought I'd hit my head."

"It's a wonder you didn't." A nervous smile played at his lips. "Things could have turned out a lot worse."

A baffled Rae looked from Wes to Laurel and back again. "Um, why am I getting the feeling you two already know each other?"

Laurel continued to watch him with those eyes that lived in his memory, as though studying every nuance of his face. "We met in Las Vegas a couple of years ago. We were both there for conventions."

Something Wes would never forget. Watching a frustrated Laurel plop down on the edge of that hotel pool in her all-business dress had been intriguing, to say the least.

Turning away, she continued. "I mistook him for a waiter and asked him to bring me a soda."

"Oh no." Christa put a hand to her mouth to cover a chuckle.

"In her defense," he said, "we were at the pool, and I was wearing shorts and a polo shirt. So it was an honest mistake."

"It wasn't until I attempted to pay him that I realized he was another guest." The color in her cheeks heightened, just the way it had that day by the pool.

Again, she looked up at him through those thick lashes he remembered so well. "I never dreamed that Rae's Wesley could be the Wes I'd met that day."

Hands perched on her hips, Rae continued to watch the two of them. "Yeah. Talk about a small world."

Laurel averted her attention then. "You'll have to excuse me. I think I need to go home."

"I don't like the sound of that." The redhead promptly stood to help Laurel. "Are you feeling ill? Why don't you let me drive you?"

"Just a little shaky. But a ride would be wonderful." Standing, Laurel held her daughter close and offered a weak smile. "I think I just need to rest for a little bit."

"Let me get that stroller for you." The one who owned the hardware store shot to her feet and started for the door. "Pop the hatch on your SUV, Paise." She waved toward Rae. "I'm going to head on back to the store." She continued outside, pausing to grab the stroller that now sat in front of the window and aimed it toward a silver SUV.

"Are you sure you don't want to go to the hospital and get checked out?" Rae visually scrutinized her friend.

"No, I'm okay. Just a little overwhelmed, that's all." Laurel glanced from Rae to Wes. "Thank you for coming to my daughter's aid out there."

"No problem. I'm glad I was there to help." Watching her, he wondered if she really was okay. Like her friends had said, sometimes things were delayed. She was obviously still dazed.

No wonder Rae watched her like a hawk—or an overprotective mother—until Laurel again gave Rae her full attention. "I just need to rest for a little while."

"All right, sweetie." Rae gave her a quick hug and kissed the baby's cheek. "I'll be by to check on you later."

Rae watched as the women emptied out of the shop before moving behind the counter to start a fresh pot of coffee. "I guess you and Laurel didn't stay in touch, huh?"

"Why would we?" He pushed in the vacated chairs

and gave the table a quick wipe with the rag he still held. "We only met once." Not that he wouldn't have contacted her if he'd known how. Then again, with all of his regrets about that night, it was probably just as well.

"When was that again? That the two of you met."

"A couple of years ago." He started toward the counter. "Not long after I got out of the navy."

"I see." As the coffee brewed, filling the café with its enticing aroma, Rae narrowed a scrutinizing gaze on him.

"Why are you looking at me so weird?" Moving behind the counter, he handed her the rag.

One capable shoulder lifted. "No reason." She leaned her backside against the counter. "So, did anything happen after you and Laurel met, or did you just shake hands?"

He shot her a warning look. "We had dinner, all right." They were two lonely people in need of a friend. Laurel was easy to talk to. She made him smile. And stirred feelings in him that he'd never had problems ignoring before. "There's no need to worry, though. I promise not to reveal anything to her husband."

"Husband?" Rae's expression morphed into something incredulous. "Laurel isn't married."

"She's not?" Why did that bit of information spark hope inside him? "I mean, I just assumed, with the baby and all."

Rae continued to study him. "And all, huh?"

"What is up with you? Why are you giving me the third—?" Wagging a finger toward her, he dared a step closer. "Wait a minute. I don't know what kind of cockamamie ideas are rolling around that pretty head of yours, Rae, but if you're trying to play matchmaker, you can just forget it. Yes, Laurel is a sweet person. And, yes, she's attractive, but I'm not interested in a relationship with Laurel or anyone else."

Scowling, she crossed her arms over her chest. "Because you think you're not worthy of a family."

"No, because I know I'm not. Now, if you'll excuse me—" he turned and started toward the stairs "—I have a wall to destroy."

Chapter Two

Wes was in Bliss. And he was Rae's brother?

Wearing a path in the hardwood floors of her living room while Sarah-Jane played with her toys in her portable playard later that afternoon, Laurel was still trying to wrap her brain around the whole thing. All she knew was that coming face-to-face with Sarah-Jane's father was something she'd never anticipated. Not in her wildest dreams. After all, when they'd met, she was living in Dallas and he was somewhere in Florida. Yet they both ended up in the tiny town of Bliss?

Only God could orchestrate something that crazy.

But why now? Laurel had built a life for herself and her daughter, one grounded in faith. Besides, according to Rae, Wes was moving to Iraq. Not only was that another country, it was the other side of the world. How unfair would it be to tell him he had a child when he was leaving?

Shaking her head, she dropped her face in her hands. Why had she allowed that night to happen? But then, if it hadn't, she wouldn't have Sarah-Jane. And she couldn't imagine life without her.

She turned as her daughter picked up a small baby doll and hugged it against her chest. Laurel had two regrets in her life—never having known her father, and the knowledge that Sarah-Jane would never know hers. Now Laurel suddenly had the power to change Sarah-Jane's life, to give her daughter the one thing Laurel never had. What would that look like, though? How would bringing Wes into their lives impact Sarah-Jane? She could only assume he was a Christian, given that he was working for a mission organization, but what if he wasn't?

A knock at the front door startled her. She pressed the pause button on her thoughts and crossed to the wooden door with arched glass at the top, her steps halting beside the pale blue sofa. What if it was Wes? What if he'd figured out that Sarah-Jane was his daughter? What would he say? What would he do?

Easy, it's not like you did anything wrong. You didn't deliberately keep his daughter from him.

True. Actually, there was a part of her that had always wanted to tell him. He was a nice guy. And even if he wasn't interested in being a father, he deserved the opportunity to decide that for himself.

But she hadn't been able to do that because she'd known nothing about him. Including his last name.

Another knock had her sucking in a deep breath. She took one more step and tugged open the antique door, relieved when she saw Rae on the other side.

"I came to check on you." Her curious friend held out a foam box. "And bring you some nourishment. Beef tips and noodles were today's special."

"My favorite." Smiling, Laurel swung the door wide. "You didn't have to do that."

"Yes, I did." Rae handed the food box to Laurel as she passed. "Because I need to talk to you."

Laurel's insides tightened. Rae was her best friend, and a rather perceptive one at that.

Closing the door, she went into the adjoining kitchen for a fork and napkin, while Rae scooped up Sarah-Jane.

"You should know, I grilled my brother after you left."

Laurel's steps slowed as she approached the living room. "About what?"

"Your previous meeting." Rae eased into the off-white glider near the large front window. "Look, I'm just going to cut to the chase." She settled the baby in her lap before fixing her blue eyes on Laurel. "And I'm asking this as a friend, not Wesley's sister."

Laurel nodded, her body tense as she prepared herself for— Wait, what was she preparing for? This was Rae. Her best friend. Laurel had nothing to be afraid of.

"Is my brother Sarah-Jane's father?"

Okay, so she wasn't afraid. However, she was definitely uncomfortable. Not once had she ever spoken to anyone about Sarah-Jane's father or the night she met him. All this time, she'd kept it inside. Wes was different than most guys. He hadn't gone out of his way to try to impress her or pretended to be someone he wasn't. Perhaps it was because he was a little older. Whatever it was, she'd often wished she could see him again.

But now that she had…

Nodding, she set the foam container on the small, marble-topped peninsula that separated the cooking space from the dining area. "He figured it out, didn't he?"

"Are you kidding?" Rae puffed out a laugh. "My

brother assumed you were married." She smoothed a hand over Sarah-Jane's soft blond hair, lifting a shoulder. "However, after seeing him and Sarah-Jane together, and narrowing down the timeline, I had my suspicions."

Laurel released a sigh and made her way to the couch. "Her eyes definitely belong to Wes." She dropped onto the cushions, a tangled web of emotions closing in around her.

Rae turned the child to face her. "They sure do." She kissed Sarah-Jane's chubby cheek. "You sweet baby. No wonder you've always held such a special place in my heart. I truly am your aunt." The woman who had been Laurel's birthing coach and was there to see Sarah-Jane take her first breath swiped away a tear.

After a long moment, she addressed Laurel again. Yet while her gaze remained warm, it held an ache that hadn't been there before. "Are you planning to tell him?"

"Yes." Grabbing the Pray More, Worry Less pillow beside her, Laurel hugged it against her middle. "Not that it's going to be easy. I mean, 'Congratulations, you're a father' isn't something you just blurt out." Chagrin washed over her, and her insides twisted. "It wasn't like I was trying to hide it from him or anything. I mean, I had no way to get in touch with him. We didn't exchange numbers or any personal information." Just the way she'd wanted it. That was, until she was gone.

Head cocked, Rae watched her intently. "Laurel, are you afraid?"

She looked at her friend. "Not afraid—more like ashamed. That night. That wasn't like me. But my grandmother had just died, I was fed up with my boss and, I guess, I just…needed someone. Some*thing*. And I think Wes did, too."

"Yeah, you needed Jesus." Rae was nothing if not blunt, though her tone held no accusation.

"I know that now. And it was in large part because of that night that I finally found Him. As I struggled to come to terms with the reality of my pregnancy, all those things my grandmother had tried to instill in me finally sank in. For years, I kept thinking I could rely on myself. Boy, was I wrong." Restless, she tossed the pillow aside and resumed her pacing. Rubbing her suddenly chilled arms, she said, "What if Wes doesn't believe me or thinks I expect money or something? What if he doesn't want to be a part of Sarah-Jane's life?"

"I guess we'll cross that bridge when we come to it." Standing, Rae settled Sarah-Jane back among her toys. "Though, honestly, I suspect Wesley is going to have a tough time coming to terms with this new reality."

"Who wouldn't? Wes has built a life for himself. Now he's about to learn he has a child."

Rae looked uncharacteristically distressed as she approached. "Laurel, my brother believes that he doesn't deserve a family."

She halted her pacing and stared at her friend. "Why?"

"Because he blames himself for our parents' deaths."

"But that was years ago, right?"

"Between Wesley's sophomore and junior year of high school."

The ache that filled Laurel's heart was unexpected. "Oh, Rae. That is so sad."

"It really is. Because it's a lie that has dictated the rest of his life." Rae eyed the baby once more. "Maybe

God can use Sarah-Jane to free him from that lie." She sniffed. "If you need me to watch her so you and Wesley can talk, just let me know."

"I will." Laurel hugged her friend, knowing she had a monumental task before her—one that couldn't wait. She could only pray that God would give her the words Wes needed to hear.

Wes did not want to think about Laurel. Yet no matter how hard he tried, she kept invading his brain. How did she end up in Bliss? Why wasn't she married? And why had she left so suddenly yesterday? Was it because of the accident, like she said, or had his presence made her uncomfortable?

His heart twisted. While Wes would never regret meeting Laurel, he'd definitely been humbled by his actions. He'd always tried to be an honorable man. For two years he'd wished for the opportunity to apologize to Laurel. Now God had actually presented him with that chance. But when? How? At least knowing she wasn't married might make things a little easier.

"Why are you torturing yourself, Bishop?" Standing in Rae's living room, he swung his sledgehammer, knocking another two-by-four free. He'd been up before the sun, removing the Sheetrock from the wall that separated Rae's kitchen and living spaces. Something he'd intended to do yesterday, but by the time he'd moved the furniture from the living room into the spare bedroom and covered the kitchen cupboards, appliances and countertops with plastic sheeting, it had been too late to get started.

He tossed the wood aside. "You don't do relationships, remember?" Even if he did, he was moving to Iraq, so what would be the point?

As the ranchers finished their coffee downstairs at the café and headed back to their herds, Wes freed the last two-by-four and stood back to admire the new wide-open space. The living area sat at the front of the building, where a wall of windows overlooked the courthouse square and infused the space with natural light. The kitchen, however, had been closed off, leaving it dark, cramped and uninviting.

But not anymore.

"So much better." Fortunately, the exposed brick walls had remained untouched everywhere except for the bedrooms, and the original wood floor still spread throughout the entire apartment.

Now his sister had an updated space that was bright and inviting. At least, she would once he got things cleaned up and added a fresh coat of paint, anyway. After all he'd put Rae through, it was the least he could do. There weren't many young women who would put their college experience on hold to raise their sixteen-year-old brother. Yet that's exactly what Rae had done.

Regret hit him in the gut, the way it did every time he thought about Craig and Jane Bishop's untimely deaths. He was the reason they'd been on the road that night. All because he hadn't thought before he acted.

With a shake of his head, he willed the unpleasant thoughts aside, knowing he had a job to do. He'd promised Rae he'd get this done, and he would not disappoint her.

Trading his hammer for the shovel he'd tucked into the corner beside one of the windows, he started scooping up the pieces of Sheetrock that littered the tarp-covered floor as memories of Laurel again pelted his brain. At this rate, he was going to drive himself nuts. He may as well just find out where she lived and apologize already.

"Hello?" A woman's voice echoed from the back of the apartment where the stairs were located.

"In here." Turning, he saw Laurel pushing past the plastic sheeting he'd hung over the hallway to prevent dust from leaching into the bedrooms. And his heart skidded to a stop.

While she was dressed in a simple T-shirt and jeans, her honey-blond waves swayed around her shoulders as she tiptoed through the chunks of Sheetrock that littered the kitchen floor. She sure was beautiful, but it was more than her physical appearance that made her so attractive. In their brief time together, Wes had been privileged to get a glimpse of Laurel's heart—a heart that yearned to love and be loved. So, given that she had a child, he was kind of surprised she wasn't married. Unless she was divorced, or the father was a deadbeat. Both were things that happened far too often in today's world.

"Hi." She stopped in front of him, biting her lip as though she was nervous.

He longed to say something profound, something that would put her at ease, yet all he managed was "How are you feeling?"

"I'm good." She poked at a broken piece of drywall with the toe of her short boot. "Maybe a little achy, like Paisley said." Peering up at him, she added, "But don't tell Rae I said that."

Fully aware of just how bossy his sister could be, he couldn't help smiling. "Your secret is safe with me.

That is, so long as you promise to let someone know if it gets any worse."

"I promise."

He knew what he should say next. That he should apologize and let her know that, by the grace of God, he was a different man now. Yet instead of saying that, all he could muster was "Where's your baby?"

"She's with Rae." She poked a thumb over her shoulder. "I, uh, wanted to talk with you alone."

Alone? Sounded more like God was giving him a kick in the pants, urging him to say those things Wes had rehearsed in his head for the past two years each and every time Laurel crossed his mind.

Sucking in a breath, he said, "Laurel, about that night—"

"Sarah-Jane is your daughter." Shoulders squared, she looked him in the eye.

As his brain struggled to comprehend what she'd said, he simply stood there for the longest time, leaning against his shovel. He must not have heard her correctly. "I'm sorry. Could you, please, say that again?"

"No, I'm the one who should be sorry." Shaking her head, she looked suddenly frazzled. "I'm saying this all wrong." She drew in a deep breath and exhaled before tentatively meeting his gaze. "My daughter, Sarah-Jane. She's your daughter, too."

Thoughts of the frightened infant he'd tried to console yesterday sifted through his mind, stealing his breath. "But, she's so…small."

"She's fourteen months old."

That old, huh? With all the chaos, it wasn't like he'd really gotten a good look at her. And then at the restaurant, he'd been so focused on Laurel. "So you mean your—my—" He stared at the woman before him, laboring to comprehend. "We have a daughter?"

Laurel nodded. "I would have told you, but I didn't have any idea how to contact you." Her words seemed to tumble out.

Half wandering, half stumbling, he dragged the shovel behind him as he moved toward the windows and lowered himself onto the top of a five-gallon paint bucket. He had a child? How could this be? Okay, he knew how, but why? *God, You know I never wanted a family. I don't* deserve *a family.*

Laurel remained where she was, her hands clasped tightly together. "Look, I know this is a shock. And to be clear, I don't expect anything from you. I just—" one shoulder lifted ever so slightly "—thought you should know."

Half a dozen feet away, Wes just sat there, feeling as though he'd been run over by a tank. What did he do now? He didn't know the first thing about babies or being a father.

Thoughts of his own dad and the intensity with which he'd loved Wes and Rae played across his mind. Was Wes capable of that kind of love? What if he let his child down? What if he failed?

"Can I see her?" He stood, sending the shovel crashing to the floor in the process, and wondered why he'd asked that particular question. Babies had never interested him.

This is your *baby.*

Maybe so, but he wasn't sure he was worthy of her.

A slight smile touched Laurel's lips as she nodded. "She's downstairs."

He followed her out of the apartment and to the café,

uncertainty knotting his entire being. Laurel had a baby. His baby. And he hadn't been there to help.

The realization made him wince. Laurel was alone. A single mom. That couldn't have been easy, and it was his fault. He'd been weak, and Laurel had been forced to live with the consequences.

The café was empty when they reached the bottom step, something he was more than a little grateful for. Rae held the child—his child, he reminded himself—in her arms and was dancing among the tables, swaying to and fro.

She stopped when she saw them. "Aw, who's that, Sarah-Jane?"

The beautiful little girl with hair the color of honey and the same blue eyes as his smiled as her mother approached. A moment later, that smile shifted to him, flipping his insides and his entire world upside down.

Mesmerized, he continued across the wooden floor, not knowing what to do or say.

When he stopped beside the pair, Sarah-Jane reached out her hand and offered him her cookie. How could he refuse? He pretended to nibble. "Yummy, thank you."

The grinning child seemed pleased with herself. Or him. And for some reason, that mattered. Because despite having just met her, he was smitten with this pint-size charmer. Sarah-Jane was everything good in this world—innocence, pure and simple. Her only expectation was that he would accept the cookie she'd offered. In exchange, he'd offered up his heart, and she'd snatched it without question.

And in that moment, Wes knew his life had been changed forever.

Chapter Three

Laurel had told Wes that Sarah-Jane was his daughter. Now what?

She'd hung around the café for a while, allowing Wes and Sarah-Jane to interact until Sarah-Jane got fussy and the lunch crowd started to move in. Still, Laurel would never forget the look of complete awe on Wes's face when Sarah-Jane offered him her cookie. It was a moment Laurel would cherish forever.

Where did they go from here, though? And how would Wes feel further down the road when the euphoria wore off and reality set in? Sarah-Jane had been on her best, cutest behavior this morning. However, she wasn't afraid to voice her displeasure of things, either. What would Wes think when he witnessed an all-out hissy fit?

The more Laurel thought about it, the clearer it was becoming that she hadn't thought this scenario all the way through. Instead she'd been so enamored with the thought of Sarah-Jane knowing her father, not to mention overwhelmed by yesterday's hullabaloo, that she'd simply acted.

Because you thought you were doing what was best for your daughter.

"Mah!" Sarah-Jane hollered from her playard in the living room.

Laurel looked up from the potatoes she was peeling for dinner and peered over the kitchen counter to see her daughter holding on to the side of the hexagon-shaped enclosure with one hand and a set of toy keys in the other. "What is it, baby?" At fourteen months, Sarah-Jane had mastered pulling up, but she had yet to show any real interest in walking.

Her daughter jabbered, a smile teasing at her slobber-covered lips as she watched Laurel.

"Let me get these potatoes on to boil and I'll come play with you, okay?"

The meat loaf Drenda had dropped off earlier was already in the oven, and it smelled divine. However, the green beans and corn she'd brought to accompany it weren't quite enough to properly round out this meal. With the stress of these last two days, Laurel needed some serious comfort food. And potatoes always topped that list. Mashed, with lots of butter and a little bit of cream cheese, just the way Grandmama used to make them. Besides, they were Sarah-Jane's favorite, too.

Her daughter chattered some more before plopping down on her bottom and moving on to the next toy.

Laurel felt beyond blessed to have so many people thinking of her. Last night's dinner had been courtesy of one of the ladies at church, and another friend had dropped by with a big ol' chocolate sheet cake. Laurel was almost ashamed to admit that she'd polished off nearly a third of it already. Perhaps she should consider putting the rest of it in the freezer. Less tempting that way.

She swapped her peeler for a knife and cut the russets into chunks, her thoughts drifting back to Wes. She'd done the right thing in telling him about Sarah-Jane. Unfortunately, the move had left her with a lot of uncertainty, too. Something she hadn't anticipated.

Suddenly there were so many things to consider. Things that had never crossed her mind before. Until yesterday, she'd never expected to see Wes again. Throw in the fact that he would be leaving soon to go to Iraq, and she wasn't quite sure how to approach this whole situation.

She tossed the potatoes into a pot and set it under the faucet to fill. Did Wes even want a role in his daughter's life? And how would Laurel handle that? After all, until now, it had only been her and Sarah-Jane. Yes, she wanted Sarah-Jane to know her father, but that would also mean entrusting her daughter to someone who was, for all practical purposes, a stranger. It wasn't just about him getting to know Sarah-Jane. He and Laurel had to get to know one another, too. They'd need to discuss expectations and boundaries.

There you go assuming again.

She huffed out a frustrated breath, set the pot atop the stove and turned the burner on high. The only way she'd know for sure about Wes's intentions was to ask him. And that might be even more difficult than telling him he had a daughter, because she'd probably come off sounding like a dictator.

The jingle of her phone had her glancing toward the counter, where Irma's name appeared on the screen. Despite the fact that Irma was old enough to be Laurel's grandmother, the two had forged a friendship. Probably because Irma reminded Laurel of her grandmother. "Hi, Irma."

"Hello, Laurel. How are you feeling this afternoon?" Irma had called early this morning to check on her, too. Laurel had been tied up in knots about telling Wes and definitely hadn't been herself, which was probably why Irma called again.

"About five pounds heavier, thanks to that cake of yours. What were you thinking, bringing me the entire pan?"

Irma chuckled. "Baking for others brings me joy." As with many of the women in the church, cooking was Irma's love language.

"I know, but it's just me and Sarah-Jane. And I'm trying to be a responsible parent and teach my daughter good eating habits."

"What about your eating habits?"

Laurel frowned. "Completely uncontrolled when it comes to your chocolate sheet cake. I don't know what your secret is, Irma, but it's no wonder everyone clamors for it at church potlucks."

"Well, I'm pleased to hear you're doing better. You gave us all quite a scare."

"Don't blame me. It was Mildred Godwin—"

A knock sounded at the door.

"Irma, I'll have to call you back. Someone's here."

Ending the call, she quickly added a lid to the pot before padding to the door in her bare feet. "Who do you suppose it is, baby?" Perhaps someone was bringing more food.

Sarah-Jane abandoned the shape sorter she was playing with and pulled herself up again, seemingly as curious as Laurel.

When Laurel opened the door, she didn't have to pretend her surprise at seeing Wes on her front porch. And, man, did he look good. The torn, dust-covered jeans and paint-spattered T-shirt he'd had on earlier had been replaced with a pair of stone-colored trousers and a nicely fitted dark gray polo.

"Wes." Laurel clung to the doorknob as though it was a lifeline. If nothing else, at least it would prevent her from falling when her knees decided to buckle.

"May I come in?"

"Yes, of course." Closing the door behind him, she did her best to calm her suddenly flailing nerves. *Stop acting like a teenager.*

With blue eyes so much like his daughter's, he took in the living room of her little bungalow. "Nice place you've got here."

"Thank you." She instinctively scanned the room, grateful it wasn't too much of a mess. "It's a work in progress." With Drenda's help, she was slowly but surely getting things to look the way she wanted.

Still standing behind the couch, Laurel could tell the instant Wes's gaze landed on Sarah-Jane. The sudden smile that spread across his face warmed her heart.

"Is she walking?"

She watched her daughter. "No, not yet. But we're getting close."

Shifting from one foot to the next, Wes ran a hand through his damp dark hair as he faced Laurel. "Look, I have a ton of things I want to say to you, but I guess the biggest thing is, I'm sorry. I allowed one of the best nights of my life to be tarnished with regret because of my actions." His focus again drifted to Sarah-Jane. "And altered your life forever."

Laurel blinked, feeling rather dumbfounded. Yet while there was a lot to unpack in Wes's statement, there was only one thing he needed to know. "My life wasn't just altered, Wes, it was transformed. Learning I was pregnant brought me to my knees, and that was precisely where God needed me to be."

One corner of his mouth lifted as he regarded her. "Interesting. Because God used that night to set me on a different path, too. A path that led me not only to Him, but back to you." He cast a glance toward his daughter. "And Sarah-Jane." Drawing in a deep breath, he again met Laurel's gaze. "There's just one problem."

She studied his face. The square jawline, the barely there stubble that darkened his chin. "What's that?"

"I can't be Sarah-Jane's father."

The words had Laurel recoiling as indignation sparked to life, simmering in her gut. And here she'd thought he was different. That he might actually care that he had a daughter. But he was no different than Jimmy Donovan, the man who had turned his back on Laurel when she was just a baby.

Crossing her arms over her chest, she felt her nostrils flare. "Can't or won't?" In that instant, the reality of his words smacked her upside the head. Was he insinuating someone else had fathered her daughter?

That simmer turned into a full, rolling boil. "Wait a minute, are you calling me a liar?"

Wes had stood face-to-face with the enemy on the streets of Iraq and numerous other places around the globe, yet even then he hadn't been shaking in his boots the way he was right now.

Frustration coursed through every fiber of his being as he searched for a way to redeem himself. He had never been good at expressing his feelings. And his propensity for making a mess of things was on full display.

Laurel continued to glare at him, and he couldn't say he blamed her. The way his words had come out would have offended anyone.

"Not that it really matters." Her chin jutted out defiantly. "Sarah-Jane and I have done just fine without you."

He was certain the comment was intended to hurt him, and she had definitely succeeded.

Lowering his head, he desperately tried to gather his thoughts and prayed he would verbalize them correctly. "Laurel, I—"

"Why don't you just leave?" She brushed past him and he could almost feel the steam radiating from her as she yanked the door open again. "I can't believe you would come into *my* house and insult me in front of *my* daughter." When she looked up at him, he saw fire flaring in her gray-green eyes. "And to think, all this time I thought you were an honorable man."

Wes scrubbed a hand over his face. He was going about this all wrong. "Laurel, please." Standing in front of the open door, he stared down at her, imploring her to listen to what he was really trying to convey. "I was not trying to insult you. The only thing I'm guilty of is shoving my big, fat foot in my mouth."

"Congratulations, it seems to fit quite well." With one hand still on the door, she sneered.

He sucked in a breath. *Lord, help me out here.*

Please? "Look, communication is not my forte, all right. What I was trying to tell you is that I don't know *how* to be a father." His heart thundered against his ribs until Laurel's stance became slightly less rigid. "I never imagined I would ever have a child of my own. I don't know how to care for a baby, or even how to change a diaper. I'm clueless, Laurel."

"Well, welcome to the club." She eased the door closed, and he breathed a sigh of relief. "You know, Sarah-Jane didn't come with an owner's manual telling me what I was supposed to do. Before she was born, I'd never been around babies, either. See that bookcase over there?" She pointed to the wall at the far end of the living room and the shelves flanking the empty fireplace. "It's full of nothing but baby books, so feel free to borrow—"

A loud hissing sound echoed from the other room, and a look of panic flitted across Laurel's face.

"Oh no!" She rushed into the adjacent kitchen.

The urgency in her voice had him following her into the small, partially open space with white cabinets and marble countertops.

Pausing near the short peninsula that separated the cooking area from the dining, he traced the sound to a pot that was boiling over on the stove. Yet, for some reason, Laurel just stood there watching it, as though she wasn't quite sure what to do.

Moving past her, he turned off the electric burner, then grabbed a towel from the counter and transferred the pot to another burner as Sarah-Jane whimpered from the living room. Poor kid. Between this chaos and their elevated voices, they'd probably scared her.

"You get Sarah-Jane," he said, "and I'll take care of this."

While Laurel stepped away to see about their daughter, Wes grabbed a dishcloth from the stainless steel sink and started wiping up the starchy water that now covered a good portion of the stovetop.

"You don't have to do that."

He turned to find Laurel standing behind him, holding Sarah-Jane. And all eyes seemed to be on him. "It's only fair since I was the one who distracted you."

Her expression was much softer now. "You know, being a parent isn't so different than what you're doing right now."

He rinsed the cloth under the faucet. "What do you mean?" Turning off the water, he resumed his wiping.

"You saw a problem, and you addressed it."

Though he tried to follow her train of thought, he was still lost. "What does that have to do with parenting?"

"Well, when a diaper is dirty or wet, you change it. And trust me, there is a slight trick to that, but it's not rocket science."

Setting the rag beside the sink, he leaned against the countertop, unable to stop the soft chuckle that escaped his lips.

"When Sarah-Jane is hungry, I feed her. When she's thirsty, I give her a drink."

Sarah-Jane turned from watching him then and looked at her mother, all the while rubbing one hand in a rough circular motion over her chest.

"What is she doing?" Wes had never seen that before.

"She must have heard me say *drink*." Laurel gave the child her full attention. "Do you want a drink?"

There went the rubbing again.

"This—" looking at Wes, Laurel mimicked Sarah-Jane's motion "—is sign language for *please*. She's telling me she wants a drink."

"No kidding." He'd never heard of an infant using sign language. "How did you figure that out?"

"I taught her."

She moved Sarah-Jane onto the opposite hip. "This means *more*." She tapped the tips of her fingers on both hands together. "And this means *all finished*." She awkwardly waved her hands in the air.

Sarah-Jane must have been amused by her mother's actions, because she giggled and bounced.

"All right, baby. I will get you your drink." Laurel slid Sarah-Jane into her high chair beside the table before retrieving a lidded cup from beside the sink. "Of course, there are a few other things that are imperative to parenting." She moved to the refrigerator and filled the cup from the dispenser while Wes's entire body tensed.

He just knew these were going to be the things he'd never be able to live up to. "And they are…?"

"Well, trusting God to get you through it all is number one." She twisted the cup's lid on. "Because there will be days when nothing goes right."

Rubbing the back of his neck, he said, "Hmm, I can't relate to that at all."

She laughed then, the sound putting him at ease. "And then there's love." She continued toward the table and handed the cup to Sarah-Jane. "Kids need to know that they're loved unconditionally. That no matter what they do, there's someone who still cares and they can count on to be there for them."

"Like your grandmother was for you."

Turning, Laurel looked up at him, blinking. "I can't believe you remembered that."

"There's not much you said that night that I don't remember." Probably because he'd replayed it over and over in his mind for the past two years.

A smile tilted the corners of her pretty lips. "You were a good listener, and that was what I needed."

"I guess I was blessed to be in the right place at the right time."

She nodded. "Now here we are again."

"With a daughter, no less." He winked at the precious child they'd unwittingly created. "So, where do we go from here?"

"I've been wondering the same thing." She leaned against the French door that led outside. "I suppose we could discuss our predicament over supper. That is, if you'd care to join us?" Laurel glanced toward the stove. "Assuming it's still edible."

His gaze drifted to the beautiful child he'd never known existed. "I think I'd like that very much."

Chapter Four

Laurel woke up Wednesday morning feeling a sense of relief. Wes hadn't rejected her daughter. However, his text message at eight thirty this morning, asking her to meet him at the café, had her wondering if he'd changed his mind. His message had been short and to the point. Not nearly as friendly and forthcoming as the man who'd had dinner with them last night.

While they enjoyed Drenda's meal, Wes had asked question after question about Laurel's pregnancy, Sarah-Jane's birth and her first year, as though wanting to know everything he'd missed. He'd even broached the topic of child support, saying he wanted to care for his daughter in every way, including financially. Later, he and Sarah-Jane had played while Laurel cleaned up the kitchen. All in all, it had been an unexpected yet pleasant evening. For all practical purposes, Wes was the same friendly, easygoing guy she'd met two years ago.

But his text was different. Strictly business. So, as she parked Sarah-Jane's stroller outside Rae's place, anxiety pulsed through Laurel's veins. If Wes turned his back on her daughter, she would…

A sigh escaped. She would go on just the way she had before he came to Bliss. Except she'd be carrying the ache of her daughter's rejection right along with her own.

The morning air was already warm as she lifted Sarah-Jane out of the stroller. They continued inside, where the enticing aroma of coffee beckoned Laurel toward the counter.

"Good morning." Rae smiled as they approached. "And how is the most adorable little girl ever doing this morning?" She leaned across the counter to give Sarah-Jane a kiss.

The child grinned and reached for Rae, who readily obliged.

"Happy to see you, apparently." Laurel glanced around the restaurant, noting four ranchers still nursing their morning ritual and a couple of other folks enjoying a late breakfast, but no Wes.

"He's upstairs." Rae's perceptiveness really bugged Laurel sometimes. It was almost impossible to get anything past her. "Told me to let you know he'd be down in a minute."

"Good." Laurel faced her friend. "Just enough time for you to whip up my usual."

"You got it." She passed Sarah-Jane back to Laurel. "Better check out Paisley's pastry offerings before they're all gone."

"Ah…" As Rae set to work on Laurel's Americano, Laurel shifted her attention to the chalkboard that hung on the exposed brick wall behind the counter, ignoring the fact that she had almost half of a chocolate sheet cake at home. "Strawberry cupcakes, oatmeal-cranberry cookies and her Blissfully chocolate brownies."

All grab-and-go treats. Just the way folks liked it. They could stop in, pick up some goodies and be on their way.

"Laurel, I'm glad you're here."

She turned as Wes approached, wearing a gray Navy Seabees T-shirt and faded jeans, her desire for sweets waning. The pucker in his brow and the laptop in his hands said this meeting was, indeed, strictly business—at least until his gaze shifted to Sarah-Jane and a smile blossomed.

"May I?" He set his computer on a nearby table and held out his hands as though he wanted to hold her daughter.

"Uh, yeah. Sure." She didn't have to coax Sarah-Jane, who readily leaned into her father's waiting arms, a sight Laurel found as endearing as she did troubling. "What did you want to talk about?"

Her phone rang before Wes had a chance to respond. She tugged it from the back pocket of her jeans and looked at the screen. Irma. She must be calling to check on Laurel again. Yet as she started to tuck the phone away, something urged her to answer.

"Excuse me," she said before swiping her finger across the screen and placing the phone to her ear. "Irma, can I call—"

"Help me, Laurel! My house is caving in!" Laurel's worries about Wes faded into oblivion as her heart skidded to a stop. Irma wasn't one to make mountains out of molehills.

"What do you mean?"

"I was in the kitchen washing up my breakfast dishes when I heard this horrible crash. The upstairs bathroom is in my family room."

Concern coursed through Laurel. "Irma, are you all right?"

"I'm not hurt, but I have no idea what to do." Irma's normally calm voice trembled. "There's water everywhere, and it just keeps coming. I'm outside on the porch, and I don't know what to do. I need help, Laurel."

"Don't worry, Irma." Her gaze drifted to Wes. "I'll be right there."

Ending the call, she relayed the information to Rae and Wes.

"That's a pretty old house." Rae handed Laurel her drink before glancing toward her brother. "There's no telling what could have happened."

"How does a house just cave in?" Laurel inadvertently deferred to Wes, knowing he was in the construction business.

"I won't know until I see it. But I suggest we get over there now." Moving around the counter, he passed Sarah-Jane into his sister's waiting arms.

Uncertainty had Laurel lifting a brow. "We?"

"Yes. I want to make sure things are structurally sound before you step inside that house."

The impact of his words wound around her heart. It was as though he cared about her.

"Come on." He started toward the door while Laurel simply watched him.

At least, until Rae motioned for her to follow. "I'll keep Sarah-Jane, you just go."

"We'll take my truck." Wes pointed toward the charcoal-gray pickup as she raced outside under the mid-morning sun.

"Considering I walked, that seems like the best option." She hopped into the passenger seat as he climbed behind the wheel.

Starting the engine, he glanced her way. "Not to mention that I have tools. And with water spewing, it's likely I'll need them."

"Good point."

After checking to make sure things were clear behind him, he backed into the street. "Which way am I going?"

"Make a right at the corner." She watched him across the cab. The determined set of his jaw. Wes was one of those guys who approached things sensibly, without getting wound up. Unflappable, as her grandmother used to say. But Laurel had certainly thrown him for a loop when she told him about Sarah-Jane. And, as far as she was concerned, the jury was still out on the outcome of that situation. "Take another right up here."

It wasn't that she didn't want to trust Wes, she just wasn't sure she could. Just like she couldn't trust her mother whenever she promised that things would be different. Aside from Rae, Christa and Paisley, Grandmama was the only person who'd ever earned Laurel's trust. She had been the one constant in Laurel's life. When Brenda and Jimmy Donovan turned their backs on Laurel, Grandmama was always there with a warm embrace and fresh-baked cookies.

Two minutes later, Wes eased the truck to a stop in front of the pale yellow Victorian with white trim where Irma paced the graceful front porch, wringing her hands.

Wes let go a low whistle. "That's a lot of house for one person."

Laurel reached for the truck's door handle. "Maybe,

but it's been in her family for over a hundred years." She slid onto the curb, tossing the door shut behind her before rushing up the walk to her friend.

The eighty-year-old, who had more spunk than most people half her age, met Laurel at the top step, her brown eyes brimming with unshed tears. "My beautiful house is ruined, Laurel."

Unable to stop herself, Laurel wrapped her arms around the petite, silver-haired woman. "I'm so sorry." She held her for a moment before releasing her. "I brought a friend with me, Irma." Motioning Wes closer, she continued. "This is Rae's brother, Wes. He knows all about construction, so he's going to take a look at things."

Irma lifted her wire-framed glasses to wipe her eyes. "Oh, thank you."

"Laurel says there's a water leak."

Depositing the tissue into the pocket of her baggy pants, Irma said, "More like Old Faithful. Go see for yourself." She poked an arthritic thumb toward the door. "The whole house is liable to float away."

Wes nodded. "I'm on it."

"Irma, you wait out here," said Laurel. "I'm going to go with him."

"All right, but you be careful. I wouldn't want to be responsible for leaving that sweet little girl of yours without a mama."

Laurel's heart cinched as she inched toward the screen door. Could it really be that bad?

Wes waited at the entrance. "I told you I wanted to check things out first."

"And I said I'm going with you." Fists firmly planted on her hips, she dared him to argue.

After a long moment, he creaked open the screen door and moved into the dimly lit entry hall.

"The family room is straight ahead." Following close behind, she pointed beyond the staircase that hugged the wall to their right.

"I can hear the water."

"Me, too." Glancing to her left, she found the parlor and all of its vintage furnishings untouched. "That's probably not good, though, is it?"

"No, it's not." He stopped halfway down the hall, aiming a flashlight she didn't even know he had at the longleaf pine floors. "And it's already made it this far."

Looking down, she noted the water spreading in every direction. Her anxiety heightened as Wes picked up his pace and continued into the family room.

As her eyes adjusted, a sick feeling seized Laurel's stomach. "Oh no." She turned this way and that, trying to take it all in. "This is horrible." Bits of plaster and shards of wood floated over the floor, and a commode lay shattered in front of the antique bookcase that lined one wall. Not far from the toilet, a claw-foot tub lay on its side in front of the window. Meanwhile, water poured from the second floor like a faucet.

Wes aimed his light overhead, moving it right and left. "Pipes are broken. I gotta get this water turned off." Doing an about-face, he urged Laurel back toward the front door and onto the porch. "Irma, where's your water cutoff?" He was already down the steps.

"Somewhere between the sidewalk and street." She pointed toward the narrow section of grass. "It's bad, isn't it?" Laurel could feel Irma watching her as Wes retrieved something from his truck.

"It certainly is a mess." She turned her attention to

the older woman. "One that seems insurmountable at the moment, but, I promise, we'll get it figured out."

Irma shook her head, her expression pinched. "I guess this is what insurance is for."

Laurel couldn't stop the laugh that puffed out. "Yes, this is definitely what insurance is for." Slipping an arm around the woman's shoulders, she pondered all that would need to be done. Starting with a call to Irma's insurance agent and a water-removal company. She was also going to need a place to stay until the repairs were complete. No telling how long that would to take, so Laurel should probably contact the church, too.

A breeze swept over her bare arms as she gave her friend a squeeze. "Don't you worry, Irma. I'm going to see to it everything is taken care of." If only she could say that about her situation with Wes. She still had no clue why he'd asked to meet with her this morning. And, at the moment, it didn't look like she was going to find out anytime soon.

Between Laurel's accident and the debacle at Irma's, Wes was starting to see that his vision of Bliss being a quiet little town was sorely misguided. Then again, if his time in the military had taught him anything, it was that there were struggles everywhere.

After turning off the water, he'd gone back inside Irma's supersize Victorian home to try and get a better handle on not only the cause of the collapse, but the extent of the damage. Unfortunately, the water only added insult to injury. Water had a way of reaching in, around and under everything in its wake. And the longer it remained, the more damage it would do. He suspected that at least half of the books on the shelves, many of which looked as though they could be antiques, were already damaged.

Now, while Laurel remained outside with Irma, making phone calls, Wes stood atop an old wooden ladder he'd found in Irma's garage, staring into the gaping hole in the ceiling with the aid of his flashlight and trying to figure out what had happened. Houses didn't simply collapse. There had to be a cause.

He studied the joists, in particular. While most appeared perfectly normal, other areas looked as though they'd suffered extensive water damage, making him wonder if there could have been a leak somewhere. Given the condition of the wood, it must have gone on for a long period of time. It was likely a slow leak no one had ever noticed because the wood soaked it up.

As he continued his examination, he noted the mud-like coating following the grain of the wood. A sure sign of termites. He swept the area with his flashlight. Between the water leak and the termites, the integrity of the wood must have deteriorated significantly. And when you've got something as heavy as a cast-iron tub and a toilet full of water, well, it's only a matter of time.

The good news, if one wanted to call it that, was that repairs shouldn't take more than a few weeks. No matter what, though, the first thing they had to do was get all of this water out of here so things could start drying out.

"Wes?" Laurel's voice echoed down the entry hall.

He stepped off the ladder into a puddle and met her as she entered the room with Irma and two men. "Right here."

"Oh, good." Motioning to the first man, she said, "This is Dwight Chastain, Irma's insurance agent."

Wes couldn't hide his surprise. "You got here quick."

The burly fellow with light brown hair and a goatee chuckled. "My office is only a couple of blocks away. And when there's water involved, we certainly don't want to waste any time."

"That's for sure." Wes eyed the other man clad in jeans, a chambray work shirt and a dirty ball cap.

"Mason Krebbs." Younger and leaner than the first guy, Mason held out his hand and Wes took hold. "I'm a local contractor."

"Mason was at the office when Laurel called," said Dwight. "Thought it might be a good idea to bring him along. You know, get a contractor's perspective."

"Actually, Wes is a construction manager," Laurel was quick to point out, obviously unimpressed by Mason's credentials. Slipping her hands into the pockets of her skinny jeans, she added, "He's also Rae's brother, and he's been on top of things since we got here."

While Laurel remained beside a distressed Irma, the two men moved deeper into the room, scanning floor to ceiling.

"Were you able to find anything?" Dwight craned his neck, eyeing the six-foot chasm overhead.

"Yes, sir. There are definite signs of both water and termite damage."

Mason climbed the ladder to do his own investigation. "While I'm not necessarily one to disagree, Wes, termites and water damage don't usually result in something this drastic. I mean, wouldn't ol' Irma have noticed some weak areas in the bathroom floor or seen water spots on the ceiling?"

"I don't recall any water spots," said Irma. "And I'm in here all the time. I don't usually go upstairs, though.

Only if I'm going to have company, and then it's only long enough to change out the sheets and the towels."

"From the looks of things, this has been going on for a prolonged period of time," added Wes. "We're talking years."

"Yeah, I can definitely see termite trails," Mason conceded. "They sure made a mess of this old wood." Stepping down, he addressed the agent. "The remaining wood will need to be treated for termites before new joists are added. Then the whole bathroom will likely need to be redone, the ceiling down here replaced and whatever damage was done by all this water fixed." He motioned toward the floor. "May need some new Sheetrock, carpet... And if we don't get this wood dried out right away—"

"Hello?" A woman's voice filtered down the hall.

"That's Christa." Laurel hurried to the doorway and waved her friend in.

Sporting jeans and a bright blue Bliss Hardware T-shirt, Christa stepped into the room. "Whoa. What a mess." She hugged Irma. "I'm so glad you weren't hurt." Releasing the older woman, she took in the other faces. "Wes." She nodded. "Dwight. Mason." Her attention returned to Laurel. "I've got a shop vac in the truck, along with three air movers. And there are at least three other people who will also be dropping off shop vacs. The faster you can get things dried out—"

"Her insurance will pay to bring in a water-removal company from the city."

Christa looked at Dwight very matter-of-factly. "That's fine and dandy, but they're not here now. And by the time they are, we could have most of this water squared away. The longer it sits, the more damage it's going to do."

Wes found himself slightly amused by the exchange. "Like you said, Dwight, when there's water involved, we don't want to waste any time. However, we will need a dumpster of some sort, because once you've gathered whatever information you need—taken pictures and such—we'll start emptying all of the impacted rooms, and we're going to need someplace to put this debris."

"That's right. And my guys and I could probably get started on the reconstruction in a week or so." Mason appeared to study the situation. "Shouldn't take us more than six weeks to get 'er done."

"Six weeks?" Wes, Laurel, Christa and Irma said collectively.

Wes knew it wouldn't take anywhere near that long. Especially with a crew. Sounded like Mason was just trying to pad his wallet by stretching things out.

"Where on earth will I stay?" Irma's bottom lip trembled.

Wes hated that this guy was trying to take advantage of her. He wasn't even sympathetic.

"We could try for five," Mason countered. "It's hard to tell until you get going on things, though." He smiled as if everything was just peachy. "I'll drop off an estimate later."

The man had barely even assessed things.

"Right now, though, I need to run. Can't keep the little woman waiting."

No, but he sure didn't have any problem making Irma wait.

Mason touched the brim of his ball cap before strutting back down the hallway. "Howdy, Ms. Parsons."

"Mason, you'd better not be here to take advantage of my friend."

Laurel and Wes exchanged a look as a white-haired woman eased into the room with a large multicolored purse dangling from one elbow.

She tsked several times as she took in the room. "This is quite a mess."

"It's more than a mess, Joyce," said Irma. "It's horrible. They're telling me I can't stay here."

"Well, of course you can't. Anyone can see that. So you may as well pack your bags."

"I don't know where I'd go." Irma continued to wring her hands.

"I have three empty bedrooms. You just take your pick."

"Oh, that is so sweet of you, Joyce."

"No, it's just one problem solved. Now—" the woman waved an arm "—what are you going to do about the rest of this?" Her gaze landed on Wes then, and narrowed. "Who are you?"

He cleared his throat. This woman was more intimidating than most of his superiors in the navy. "Wes Bishop, ma'am."

She moved closer, not the least bit intimidated by the standing water. "You're not from around here, are you?"

"No, ma'am. Rae Girard is my sister. I'm here to visit her."

"How come the two of you have different last names?"

"Rae was married. Her ex-husband was a Girard."

She peered up at him through her bifocals. "I like Rae. And I like that you say *ma'am*. You have manners."

He found himself standing at attention. "Twenty years in the military will do that."

"What branch?"

"Navy."

"My husband served in the navy." Taking a step back, she continued to size him up. "I'm Joyce Parsons." She smiled then. "You know I'm messing with you, right?"

"Yes, ma'am." Okay, he may have fibbed a little on that one.

"Good." She looked at the others now. "So, what's the plan, Dwight?"

The man appeared more than a little nervous. "We're going to get Irma fixed up just as quick as we can."

"And how quick is quick?" Hands clasped, Joyce waited.

"Mason said six weeks."

"Mason doesn't know his head from a hole in the ground," she said. "He's an opportunist."

Wes was liking Joyce more all the time. And he was certain that Mason's bid would be ridiculously high. Yet while Wes was more than capable of handling the job himself, he was only in Bliss for three weeks. He might be able to do it, providing any subs he'd need— termite people, a plumber and flooring people—were available. Worst-case scenario, he could do the flooring himself, but a licensed plumber was a must. As was the termite treatment. And if any of these wood floors had to be refinished, that would take time Wes didn't have.

He looked at Irma again, his heart going out to the poor woman. *Lord, what should I do? I'd hate to let her down.*

What if he wasn't able to finish the job before it was time to leave? Then again, if the downstairs was complete, Irma could still move back in. And if he had folks lined up to handle those final details of plumbing and flooring, perhaps Laurel could oversee them.

He caught Laurel's eye. "Could I see you outside for a minute?"

She nodded, then looked at the others. "Excuse us, please."

They moved down the hall, through the screen door, across the porch and onto the lawn before he said anything.

"I want to help Irma." He shoved a hand through his hair, eyeing the sprawling tree branches overhead. "I'm just not sure I can."

"Wes, you don't have six weeks."

"No, but I have almost three. And the job shouldn't take any more than that." He looked her in the eye. "It just depends on how long it takes us to get things out of here and dry before the work can begin."

"I've already contacted the church. The pastor is out of town, but Roxanne, the church secretary, is lining up volunteers to help us move stuff right now. I told her I would oversee things."

Wes couldn't help frowning. "Why would you do that? What about Sarah-Jane?"

"Because Irma is my friend, and her kids all live out of state. Besides—" she lifted a shoulder "—she reminds me of my grandmother."

Given that Laurel had thought the world of her grandmother, that statement explained a lot.

"As far as Sarah-Jane, I'll figure it out. Rae's keeping her for the rest of today, though."

He stared at the determined woman whose long hair was now pulled back into a ponytail. "You're familiar with the area. Could you help me find a plumber and termite people?"

"Sure. Brandt Hefley goes to my church. He's a plumber. And he has a big heart. I have no doubt he'd be more than happy to help Irma."

"Good."

She watched him. "So, are you going to extend the offer?"

He couldn't help grinning. "Well, as my old buddy Eddie would say, some things are worth fighting for." He nodded toward the house. "I can't let that Mason fellow take advantage of her."

"Who's Eddie?"

"He was my boss in the navy, then I went to work for him again after I retired. He's the reason I was in Vegas. But he also got me back into the church and become my spiritual mentor. He's the one who recruited me for Servant's Heart."

"Sounds like a very special friend."

"I'm blessed to know him."

Laurel's expression softened, a smile teasing at her pretty lips. "Shall we go see what Irma thinks then?"

He motioned toward the house. "Lead the way."

Chapter Five

Laurel had never ached so much in her entire life. Here she'd thought lugging a fourteen-month-old around was keeping her fit. She was obviously delusional, because removing everything from the impacted areas at Irma's had taken its toll. The debris, furniture, books… It had taken a group effort to move that old cast-iron tub out to the front porch.

God had provided them with lots of help, though. No fewer than ten people had chipped in throughout the day, helping them empty the affected rooms and move as much as they could into the parlor and dining room. Since water had leached into Irma's bedroom, soaking the carpet, it had been lifted and the pad cut away. Wes had removed all of the baseboards so no water would be trapped. Then, with the aid of shop vacs, they'd managed to rid the place of any standing water. By the time the water-removal crew Dwight had insisted they call in arrived from the city, all they had to do was add a few more air movers to the mix to speed up the drying process.

The only break they'd taken was when a group of

women from the church brought them all King Ranch casserole and peach cobbler for dinner. Considering Wes and Laurel had skipped lunch, that meal was a welcome treat.

Now, as Laurel sat in the cab of Wes's pickup with a country music station playing low on the radio, she was almost too numb to think. All she wanted was to get home, hug her baby girl and crawl into bed. Then she recalled how her day had started—with Wes asking her to come to the café to discuss something. She still didn't know what that something was. And while she was appreciative for all Wes had done today—his take-charge attitude and offering to do the repairs to Irma's house—Laurel's heart was weighted down by that one unknown. Because it could determine the course of her daughter's future.

The sun was low on the western horizon, shading the tree-lined streets of Bliss as they made their way back to Laurel's where Rae waited with Sarah-Jane. Looking at Wes, Laurel couldn't help noticing that he didn't appear anywhere near as exhausted as she felt. Then again, he was probably used to this sort of stuff. Honestly, she was glad he'd been with her today. She might know how to organize a work crew, but she knew nothing about building.

Knowing they were only minutes away from her house, she mustered her courage. "What was it you wanted to talk to me about this morning?"

He shook his head and gave a slight smile. "So much has happened since then, I'd almost forgotten."

Great. While she couldn't say she'd stressed all day, she had stressed. And yet he'd forgotten?

"I guess it'll have to wait now, but I wanted to get

the information for your bank account so I can set up an automatic transfer. That way, money for Sarah-Jane will come to you every month and I won't have to worry about missing a payment."

While she appreciated his commitment, "You couldn't have asked me that over the phone?"

"I didn't think you'd want to put that kind information in a text."

"No, but you could have called." Unless he was one of those people who hated talking on the phone.

"Actually, in this world of identity theft and cyber-security, I thought you might prefer to type in the info yourself. That's why I had my laptop at the café."

She could see his point, but still. "This is exactly why texting isn't necessarily the best means of communication. If you'd have just called and told me all of that, you could have saved me a lot of worry."

His brow creased. "Why were you worried?"

"Because I thought—" Thankfully she caught herself before revealing the truth—that she was afraid he'd reject Sarah-Jane the way her father had rejected her. "I just was, that's all." They pulled up to her house then, and she hopped out before he could question her any further.

Unfortunately, he followed her. Never mind that they'd spent almost the whole day together. Not that it was Laurel he wanted to be with. He wanted to see Sarah-Jane.

She gave herself a stern shake. She was getting cranky. And after all Wes had done, he didn't deserve to be the object of her ire.

However, the moment she stepped through the back

door and saw Sarah-Jane crawling toward her, her spirits lifted.

"There's my girl." Lifting her daughter to her, she kissed her cheek. "I missed you so much."

"Laurel?"

She turned to see Wes standing in front of the kitchen sink.

"You might want to wash up first."

"Ew, yes, you're right." She held Sarah-Jane at arm's length. "Here, Rae. There's no telling what could be all over me."

Rae took hold of the child. "Were you able to accomplish much?"

Laurel had contacted Rae earlier in the day, letting her know the initial assessment. "I think so." She smiled at Sarah-Jane. "I'll be right back, baby." She joined Wes at the sink, his nearness making it difficult to think. He smelled like hard work and peaches, so she was grateful when he started filling his sister in.

"I was impressed at how many people volunteered to help." He soaped up his hands before scrubbing his forearms, a move Laurel mimicked over the adjoining bowl. "Not just to pitch in and help with the grunt work, but to bring food, bottled water, shop vacs. I've not seen that kind of generosity outside of the military."

"Only one of the reasons we love Bliss so much, right, Laurel?"

"You know it, Rae." She scrubbed her fingernails. "But even I was surprised. And I'm glad Wes was there. Especially when Mason Krebbs showed up."

"Looking for business, no doubt." Rae stood near the table now. "He's such a creep."

Wes shook the excess water off his hands before

reaching for a towel. "I don't care for people who try to take advantage of others' misfortune."

Laurel ran her arm under the faucet to remove the soap. "It was obvious that Wes was far more knowledgeable than Mason." Yet he didn't demean Mason. Wes simply stated the facts, even when he had a bad feeling about the guy.

"That's because Wes has built more things in more places than Mason could even imagine."

Laurel accepted the towel from Wes and quickly wiped her hands. "Now where's that baby?"

A smiling Sarah-Jane practically threw herself into Laurel's arms. Yet as Wes took a seat in one of the four dining chairs, her daughter squirmed to get down.

"Okay, fine." No sooner had she set Sarah-Jane on the floor than she took off toward Wes and pulled up on his legs.

"Well, hello there." He picked her up, his face lighting with amusement.

That left Laurel in a quandary. She'd always regretted not having a father and hated that Sarah-Jane was facing that same fate. But seeing her little girl in Wes's arms brought out Laurel's instinct to protect. Could Wes be trusted? Sure, he was Rae's brother, not to mention former military…

"Shall we go play?" Still holding her daughter, Wes stood and went into the living room where Sarah-Jane's toys were.

Okay, so Laurel wasn't concerned about her daughter's physical safety, but there were plenty of other things to worry about. Such as betrayal. What if Wes decided he didn't want to be involved in his daughter's life? Simply paying child support did not make someone a parent. What if he walked away like Laurel's father had? Did she even want him around Sarah-Jane until she had the answers to those questions?

Rae nudged her elbow and pointed to Wes and Sarah-Jane. "I think that's about the sweetest thing I've ever seen."

Wes lay on the floor, grinning at Sarah-Jane, while she sat atop his belly, laughing as though she'd conquered a mountain.

The sight was, indeed, heartwarming, and one Laurel had longed for all her life. Yet from where she stood now, it was also one of the scariest.

"Two weeks?" Phone pressed against his ear just after nine the next morning, Wes paced Irma's front porch, his frustration mounting. It had been bad enough that the other four pest-control companies he'd contacted had said a week to ten days. But two weeks? He didn't have that kind of time. Yet even after he'd explained the situation, they all acted as though coming to Bliss was the equivalent of going to another country. "Sorry, that's not going to work. Thank you."

Ending the call, he dropped into one of two rocking chairs that had been relegated to a corner because of the bathtub. He'd made a commitment to Irma, but now it didn't look as though he'd be able to see it through. He couldn't add the new floor joists until the remaining wood had been treated for termites. And without those joists, everything else was at a standstill, which left him with just a little more than a week to do the remainder of the work. Even if he managed to get some of the downstairs squared away beforehand, he still wasn't likely to finish the job.

Not that he considered it a job. On the contrary, he'd been in his element yesterday as he, Laurel and the folks from church worked to empty Irma's house. Serving others was what Wes was created to do, and it felt good to be working with a purpose again. And that was precisely why he'd signed on with Servant's Heart to go to Iraq. Working simply for a paycheck didn't really suit him, but knowing that he was helping someone, making a difference in their lives... That's what drove him.

Except now it looked as though he wasn't going to be able to help Irma, after all. And if he didn't, who would? Sure, Mason would probably be more than willing to swoop in and do the job, but at what cost to Irma?

With a sigh, Wes slumped back in the chair and watched a pair of cardinals making their way around the sun-speckled front yard, flitting from one tree or bush to another in search of twigs and other nest-building materials. *Lord, did I misunderstand You? All that prompting yesterday. The rationalizing.* Perhaps Wes wasn't supposed to be the one to help Irma.

The sound of a vehicle pulled him from his thoughts, and he looked up to see Laurel's SUV easing alongside the curb. He might as well tell her the bad news. Perhaps she would know of someone other than Mason who could take over.

After exiting her vehicle, she started up the walk. Her hair was pulled back in a long ponytail, and she looked ready to work in a pair of faded jeans and a Dallas Cowboys T-shirt. A moment later, she spotted him, and her gaze instantly narrowed.

Strange to think that two years ago, Laurel had trusted him and they'd connected as though they'd known each other for years. But last night, when he was playing with Sarah-Jane, he'd seen nothing but distrust in her eyes. Then again, he couldn't say that he blamed her. They were, for the most part, strangers. And she had Sarah-Jane to think about. He'd hoped to prove her wrong, to win at least a morsel of her trust. However, this latest development hadn't done him any favors.

"What's wrong?" She moved slowly up the steps.

"I've hit a snag."

Her eyes went wide. "What? Did something else happen inside the house?" She took a step toward the door.

"The house is fine," he said. "Well, not *fine*, but unchanged." He rested his hands on his hips. "It looks as though I'm not going to be able to do the work for Irma after all."

Her gray-green gaze searched his. "Why? What's the problem?"

He blew out a sigh. "I've called five pest-control companies, and the earliest any of them can get out here is late next week. And, unfortunately, any work on that bathroom hinges on getting the remaining wood treated for termites."

"Who all have you called?"

He listed the names, her face contorting more with each one.

"Why would you call them?" She looked at him as though he'd lost his mind.

"Because that's what came up when I did a search for pest control in Bliss, Texas."

"I thought finding a termite person was something you wanted me to help you with. Those folks may be *near* Bliss, but they're not *in* Bliss." She pulled her phone from her back pocket. "You need to call Frank Wurzbach."

"Who's he?"

She looked intently at her phone. "Town council-man, who also happens to own Wurzbach Pest Control."

"I saw the name in my search, but they didn't have a website, so I skipped it. Is he any good?"

Glancing up at him, she frowned. "Wes, Bliss may be small, and a lot of people are old-school, but don't be so quick to discount them. What we lack in quantity, we make up for in quality." Sounded like something his sister would have said.

"Do you have his number?"

Laurel again focused on her phone. "I've got it here somewhere." A couple of finger taps later, she said, "There. I just sent it to you." She tucked her phone away as his vibrated in his hand.

"Thanks."

"Be sure to tell Frank you're working on Irma's house. I guarantee that'll get him out here right away."

"Well, we need to let the wood dry over the weekend, but that's good to know." He logged the number into his contacts. "So, what are you doing here?"

She poked a thumb over her shoulder in the general direction of the front door. "I need to check on those books and other things the ladies and I set out to dry last night."

"Where's Sarah-Jane?"

"Irma and Joyce are watching her."

The thought of two elderly ladies caring for an ac-tive infant who happened to be his daughter made him uneasy. "Where?"

"At Joyce's house."

"Wouldn't it have been better for them to come to your place?"

"Perhaps. But I didn't want to inconvenience them. Besides, Joyce has a little dog, and Sarah-Jane loves dogs."

Maybe so, but some dogs weren't too fond of little kids. "Do you think she'll be okay with them?"

"Why wouldn't she be?" Exasperation wove its way through her words. "The two of them will probably dote on her so much she might never want to come home. And just for the record, if I thought she was in any danger, I wouldn't have taken her over there in the first place."

"But what if Sarah-Jane wears them out?"

"Then I guess they won't offer again, will they?" Nostrils flared, she turned and pushed through the front door, where the roar of the air movers drowned out everything else.

That didn't stop him, though. He followed her into the parlor, the smell of old house circling around him as he stepped in front of her. "Why are you so upset with me?" He had to raise his voice to be heard over the incessant rumble. "You act as though it's a crime for me to be concerned about my daughter."

"I have no problem with your concern for Sarah-Jane," she countered. "But what I don't appreciate is you coming in here and questioning my judgment. I've been taking care of Sarah-Jane since the day she was born—quite well, I might add—with no help from you, thank you very much."

"And whose fault is that?" As soon as the words left Wes's mouth, he wished he could take them back. And the tears that sprang to Laurel's eyes didn't help.

Frustrated, he strode into the entry hall and turned off the blower in there before continuing into the family room and doing the same with the three in there. On his way back, he went into the bedroom and killed the two units that were drying the carpet.

Surrounded by virtual silence, save for the blowers upstairs and the sound of his boots against the wooden floorboards, he crossed to where Laurel still stood, feeling like a major jerk. "I'm sorry. I didn't mean what I said. I know you had no way to get in touch with me. And I shouldn't have pushed you so hard. You're a good mother. I know you would never put Sarah-Jane in any kind of danger."

Arms wrapped tightly around her middle, she nodded without ever looking at him. "We both have work to do." With that, she continued into the dining room, leaving Wes to wonder if he'd just dug himself a hole he might not be able to climb out of.

Chapter Six

The stress of the last two days had finally caught up to Laurel. Wes's sudden appearance had her drifting into uncharted waters. And for a moment today, she'd felt as though she might drown.

She couldn't blame Wes, though, not when she'd thrown the first punch. Yet while he'd been quick to apologize, she had yet to say a word. Even now, as she was ready to leave Irma's, she wasn't sure she could muster the courage to say she was sorry.

Despite the incessant droning of the fans threatening to drive her crazy, her steps halted as she approached the front door just after noon. Wes was on the other side. He'd informed her half an hour ago that he was going out there to make some phone calls. Perhaps he'd be on the phone now, allowing her to simply wave as she escaped to her vehicle.

Unfortunately, when she opened the door, he was standing on the other side.

His blue eyes seemed fixed on her as he stepped aside, allowing her to join him.

"I, uh, I'm going to head out." She somehow managed to move the words past her suddenly tight throat. "I need to get Sarah-Jane down for a nap." And maybe even grab one herself. Except she had work to catch up on. As a CPA who specialized in working with ex-pats, she prided herself on addressing their needs in a timely manner. And after being out of the office all day yesterday, there were things that required her attention.

"Yeah, I'm going to cut out shortly myself." His voice sounded strained, as though he was uneasy. "By the way, I called Frank, and he'll be out here on Monday."

"Oh, that's good." She nodded repeatedly, probably looking like a bobblehead doll.

"Yeah. So it looks like I'll be able to do the work after all."

"That's great." Actually, it really was, because the busier he stayed, the less time Laurel would have to spend with him.

But what about Sarah-Jane?

"Would, uh, would you mind if I stopped by to see Sarah-Jane later? After her nap."

"I don't know." Conflicted, she shifted from one sneaker-covered foot to the next, watching the leaves on a large oak tree sway in the breeze. "I was really hoping to make it an early night."

"Me, too. Yesterday kind of wore us out. However, I'd still like to see her. I've only got a couple more weeks, and I'd like to use them to get to know my daughter."

Her gaze jerked to his. *My daughter.* He wielded those two words as if they'd gain him access. Not that she would deny her daughter a relationship with her father. But that relationship was still in its infancy, and Laurel wanted to make sure Wes was in it for the long haul before she gave him carte blanche.

"I'll even bring dinner," he added.

All right, now he was playing dirty. Because the mere thought of planning, let alone preparing, a meal sucked what little life was left right out of her. "What did you have in mind?"

"Rae says there's a burger joint around here that's hard to beat."

Bubba's. Laurel's mouth watered, and her stomach growled just thinking about it. Wes did not play fair.

With a fortifying breath, or, perhaps, one of resignation, she said, "In that case, I'll take a loaded cheeseburger with a large fry and a chocolate milkshake."

"And Sarah-Jane?"

"Chicken nuggets, of course."

His smile was genuine as she strode off the porch, headed for her SUV. "All right, then I'll see you around five thirty?"

"Sounds good." Or at least the meal did, anyway.

When she picked up Sarah-Jane, Irma and Joyce gushed about what a good baby she was and how much they'd enjoyed spending time with her. But Sarah-Jane's good mood was quickly coming to an end. After being up later than her usual eight o'clock bedtime last night, she was more than ready for a nap and fell asleep on the way home.

Over the next two hours, Laurel managed to distract herself with work, emailing a couple of clients and following up on an outstanding case with the IRS. Then, after Sarah-Jane had awoken, the two of them played and Laurel did a load of laundry, all the while pondering the things she'd like to tackle at Irma's. While picking up Sarah-Jane, Laurel had mentioned to Irma that Wes was hoping they could salvage the carpet in the bedroom. However, Irma had quickly told her to instruct him not to bother, because she hated the ugly brown stuff. And that got Laurel to thinking. Maybe there were other cosmetic things that could be done to refresh some of the spaces impacted by the collapse.

Those thoughts seemed to fade away as five thirty drew nearer, though, replaced by a whole lot of angst. How could she spend the evening with Wes with her spiteful words still hanging between them? Conflict was not something she relished. She was an only child, for crying out loud. She'd had no siblings to argue with. Or, more to the point, to make up with. How did she tell Wes she was sorry?

Pride goeth before the fall.

Pride? Was that really her problem?

Only where Wes was concerned.

Laurel prided herself on being a good mother to Sarah-Jane. So, when he'd started questioning her about leaving her daughter with Irma and Joyce, ladies Laurel trusted, she'd lashed out, wanting to discount him the way she thought he was doing to her. Now she was left with the bitter taste of regret. And that was not going to go well with her Bubba burger.

She had just finished changing Sarah-Jane's diaper when someone knocked on the door. Checking her watch, she noted that Wes was right on time. Another trait that had carried over from his military career, no doubt.

"Are you ready for some dinner, baby?" She held Sarah-Jane in one arm while she opened the door with the other.

Wes clutched a white paper bag in one hand and a drink carrier in the other, his face lighting up when he saw Sarah-Jane. "There's my favorite girl." He pressed a kiss to her chubby cheek as he entered. "I hope you two are ready to eat—" he continued into the kitchen "—because the smells coming from this bag are making my stomach grumble."

Laurel set a wiggling Sarah-Jane on the floor before closing the door. "We sure are."

After setting the food on the rustic wooden table, Wes intercepted a speed-crawling Sarah-Jane at the opening between the living room and dining space. "Let's get you in your high chair."

Laurel watched him slip the child into her seat and carefully strap her in. Like her, all Wes wanted was what was best for Sarah-Jane. How could Laurel fault him for that?

While he finished up, Laurel emptied the contents of the bag onto the table. She popped a fry into her mouth before breaking up another and setting it on Sarah-Jane's tray.

"What about me?" Wes looked at her expectantly. "I think I have some fries in there, too."

Puffing out a laugh, Laurel grabbed another fry and handed it to him.

"Thank you." He popped it into his mouth, his playful gaze never leaving hers, reminding her of the man she'd met two years ago. The one who made her laugh and whose company she truly enjoyed.

With him standing close enough for her to smell the clean aroma of his soap, she stared at her hands. "Earlier today, at Irma's, I said things to you that I shouldn't have." She looked up at him. "I'm sorry. I had no right to accuse you of something you had no control over."

"It's all right. I think tensions were rather high for

both of us this morning. I was frustrated, and you were worn out from yesterday."

"You don't have to make excuses for me. I'm big enough to admit that I was wrong." She lifted a shoulder. "Eventually, anyway."

"If I say you're forgiven, can we eat?"

She shook her head. "No, I'll probably eat regardless."

"Good, because there's nothing to forgive." He pulled out a white chair and sat down beside Sarah-Jane.

Moving to the other side of their daughter, Laurel took a seat, watching the man who seemed to truly want to be a part of his daughter's life. Yet there was one thing she couldn't seem to forget.

Wes believes he doesn't deserve a family.

For now, he seemed to have forgotten that. But what would happen when he remembered the lie that haunted him for much of his life? And how would the fallout impact Sarah-Jane?

Wes stood atop a new, much more stable ladder in Irma's family room Friday morning, peering into the gaping hole overhead and evaluating the joists—partial joists, in some cases—that remained. Anything that wasn't sound, he cut away, leaving the rest to be treated.

Reciprocating saw in hand, he trimmed another section, his mind drifting back to last night. Who knew babies could be so therapeutic? Certainly not him. Of course, he'd never really been around babies before. Yet having a chance to spend time with Sarah-Jane had been exactly what he needed to vanquish the stress of the past couple days. And he was surprised by the feelings she stirred inside him. They were unlike anything he'd ever felt before. She was his own flesh and blood—a hefty concept that sparked all sorts of unfamiliar instincts.

Even Laurel had seemed to enjoy herself, at least for a short time, reminding him of the woman who'd lived in his mind for the past two years and making him wonder what might have happened had he known about Sarah-Jane from the beginning. Would he have tried to explore a relationship with Laurel? With them living in two different states, it wouldn't have been easy. Not to mention his vow to never have a family. His bad choices had killed his parents and changed Laurel's life forever. He couldn't risk hurting someone again.

Still, there was no way he would have turned his back on his own child.

He wanted to be a part of her life. How would he do that, though, when he'd be living on the other side of the world for the next year? And what about when he came back? To be a real father, he'd need to live close enough to see Sarah-Jane every day. Could he make a home in Bliss? And how would Laurel feel about that?

He couldn't worry about that now. He needed to get things squared away here before he headed back to Rae's to help her with some painting. With both of them pitching in, they might be able to get the bulk of it done tonight. And while it would mean time away from Sarah-Jane, at least it would free him up for the weekend. With Irma's home still in the drying process, he was hoping to do something fun with Laurel and Sarah-Jane.

"Wes?"

He barely heard his name over the roar of the blowers that had been running around the clock since Wednesday.

"Family room," he hollered before making his way down the ladder.

"Hey." Though Laurel smiled as she entered the empty space, there was a hesitance about her. Moving beside him, she said, "I need to talk to you about something."

Nodding, he held up a finger to indicate he needed a moment. After setting the saw on the tarp he'd laid down to catch the rotted wood and protect the floor, he turned off the air movers in the family room and hall. Since he'd already turned off the upstairs units to keep wood from flying everywhere, things were almost silent, except for the distant sound of the two in the bedroom down the hall.

"You were saying?"

"I've been thinking, as long as we're having to do all this work—" she motioned around the room "—what if we also refreshed things a little bit?"

Having worked with several hard-to-please homeowners since leaving the military, he couldn't help wondering just how little a little bit meant. "What did you have in mind?"

"Mostly cosmetic stuff. Maybe repaint this space and her bedroom, since those two rooms are where she spends most of her time."

"That's easy enough."

"Oh, and Irma said for you to go ahead and deep-six the carpeting in her bedroom. Apparently her late husband picked it out and had it installed to surprise her." Laurel giggled, and he couldn't help thinking how cute she sounded. "She said she was surprised, all right, but not in a good way. However, she didn't have the heart to tell him, so she's lived with 'ugly brown'—" she did air quotes with her fingers "—ever since."

"How long were they married?"

"Fifty years."

"After all that time, you'd think he'd have had enough sense to consult with her first."

"You would think." She motioned for him to follow her before starting down the hall.

He did so, detouring into the bedroom to kill the blowers in there before joining her in the parlor. For the umpteenth time, he eyed the stacks of boxes that covered a third of the space. "I can't believe all of this came out of her bedroom." His gaze drifted to Laurel. "This could border on hoarding, you know."

"Hardly." She flipped open one and pulled out a stack of photos. "These are memories, Wes." She waved them as if to emphasize her point. "High school yearbooks, baby books, baby clothes… I even found Irma's wedding dress." She pointed to a stack of boxes nearest to her. "Every one of these is filled with photographs. Her parents, her kids, wedding photos. And to Irma's credit, every single picture is labeled." Laurel shook her head. "I sure wish Grandmama had done that. I can't tell you how many pictures I tossed because I had no clue who the people were."

"But what good is all this stuff if it just lives in a box?"

"Exactly! That's why I've been doing so much digging. I thought that, maybe, when we put things back together, some of these things could be displayed."

"Even the wedding dress?"

"Maybe, if I could get my hands on a dress form."

She touched a finger to her lips. "Hmm, I wonder if Drenda might have one of those at her shop?"

"You know I was kidding, right?"

"Yes, but it's still a great idea."

Leaning against the bookshelf that had been moved from the family room, he couldn't help admiring her enthusiasm. "Do you take many pictures?"

"Ha! You have no idea. My phone alone is an album of Sarah-Jane's entire life."

He straightened then. "Can I see them?"

She looked up from a box, blinking. "I guess you would be curious about that, wouldn't you?"

"I may not have been here to experience her first fourteen months—" he moved closer "—but I could live vicariously."

"All right. Then I guess we should start from the beginning." She pulled her phone from the back pocket of her shorts, and a few finger taps later, he was looking at a black-and-white image of a bean. "This was the very first time I saw her. It was taken at my first OB appointment." She pointed to the bean. "That's Sarah-Jane right there."

Her enthusiasm was contagious. Yet as he watched this strong, independent woman, he couldn't help realizing how difficult that moment must have been. She was pregnant by someone who not only wasn't in the picture but was, for all intents and purposes, a stranger. "Were you scared?"

"Yes. But thinking of that little life growing inside me made me unbelievably happy."

"I wish I could have been there to share it with you. To help you."

She lifted a shoulder. "We can't change the past, Wes."

He was probably more aware of that than she knew. Still— "No, but the future is up for grabs. And I'd like to be a part of Sarah-Jane's future. I want to teach her how to ride a bike and be the one who puts the bandage on her knee when she falls off."

"Wait, you're planning to let our daughter fall?"

He grinned. "I want to be there to see her off on her first date. Of course, that won't happen until she's at least thirty-one." He laughed. "And to see her graduate from high school, college… I want to walk her down the aisle when she gets married."

Laurel held up a hand, cutting him off. "Okay, stop. I am *so* not ready to think that far ahead. She's not even walking yet."

"Well, maybe she'll do that while I'm here. And it can be the first of many firsts."

As she watched him, there was an uncertainty in her eyes. "I guess we'll just have to wait and see."

Chapter Seven

He wanted to give Sarah-Jane away at her wedding?

Almost twenty-four hours later, Laurel still couldn't believe Wes had actually said that. Not only was she nowhere near ready to think about Sarah-Jane getting married, but who was to say Wes would even be around then? Sure, it might sound nice now, but he was about to leave for a year. A lot could change in twelve months. He might decide he didn't want to come back to Bliss. That he didn't want to be a father.

But what if he does?

She didn't want to think about that, either. She and Sarah-Jane had plans this morning, and they didn't include Wes. For all she knew, he was still busy painting at Rae's. Yesterday, that had afforded Laurel her first night without him since he learned about Sarah-Jane four days ago. And while she appreciated his commitment, no matter how short-lived it could potentially be, she also liked having a relaxing evening to herself. Because, let's face it, having someone who could impact the life of your child around was stressful. And she'd had more than enough stress for one week.

With the midmorning sun filtering through the oak tree in her front yard, she blew out a frustrated breath and settled Sarah-Jane into her stroller. "Want to go to the farmers market? Maybe they'll still have some dewberries so Mommy can make another cobbler."

Not that she needed another cobbler, especially since she'd just polished off the last of Irma's chocolate cake. But Grandmama's dewberry cobbler was her favorite and brought back such fond memories.

Stooping to fasten the straps around Sarah-Jane, Laurel pondered the woman who'd been the one constant throughout her life. Actually, Laurel had her to thank for ending up in Bliss. Having inherited her grandmother's house in Dallas and a decent life insurance policy, Laurel had finally been able to leave her corporate job and branch out on her own. Then she'd found out she was pregnant. And while Dallas was a nice place to live, Laurel wanted a different kind of life for her child. A simpler life.

She straightened, admiring her sweet slate blue house with the inviting front porch. Thanks to her grandmother, she'd found that life in Bliss. Though with the appearance of Wes, things had definitely gotten more complicated.

Shoving the thought aside, she started along the sidewalk, savoring the blissful weather this last Saturday of April had brought. Neither she nor Sarah-Jane needed a jacket. The sun was bright, the temperature not too hot and not too cold, which made their journey to the courthouse square beyond pleasurable. If only every day could be like this. Of course, then she'd never get any work done, because it would be sheer torture to stay cooped up inside.

Ten minutes later, they arrived at the square where people were selling farm-fresh eggs, baked goods, plants, produce and, yes, dewberries. Well aware that the season was coming to an end, Laurel decided to buy an extra bag to freeze. That way, she could enjoy her favorite cobbler later in the year.

"How much do I owe you?" In the shade of a magnificent old live oak that dripped with Spanish moss and swayed with the gentle breeze, Laurel eyed the blonde on the other side of the table.

"I've got it."

She turned as Wes passed a twenty to the lady.

"I love blackberries," he said.

"Those aren't blackberries," Laurel informed him. "They're dewberries. And I can pay for them myself." She stretched a hand with her own twenty toward the woman, nudging Wes's out of the way.

Though he withdrew his money, he didn't look happy about it. "I don't think I've ever heard of dewberries before."

"Probably because you're not from Texas. They grow wild." She held the bag open. "Go ahead. Try one." Watching as he grabbed one, she tried not to laugh. Dewberries might look like blackberries, but they were quite tart.

He popped a couple in his mouth and promptly puckered. "Ooh, those are sour."

"Just a little. But they make a great cobbler."

"Wait, you cook?"

"On occasion." She closed the bag. "Depends on the motivation."

"And you're motivated by cobbler?"

"Dewberry cobbler, yes. Don't worry, it has plenty of sugar."

Laurel accepted her change while Wes crouched beside the stroller.

"I missed seeing you yesterday, sweetheart."

A smiling Sarah-Jane offered him a bite of her graham cracker, which he pretended to nibble.

"It's a beautiful day." Standing, he faced Laurel again. "What do you say we all go do something?"

And give her another opportunity to get a glimpse of how wonderful he could be. The way she had the other night at dinner, when she'd carelessly let her guard down. "Like what?"

"I don't know. Something Sarah-Jane would enjoy."

She'd already been contemplating taking Sarah-Jane to Founder's Knoll. Not only did it have a beautiful view overlooking the river, between the nature trails and the playground, there was plenty to keep Sarah-Jane entertained. Except, when the thought had popped into Laurel's head, Wes hadn't been part of the equation. But now that he was here and being rather insistent, she supposed an extra set of eyes would be beneficial.

Depositing the berries and her wallet in the basket beneath the stroller, she said, "I have an idea. It's not far, but we'll need to drive."

"My truck is right there." He pointed toward the café on the other side of the street.

"You don't have a car seat, though. Besides, I'll need to grab the diaper bag and some snacks for Sarah-Jane."

Wes accompanied them back to their place, and a little more than an hour later, they were strolling along a wide dirt trail bordered with lush green foliage.

"This is amazing." Wes gazed at the expansive oak canopy.

Hands shoved in the pockets of her jeans, Laurel breathed in the fresh air, hoping for a calm she hadn't had since Wes showed up at the square. "Founder's Knoll is one of Bliss's most overlooked treasures."

"I guess that's both good and bad." He turned his attention to Laurel. "Good for us because it's not crowded, but bad for those who've missed out on something so beautiful."

"This is nice, but wait until we reach the top."

"Well, that's intrig—" His eyes suddenly lit up, and he knelt to the ground. He looked as though he was picking up something.

So long as it wasn't a snake.

"Look, Sarah-Jane." Moving in front of the stroller, he lowered his hand. "It's a little lizard." He held the tiny creature between his finger and thumb as Sarah-Jane looked on in wonder.

Laurel pulled her phone from her pocket and snapped a picture. "What do you think about that, baby?"

Her daughter reached out a finger to touch it, grinning when it flicked its tail.

"Be gentle." Wes's voice was tender, and Laurel was impressed that her daughter actually seemed to understand, slowing her movements.

"That's right." Wes smiled as she carefully touched the creature. "Okay, we have to let him go now." He set it on the ground, and Sarah-Jane leaned over to watch the lizard scurry off into the ground cover.

As they continued on, Wes turned his attention to Laurel. "Does having me around bother you? I mean, things were so easy between us in Vegas. Now you seem…tense."

Last week at this time she'd been just fine, but now… "I'm the same person I've always been, but I'm a mother now, and I have to protect Sarah-Jane."

"You think I pose a threat to her?"

Laurel's steps slowed as they came to the open area atop the bluff that overlooked the river and the rolling hills that surrounded Bliss. She might not like conflict, but all of this tiptoeing around, torn between wanting Sarah-Jane to know her father and fearing he'd eventually reject her the way Laurel's father had done with her, was eating her up. She needed to just get everything out in the open.

"Well, you are leaving soon."

He squinted against the sun. "But I'll be back."

"Will you?" She continued toward a picnic table situated beneath a tree and forced herself to look at him. "A lot could change in a year, Wes."

"I can't believe this. You act as though I don't want to be with her."

Laurel opened her mouth to argue, but he continued.

"Have you ever stopped to think that, maybe, you're not the only one who's worried? I mean, here I am, suddenly in her life, yet in two weeks, I'll be gone. How is that going to impact her? And what about when I come back? Will she even remember me? Will she wonder where I've been and if I'm going to leave again?" He rubbed the back of his neck. "I don't want to mess with her or have her grow up thinking her father doesn't want to be with her—because I do. More than anything. And if I wasn't already committed to going to Iraq, I wouldn't leave at all. Unfortunately, I am committed.

So, tell me what I should do, Laurel, because I don't want to do something that's going to hurt my daughter in the long run."

Laurel just stood there, blinking up at him. He really had looked at the big picture. And not just the good parts, like walking Sarah-Jane down the aisle. He'd actually considered the effects of his actions.

She swallowed hard, her heart twisting. How was it possible to go from feeling skeptical to being completely enamored with someone in the span of thirty seconds?

Easy. Wes loves his daughter.

And that had melted her heart faster than butter in the Texas summer sun.

Reluctant to allow her mind to go down that path, she drew in a deep breath and willed her pulse back to a normal rate. "You know, technology is a wonderful thing. Even though you'll be half a world away, you and Sarah-Jane will still be able to see each other via video calls. I assume you'll have internet."

"Yes. Though I'm not sure to what extent."

"Then there you go. I Skype with my clients all the time. So it won't be as though you're disappearing from her life."

He ran his fingers over the stubble that lined his chin. "I hadn't thought of that." A smile lifted the corners of his mouth, erasing the lines that had creased his forehead as he knelt beside his daughter and reached for her hand. "Technology isn't necessarily my forte, but I'm willing to learn. Because being able to see each other would certainly make our time apart easier." His eyes never left his daughter. "And I can continue to see her while I'm here." He hesitated then. Standing again, he looked at Laurel. "If that's okay with you."

Her daughter was being granted the one thing Laurel had always wanted—a father who loved her and wanted to be with her. So what else could she say?

"Fine by me." However, given the sudden condition of her heart, his leaving might end up being harder on her than she ever imagined.

Wes felt better knowing that he and Sarah-Jane would still be able to see each other while he was in Iraq. Even if it was on a computer screen, that was better than nothing. What he couldn't understand, though, was why Laurel would think he wasn't coming back when his year was up. Granted, living in Bliss, Texas, had never blipped on his radar before, but then, he'd never planned to have children, either. However, now that he knew about Sarah-Jane, wild horses couldn't keep him away.

Why would Laurel question that? Even if he still couldn't see himself with a wife and kids, what's done was done. He wouldn't turn his back on his daughter. He'd just have to accept that God had a different plan for his life and then try to be the best father Sarah-Jane could ask for.

In the parking lot of Bliss's lone grocery store, he loaded plastic bags into the back seat of his truck, suddenly curious about Laurel's father. While he'd heard her mention her mother and grandmother before, there hadn't been a word about her father. And since it had been Laurel's grandmother who had raised her after her mother died, Wes couldn't help wondering what the story was with her father.

Sarah-Jane and I have done just fine without you.

He closed the door, recalling the determination in

Laurel's voice that night Wes had tried to explain his trepidation over being Sarah-Jane's father. Could the absence of her father have been why Laurel had reacted so strongly?

The only way Wes would ever know was to ask her. Yet while they'd been honest with each other regarding their individual concerns about his future with Sarah-Jane this afternoon, asking Laurel about her father could threaten their fragile friendship.

With his groceries loaded, he climbed behind the wheel and headed back to Laurel's. After a couple of hours at Founder's Knoll, Sarah-Jane had become grumpy. The kind of grumpy no amount of snacks could appease, a good indicator that she was ready for a nap, according to Laurel. After returning to her place, Wes discovered a great backyard complete with a deck and grill. Considering what a beautiful day it had been, he offered to grill some steaks for dinner and was pleased when Laurel not only said yes, but that it gave her an excuse to make that dewberry cobbler she'd talked about. He was curious to try it, despite his less-than-favorable opinion of the fruit.

So, while Sarah-Jane napped, Laurel called Rae to invite her to join them, and Wes headed to the store for rib-eye steaks, potatoes for baking, salad and some vanilla ice cream to go with the cobbler. Now, as he returned to Laurel's, he hoped he could find a way to get her to open up about her father—without her shutting down or ending up mad at him.

Lord, You've granted me a precious gift in the form of Sarah-Jane. Please don't let me do or say anything that might hurt her mother.

"These are some nice-looking steaks," Laurel said as

she removed them from the bag in her kitchen a short time later. "What type of seasoning do you use?" She opened the stainless steel refrigerator and set them inside.

"A little bit of salt, some pepper and a touch of garlic powder." He set the large baking potatoes on the marble counter. "Just enough to bring out the flavor of the meat, not cover it up."

Smiling, she rested her hip against the counter, watching him as he unloaded sour cream, cheese and bacon bits for the potatoes. "Sounds like you've done this a time or two."

"What can I say? I appreciate a good steak."

"I'm sure the cattle ranchers of Bliss will thank you for that." A slight noise drew her attention to the video monitor sitting on the opposite counter.

He turned toward the small screen, watching his daughter rouse from her slumber. "That's a pretty cool gadget you've got there."

"I know, I love it. Saves me from having to guess what she's doing in there or disturbing her by trying to sneak a peek." As she spoke, Sarah-Jane moved to her knees, then pulled up on the side of the crib. "Guess I'd better go get her."

He gathered up the items that needed to go into the fridge. "I'll be checking on the grill to see if it needs to be cleaned. When was the last time you used it?"

Her face contorted as she thought. "New Year's Eve, when Rae, Christa, Paisley and I rang in the new year."

"Sounds like fun."

"It was." Smiling, she headed down the hall.

After depositing the items in the refrigerator, he made his way onto the wooden deck that overlooked a decent-size backyard with a lush lawn. A couple of well-established trees sat near the back of the property, their deep green leaves dancing in the slightest of breezes. Man, it was a beautiful day. One you wanted to set on repeat to play over and over.

A sweet fragrance touched his nose then, drawing his attention to the wisteria-covered fence on the other side of the driveway. The vines dripped with clusters of purple flowers in a spectacular show of color.

Lifting the lid on the gas grill, he noticed the wire brush dangling from a hook. One glance at the grates told him he was definitely going to need that. He'd just started scrubbing when the back door opened, and Laurel emerged holding Sarah-Jane.

"Somebody's in a very good mood." A smile lit Laurel's gray-green eyes as she stood the child in front of her, keeping hold of her hand.

Wes knelt opposite his daughter. "Did you have a good nap, Sarah-Jane?"

She smiled and bounced. Seconds later, she let go of Laurel's finger and took a step.

Laurel's quick intake of air was hard to miss as she watched her little girl.

Still kneeling, Wes stretched his hands toward Sarah-Jane. "Come on, sweetheart, you can do it."

She stepped once more, then bobbled, but caught herself before continuing. Several steps later, she collapsed into Wes's waiting arms.

"You did it, Sarah-Jane!" He hugged her tight, pride weaving through him.

"I can't believe it." Laurel pressed a hand to her cheek. "That's more steps than she's ever taken. She was actually walking all by herself."

"I guess you just had to strengthen up those legs, didn't you, Sarah-Jane?" Still holding his daughter, he stood.

"Or have the right motivation."

He looked at Laurel to find her smiling as she approached.

She took hold of her daughter's hand. "Were you showing off for your daddy?" Laurel froze then and so did he.

Their eyes met.

"I—I'm sorry." She took a step back. "That just kind of slipped out."

"No, it's okay." He smoothed a hand over his daughter's back. "Daddy is a distinction I will wear proudly." But could Laurel say the same about her father?

She started to turn away.

"Laurel?"

"Yes?" She faced him again.

Suddenly he was nervous. This wonderful moment could be blown to smithereens if he put his foot in his mouth again.

Lord, help me get this right.

"You've told me a little bit about your mother and your grandmother. But what about your father?"

Her eyes seemed to search his before falling to the weathered boards beneath their feet. And when she wrapped her arms around herself, he wished he hadn't brought it up.

"That's okay, you don't have to—"

"He went to jail when I was a little younger than Sarah-Jane." She rubbed her arms now. "It was only supposed to be for six months, but he didn't come back for us. My mom and I, we never saw him again."

He didn't come back for us. Those six words hit him like a ton of bricks. No wonder she had such concerns about Wes leaving. She was convinced he was going to do the same thing. Leave and never come back for Sarah-Jane.

In two steps, he closed the distance between them, determined to make her understand that he was not like her father. "Laurel, I'm sorry. I shouldn't have pried like that."

"It's fine, Wes. You weren't prying."

He looked at the child he still held in his arms. "I promise you right here and now, unless the good Lord decides to take me home, I will be back. Sarah-Jane is my daughter. And while the role of father may be one I was hesitant to take on, I would never turn my back on my own flesh and blood. The love I feel for her is something I still can't fathom, but it's there and it's strong and it's more real than anything I've ever felt before."

Lips pursed, she smiled, nodding repeatedly. She didn't believe him. And, unfortunately, it would be a year before he could prove himself, which meant he'd have to work all the harder now to convince her that he was a man of his word. But that was proving to be more difficult with each and every day, because keeping his word to Servant's Heart meant stepping away from the most important role of his life. And that might prove to be the most difficult thing he'd ever done.

Chapter Eight

For the life of her, Laurel couldn't figure out why she'd told Wes about her father. That was so not like her to open up to someone she barely knew, yet she seemed to do it over and over—first in Vegas, and then yesterday. Just because he'd asked about her father didn't mean she had to tell him. But did that stop her? Not one bit.

The love I feel for her is something I still can't fathom, but it's there and it's strong and it's more real than anything I've ever felt before.

Even now as she sat in the sanctuary of Bliss Community Church, those words brought tears to her eyes. And while they could be just that—words—the depth of sincerity in Wes's voice and his expression had told her that Sarah-Jane was one blessed little girl. A little girl who was now walking. Laurel still couldn't believe it.

If only she hadn't referred to Wes as *daddy*. Even though it may be true, there was something about saying it out loud that had felt rather intimate, like a term of endearment shared between a couple. Something she and Wes definitely were not. Instead, they were barely friends. Not that there weren't times when she wondered what it might be like if they were more.

Like right now as she sat in the pew, wedged between him and Rae during Sunday morning worship service.

She surreptitiously glanced his way, taking in the sound of his baritone voice as he sang, the scent of soap and raw masculinity, and the blue plaid shirt that matched his eyes… To top it all off, the man was oblivious to how attractive he really was, which made him even more appealing. Yet while she'd admittedly allowed herself to fall for him once, she couldn't afford to do it again. Not when it meant she could get hurt. While Wes might be accepting of his daughter, Laurel and Sarah-Jane weren't a package deal. And if her parents had taught her anything, it was that Laurel was disposable.

"I like that pastor." Wes followed Laurel and Rae out of the sanctuary after the service and into the long hallway that led to classrooms and the fellowship hall. "He's not all flowery and doesn't try to impress everyone with his knowledge. He just tells it like it is."

Even though Laurel's mind had been too preoccupied to listen to the sermon, she agreed wholeheartedly. Bliss Community was not the first church she'd visited when she arrived, but it was where she'd felt at home.

"One of many reasons we will do whatever is needed to keep Pastor Kleinschmidt around," said Rae.

"Rae!"

All three of them turned to see Anita McWhorter hurrying to catch up. The woman in her midforties with short sandy-colored hair pulled some papers from her Bible. "Here's that information I promised you about becoming a foster parent."

Rae, who was in her early forties and had never had children, smiled as she accepted the papers. "Oh, good. I've got a couple of questions I'd like to ask you, though. Have you got a minute?"

"Sure."

Rae glanced at Wes and Laurel. "You two grab Sarah-Jane. I'll catch up."

Wes leaned toward Laurel as they again moved down the hallway. "Foster parent?"

"Yes. There's a huge need right now." Something that always broke Laurel's heart. If she didn't legally name a guardian for Sarah-Jane and something happened to Laurel, her daughter would be one of those kids. Unfortunately, between the accident and Wes's sudden appearance, she had yet to take action.

"But why would Rae want to do that?"

Stopping, Laurel looked up at him curiously. "Because she loves kids. She's a born nurturer, and since she never had any children of her own…"

He glanced back at his sister with a fondness Laurel hadn't seen before. "Rae is definitely a nurturer. Yet that louse of a husband she had never wanted kids." His gaze shifted to Laurel. "At least, not with her."

That was obviously a reference to the fact that Rae's ex had married his pregnant mistress and then gone on to father two more children with her.

"Well, from what I've been able to gather," said Laurel, "she's better off without him."

"That's for sure." The corners of Wes's mouth tipped upward as they started walking again. "I guess this foster thing is why she's so eager to get her apartment fixed up."

"Probably."

The sounds of children at play drifted into the hall as they approached the nursery. One of the workers was holding Sarah-Jane when they stopped outside the brightly colored room. As always, Sarah-Jane's smile was wide as she reached for Laurel.

"Here's her diaper bag." The worker passed it over the half door.

"I can take that." Wes reached for the backpack.

"Say goodbye, Sarah-Jane." Laurel encouraged the child to wave, but Sarah-Jane wasn't having any part of it.

With a final farewell, Laurel again started down the hallway and almost bumped into Pastor Kleinschmidt. "I'm so sorry."

"No, no, you're the one with the baby," said the pastor. "I simply wasn't watching where I was going." The balding man in his late fifties turned his attention to Wes. "I don't believe we've met. I'm Ron Kleinschmidt."

"Where are my manners?" Laurel looked from one man to the next. "Pastor, this is Wes Bishop. He's—" She saw the way the pastor's eyes shifted from Wes to Sarah-Jane. Was this the right time to introduce Wes as Sarah-Jane's father? After all, Bliss was a small town. And while the pastor may not talk, if anyone else overheard… "—Rae's brother."

"Oh yes." The pastor shook Wes's hand. "Rae told me you were going to be in town for a few weeks. I also hear you're taking care of the repairs over at Irma's."

"Yes, sir." Wes looked from the pastor to her. "Though it's Laurel who's calling the shots."

Pastor Kleinschmidt's gaze homed in on Wes. "Rae

mentioned that you'd accepted a job with a mission organization in Iraq."

"Servant's Heart, yes. I'll be working on some rebuilding projects." He slung Sarah-Jane's pack over one shoulder. "Having served over there, it'll be nice to aid the Iraqi people in a less intimidating capacity."

"Well, the church will certainly keep you in our prayers."

"Thank you. I'd appreciate that, sir."

Sarah-Jane chose that moment to start fussing. She rubbed her eyes.

"Looks like I'm not the only one who's ready for a nap." The pastor patted the child on the back.

"Probably." Laurel finger combed her daughter's hair to one side. "She had a lot of excitement yesterday." Her gaze inadvertently drifted to Wes. "She took her first steps."

"Uh-oh." The pastor's expression turned serious. "If you thought you were busy before…"

"Trust me, I've already thought about that." She shifted her daughter to the other arm. "Come on, sweet pea. Let's get you home."

"It was nice to meet you, Wes." The pastor waved as they walked away.

Wes held the door for Laurel as they continued outside.

"Thank you." A bird's song carried on the gentle breeze as she stepped into the midday warmth. The weather was almost a carbon copy of yesterday's, though perhaps with just a tad more humidity.

Stopping, Wes faced her, his expression suddenly serious. "So, is that how it's going to be, Laurel? I'm

Sarah-Jane's daddy behind closed doors, but in public I'm Rae's brother?"

Laurel's whole being cringed as she recognized the hurt etched across his handsome face. While he'd been there to witness Sarah-Jane's first steps, he hadn't been able to share the joy when Laurel had talked about it because she'd been too busy worrying what someone else might think. Why hadn't she considered Wes's feelings?

"Wes, I didn't mean—"

"Yes, you did, Laurel. I saw you hesitate. But I get it. This is new territory for both of us. Yet while I may be leaving for a year, I *will* be back. So you'd better get used to it." He kissed Sarah-Jane's cheek. "I'll see you later, sweetheart."

Laurel's stomach twisted like a pretzel as she watched him walk away. How selfish could she be? The pastor and most everyone else in town knew she was a single mother and that she'd never been married. So why had she been so afraid to tell the truth about Wes? And how would that decision impact Sarah-Jane?

Her eyes momentarily closed. *Oh, Lord, please help me find a way to make this right.*

Wes eased his truck to a stop in front of Irma's house a few hours later, after lunch with Rae. He'd never been prouder than when Laurel referred to him as Sarah-Jane's daddy yesterday. The way it seemed to just tumble out sounded so natural. So when she introduced him to the pastor as Rae's brother, it had felt like a kick in the gut. And here he'd thought their relationship was improving, especially after she'd told him about her own father yesterday.

Getting out of his truck, he threw the door closed and

started up the walk, eyeing a squirrel that darted across the lawn. He had done everything he could to assure her he was all in for Sarah-Jane. Yet Laurel still didn't trust him. Either that, or she didn't want him in the picture. Didn't want someone else to have a say in Sarah-Jane's life. Laurel was used to going it alone, after all. What if she saw him as a threat? One she hoped to stop.

He would not let that happen.

What can I do when I'm half a world away?

The only thing he could—trust God to go to battle for him.

With a sigh, he climbed the steps onto Irma's front porch. Yesterday things had appeared so promising. Now he and Laurel had to find a way around this new pothole in their relationship.

Unlocking the front door, he strode inside the old Victorian home, noting that the humidity in the house had lowered considerably. Just what he'd been hoping for when he decided to keep the place closed up for the weekend, leaving the blowers and air conditioner running for the past forty-eight hours. The lower the humidity, the faster things would dry out.

After depositing the keys and his notepad atop the nearest box in the parlor, he retrieved the moisture meter from his back pocket and headed into the family room, where the bulk of the water had been. Fortunately, the joists that remained had only been impacted by water from the collapse itself, as opposed to the wood that had been absorbing moisture from the leak for who knew how long. That wood now rested at the bottom of the dumpster in Irma's driveway.

The drywall was another concern, however. Despite having pulled off the baseboards that first day, it was hard to tell how much water could have leached up any given wall prior to that.

Dropping to one knee on the wooden floor, he touched the sensor pins to a lower section of the wall that had been home to the bookcases. Pleased with the reading, he tested one of the wooden planks on the floor. Damage to the floors had actually been one of his greatest fears. If any of them were warped, they'd have to be sanded and refinished. Not only would that take more time than he had, it also meant Irma would be displaced even longer. His hope was that, since they'd been able to attack things so quickly with the shop vacs, they'd be fine. And from the looks of things in the family room, it appeared he just may have gotten his wish.

He continued with the meter, into the hallway and around to the bedroom, until he was convinced they'd actually be able to get started on the repairs this week. Then he returned to the parlor and scooped up his notepad to start making a list of supplies.

"Hello."

Wes lifted his head at the unfamiliar voice.

"Wes, are you in here?"

Leaving his notes atop a box, he turned and moved into the entry hall to see Pastor Kleinschmidt poking his head through the door.

"Oh, there you are." The man who looked to be ten to fifteen years older than Wes's forty years smiled and slipped inside. "I knocked, but I guess you didn't hear it."

"No, these air movers make it kind of difficult to hear anything." They practically had to yell to be heard. "Stand by." With that, Wes moved into the bedroom and family room to turn off the units, all the while wondering why the pastor would be looking for him.

With only the hushed sounds of the blowers upstairs remaining, he rejoined the man in the entry hall.

"Your sister told me you were here." The pastor's suit from this morning had been replaced with jeans and a polo shirt, and a pair of sunglasses were perched atop his bald head, making him appear much more casual. "I hope you don't mind me just dropping by like this."

"Not at all." Though Wes was definitely curious.

The man's dark gaze drifted to the parlor, his eyes widening as he took in everything from furniture to boxes to a queen-size mattress. "Looks like you all had quite an undertaking."

"We certainly did, especially since time was of the essence. But thanks to your congregation, we got it done quicker than I'd ever imagined."

"They are a wonder. I'm just sorry I wasn't able to help out." He looked at Wes. "I was down in south Texas at a church conference."

"Well, it's not like anyone planned for this, but God provided. And, thankfully, Irma wasn't injured."

"That's for sure." The man shook his head. "I'm also grateful God placed you here in Bliss at just the right time. Your willingness to help a stranger says a lot about your character, Wes."

Too bad Laurel didn't see things that way.

He shrugged. "It'll give me something to do while I'm here."

"Oh, I'm sure you've got plenty to keep you busy. Spending time with your sister…and Sarah-Jane."

His gaze shot to the pastor's.

"Laurel sought me out after you left and filled me in on the rest of your story."

Despite the man's matter-of-fact tone, Wes shifted from one booted foot to the next. "She…she did that?" Suddenly he had that uneasy feeling that must've kept Laurel from telling the truth in the first place. Owning up to sin was always tough. Admitting to that sin in front of a man of God was downright unnerving. "I only learned about Sarah-Jane after coming to Bliss. Laurel and I, well, it shouldn't have happened."

The pastor held up his hands. "I'm not here to judge, Wes. That's God's job. The good news is that He's a gracious God Who can turn even our biggest mistakes into our greatest blessings."

"He certainly did in this case. Sarah-Jane is…" Watching the rainbow of colors the sun's rays cast through the front door's leaded glass, he pondered how to describe how he felt about his daughter. "She's a blessing I'm not sure I deserve."

"God must not have seen it that way, Wes. Otherwise He wouldn't have brought you to Bliss."

"Humph. I thought the same thing myself. The part about Him bringing me to Bliss, anyway."

"Well, there are no coincidences where God is concerned. Which brings me to the real reason I came by." Hands perched casually on his hips, the pastor kept his focus on Wes. "We're having a men's prayer breakfast at the church on Saturday morning, and I wanted to extend an invitation. I was hoping that, perhaps, you could share what it is you'll be doing in the mission field. Give our men the opportunity to pray for you."

The notion of standing up and talking to a bunch of strangers made Wes a little uncomfortable. However, it wasn't like he was going on vacation. He was going to a war-torn country where peace was about as fragile as fine antique crystal. So, yeah, he'd take all the prayers he could get.

"I appreciate that. Yes, I can make it."

"Great. We meet in the fellowship hall at 7:00 a.m."

"I'll be there."

The pastor reached for the door. "Oh, and come hungry. We'll have a lot more than just doughnuts."

Wes chuckled. "Sounds good to me."

Watching the man retreat, Wes felt like a heel for coming down so hard on Laurel. Yes, he was just being honest, and yes, he was hurt, but he could have been a little more tactful. At this rate, he would never earn her trust.

Chapter Nine

In south central Texas, a seventy-five-degree day without the threat of spring storms was one to savor. And Bliss had had its share of glorious days lately. Yet while this one had started out promising, things had quickly gone downhill for Laurel. Ever since that falling-out with Wes, she'd been in a funk. All because she'd been afraid to tell the pastor the truth. Even though she'd since corrected that faux pas, she was still out of sorts because she had no clue how to smooth things over with Wes.

After Sarah-Jane's nap, Laurel loaded her daughter into the stroller, and they were now on their way to Joyce's to inform Irma of the tentative timeline for the work on her house. Perhaps the visit would help improve Laurel's mood.

"She's getting so big." Irma watched Sarah-Jane walk into Joyce's 1970s ranch-style house, holding on to Laurel's hand.

"This walking thing is brand-new, too." Laurel directed her daughter toward the living room to their right, trying not to think about those first steps she'd taken to Wes. "Where's Joyce?"

"She had a family reunion in Austin today."

Laurel scanned the space, eyeing the dark paneled walls and mottled tan carpet as she searched for Joyce's dog. "I'm guessing she took Henry with her."

"Yes." Irma perched on the edge of the brown-and-gold sofa. "She treats that pup like it's her baby."

Still holding Sarah-Jane's hand, Laurel joined her friend. "I wanted to give you a heads-up on what's happening over at your place." She watched the way Irma's dark eyes lit as Sarah-Jane moved toward her. "Seems you had a little termite problem in that upstairs bathroom, so Frank Wurzbach will be by tomorrow to treat the wood. Once that's done, Wes can get started on the repairs. We're also going to do a little painting for you in the family room and bedroom to freshen those spaces."

"Oh—" Irma reached her hands out for Sarah-Jane to grab hold "—that would be lovely."

"Now about that carpet in the bedroom."

Irma gave Laurel her full attention then. "Good riddance is all I have to say about that."

Laurel couldn't help laughing at the demure woman's adamant tone. "We'll need to decide what we want to do in its stead. Do you want to replace the carpet or stick with just the wood floors and, perhaps, a large area rug?"

The conversation continued as Irma vacillated on whether area rugs were a good idea for someone her age.

"I still can't believe Wes is willing to do all of this work for me." The older woman lifted Sarah-Jane into her lap. "He's supposed to be visiting his sister, after all. But then, he is headed into the mission field. That right there tells me he has a giving heart."

"Yeah, Wes is a good guy."

Twisting, Irma lifted a brow. "Do I detect a hint of attraction, Laurel?"

Laurel felt her eyes widen. "What? No. I mean, maybe at one time, but—I don't date. My daughter is my focus." Unlike Laurel's mother, whose dates sometime lasted for weeks.

"What do you mean 'at one time'? Were you and Wes in a relationship before?"

Laurel bit her lip. She'd stepped in it now. "No, no relationship. Just…" Did she dare tell Irma? She'd already told the pastor. And as word got out—not that Laurel thought the pastor was going to go blabbing—Irma would hear about it anyway and be hurt that Laurel hadn't told her herself.

Sarah-Jane reached for Laurel then. Taking hold of her, Laurel said, "Irma, Wes is Sarah-Jane's father. It was a chance meeting in Las Vegas two years ago."

"Oh. Well. Evidently what they say isn't true then, because what happened in Vegas did not remain there."

Laurel puffed out a laugh as she smoothed a hand over her daughter's soft hair. "No, it definitely followed me home."

"Did Wes know about Sarah-Jane?"

Laurel grimaced. "Not until five days ago."

"I see. Well, that does complicate things, doesn't it?" The older woman didn't act the least bit put off by Laurel's news.

"Tell me about it. Not only did he turn out to be Rae's brother, but I didn't expect him to be so willing to embrace his role as a father."

"But that's a good thing for Sarah-Jane, don't you agree?" Her dark eyes were fixed on Laurel.

"I suppose." Biting her lip, Laurel couldn't help thinking about all the ups and downs of these past few days as she and Wes tried to find a level playing ground.

"You don't want to share her, do you?"

"Would you want to share your baby with a stranger?"

"You must have seen something good in him at one time."

Laurel thought back to their first meeting, when she'd tried to pay him for that Coke. She'd been so embarrassed.

"I have to do something to say thank you."

"No, you don't." He briefly looked away, as though he was nervous. "However, I just ordered up a big basket of wings. I'd welcome the company, if you'd care to join me."

When he'd looked at Laurel again, there had been an honesty in his eyes she wasn't accustomed to seeing in people. Wes had never set out to impress her or anyone else. And that had endeared her to him more than she wanted to admit. Even to herself.

"He was kind," she finally said. "A good listener. He's the one who gave me the courage to leave my corporate job and follow my dream of starting my own company." A sigh escaped her lips. "He was unlike any guy I'd ever met."

Irma's brow hiked a little higher. "And you're not interested why?"

Laurel shook her head. "Doesn't matter, Irma." She stood, bringing her daughter with her. "Like I said, I don't date."

After bidding Irma goodbye, Laurel returned Sarah-

Jane to her stroller and pushed her home, trying not to dwell on all those wonderful things she'd remembered about Wes. Yet when she arrived at her house, he was on her front porch.

"There you are." Turning, he started down the steps as anxiety rose inside Laurel.

"We, uh, went over to see Irma so I could update her on things." She peered up at him. "I didn't expect to see you today." Then again, he probably just wanted to spend time with Sarah-Jane.

"I owe you an apology for acting like a jerk at church."

"You weren't a jerk. You—" Lowering her gaze, she noticed something in his hands. "What's in the bag?"

"A peace offering." He held it up. "Butter pecan ice cream."

Her favorite. And if memory served her correctly— "Isn't that your favorite, too?"

"You remembered."

Unfortunately, after talking with Irma, she remembered far more than she wanted.

"You take this—" he handed her the bag "—and I'll free Sarah-Jane."

She looked inside the bag as he unhooked the clasps. "Blue Bell. You got the good stuff."

He lifted his daughter to him as though he'd done it all of Sarah-Jane's life. "That's the official ice cream of Texas, right?"

"If it's not, it should be." She started up the steps. "Come on in."

In the kitchen, she set the ice cream on the counter and grabbed two bowls from the cupboard. "Wes, I'm the one who owes you an apology. I should have told the pastor who you were to Sarah-Jane and me instead of trying to cover."

"It did sting." Still holding Sarah-Jane, he watched her from the other side of the peninsula. "But I understand why you did it."

Reaching for an ice cream scoop, she watched, waiting for him to continue.

"I ran into the pastor at Irma's. He told me you sought him out after I left. Knowing the pastor knew what had happened between us was a little unnerving."

She scooped ice cream into the first bowl. "What did he say?"

"He said it wasn't his place to judge. And that he was there to invite me to speak at some men's prayer breakfast." He paused then, his forehead furrowing as though he was distressed. "Has anyone ever judged you for being a single mom?"

"I suppose there may have been a few eyebrows raised along the way. But by and large, the people of Bliss have been nothing but good to me."

"Good. I'd hate to think of someone treating you badly." The look on his face, the sincerity in his voice… That was why she'd fallen for this man. Except things had been safe in Vegas. She knew she'd be leaving the next morning, so she didn't have to worry about getting her heart broken when he turned his back on her. And if she didn't watch herself, she was apt to fall again. Only this time, she was certain not to come out unscathed.

Wes stood at the double front doors of Joyce's sprawling rambler Tuesday evening, wishing he'd had the nerve to turn down Irma's dinner invitation when she'd stopped by her house earlier in the day. But when she'd started talking about love languages and how hers was cooking and dinner was the only way she'd be able to properly thank him for all he was doing, well, he couldn't bring himself to say no.

So here he stood, holding a bouquet of flowers he'd picked up at the grocery store, feeling like he'd been summoned by the admiral.

He sucked in a breath, worked the kinks out of his neck and lifted his hand to knock.

She's a nice lady who just wants to say thank you.

That's right. Except Joyce would probably be here, too. That woman would give Rae a run for her money when it came to interrogation. Rae was less intimidating, though.

He swallowed hard and was about to knock when he heard a vehicle behind him. Turning, he saw Laurel's SUV rolling to a stop in the circular drive of the brick house. Had she been invited, too?

Man, he hoped so.

She emerged from the vehicle, eyeing him over its roof. "What are you doing here?"

"I was invited for dinner."

"Huh. Sarah-Jane and I were, too." Tossing her door closed, she opened the back door to retrieve their daughter.

Wes joined her. "Let me guess, Irma wanted to say thank you for helping her?"

Her gray-green eyes met his. "Cooking is her love language, you know?"

He couldn't help laughing. "So I've been told."

"Were you able to get those joists replaced?" Approaching the door, she cast him a sideways glance.

"Yep, they're all in." Yesterday the wood had been

treated for termites, allowing Wes to get in there today with the replacements. "And the plumber will be by in the morning to work on the pipes. After that, things are in my hands."

The front door opened as they approached, and a little white dog wandered outside.

"I thought I heard voices out here." Joyce's gaze moved between them. "You two are right on time." She held the door wide, allowing them to enter.

Sarah-Jane twisted in Laurel's arms, seemingly fixated on the dog.

"Come on, Henry." Joyce waved the animal inside, too.

"These are for you." Wes held out the flowers. "Or Irma." He hesitated, feeling like a fool. "Who's doing the cooking?"

"We both pitched in." The corners of Joyce's mouth quirked upward.

"That's good—" still holding a distracted Sarah-Jane, Laurel leaned in "—because the flowers are for both of you to enjoy."

Phew. He'd have to remember to thank her later.

Laurel set Sarah-Jane on the floor and held her hand as they followed Joyce and some very enticing aromas into the outdated kitchen. Obviously the '70s weren't lost on Joyce. Orange, brown and gold dominated every surface, including the countertops.

"Hello, hello." Standing beside the ancient downdraft cooktop, Irma waved before shifting her attention to her friend. "Joyce, which serving bowl would you like me to use for these mashed potatoes?"

"It's right up—" Still holding the flowers, Joyce turned toward him. "Wes, would you mind getting that bowl for me?" She opened the dark walnut cupboard over the pass-through to the family room and pointed to the top shelf.

"Sure." He reached to grab it.

"It's so nice to have a man around," he heard Irma say behind him. "Wouldn't you agree, Laurel?"

Handing the bowl to Irma, he couldn't help noticing the pink that had crept into Laurel's cheeks.

A short time later, they moved into the dark wood-paneled dining room for a meal of chicken fried steak, mashed potatoes, corn and broccoli. Laurel settled Sarah-Jane into the waiting high chair before taking the seat beside it, while Wes pulled out a high-backed chair across from her.

"Why, thank you, Wes." Joyce eased into the seat, leaving him standing there, feeling like a bump on a log. As Irma took the chair beside her, Joyce looked up at him. "You can sit next to Laurel."

He wasn't about to argue. Not that he minded sitting beside Laurel, but this was turning into one really awkward evening. Especially when Irma insisted they all hold hands while they said grace.

"Wes, what are your plans when you come back from Iraq?" Irma cut into her meat.

With a bite of mashed potatoes waiting on his fork, he said, "Well, I have a year to consider my options, so I'm not a hundred percent certain yet."

"You'll be coming back to Bliss, though. Right?" There was a sense of urgency in Irma's voice. "I mean, Sarah-Jane needs her father."

Laurel nearly choked on the sip of water she'd been in the midst of swallowing.

Lowering his fork, he passed her a napkin, this whole

evening suddenly becoming crystal clear. Laurel must have confided in Irma. Now the woman—his gaze drifted to an expectant Joyce—make that *women* were doing everything they could to bring him and Laurel together.

"Yes, ma'am. I am definitely considering making a home in Bliss."

Joyce set down her fork. "Laurel, have I shown you my granddaughter's wedding photos?"

Boy, talk about subtle.

"No, but—"

The white-haired woman stood and retrieved something from the adjoining living room. "It was such a lovely spring wedding."

"Spring weddings are always nice." Irma watched as Joyce handed a stack of pictures to Laurel. "But then, fall weddings are beautiful, too." She chuckled. "Come to think of it, there's really not a bad time for a wedding. Except maybe Christmas. Everyone is so busy then." She regarded Laurel. "Laurel, when do you think is the perfect time to get married?"

Flipping through the photos, her eyes went wide. "Um, I guess I've never thought about it."

"Of course you have," Joyce corrected. "Every young girl dreams of her wedding."

"Sorry." Laurel handed the pictures back. "I'm too busy being a mom to think about a wedding." She offered Sarah-Jane a bite of mashed potatoes, but the child only had eyes for the dog pacing around her chair. "I think somebody is quite smitten with Henry."

"Can't say as I blame her." Joyce scooted her chair away from the table. "I am, too." Rounding the table, she looked down at the dog. "If you'll be nice to Sarah-Jane, I'll take you outside so the two of you can play."

"I'll help." Irma was on her feet in no time.

"That's all right." Laurel pushed her chair away from the table. "I can go with her."

"Nonsense." Irma patted her on the shoulder. "You and Wes stay here and enjoy your dinner. *Alone*."

Laurel looked as though she wanted to crawl under a rock. As the women departed with Sarah-Jane, she dropped her head in her hands. "This is my fault."

"Why do you say that?"

"I told Irma you're Sarah-Jane's father." Lifting her head, she pushed the hair out of her face.

"You told the pastor, too."

"Yes, but he's not prone to playing matchmaker."

"Oh. Well, at least they're great cooks." He ate another bite of steak.

Laurel scanned the table. "I guess we could clear the dishes."

"And ruin our *alone* time?"

Her laugh was genuine. She sure was pretty when she did that. "You know, if you do move to Bliss, you can expect more of this."

"Dinners?"

"Matchmaking." She stabbed a piece of broccoli with her fork. "These ladies, not to mention several others, have been beside themselves since Rae, Paisley, Christa and I came to town." She took a bite.

"Fresh meat?"

"Pretty much. At least I have Sarah-Jane to use as an excuse."

"You mean, no dates?"

Setting her fork on her plate, she grabbed her glass

and leaned back. "I've never been much into the whole dating scene."

"Why not?"

She shrugged. "After my dad left, my mom spent her life bouncing from guy to guy, thinking one of them would make her happy. I'd rather make my own happiness."

"My parents had a great marriage." He wasn't sure why he said that, but he kept going anyway. "They always seemed so in sync with each other. That didn't mean they didn't each have their own goals and desires, but they supported each other and had similar values that permeated everything they did."

"You were blessed to have such a great example."

"Yeah." He foolishly allowed his mind to drift back to before the accident. "I used to hope I'd find a partner like that one day." He probably shouldn't have said that out loud.

"Does that mean you stopped?"

"I guess my dream died when they did." At least, until he met Laurel.

"Sarah-Jane—" Joyce chuckled somewhere in the vicinity of the kitchen "—we'll just have to talk to your mama about getting you a puppy."

And just like that, the moment was gone. But not before Wes realized that Laurel could be the partner he'd always dreamed of.

Chapter Ten

After dropping Sarah-Jane with her regular sitter Mary Lou on Wednesday morning, Laurel headed over to Bliss Hardware with thoughts of last night still tumbling through her mind.

Why didn't she date? Because she was afraid of falling in love and having her heart broken. Between her mother and her father, she'd endured enough rejection. There was no way she'd tell Wes that, though. No matter how much she might want to. Instead, she needed to work harder at keeping her heart in check. Especially after Wes had all but said he'd given up on the idea of marriage.

I guess my dream died when they did.

Dreams were fragile things. One little slip and they could shatter into a million pieces.

"All right, your color gurus are present and accounted for." Paisley's sweet southern drawl was unmistakable.

Laurel tore her gaze away from the wall of paint chips to hug Christa and Paisley. Since Christa owned Bliss Hardware and Paisley had a flair for decorating that would put even professional designers to shame, it seemed only logical that they help her choose the paint colors for Irma's bedroom, bath and family room.

"You must be busy at Irma's." Christa slid her hands into the back pockets of her jeans. "I've barely seen you since that day Mildred ran you down."

At the moment, that whole incident seemed like forever ago. Yet it had only been nine days. And, my, how things had changed since then.

"I couldn't help noticing you sitting beside Rae's brother at church on Sunday." Paisley lifted two perfectly arched brows. "Wesley sure is easy on the eyes."

A grinning Christa added, "I heard he's doing the repairs at Irma's, too, so I guess the two of you are spending a *lot* of time together."

Before Laurel could cringe at the implications, she realized that she'd not told them about Wes. What kind of friend was she, telling a matchmaking Irma when she hadn't even told her best friends?

"Oh boy." She rubbed her forehead.

"What is it, darlin'?" Paisley took a step closer.

Shifting her attention to Christa, Laurel said, "Any chance we could talk in your office?"

"Sure." Christa's hazel gaze narrowed. "Is everything all right?"

"Yes, there's just something I need to tell the both of you."

Christa wasted no time in hustling them across the store, past the power tools, hummingbird feeders and door locks.

"Annie," she hollered over her shoulder to the gal behind the counter, "I'll be in my office for a bit."

While the rest of Bliss Hardware was very utilitarian, Christa's office had a cozy farmhouse vibe going on, with warm white shiplap walls, a colorful area rug and a modern-yet-rustic wooden desk with a sawhorse-style base.

Laurel eased into one of two trendy metal side chairs as Christa closed the door in such a hurry that the black-and-white-checkered valance over its window stuck straight out for a moment.

Paisley took the second chair, crossing her denim-covered legs, her cornflower blue eyes fixed on Laurel. "All right, darlin', what's going on?"

With Christa leaning her backside against the desk, Laurel looked from one friend to the other. "Wes is Sarah-Jane's father." Saying it seemed to be getting easier, though the looks on her friends' faces had her wincing.

"How long have you known this?"

Paisley shot Christa an annoyed look. "I can't believe you asked that."

Christa cringed. "I know. That didn't come out right."

"I'll say." Paisley shifted her attention back to Laurel. "The question is, how long has Wesley known?"

"Oh, a little over a week now."

"You know—" Christa's mouth twisted "—that day at the café, I thought there was something familiar about him."

Laurel and Paisley both looked at her.

"His eyes! Sarah-Jane has his eyes."

"That she does," Laurel conceded.

"I'm assuming Rae knows." Paisley's gaze seemed riveted to Laurel's.

"Yes. Our perceptive friend managed to pretty much figure it out on her own."

"Wow." Christa pushed away from the desk and began to pace. "This is just crazy."

"You're telling me." Standing, Laurel crossed to the row of two-drawer white file cabinets against the opposite wall and grabbed a piece of chocolate from the small galvanized bucket labeled In Case of Emergency.

"What are the two of you going to do?" Paisley cocked her head, sending her red hair spilling over one shoulder. "Now that Wes knows, is he going to pay child support? Do you think he'll want partial custody?" She held up a finger. "Wait, he's on his way overseas."

Laurel tore the golden wrapper away from the candy. "I think each of those topics has been touched on at some point. But, for now, he and Sarah-Jane are just getting acquainted." She bit into the chocolate, caramel and cookie goodness.

"And how is that going?" Ankles crossed, Paisley gripped the sides of her chair.

When she'd finished chewing, Laurel said, "Quite well, actually. Sarah-Jane took to him right away. Oh, and she's finally walking. Her first steps were in an effort to get to him."

Christa fingered through the bucket now, in search of her favorite candy. "And how do you feel about that?"

"I'm…conflicted." Laurel returned to her chair. "On the one hand, I want Sarah-Jane to know her father. To have a relationship with him." One shoulder lifted. "I mean, I've dreamed of that for myself my entire life. But at the same time, I'm afraid for her. What if Wes decides he doesn't want to be a father? What if he goes away and never comes back?"

"The way your father did." Paisley watched her.

Lips pursed, Laurel simply nodded.

"Well, cautious is good." Christa tossed her candy wrapper in the trash. "After all, we don't call you Mama Bear for nothing."

Paisley remained silent, looking rather thoughtful.

"You're too quiet, Paise." Christa dropped into her desk chair. "What's going on in that pretty head of yours?"

"I don't want the two of you jumping all over me for this, however, I am the romantic in our little group."

"Here we go again." Christa rolled her eyes and spun her chair around.

"Laurel?" Paisley's gaze bore into her. "Is there any chance you, Wes and Sarah-Jane could be a real family? Not right now, but eventually."

Christa brought her chair to an abrupt stop. "You think Laurel and Wes should get married?" While Paisley may be the romantic one, matters of the heart never seemed to blip on Christa's radar. At forty-two, Christa not only had never been married, but she was adamant that she never would. Probably why she and Laurel got on so well.

"Not right now," Paisley was quick to add. "But somewhere down the road, maybe after he gets back from Iraq?"

Laurel reached for her friend's hand. "Paisley, I love that you're a romantic, and I wish I were more like you, but no. I'm not interested in settling down with Wes or anyone else. And neither is Wes."

Both pairs of eyes settled on her.

Christa's were round. "Does that mean you've discussed it?"

Maybe in a roundabout way, last night at Joyce's, but

Laurel wasn't going to bring that up. "No. But Rae says Wes thinks he doesn't deserve a family."

"Because he believes he's responsible for their parents' deaths." Paisley nodded. "I've heard her say that, too. So sad."

"Except he does have a family." Christa shrugged. "Two, actually. First it was he and Rae, and now he has Sarah-Jane."

"This is true," said Paisley. "So, as he spends more time with Sarah-Jane and, by extension, you, he could change his mind." She looked at Laurel. "What would you do then?"

Either fall into his arms or run the other way.

"Look, we could sit here and play what-ifs all day long." She pushed out of her chair. "But we have work to do." Jerking the door opened, she added, "So are y'all going to help me pick out paint colors or what?"

By three o'clock that afternoon, the plumber had finally finished repiping the upstairs bathroom. Unfortunately, he hadn't been able to get there as early as Wes would have liked, thanks to an emergency at one of the businesses in town, which left Wes to putz around with whatever he could find, trying not to think about Laurel. Yet no matter what he did, he couldn't get her out of his mind.

If last night had shown him anything, it was that he and Laurel were cut from the same cloth. Both were determined to avoid romantic relationships. Yet here they were with a daughter. How was it they'd both wavered from their resolve that night in Vegas? And why couldn't he seem to stop thinking about her?

He needed to work, to occupy his mind with something besides the pretty blonde accountant and the adorable baby they shared, because the two of them together created too tempting a picture. One he wasn't worthy of. His parents had paid for his mistakes with their lives. Rae had sacrificed because of those same mistakes and he wasn't willing to put anyone else he cared about in jeopardy.

Standing in Irma's upstairs bathroom, he studied the hole that was now crisscrossed with wood and PVC pipe. Tomorrow he'd add the subfloor up here and drywall to the ceiling below. He wasn't sure what Laurel had planned for flooring in the bathroom, but once the subfloor was in, he could safely remove the old sheet vinyl without fear of ending up in the family room.

"Wes?" Laurel's voice drifted from the entry hall downstairs.

As if he hadn't spent enough time with her already today. She just wasn't aware of it.

"Up here."

A few moments later, she stood in the doorway, wearing a pair of skinny jeans, a maroon Texas A&M T-shirt and a pair of slip-on canvas sneakers. With her blond waves spilling over her shoulders, she was about the prettiest worker he'd ever seen.

"How's it going?"

"Well, the plumber finished." He pointed toward the hole in the floor.

She tiptoed into the small space.

"Careful—"

Before he could finish his warning, her foot caught on a strip of the old flooring, and she lost her balance.

Wes made a quick side step and managed to catch her. "Sorry, I should have warned you sooner."

Her cheeks were red as she straightened. "I'm too clumsy for my own good."

With one arm still around her waist, he brushed the hair out of her face. "Clumsy never looked so beautiful." Or smelled so good.

Realizing what he'd just said, he let her go. Those were the things that had gotten them into trouble the first time around.

Regaining her composure, she shifted her gaze from the floor to him. "So, what's next?"

He explained his plans for tomorrow. "That reminds me, I haven't heard you mention what you're doing for flooring in here."

Her eyes went wide. "That's because it completely slipped my mind."

"Which means you probably don't have anyone lined up to install it, either."

"Of course I don't." Hands on her hips, she moved into the hall and began to pace. "And whatever I do decide on is probably going to take at least a week to get here." She groaned, planting a palm against her forehead. "I can't believe I forgot."

He hated to see her being so hard on herself. Joining her in the hallway, he said, "All right, let's just settle down for a second. First question, what do you envision on the floor in this bathroom? Sheet vinyl or something else? I mean, for an application like this, you could do vinyl plank or tile."

Stopping, she turned to face him. "Actually, I did have an idea."

He lifted a brow, waiting for her continue.

"I saw this woman on TV who renovates a lot of old houses and she always used those black-and-white mosaic tiles. You know, like the small squares or hexagons."

He nodded. "Yeah, I know what you're talking about. And you're right, that would look good in here. It's a small space, and the style would fit in with the character of the house."

"Much better than that faux-brick vinyl." She motioned toward the bath. "But where does one find something like that?"

"The big home improvement centers usually carry them."

"Really? That sounds easy enough."

"Yeah." He checked his watch. "And since there's really not much I can do here today, we could grab Sarah-Jane and make a run right now. Where is she, anyway?"

"At her regular sitter's. But why do we all need to go?"

"Well, *you* need to be there to make sure you get what you want, and if Sarah-Jane doesn't go, I won't get any time with her, since we'll likely be gone for a few hours. And finally, I'm the guy with the truck."

"Oh." The way her brow furrowed was dealing a blow to his ego.

"Plus, if we get the stuff now, I'll have time to install it myself."

Her suddenly hopeful gaze jerked to his. "You can do that?"

Now she was impressed. "When it comes to construction, there's not much I can't do, Laurel. Except those things that require a license, like plumbing and electrical. So, what do you say?"

"Let me pick up Sarah-Jane and I'll meet you at the house in thirty minutes."

Two and a half hours later, after a fast-food dinner they hoped would keep Sarah-Jane in a good mood, Wes pushed an industrial cart filled with backer board, mortar, tile, grout and everything else he would need to complete the flooring project in Irma's upstairs bath toward the checkout counter of the home improvement center. Of course, Laurel had to pause at least half a dozen times to look at home decor stuff. Wes didn't complain, though. He was having too much fun entertaining Sarah-Jane, who was strapped into the seat of a regular shopping cart. She really was a good baby. Always quick with a smile. And the fact that he seemed to be able to do no wrong in her eyes was an added bonus.

Darkness had already descended over Bliss by the time they made it back to Laurel's, and Sarah-Jane was asleep in her car seat.

"I'll get her," he told Laurel as she hopped out of the truck. Opening the back door, he carefully removed the straps that kept his daughter safe and lifted her to him.

With a contented sigh, she snuggled against him, and he couldn't help holding her a little tighter as they made their way toward the house.

Laurel ascended the porch before him and unlocked the front door.

Despite Laurel removing her little shoes and pants, Sarah-Jane remained asleep, even when he laid her in her crib.

"She must be tuckered out," he whispered to Laurel.

"All that excitement. You're quite the entertainer, you know." Laurel started for the door, but Wes couldn't seem to make himself move. Instead, he just stood there, watching his daughter sleep. So innocent. Such a precious gift from God.

He didn't know how long he'd been there when he felt a hand on his arm.

Laurel was beside him again. "I have done this same thing many a time. There's just something about a sleeping baby that's so peaceful."

His gaze lowered to his daughter. "Definitely."

When he managed to pull himself away, they moved into the hall, and Laurel softly closed the door behind them.

"I'm curious," he said as they moved into the living room. "How did you come up with the name Sarah-Jane?"

"Sarah was my grandmother's name. It means princess." She gathered a few toys that littered the floor. "However, I like the name Jane because it means God is gracious." She tossed the toys into a basket before leaning against the end of the sofa. "I felt as though God had been so gracious, allowing me to be a mother to this little princess…" Though her voice cracked, she smiled, blinking repeatedly. "It just fit."

"Yes, it does." He longed to touch her, to let her know she wasn't in this alone. Instead, he shoved his hands into the pockets of his jeans. "Has Rae ever told you that Jane was our mother's name?"

Laurel straightened, her composure returning. "Now that you mention it, yes. I'd forgotten. Probably because it didn't mean as much then, but now…" She paused before looking up at him, blinking. "Wes, God's hand has been all over this baby's life, even when we were unaware."

"Yeah. And He brought me here, to Bliss." He studied the curve of her face, the freckles that dotted her nose. "You know, I've never forgotten you, Laurel.

At the most random times, something you said or did would play across my mind."

"Like when I ordered you to bring me a Coke?"

He couldn't help laughing. "Oh, I've thought about that one a lot. But you didn't order me—you were very polite."

"I still can't believe you actually bought the drink yourself and brought it to me."

"Seeing you sitting there with your feet dangling in the pool in your tailored dress told me that you were not some high-powered exec who was used to getting her own way."

Standing, she tilted her head, watching him with such an intensity it nearly took his breath away. "What did it tell you?"

"That you appreciated the simple things in life. That you didn't take things too seriously and you liked to have fun."

"Wow, you're good."

He lifted a shoulder. "It's a gift."

"I thought construction was your gift."

"Can't a guy have more than one gift?"

"I think you have plenty, Wes Bishop. Including being a wonderful father."

"What makes you say that?"

"Because you're a man who genuinely cares and views being a part of his daughter's life as a privilege, not an obligation."

"It is definitely a privilege." Staring into her gray-green eyes, his throat clogged with emotion. Just knowing that was how she saw him meant more to him than she would ever know. And the feelings he had for her, the ones he'd been trying to squelch ever since that first day he saw her in the street, rose to the surface, refusing to be contained any longer.

He forced himself to look away. He wasn't worthy of Laurel's praise, any more than he was worthy of that precious little girl sleeping down the hall. Yet that hadn't stopped him from falling in love with his daughter. Now he was dangerously close to falling for her mother, too.

He couldn't let that happen.

Taking a step back, he said, "I need to run that stuff over to Irma's before it gets too late."

Chapter Eleven

Laurel set Sarah-Jane in her playard late the next afternoon, then headed into the kitchen to fill her sippy cup. Wes would be here soon, and that concerned Laurel even more than the ominous gray clouds gathering to the west. While she wasn't able to make it over to Irma's today because of work commitments, that hadn't kept her thoughts from drifting to Wes and their conversation last night.

She'd meant what she said about him being a wonderful father. She just wished she had kept that particular thought to herself, because the look in his eyes had nearly been her undoing. Coupled with that little stumble she'd taken at Irma's…

Filling Sarah-Jane's cup with water from the dispenser on the refrigerator, Laurel recalled the feel of Wes's strong arms around her and the way he made her feel safe, protected. The same way he had that night two years ago. No one else had ever made her feel like that before.

A knock at the front door startled her. She quickly put the lid on the cup and passed it to her daughter on her way through the living room where Wes, no doubt, stood on the other side of the door. Pausing, she drew in a deep breath. *Lord, help me to keep these crazy, mixed-up emotions in check.*

When she opened the door, though, the man on her porch wasn't Wes. He was older, tall, thin and clean-shaven with short gray hair. Hands in the pockets of his sharply creased medium-wash jeans, he looked nervous. And, while she couldn't put her finger on it, there was something familiar about him.

With Sarah-Jane safe in her playard, Laurel stepped into the humid air, pulling the door closed behind her. "Can I help you?"

He simply stared at her for a moment before saying, "Are you Laurel Donovan?"

"Yes."

The man's faded green eyes teared as a smile quivered at his lips. "My name is Jimmy Donovan."

Laurel felt her own eyes grow wide. Her nostrils flared as a jumbled ball of emotions slammed into her gut. Her breathing intensified. "*Get* out of here." Every muscle in her body tensed. How dare this…this—

"Please, let me—"

"No!" The word spewed from her mouth with a vehemence she'd never experienced. "I don't believe you." She dared a step closer, fists clenched. "What are you? Some kind of sicko? Have you been stalking me, gathering information so you can blackmail me or something?"

"No, I would never…" Lines creased his tanned brow, and he appeared confused. Panicked even. Yet he made no effort to move.

Fortunately for her, she spotted Wes's truck easing

toward the curb. He'd take care of this pathetic excuse for a human being.

"You wait right there." Taking two steps back, she pointed toward the stranger, as though her finger alone would prevent him from fleeing.

To his credit, the guy looked genuinely freaked out as she motioned with her other hand for Wes to hurry.

Thankfully, Wes caught her drift, slammed his truck into Park and practically ran toward her, taking the porch steps in a single leap. "Is there a problem?"

"This—" she wagged her finger at the stranger "—this…*jerk* says he's my father."

Looking as though he'd pummel the guy if he made one wrong move, Wes cast a wary glare at the man. "State your business, sir." Suddenly Laurel was thankful Wes was a military man.

The stranger lifted his hands in the air. "My name is Jimmy—James—Donovan. I'm not here to make any trouble. I hired a private investigator to find my daughter, Laurel. You can check my ID and the returned letters I sent to her mother."

Laurel's heart squeezed, and she sucked in a sharp breath. "You have letters?"

"Yes." He kept one hand in the air while the other slowly reached for his back pocket.

Laurel shot a glance at Wes, who closely watched the man's every move like a lion ready to pounce.

The stranger's hand was shaking as he held out a small stack of envelopes.

Wes snatched them, giving them a quick once-over before passing them to Laurel.

Looking at the top one, she saw her mother's name, along with her grandmother's address and the words

Return to Sender. Whether it was from the implications of these letters or the thunder rumbling in the distance, a shiver skittered down her spine.

With both hands again in the air, the stranger said, "My wallet with my ID is in my other pocket."

Wes didn't hesitate to retrieve it.

Confusion swirled through Laurel like gathering storm clouds as Sarah-Jane squawked inside. Could these letters be real? And what would it mean if they were?

She looked at Wes. "You okay for a minute?"

He nodded, pulling the man's ID from his wallet.

With a parting glance, she escaped inside, knowing she was not about to expose Sarah-Jane to this man Wes had in check. At least, she hoped he did. But considering how fit Wes was, her concern was probably for naught.

Moving around the sofa, she saw Sarah-Jane standing at the edge of her playard, holding on to her cup.

"What is it, baby?" Laurel set the envelopes on the counter and grabbed the small bowl of fish crackers. "Are you hungry?"

Her wide-eyed daughter did the "more" motion.

Even in the midst of this momentary crisis, Laurel couldn't help but smile. "I love you so much, baby." She kissed her daughter's head then handed her the bowl.

As Sarah-Jane plopped back down, curiosity pinged through Laurel's brain. What if this man was her father?

Retrieving the letters, she riffled through the small stack. Every one of them was postmarked thirty-two years ago. She would have been Sarah-Jane's age.

Setting the others aside, she opened the first envelope, pulled out a sheet of yellow legal paper and read.

"My beloved, Brenda. I miss you more than you will

ever know, and I can't wait for you and Laurel to join me. I know I messed up but, thanks to your mother, I'm back on my feet. I'm working in the oil fields and am making more money than I ever imagined."

Something stopped her then. She again looked at the envelope.

Return to Sender. The writing was her grandmother's. She picked up the other four letters. They were all unopened with *Return to Sender* in her grandmother's script.

A sick feeling churned in Laurel's belly. Had her mother even seen these letters? And if what this man said was true, if he really was her father, where did she go from here?

Her eyes momentarily closed. *Lord, give me wisdom.*

With Sarah-Jane content, Laurel again slipped onto the porch. Wes was still on high alert, towering over the man who now sat on her wicker love seat, his hands in his lap, concern carving deep lines into his brow. And for the first time, she noticed that he looked…frail.

She drew in a bolstering breath, looking at Wes. "It's all right."

He nodded. "Are you okay if I check on Sa—?" His gaze momentarily shifted toward the stranger. "Our daughter?"

She appreciated his concern for Sarah-Jane. Not only that, but the way he said *our daughter* suggested that Laurel didn't live here alone. "Yes, I'll be fine."

With a parting glance, he said, "I'm right inside if you need me."

A multitude of questions played across her mind as she pulled up a chair and sat down opposite the man. She studied him a moment, realizing why he looked so familiar. It was his eyes, though she wasn't ready to admit how much they looked like hers.

"If you are my father, why didn't you try to find me sooner or come back to see me when I was little? I mean, couldn't you have at least called? Didn't you want to see me?"

"More than you can imagine. And yes, I did think about coming back, wanting to reclaim what was rightfully mine." He shook his head repeatedly. "But shortly after those letters were returned to me, I received another envelope with divorce papers. Your mother had signed them and expected me to do the same." Something akin to heartache passed across his expression. "It about killed me, but I figured she'd moved on, so I signed them and sent 'em off."

Try as she might, Laurel was struggling to understand what he was saying. It was as though she was trying to put together a puzzle with only half of the pieces. "That doesn't make any sense. You left me and Mom without even saying goodbye."

His shoulders slumped. "Is that what they told you?"

She nodded. "Mom said you went to jail, and when you got out, she never heard from you again."

He dragged a weathered hand over his face. "I guess I'd better start from the beginning. That is, if you have time." He nodded toward the door. "With the little one and all."

"She's with her father." Laurel had never imagined herself saying that before. Or that she'd be sitting on her porch with a man that could possibly be *her* father. "And yes, I need to know the whole story." Not that she was ready to believe everything this stranger said.

Drawing in a deep breath, he stared out across the

lawn as clouds overtook what had been a brilliant blue sky. "Your mother and me, we were young. Fell in love in high school and married before the ink was dry on our diplomas. Of course, your grandmother wasn't real pleased about the fact that we snuck off to the justice of the peace as opposed to having a formal church wedding. But we didn't care. We had big dreams for ourselves."

Laurel leaned back in her chair, though she was anything but relaxed as she tried to envision a younger version of this man and her mother together. "Such as?"

"I wanted to work in the oil industry. Wanted to build my own company. But then your mother got pregnant and couldn't work for a while when the doctor put her on bed rest. I managed to pull some overtime with my warehouse job, but the company folded shortly after you were born, and your mother got let go from her job." He met her gaze now. "My pride took a major hit when we had to move in with your grandmother. Don't get me wrong, I was grateful to Sarah Corwin for giving us a roof over our heads, but I wanted to provide for my family, and those temporary jobs I'd been taking weren't cutting it." His expression clouded. "I got desperate and started selling drugs, thinking I could make some fast money. Ended up going to jail instead. I spent the next six months trying to come up with a way to take care of my family, but when you're on the inside, the future doesn't always look so bright. Then, shortly before I was released, your grandmother came to see me and made me an offer."

Laurel's gaze narrowed. "What kind of offer?"

"She said Brenda had told her about my desire to work in the oil fields and that she'd talked to a man who was willing to hire me as a roughneck. Said she'd cover my fine and pay for a bus ticket and two weeks' worth of hotel, but I'd have to leave the moment I was released or else the fella would give the job to someone else."

Laurel recalled her grandmother's handwriting on those envelopes. "You mean, you couldn't even say goodbye to us?"

"Your grandmother said there wasn't time, that I had to be on that first bus out. So I thanked her and promised I wouldn't let her down." The way his voice trailed off made it seem as though that was the end of the story.

Laurel gripped the arms of her chair. "Okay, so what happened then?"

"Everything came together just the way your grandmother had said. I got out, moved to west Texas and became a roughneck."

"All right, but what about my mom and me?"

Elbow on the arm of the settee, he rubbed a finger across his lips as tears again filled his eyes. "I never saw either one of you again." His voice cracked, making his sorrow seem so deep and real.

Despite the increasing thunder that seemed to insist she go inside, Laurel wasn't ready. There were things she still needed to know. "Did my mother visit you while you were in jail?"

He lifted a shoulder. "Not very often. But then, she had you to care for. After your grandmother's visit, I wrote Brenda a letter, explaining the plan, and told her I'd bring the two of you out to be with me just as soon as I had a place for us to live."

Laurel was almost afraid to ask. "So why didn't you send for us?"

"I did." He gave a slight shake of his head. "But the letter was returned just like the others."

Laurel's head was swimming. She'd thought that hearing the whole story would help clarify things, but her mind kept going back to her grandmother's handwriting on those envelopes. If what this man—Jimmy—said was true, then her grandmother had sabotaged her parents' marriage. And everything Laurel had ever believed was a lie.

The wind kicked up then, tinged with the smell of ozone.

She needed to go inside before the storm hit. But not before she had the answer to one last question. "Why did you decide to find me now?"

He stood, as though he was ready to evade the storm, too. "Because I'm dying."

Chapter Twelve

Wes was up early Friday morning. Not that he'd gotten much sleep. He was worried about Laurel. Having her father show up after thirty-plus years had to be a huge shock—even more so than when Wes first appeared in Bliss.

After the man left, Wes had remained at Laurel's until the thunderstorm had passed. At least that had been his excuse. Truth was, he wanted to be there in case Laurel needed him. Instead, he'd spent his time entertaining Sarah-Jane and making sure both she and Laurel ate.

What Laurel wanted, though, was to be alone. She'd been in a daze, no doubt processing the information she'd been given. Wes had no clue what was in those letters Jimmy Donovan gave Laurel, but there must have been some facts that were difficult to ignore, otherwise she wouldn't have spent so much time talking with him.

Wes was just glad he was there to take care of Sarah-Jane because, as of right now, Wes didn't want that man anywhere near his daughter. After returning to Rae's, Wes had spent the rest of the evening researching the person who claimed to be Laurel's father. He even sent the photo he'd taken of Jimmy's driver's license to an old navy buddy who worked for the FBI, but Wes had yet to hear anything.

Now, armed with two large Americanos, he headed to Laurel's a little before eight. After he'd told Rae what had transpired last night, his sister had encouraged him to give Laurel time, saying she'd talk when she was ready. But he wanted to see for himself how she was doing. If nothing else, it would at least alleviate his anxiety.

When he pulled up to the bluish-gray Craftsman-style home, he put his truck in Park and paused. *Dear Lord, I know Laurel is confused and hurting right now. I pray that You will comfort her and give her wisdom to know the truth about this man who claims to be her father.*

Killing the engine, he grabbed the coffees and made his way up the walk. The morning sun filtered through the established trees. A few leaves littered the ground, the only evidence of last night's storm. The one out here, anyway.

At the door, he knocked, and Laurel opened it a few moments later with Sarah-Jane on her hip. Wearing black yoga pants and a two-sizes-too-large T-shirt, Laurel stared at him through puffy eyes. And her hair was a mess.

"I wasn't expecting you," she said.

"I know. But I thought you could use this." He held out a cup. "One Americano, just the way you like it." For a second, he thought she was going to turn him away. Then Sarah-Jane reached for him. "How about we trade?"

She hesitated a split second before taking her drink, leaving him a free arm to grab Sarah-Jane.

Following Laurel into the dining area, he dared to ask, "How are you doing?"

"Fine. I'm just busy." She set the cup on the counter and moved around the peninsula into the kitchen. "Sarah-Jane needs to eat so I can take her to the sitter."

"Oh. I thought she only went once a week?"

Laurel plucked a banana from the bunch on the counter. "I called Mary Lou this morning to see if she could take her again."

"Why?"

"Because I happen to have a job." She hastily opened the cabinet, grabbed a small plate, then let the door slam closed. "As if it's any of your business."

Oh, she was stressed, all right.

His phone dinged then, so while Laurel prepared Sarah-Jane's breakfast, he took his daughter into the living room to check the text he hoped was from his friend. Pulling the device from his pocket, he looked at the screen.

Check your email.

Just what Wes had been waiting for.

Opening the screen, he tapped a few buttons to bring up his email, then quickly scanned the information.

"Wes, I need Sarah-Jane in her high chair so she can eat."

"I'm on it." Turning, he closed the screen and tucked the phone away. "Are you hungry, sweetheart?"

She rubbed her chest.

"Mommy's gonna get you all fixed up." He slid the child into her seat.

"Wes, I appreciate the coffee, but I think you should go now." She set the plate with cut-up banana on Sarah-Jane's tray then moved back into the kitchen, pausing at the refrigerator to grab the milk.

"Okay, but I'm a little confused as to why you're in such a hurry. Do you have a video chat or something?" Or did she simply want to wallow in the turmoil that was, no doubt, raging inside her? Since things had gotten better between them, he'd thought she might talk to him. Obviously he was mistaken.

"No." She removed the lid from a sippy cup. "I just need you to leave, all right?" She began to pour the milk with a shaky hand.

"Here—" he reached for the milk "—let me help you."

She jerked away, though, sending milk spilling onto the floor. Within seconds, her eyes filled with tears. She slammed the jug on the counter and grabbed a rag. "See what you made me do."

Wes quickly moved around the peninsula and tried to take the rag. "I can get this."

"No!" She jerked away again, but this time tears poured onto her cheeks. "I don't need your help." Her whole body shook. "I don't need anybody."

Wes couldn't take it anymore. Stepping over the small puddle, he wrapped his arms around Laurel.

Her body was rigid at first, but he refused to let go.

"Whether you need me or not, I'm here, Laurel. I'm here." Stroking her hair, he continued to hold her.

Finally, the tension seemed to flow from her, and she clung to him.

"I don't know what to believe." Her words were muffled against his shirt. "I'm so confused."

"Confused about what?" He didn't know if she'd confide in him or not, but he had to try.

A whimper sounded from Sarah-Jane.

"I must have scared her." Sniffing, Laurel took a step back so she could see her daughter. "Mommy's okay, baby." She forced a smile.

"Go sit with her," Wes encouraged Laurel. "Drink your coffee while I get her drink and clean up." To his surprise, Laurel nodded her agreement and went to sit by their daughter.

A few minutes later, Wes handed Sarah-Jane her cup before joining them at the round table.

"I'm sorry I went off on you like that." Laurel wrapped her fingers around her cup. "You didn't deserve it."

"No, but I also know you didn't mean it, so we're good. However, I have something I need to tell you."

Straightening, she lifted her cup. "Go ahead. I doubt it could be anything worse."

"I took a picture of Jimmy's ID yesterday and sent it to a friend of mine who ran a background check."

Her suddenly wide eyes searched his. "And?"

"From all appearances, Jimmy Donovan is a stand-up guy. He owns a drilling business out in the Permian Basin, and his only run-in with the law was over thirty years ago, when he served six months for possession with intent to distribute a controlled substance."

Nodding, she leaned back in her chair. "I guess he was telling the truth, then. At least about that part."

Did Wes dare press her to let him in? To tell him about what she'd learned yesterday?

He took a deep breath. "What else did he have to say?"

Over the next several minutes, Laurel opened up, revealing her grandmother's offer to help Jimmy when he got out of jail and how his letters to her mother were not only returned but followed by divorce papers.

"I feel like I've been lied to all my life. I can't believe my grandmother would deliberately try to keep my parents apart. I thought she was the only person I could trust. Now it appears she was simply the puppeteer manipulating everyone else for the outcome she wanted."

While a part of him wanted to agree, he said, "I'm sure she had her reasons. Probably thought she was protecting you and your mother."

"By tearing apart my family?" She huffed. "What kind of person does that?"

Of course, this was assuming Jimmy was telling the truth. But he also could have been trying to deflect responsibility. "Does Jimmy blame her?"

Laurel thought for moment, emptied the last of her coffee. "If he does, he didn't say it. He simply laid out what I assume are facts."

Wes had to give the guy credit for that.

"I don't understand why my grandmother would return those letters without ever giving them to my mother."

"I'm sorry to say, that's something you'll probably never know."

Her gaze drifted to Sarah-Jane. "Are you all finished, baby?"

The child waved her hands in the air.

Laurel chuckled. "Good girl."

Wes stood and went into the kitchen to dampen a

paper towel, then came back to wipe off his daughter's hands and face. When he was finished, he lifted Sarah-Jane out of her chair and set her on her feet. She promptly headed into the living room.

"He said he's dying, Wes."

He faced Laurel.

Standing, she continued. "That's why he wanted to find me."

"Wow." He shoved a hand through his hair. "How do you feel about that?"

"That's just it—I don't know how I feel. I mean, I thought I knew everything. I thought he walked out on me and my mother. I thought he rejected me. Now it appears that wasn't the case at all."

"Do you plan to talk to him again?"

"I don't know. He said he's staying at the Bliss Inn for a few days, in case I wanted to talk, and he gave me his number. But... I just don't know."

"I understand your hesitation. However, you might want to ask yourself this. How are you going to feel if you don't? Especially since you know he's dying."

"I'll probably regret it. But I'm not sure I want to expose Sarah-Jane to him. At least not yet. Not until I'm sure."

"I'm in complete agreement with you there. Why don't you ask him to meet you for lunch somewhere so there will be other people around? I mean, you're already taking Sarah-Jane to the sitter. And if you want me to go with you, I will."

She blinked at him. "You'd do that?"

At this moment, there wasn't a whole lot he wouldn't do for her. He cupped her cheek. "In a heartbeat."

She pulled away then and smiled. "I appreciate that."

Drawing in a long breath, she continued, "But I'm afraid this is something I'm going to tackle alone."

He couldn't say that he blamed her. Still, "In that case, I'm only a phone call away if you need me."

Laurel opted to meet Jimmy at Rae's Fresh Start Café. Given how difficult their conversation was likely to be, Laurel decided it might encourage her, at least, to have it in familiar territory. Not that her porch hadn't been familiar. She knew what she was getting into today, though. Or hoped so, anyway. She wasn't sure she could handle any more bombshells.

She arrived early so she could inform Rae as to what was going on and then snagged a table near the back, where they weren't as likely to be interrupted every time someone walked in the door. Finally, at 11:44 a.m., one minute before their designated meeting time, Jimmy Donovan walked into the restaurant. He was a handsome man and carried himself well. No wonder her mother had fallen for him.

But there was something else about him. A sadness. Not just because of the current situation or his illness, but a deep-rooted ache. The kind that comes from a broken heart.

Shaking off the notion, and as much of her sympathy as she could manage, she stood so he could see her.

His smile grew wide when he did, albeit a tad tremulous. Moments later, he was beside her. Hands buried in the pockets of his jeans, he said, "I was kinda surprised to hear from you."

"A sleepless night left me with a lot of questions. Questions I'm hoping you can answer for me."

"I'll do my best."

She motioned for him to sit down as she eased into her chair once again. Rae promptly brought them each water and a menu. After small talk and placing their orders, Laurel was ready to dive in.

Arms crossed, she rested them on the wooden tabletop. "Tell me about my mother. What was she like?"

A faraway look glimmered in his eyes. "She was the epitome of vivacious. Fun, full of energy, always saw the best in everyone and everything. Including me." He shifted in his seat. "I'll never forget the first time I saw her. It was at a high school football game. She was a cheerleader, you know. Had that cute little skirt and sweater." His smile faded slightly, and he looked at Laurel. "She was the only person who ever believed in me, and I was determined to prove myself worthy. I ended up letting her down instead."

That last little tidbit had tears prickling Laurel's eyes, but she managed to blink them away. Still, the way he talked about her mother... He really had loved her. Perhaps still did.

"The investigator told me she'd passed on. How did she die?"

Fingering the wrapper on her unopened straw, Laurel said, "Drugs." A sigh escaped. "I was ten, so my memories of her are vague. I just remember that she was always leaving. I'd stay with my grandmother while Mom ran off with guy after guy. Then she'd come back a few weeks later, usually brokenhearted, promising that things were going to be different. Then, before I knew it, she'd be gone again."

Jimmy's countenance grew distressed. "And all these years I just assumed she'd found love again."

"I think she kept looking, she just never found it."

A myriad of conversations, none of them intelligible, swirled through the sudden silence.

Jimmy's Adam's apple bobbed up and down rapidly, and he seemed to struggle for composure. "I guess my leaving really messed her up."

"Perhaps. However, after taking in everything you told me, and looking at those letters, seeing my grandmother's handwriting on the envelopes, I'm starting to get the feeling Mom never knew the reason *why* you left. Like me, I think she thought you'd abandoned us. And as much as it pains me to say this, I think that's what my grandmother wanted us to believe."

"I'm so sorry Laurel. I let pride get the best of me—" a tear spilled onto his cheek "—and ended up hurting the two people I love most in this world."

Laurel's vision blurred. How she had dreamed of hearing her father say he loved her. That he hadn't abandoned her. Or rejected her. He'd wanted her.

"There wasn't a day that's gone by I didn't send up a prayer for you."

Reaching for her napkin, a move that sent her silverware clanging against the table, she stared at him. "You did?" She dabbed her eyes.

"I couldn't be there to watch over you, so I asked the Lord to do it in my stead."

Through tears, she said, "You have no idea how much I want to believe that."

"I understand." Straightening, he sucked in a breath. "Trust is something that needs to be earned. But I intend to use whatever time I've got left to do just that."

Here she was, in the middle of a restaurant, and the tears simply wouldn't stop. This would not do. "I'm sorry—" she sniffed "—but we're going to have to change the subject before I turn into a bawling heap."

He chuckled.

She blew her nose. "Um, so you own a drilling company?"

His brow lifted. "Sounds like you've done some research."

"Actually, Wes did." She reached for her water. "He had a friend run a background check."

"Can't say as I blame him. He was trying to protect you, like a good husband should."

"Well, he's retired military, if that tells you anything. And..." Setting her cup back down without ever having taken a drink, she wondered if she should tell him. Yesterday she hadn't wanted Jimmy to know any details about her life. But then, she'd also believed he was a fraud, someone who only wanted something from her. Now, though, she actually believed he was her father and the reasons behind his sudden appearance were sincere.

Meeting his gaze once again, she said, "Wes is not my husband."

"Oh." Jimmy looked surprised. "I just assumed."

"It's a rather complicated situation." Out of the corner of her eye, Laurel saw Rae approach.

"All right, I've got your beef tips with noodles." Rae set the plate in front of Laurel then handed the other plate to Jimmy. "And chicken fried steak for the gentleman."

"Thank you, young lady."

"Can I get you anything else?" Rae said those same words to everyone in her restaurant. But the look she sent Laurel said she was ready to provide a means of escape if Laurel needed it.

"No." Laurel winked. "I think we're good."

A smile lit Rae's blue eyes. "Glad to hear it." She patted Laurel's shoulder. "Just holler if you need me."

Laurel was surprised when Jimmy asked if he could say grace. Then, over their meal, Laurel explained her and Wes's relationship. What little of it she understood, anyway.

"It's obvious he cares about you very much." Jimmy shoved another bite of steak into his mouth.

She thought about the feel of Wes's hand touching her face. Oh, how she'd wanted to lean into it. To feel his embrace once again.

Shrugging, she nabbed a forkful of noodles. "He's an honorable man, and I happen to be the mother of his child."

"I saw firsthand how fiercely protective he was of you." Knife in one hand, fork in the other, he cut another piece of meat.

"He was protecting his daughter."

Jimmy glanced up at her. "Don't kid yourself, Laurel."

She wasn't kidding herself—she was protecting her heart. Her feelings for Wes had begun to shift, moving into unfamiliar and terrifying territory. Believing that his feelings were only because of Sarah-Jane was what Laurel needed to keep her from getting her hopes up.

"Well, it doesn't really matter, anyway, because Wes is leaving soon."

Jimmy's brow lifted in question.

"He's going to Iraq for a year to work with Servant's Heart."

"I've heard of them. However, a year's not that long, then he'll be back."

She paused, her fork in midair. "I'm not trying to be hurtful, but the concept of coming back isn't something I can easily wrap my head around."

He frowned, nodding. "Laurel, your grandmother loved you. I'm sure she thought she was doing the right thing by you. She took very good care of you. Left you her entire estate, from what I hear."

"Yes, but she took away the only thing I ever really wanted."

Chapter Thirteen

Wes needed to stop thinking about Laurel. Ever since that night they had dinner with Irma and Joyce, his resolve to steer clear of romantic relationships had seemed to be fading fast when it came to her. Perhaps all that talk about weddings had gotten to him.

Whatever the case, he needed to get a grip. Just because he and Laurel shared a daughter didn't mean that they were destined to be together. Sure, he cared about her and wanted what was best for her. But Wes wasn't the best. He'd failed his parents. He couldn't bear it if he failed Laurel, too.

By the grace of God, he'd managed to keep himself in check when she'd stopped by Irma's a little over an hour ago to let him know how things had gone with Jimmy. She seemed to be getting closer to accepting that the man was, indeed, her father, which was something Wes couldn't argue with based on everything she'd told him.

Pulling the front door closed at Irma's just after three, he twisted the key in the dead bolt before heading toward his truck. He'd accomplished everything on his list today—added the subfloor to the bathroom, removed the remaining vinyl and then did the drywall repair on the family room ceiling. He supposed he should start thinking about what he was going to say at the men's prayer breakfast tomorrow. He could make a list of the details he wanted to be sure to touch on.

But first, he owed his sister some attention. He'd been spending so much time with Laurel and Sarah-Jane that Rae had become relegated to a back burner, and that wasn't fair. Not after all she'd done for him. At least he'd managed to get in most of the painting she'd wanted done.

Rae was in her newly opened-up kitchen, folding laundry at the table when he arrived.

"You're home early." She set a towel on the table. "Did you accomplish much?"

"There's no longer a gaping hole in Irma's family room, if that tells you anything." He set his tool bag on the wooden floor, in the corner by the table, then headed to the sink to wash up.

"Sounds like progress." Adding another towel to the growing stack, she said, "By the way, I just got off the phone with Laurel. We're going to dinner with her and Sarah-Jane tonight." She grabbed another towel from the basket on the chair. "I'm craving Mexican and some time with my niece, so I figured I may as well kill two birds with one stone. And since you've been spending all of your time with them anyway…"

He turned the hot water on and squirted soap onto his hands. Just when he'd decided he should take a break from Laurel. Then again, a meal with his sister at a restaurant wasn't the same as the two of them and Sarah-Jane feeling like a family at Laurel's house.

After working up a lather, he scrubbed his hands and forearms.

Behind him, his sister continued. "How are things going between you and Laurel, anyway?"

He cringed, not wanting to talk about Laurel. "We're adjusting." He moved his arms back and forth beneath the stream of water, hoping his sister wouldn't press the conversation.

"That's not what I mean, and you know it." Glancing over his shoulder, he saw a frustrated Rae set the final towel atop the stack. "Is there any chance the two of you could, you know, have a future together?"

As if he deserved a future with Laurel or anybody else. Rae knew better. He'd cost their parents their lives. That was why he had to forfeit his.

"Not with me leaving soon." Turning off the water with his elbow, he reached for the dish towel on the counter.

"But you'll be back." Rae was not about to let this go. "Besides, I've seen the way you two look at each other."

Hands clean and dry, he threw the towel back onto the counter. "We share a child, Rae. Of course we're going to have a mutual respect for one another."

Skepticism narrowed her blue eyes. "Mutual respect, huh?" Crossing her arms over her chest, she continued to watch him.

He retrieved a glass from the cupboard. "Don't do this to me, Rae. You know where I stand when it comes to relationships."

"Then how do you explain Sarah-Jane?"

Reaching for the handle on the fridge, he froze. He hated it when she was right. Because he still couldn't understand how he'd allowed that night to happen.

He yanked open the door and filled his glass with some iced tea without saying a word. Then he slammed the door closed, went into the living room and dropped onto the leather couch, all without so much as a glance toward his sister. He could only hope she'd take a hint.

Instead, she crossed the room and sat down beside him, setting a hand on his knee. "You're a good man, Wesley. A man who's spent his entire adult life serving others. I know you feel as though you deserve to be punished for what happened to Dad and Mom, but I think your sentence has been served."

He watched her out of the corner of his eye. "Don't tell me you've never blamed me, Rae. I mean, look at all you gave up."

She stared at him. "Not once. I may not have liked it. I certainly didn't understand why, but I never blamed you or anyone else for their accident. Because that's just what it was, an accident." With a final pat, she walked away. "I saw Laurel's father today."

His sister knew him well and understood he was done discussing the previous topic. Of course, not without having her own say. "And?"

"She introduced him on their way out." Returning to the table, she began folding a pile of clothes.

"Did she refer to him as her father?" Grateful for the reprieve, he stretched an arm across the back of the sofa.

"No, she called him Jimmy, but I have no doubt that he is her father. She looks a lot like him. Same eyes, same smile."

He took a sip of his tea, the cold liquid soothing his suddenly parched throat. "Any other observations?"

"No, I tried to leave them alone. They were pretty deep in conversation. Though I did notice a few tears from both of them." She dropped the shirt she'd just picked up. "Oh, I almost forgot." Moving to the kitchen counter, she retrieved a large envelope. "A package came for you from Servant's Heart." She started toward him.

He leaned forward to deposit his cup on the coffee table with one hand while intercepting the envelope with the other. "Must be the paperwork they told me about." After digging his pocketknife from his jeans, he sliced open the top.

Pulling out the forms, he sifted through them. They wanted him to list a beneficiary, which wasn't much different from serving overseas with the military. In the past, he'd always listed Rae. But that was before Sarah-Jane.

"You look awful serious over there." Rae continued to fold. "What's in the packet?"

"The usual stuff." He lifted his head to look at her. "What should I do about the beneficiary this time?"

"What's your first instinct?"

"Laurel."

Rae shot him a smile and a thumbs-up. "I was hoping you'd say that."

"But I've always named you."

"And you think you'll be hurting my feelings." She shook her head. "Wesley, you know I don't need the money." Rae had gotten the last laugh when the judge ordered her ex-husband to pay her for her half of the car dealership they'd owned together, allowing Rae to walk away with a tidy chunk of change. "Besides, I'm not raising your child. If anything happens to you, the money should go to Laurel."

Staring at the paperwork in his lap, his new job suddenly became more real. He'd be leaving in just a little over a week. He was used to leaving, except things had changed. This time he'd be leaving someone besides Rae. Truth be told, two very important someones—Laurel and Sarah-Jane. Could he do that? Not that he had a choice. He was committed. If only he'd known about Sarah-Jane before he signed his contract.

He shoved a hand through his hair. This could be his toughest assignment yet.

Laurel was glad when Rae had called and suggested they do dinner. She hadn't had much time with her friends since Wes came to town. And with her father showing up, well, she could really use a friend about now. There were so many thoughts tumbling through her head that it was difficult to sort them all out. Perhaps a change of scenery and a listening ear would help. Even if Wes was going to be there, too.

She pulled into the already full parking lot of La Familia just as Rae and Wes were exiting his truck. Rae hurried over and hugged Laurel as she got out while Wes unhooked Sarah-Jane from her car seat. Moments later, they all made their way inside the colorful eatery, where they were greeted with the enticing aromas of fresh-made tortillas, sizzling meat and spices.

Laurel's mouth watered in anticipation.

Despite the busy Friday-night crowd, they were seated right away. Something Laurel was more than grateful for, because she was starving. With so many tears over lunch, she'd found her appetite waning. Now, it was back with a vengeance, along with a sudden craving for Mexican food.

While Wes studied his menu, Laurel had already

settled on the cheese enchiladas, so she simply sat back and took in the busyness of the place. Waiters and waitresses scurrying back and forth with large trays laden with food, patrons talking and laughing, and Rae playing peekaboo with Sarah-Jane, making the child giggle.

Grabbing a tortilla chip from the bowl on the table, she scooped up a fair amount of salsa, her gaze drifting toward the door. Somehow, beyond the throng of waiting people, she spotted Jimmy Donovan. He was alone, of course, and something about that bothered her.

She glanced toward her daughter. Did she dare invite him to join them? Would Wes be okay with that? After all, they had yet to expose Sarah-Jane to the man. But then, what if he saw them?

As she continued to stare, Wes nudged her elbow. "Do you want to ask him to come sit with us?"

Her gaze shifted to the man beside her. "I don't know. What about Sarah-Jane?"

Rae leaned across the table. "What are y'all whispering about?"

"My father is here." Only after the words left her mouth did Laurel realize that she'd referred to him as her father instead of Jimmy. Perhaps this was the beginning of acceptance.

"Why don't you invite him to join us, then?" Rae made it sound so simple. "That is, unless you don't want to."

"It's not that. It's just that he hasn't met Sarah-Jane yet."

Rae briefly glanced over her shoulder in the direction Wes and Rae had been looking. "Do you think he poses any sort of threat to her?"

"No. It's just all so…new."

"Hmm... Kind of like when Wes showed up, huh?" Rae reached for a tortilla chip. "Look on the bright side—you're surrounded by friends." She motioned between herself and Wes.

Laurel saw Rae's point, though she still found herself looking to Wes for guidance. After all, he was Sarah-Jane's father.

He smiled. "Go ask him. I'll have the waiter bring another setup and menu."

Standing, Laurel took in a deep breath and crossed the terra-cotta pavers to where Jimmy waited, aware that this would likely signal a change in their relationship.

"Jimmy?"

He looked up at her with a smile she'd seen a thousand times on Sarah-Jane.

"I didn't expect to see you here."

"I'm with Wes, my best friend, Rae, and Sarah-Jane. My daughter. Would you care to join us?"

As he stood, his smile became more tremulous. "Aw, I'd hate to intrude."

"You're not intruding. You're invited." It surprised her when she realized that she actually meant it.

"In that case, I'd be honored."

Amid the sounds of mariachi music, they returned to the table, where Wes formally introduced himself and Rae.

"And this is Sarah-Jane." A sense of pride washed over Laurel. "Your granddaughter."

He crouched beside the high chair, his gray-green eyes filled with wonder. "Hello, Sarah-Jane. You sure are a cute little thing. Just look at those pretty blue eyes."

"She has her father to thank for those," said Laurel.

"Though I don't think anyone has ever said mine are pretty." Wes bit into another chip.

"At least not since you were little," injected Rae.

Once they sat down, the conversation remained casual, just as Rae had suggested. And it was comforting to have Rae and Wes asking Jimmy questions about himself, giving Laurel more insight into the man she had so much to learn about. Like the fact that he'd never remarried. Laurel wasn't sure what to read into that, but given their conversation earlier today, it was obvious he had loved her mother very much. And from what she knew about her mother, she suspected the feeling was mutual.

When the waiter brought the check, Jimmy insisted on picking up the tab. "Y'all made me feel welcome, and I appreciate that."

Rae and Jimmy fussed over Sarah-Jane as they exited the restaurant into the steamy night air.

Moving into the parking lot, Laurel tugged Wes aside. "Do you think it would be okay to invite him over to the house for a little bit? Maybe let him see Sarah-Jane in her element. Of course, she'll be going to bed soon, so—"

"Laurel." With a grin that made his blue eyes sparkle, Wes reached for her arm. "He's your father. It's fine."

Her gaze darted to the older man, uncertainty still lingering. "Would you—?"

"Rae and I will be happy to join you."

She couldn't help smiling. It seemed Wes knew her too well.

She caught up to her father. "Jimmy?"

He turned.

"Would you like to—"

His face suddenly went ashen, his expression going blank.

She stretched out a hand, attempting to reach for him. "Jimmy, are you o—"

But before she could get the words out, he collapsed.

"Jimmy!" She dropped to her knees.

"What happened?" Wes was at her side, rolling the man onto his back.

"I don't know. The color drained from his face, then he went down." She gasped when she saw the blood oozing from a gash on his forehead. *God, please don't let my father die now. I just found him. Please.*

Tears stung the backs of her eyes as Wes checked Jimmy's pulse.

"Jimmy?" He continued to evaluate the man. "Can you hear me?" He looked at Laurel. "Do you have a rag or anything else in the diaper bag we can use for the bleeding?"

Moving the strap off her shoulder, Laurel saw Rae looking on, bouncing a blessedly oblivious Sarah-Jane.

"The hospital is right up the street, if you need it," said Rae. "It'd probably be quicker to take him than wait on an ambulance."

Hospital? Ambulance? Laurel hastily unzipped the main compartment of her bag and dug through it until she came up with an old cloth bib. "Here." She thrust it toward Wes as her father began to rouse. "Thank You, God." She fell back on her flip-flop-covered heels, grateful for Wes's combat service. She could trust him to take care of her father just as well as any EMT.

"Jimmy?" Wes waited for the man to make eye contact. "I'm going to help you into my truck and take you to the hospital, all right?"

Thankfully, her father nodded his agreement.

Minutes later, Wes, Jimmy and Laurel were on their way to the hospital, while Rae took Sarah-Jane home in Laurel's SUV. Laurel sat in the back seat with Jimmy, holding the bib to his forehead and praying like never before. She couldn't lose him. Not with everything she'd learned today. He loved her, and he'd always wanted her. She squeezed her eyes shut. *God, please.*

When they arrived at the emergency room, the aides put Jimmy on a gurney and promptly whisked him away.

"Are you all related to this man?" A young woman wearing bright pink scrubs looked from Laurel to Wes and back again.

"He's my father," Laurel managed to eke out.

Fearful, she collapsed into a nearby chair, the antiseptic smells threatening to overwhelm her. Wes joined her, reaching for her hand. Strange how she was so used to taking care of herself, and yet tonight, she appreciated Wes's take-charge attitude. And the strength of his touch was what she needed right now.

After what felt like an eternity, Laurel and Wes were accompanied to her father's exam room, where the doctor informed them that it was likely Jimmy's elevated blood pressure that caused him to black out.

"Coupled with the head wound, I'd like to go ahead and keep him overnight for observation," the doctor continued.

The news came as a relief to Laurel. The thought of her father going back to a hotel room all alone made her nervous.

She and Wes remained at the hospital until her father was settled into his room. Then they bade him goodnight with a promise from Laurel that she'd be by in the morning.

Once back at Laurel's place, they relayed all of the information to Rae, then she excused herself and went on out to Wes's truck.

Alone, Laurel reached for Wes's hand. "Thank you for staying with me. Without you, I'm pretty sure I would have fallen apart."

"Nah, you're a strong woman."

"I like to think so, but not tonight. You were my rock."

His gaze searched hers for the longest time, and she thought—perhaps even hoped—that he was going to kiss her. Instead, he took a step back and said, "Rae's waiting on me."

Turning away, she cleared her throat, doing her best to ignore the disappointment sifting through her. "Yes, you should go." Because while she'd allowed herself to get caught up in the moment, thinking Wes might actually be interested in her romantically, she now realized that wasn't the case. She and Wes were friends and nothing more. And, somehow, Laurel would have to find a way to live with that.

Chapter Fourteen

After all that scolding Wes had done yesterday, reminding himself why he should stay away from Laurel, he'd almost kissed her. What had gotten into him?

Laurel had. She'd gotten to him in a way no other woman ever had. Every time they were together, he found himself wanting things he couldn't have. Things he didn't deserve.

His frustration was still in full force when he pulled up to the church Saturday morning, and he found himself wondering why he'd even agreed to attend the men's prayer breakfast. Yes, he was heading into the mission field, but he wasn't your average missionary. He was a hands-on worker-bee kind of guy, which was why Servant's Heart had hired him to manage their shelter construction program. He not only loved what he did, he was good at it. But standing in front of a bunch of strangers and talking about his faith wasn't his style.

Yet, despite his misgivings, he still found himself in the church's fellowship hall, gathered around a long table with several men he didn't know. His belly full of some of the finest breakfast tacos he'd ever had, he talked about his upcoming venture. At least they hadn't asked him to stand.

"From what I hear, the entire country of Iraq was left in ruins." An older gentleman who looked every bit a rancher with tanned skin and a full head of white hair gripped a foam coffee cup opposite Wes.

"You may be right, sir." Under the glow of bright white LED lights, he continued, "I can personally attest to the fact that the war in Iraq destroyed many homes, neighborhoods and villages. Our rebuilding efforts are a way of showing Christ's love to the Iraqi people in a tangible manner."

The same man lifted a brow. "Did you serve in Iraq?"

"Yes, sir."

"Which branch of the service were you in?" a man about Wes's age piped up at the far end of the table.

"Navy."

"My grandson is in the navy." Another older gentleman smiled proudly.

"How long were you in?" the stocky fellow next to Wes asked.

"I was a Seabee for twenty years before retiring a couple of years ago."

"You must have joined quite young, then." The pastor watched him curiously.

"Right out of high school."

Eyeing the round black clock on the wall, the pastor said, "Fellas, this has been a great discussion." He faced Wes. "Wes, we'll keep you in our prayers. And, if you have an opportunity, drop us an email and let us know how things are going and how we can specifically pray for you during your time in Iraq."

Given the state of his attitude when he'd walked into

the church earlier, Wes was humbled. "I will do that, sir. Thank you."

After the pastor closed with a word of prayer, chairs scraped across the linoleum floor as the men stood, gathering their trash. Most paused to shake Wes's hand and thank him for his service on their way out the door.

"I'll have to add my thanks once again." With everyone else gone, the pastor gathered the sugar, creamer and a stack of foam cups from beside the coffeepot that sat on a small table set off to one side. "I know that was short notice, so I appreciate you taking the time to come."

Wes grabbed the empty box that once held the tacos and the partial box of doughnuts and followed the pastor into the kitchen. "I'll admit that I was a little apprehensive at first. But I actually enjoyed it."

"I'm glad to hear that." The older man deposited his armload on the long center island, and Wes did the same. "So, what made you decide to become a Seabee?"

To atone for my parents' deaths was the first thing that came to Wes's mind.

"I knew I wanted to serve in the military. When I went to see the recruiter, he talked about the Seabees, and I got really pumped. I had no idea there was such a thing. My dad and I used to build things all the time and I really enjoyed it, so it seemed like a natural fit." He lifted a shoulder. "Besides, I needed to give Rae her life back."

When the pastor sent him a confused look, Wes went on. "Our parents died when I was still in high school. Rae put college on hold to finish raising me. Something I know I didn't deserve."

"Why do you say that?"

Contemplating the man beside him, Wes found himself in a quandary. He could easily come up with some offhanded remark about being a teenager that might appease the guy's curiosity, or he could tell him the truth.

Not so different from the dilemma Laurel had faced last Sunday when she introduced Wes as Rae's brother. Her half-truth had not only hurt Wes, it had left her riddled with guilt. And guilt was something Wes was all too acquainted with.

Resting a hand atop the counter, he said, "I'm the reason my parents are dead." His words were blunt, he knew that, yet Pastor Kleinschmidt didn't even flinch.

Eyed narrowed, the pastor studied him. "You really believe that?"

"I do."

Lines formed on the man's brow as he continued to watch Wes. "How did they die?"

"Car crash."

"Were you driving?"

"No."

"Then how could it be your fault?"

"Because they were coming to pick me up from camp." Crossing his arms, he drew in a long breath and leaned his backside against the counter. "I was sixteen. Me and this other kid had gotten into a fight, so they called our parents to come and get us." He found himself staring at the dropped ceiling, unable to look the pastor in the eye. "It was raining really hard that night. They shouldn't have been out on the roads. But they were. Because of me." Mustering his courage, he met the pastor's concerned gaze. "Just another in a long line of bad choices I've made in my life. Except the impact of that one was far-reaching."

The pastor remained silent for a moment, as though searching for the right words. "Wes, the Bible says, 'When I was a child, I thought as a child: but when I became a man, I put away childish things.' As a sixteen-year-old boy, you convinced yourself that you alone were responsible for your parents' deaths, when nothing could be further from the truth."

Wes struggled to grasp what the pastor was trying to say. If he hadn't gotten into that fight, his parents wouldn't have been out in that storm. Dad wouldn't have lost control of the car.

"Did you cause the storm that night, Wes?"

"Of course, not. Only God can do that."

"That's right." The pastor's lips tilted into a half smile as he leaned against the opposite counter. "Wes, sometimes God allows things to happen that our feeble minds simply cannot understand. But God is still in control. And He has a plan and purpose for each of us."

Wes let the pastor's words rumble around his brain for a minute. "I understand what you're saying up here." He tapped the side of his head. "It's in here—" he pointed to his heart "—where I struggle."

"You can't make sense of your parents' deaths, so it's easier to blame yourself."

"Something like that, yeah."

"Then how about, instead of blaming yourself, you choose to trust that God was in control that night your parents died? That He still has a plan for you. And that Sarah-Jane, perhaps even Laurel, are part of that plan."

Why would he mention Laurel? Did the pastor know, could he see, how Wes felt about her? "It sounds too simple."

"Trusting means letting go, Wes. And I don't know about you, but for me, letting go is never easy."

When I became a man, I put away childish things. Could he really do it? Could he let go of the belief that he'd caused his parents' deaths? After all these years.

God, I want to believe You're in control. Help me. Please.

He eyed the man across from him. "Pastor, will you pray with me?"

"I'd be happy to, Wes."

There was nothing special in the pastor's prayer. No big words, nothing fancy. Yet when Wes walked out of the church twenty minutes later, he felt lighter. It was as though the burden of his past, the one that had weighed him down for so many years, had been lifted from his shoulders. And as thoughts of Sarah-Jane and Laurel sifted into his mind, he began to wonder if, maybe, he might be worthy of a family, after all.

"I've put the paint for each room in that particular room." With Sarah-Jane in one arm and Paisley at her side, Laurel moved from Irma's entry hall into the bedroom Saturday morning, pointing toward the cans near the window. "Rollers, trays and drop cloths are in the family room, along with that blue painter's tape, if you need it."

"Darlin', you've got nothing to worry about." Even in paint clothes, which consisted of torn jeans, a tailored T-shirt and canvas sneakers, Paisley looked like a fashionista. "I've painted more rooms in my lifetime than many professionals."

"Paisley, I really appreciate you helping me out like this." Laurel was supposed to meet her friend and a couple of other women from the church to do the painting at Irma's today. But with Laurel's father in the hospital, she'd asked Paisley if she could take charge of the task in her stead.

"Look, it's not every day a girl finds her long-lost father." Her friend draped an arm around Laurel's shoulder and gave her a sideways hug. "He needs you, so I'm happy to help."

Laurel wasn't sure what she'd done to deserve such wonderful friends, but she was blessed to have them.

After going over everything, she loaded Sarah-Jane into her car seat and drove across town toward the hospital.

Glimpsing her daughter in the rearview mirror, she said, "How do you like that, Sarah-Jane? Only a few weeks ago, it was just us. Now you have a daddy and a grandpa." Not to mention Rae. Tears attempted to blur her vision, though she managed to thwart them. "You have a family, baby." And so did Laurel. After all these years of thinking he'd rejected her, she had a father.

Lord, please don't take him too soon. She wanted the opportunity to get to know Jimmy and make memories.

Under a cloudless sky, she continued on to the hospital. Since all indications were that Jimmy would be discharged today, she wanted to be there to take him back to his hotel to rest, and maybe spend a little time with him until she knew he was settled. Even if he wasn't discharged, she wanted to be there for him. Being in the hospital alone was just plain sad. Fortunately, when she'd had Sarah-Jane, she'd almost never been alone. It seemed either Rae, Christa or Paisley was always there with her, keeping her company, bringing her coffee, pastries and a big ol' basket full of snacks for her and booties, onesies, wipes and pacifiers for Sarah-Jane.

After parking, Laurel retrieved her daughter from the back seat. "Let's go see your grandpa." She supposed she'd have to ask him what he preferred to be called. Grandpa, Pawpaw, Granddaddy...

Holding Sarah-Jane, she made her way across the parking lot and through the automatic double doors at the front of the hospital, then continued down a series of hallways until she came to his room.

"Good morn—" She stopped just inside the doorway. The room was empty. Not only that, the light was off, and the adjustable bed was stripped, as though her father had never been there.

A nurse breezed past the door just then.

"Excuse me." Laurel stepped back into the hall.

The woman sporting short, slightly graying hair did a quick about-face. "Oh, hey, Laurel."

"Ginny, hey. It's good to see you."

"Look at this baby." Ginny, someone Laurel was acquainted with from church, cooed at Sarah-Jane. "She gets cuter every time I see her." Her attention returned to Laurel. "Is she walking yet?"

"Barely, but yes." She shifted Sarah-Jane to her other arm as an aide swept by, pushing a blood pressure cart. "Um, they moved my father, Jimmy Donovan, into this room last night. Can you tell me where he is now?"

"I didn't know he was your father." Ginny palmed her forehead. "Silly me, I didn't even make the connection. He was discharged a couple of hours ago."

"Discharged?" Laurel's heart squeezed. "Did someone pick him up?"

"I don't recall seeing anyone, unless they picked him

up out front. Would you like me to see who escorted him out? Perhaps they could tell you more."

Who just walks out of a hospital? And why wouldn't he have called her? Or even waited, since she'd told him she'd see him in the morning. Unless he didn't want to see her.

"No, that won't be necessary. Thank you, Ginny."

The early May sun had turned hot by the time Laurel made it back to her vehicle. Sweat beaded her forehead. Maybe Jimmy had had someone drive him to get his truck. Then again, it wasn't like Bliss had any taxis. Still, he could have asked someone for a ride. Someone who wasn't his daughter.

She again loaded Sarah-Jane into her car seat. "I'm sorry, baby, but we need to find your grandfather."

A few minutes later, she pulled into the parking lot of La Familia. Jimmy's truck was no longer there.

The familiar ache of rejection threatened to overwhelm her. Tears pricked the backs of her eyes, and her throat tightened. He was gone. Without even saying goodbye.

Sucking in a deep breath, she continued over to the Bliss Inn, where she finally spotted his big white pickup truck, though her relief was merely replaced by angst.

She pulled into the mostly empty parking lot of the '50s-era single-story motel that had recently been renovated and eased into the space beside his truck, which was parked right in front of his door. With her vehicle still running, she said, "I'll be right back, Sarah-Jane." She locked the doors via the keypad on the driver's door before marching to Jimmy's door a few feet away.

She knocked three times and waited long enough to feel the heat rising off the asphalt. Was he even in there? What if something had happened? What if he'd passed out again?

Noting the window boxes filled with red and purple petunias, she gave three more emphatic knocks. "Jimmy?"

Panic and grief battled for her attention. But after a few minutes, she realized she'd done all she could.

Slowly, she started for her SUV, but she stopped when she heard something behind her.

"Laurel?"

Turning, she saw Jimmy standing in the doorway, wearing a T-shirt and a pair of basketball shorts. He ran a hand through his disheveled gray hair.

"I'm sorry, Laurel. I was asleep."

As much as she hated that she'd woke him— "Why didn't you let me know they released you? That you were coming back here?"

"I'm sorry. I guess I was sleep deprived. Those hospital folk were in and out of my room all night long, so as soon as they told me I could go, I did."

After sneaking a peek at Sarah-Jane, Laurel crossed her arms over her chest. "How did you get to your truck?"

"I walked."

If someone were to take her blood pressure right now, she was pretty sure it'd be off the charts.

With the hum of her car's engine echoing around her, she lowered her arms and stepped toward him. "*You walked?* After collapsing and hitting your head, you decided to walk. Seriously? Why didn't you call me?"

"It was early, and I didn't want to bother you. Especially after you were there so late last night."

"Bother me? As if thinking you'd run out on me

again didn't bother me?" She knew she shouldn't have said it, but it was out there now.

He looked distressed. "Oh, Laurel, I never expected you'd feel that way. I would never do anything to hurt you."

"Well, you did. So, obviously we're going to have to set some ground rules here."

Still standing on the carpet just inside the door, he shifted from one bare foot to the next. "Ground rules? Does this mean you're willing to have a relationship with me?"

A sense of relief washed over her. "You're my dad. Of course I want a relationship. I also want to know all about this congestive heart failure thing. Because now that I've found you, I plan to do everything in my power to see to it you're around for as long as possible."

Chapter Fifteen

Wes found himself looking out of Irma's front windows more frequently Monday morning, anticipating Laurel's arrival. Aside from the fact that they'd be finishing the painting in the family room and laying the tile in the bathroom, he wanted to see Laurel. To be with her, talk to her, see her beautiful smile. All too soon, he wouldn't have that luxury for twelve long months. And he wanted to know everything about her, the same way she wanted to know about Jimmy.

Her father had felt good enough to accompany them to church yesterday, then they'd all gone to Laurel's along with Rae for a lunch of smoked brisket, beans, coleslaw and potato salad from a local barbecue joint. The whole lot of them had spent the entire afternoon talking and playing with Sarah-Jane, reminding Wes of when he was a kid and he, Rae and their parents would go off on adventures or simply hang out.

Strange that he hadn't thought about that in years. With his parents gone, it was too painful. Now, he suddenly found himself longing for more days like that—days with Laurel and Sarah-Jane. But as the pastor had said, Wes would have to trust God's plan. He just wished that plan didn't involve him moving to the other side of the world.

Perhaps he should contact Eddie. Tell him what was going on. Maybe something else could be arranged.

No. Wes had made a commitment. Not only to his friend, but he'd signed a contract with the organization. Even if they could place him somewhere else, it wouldn't be in Bliss.

Returning to the family room, he picked up the roller he'd attached to an extension pole, dipped it into the five-gallon bucket that held the bright white paint and started his second coat on the ceiling. Paisley and the other ladies had made a big dent in the painting Saturday, finishing Irma's bedroom as well as the upstairs bath. Today he and Laurel would knock out the family room, allowing them to start moving stuff back into the space tomorrow.

Okay, so it was Laurel who was supposed to do the painting while he tackled the tile upstairs. But how could he talk with her if she was down here and he was up there? And if he helped her, this room would be finished faster, then, maybe, she could assist him with the tile, or at least keep him company.

It was strange how quickly his thoughts on a relationship with Laurel had changed. No longer was he fighting the feelings that always seemed to be there, no matter how much he tried to ignore them, which made him glad he'd opened up to Pastor Kleinschmidt. Even if it had been inadvertently, the man had hit the nail on the head. Wes couldn't make sense of what happened to his parents, so he blamed himself and did whatever he could to atone for his actions.

The front door opened then, and a wave of expectation swelled within him.

"Wes?" Just the sound of Laurel's voice made him smile.

"In here."

"Wow." Clad in denim shorts and a T-shirt, she stared at the ceiling. "That thing must have been really dingy, because it's so much brighter in here already."

He lowered the pole. "It had definitely yellowed with time."

She watched as he loaded more paint onto the roller. "Can I do some?"

"I've been trying to get this done so you can tackle the walls."

"I know." Her grin turned silly. "But this looks like fun."

"Fun?" He passed the pole to her. "In that case, be my guest."

Her gray-green eyes sparkled with mirth, like a child trying something new.

"Be sure to take off the excess paint."

She did as he instructed, then lifted the pole over her head and began moving the roller forward then back.

"Careful not to apply too much—"

A blot of paint dripped from the roller just then, hitting her on the cheek.

"Oh!" She promptly lowered the pole, which he intercepted, directing it back into the bucket.

"Pressure." He bit back a chuckle.

"Now you tell me." Laughing, she wiped a finger over the paint, but only succeeded in spreading it across her face.

"Let me help you." He pulled a rag from his back

pocket. "At least it didn't get in your hair or your eyes." Taking a step closer, he cupped her chin in one hand and began wiping her cheek with the other.

"They don't call me Grace for nothing." She puffed out a chortle but went still when her eyes met his.

He liked that she could laugh at herself. However, the sweet fragrance of her shampoo had his heart thundering against his ribs. Or, perhaps, it was their proximity. All he had to do was lower his head and their lips would meet. The taste of her kiss had lived in his memory for the past two years. What would she do if he kissed her now? Would she kiss him back or turn away?

"Laurel, I—"

A knock at the door had her stepping away. And the sudden pink in her cheeks left him wondering what was going through her head. Was she embarrassed or relieved?

"I'll get that." His voice sounded unusually raspy. Clearing his throat, he handed her the rag before making his way through the entry hall. Opening the door, he saw Laurel's father standing on the porch. "Jimmy, come on in."

"I know you're busy, Wes, and I'm sorry to interrupt you, but I need to talk to Laurel."

She was already approaching. "What is it? Are you okay?" Panic laced her tone, and after what happened Friday, Wes couldn't blame her.

"Everything is fine, Laurel. But something's come up and I need to get back to Midland right away. I didn't want to leave without saying goodbye, though."

Her expression went flat. "But I thought you were going to stay for a few more days?"

"I did, too, but there's a problem with one of my

rigs, and I need to be there to address it. I promise, I'll come back to Bliss just as soon as I can. Maybe this weekend."

"What about your heart, though? All that traveling can't be good for you."

"I'll be fine." Closing the short span between them, Jimmy rested his hands on her shoulders. "I promise I'll pull over if anything seems amiss."

Laurel searched the man's green eyes for a moment, then took a step back, wrapping her arms around her middle. "Drive safe."

"I will. You've got my number. Don't hesitate to call. If you need me, if you just want to talk." He paused a moment before adding, "I love you, Laurel."

Her quick nod said everything Wes needed to know. She hadn't just pulled away from her father physically, she'd pulled away emotionally, afraid of being let down again.

Jimmy turned his attention to Wes then and held out a hand. "It's been nice to meet you, Wes. If I don't see you before you leave, you take care of yourself."

"You, too, Jimmy."

Still hugging herself, Laurel made her way back into the family room the moment Jimmy closed the door.

Wes wished he could make her see that goodbye didn't mean forever. That what happened all those years ago with her parents was not the norm.

Except it was her norm. And now learning that her grandmother had manipulated the whole thing—tearing Laurel's family apart—had, in some ways, made things even worse.

Longing to comfort her, he followed her into the other room and found her staring out the window.

She must have heard him, because she said, "What if he doesn't come back?"

"He said he would." Moving across the canvas tarp, he stopped behind her. "And, if you'll recall, even the circumstances of him leaving the first time weren't as you believed."

"I know." In her head she might know, but had her heart had time to embrace the truth? "What if something happens to him?" She faced him now, and Wes saw the worry marring her brow. "You were there when he collapsed. What if that happens again?"

He let go a sigh. "We'll just have to pray and trust that God will bring him safely back to you."

"I don't know if he should be traveling so much. I mean, in his condition."

"He wants to be with you, Laurel." And Wes certainly couldn't fault him for that. "He wants to make up for all the time he missed."

She peered up at him, unshed tears shimmering in her pretty eyes. "I'm scared, Wes." Her bottom lip quivered.

Without a second thought, he wrapped his arms around her, tucking her head under his chin and holding her close as she cried.

Lord, please, bring Laurel's father back soon. Help her see that she is loved. Wanted. And not only by her father. Wes loved Laurel, too. The more time he spent with her, the more he wanted to build a life and a family with her. He wanted to protect her and shower her with all the love she deserved.

But all too soon, he would be leaving, too, which made convincing her his biggest challenge ever.

By Tuesday evening, Irma's place was finally starting to look like a home again. Paisley, the pastor's wife, Drenda, and a couple more ladies from the church had come by earlier to help Laurel with general cleanup and to put Irma's new bedroom together.

Since the wooden floor was still in good shape, they'd opted to add a large gray-and-white rug that encompassed the area under and around the antique bed—taking care to secure all of the edges—so Irma would have something soft to put her feet on when she got out of bed each morning. Then the sheer white curtains that covered the floor-to-ceiling windows were washed and rehung, while a couple of decorative shelves were added to one wall to display newly framed family photos, along with some trinkets Laurel had found shoved into one corner of the vintage oak dresser. Finally, they topped the room off with luxurious new bedding in a soothing pale cyan.

But what sent the room over the top and made it feel extra special was Irma's wedding dress. A dress form in the corner to the left of the windows proudly displayed the simple white satin gown with a chapel-length train, so it was one of the first things you saw when you entered the room. Laurel could hardly wait to see Irma's reaction.

Unfortunately, there was still much to do.

"Are you ready to see your daddy?" While the late-afternoon sun played peekaboo with the clouds, Laurel unhooked Sarah-Jane from her car seat in front of Irma's. Knowing Wes would be working late, Laurel had picked her daughter up from the sitter's then grabbed burgers, chicken nuggets and fries from Bubba's so they could spend a little time together before Sarah-Jane went to bed. With all he'd done for Laurel, it was the least she could do.

She'd never forget the feel of his arms around her yesterday. The way he'd held her close, trying his best to console her as she broke down. Yet, despite all of the reassuring Wes had offered her just prior, those old feelings of rejection refused to be ignored. So it came as a pleasant surprise when Jimmy called her last night to let her know that he'd made it home safely.

Lifting her daughter from the back seat, Laurel saw Wes coming toward her.

"Need a little help?" He rounded her vehicle.

"You want to take your daughter or your dinner?" She closed the back door.

"Let me see that munchkin." His tone was light and teasing as a smiling Sarah-Jane practically threw herself into his waiting arms. She was going to miss him when he left.

Laurel would, too.

Moving around to the passenger side, she grabbed the bag of food and the drink carrier and followed Wes inside.

"By the way, I finally took a look at the bedroom," he said as they moved into the parlor. "You ladies really transformed that space."

"I couldn't have done it without Paisley and Drenda, but it did come together nicely. I just hope Irma likes it."

They snaked their way through the parlor, past furniture and around boxes, until they reached the dining room table, where one end had been cleared.

"I'm sure she'll love it." Wes sat down in the high-backed chair at the head of the table with Sarah-Jane in his lap. "Are you ready for a French fry, Sarah-Jane?"

She happily clapped her hands as Laurel broke a couple into pieces and set them on a napkin in front of her daughter.

"Looks like we're going to have a busy day tomorrow." Laurel pulled out another bag of fries and passed them to Wes, along with his burger.

"Yeah, I sure hope all those guys who said they'd be here at eight show up. Otherwise, I don't know how I'm going to get that tub back upstairs."

She laughed. "It's going to be strange not seeing it on the porch."

"I'm sure the neighbors will be pleased to see it gone, though."

Taking a seat beside Wes and her daughter, she cut Sarah-Jane's chicken nuggets with a plastic knife. "I still can't believe how quickly you got it done."

"Well, I wasn't juggling any other jobs." The man was too modest.

"No, just your sister and a daughter whom you'd never met before. Not to mention having to deal with her sometimes difficult mother."

He was about to take a bite of his burger but paused. "You're not difficult." The corners of his mouth lifted. "Challenging sometimes, but not difficult."

"Good." She slid the chicken in front of Sarah-Jane. "You needed a challenge."

When he'd finished chewing, he said, "From you, I welcome it." The playfulness glimmering in his blue eyes had her heart racing the same way it had yesterday when he was wiping the paint off her cheek.

Time to change the subject.

"When do you think Irma will be able to move back in?" She took a sip of her vanilla milkshake.

"Depends how long it's going to take you to get the rooms situated."

"I've got several people helping me tomorrow, including the guys who are supposed to move the tub. I'm counting on them to get those bookshelves back into the family room. Along with the sofa."

"If they're here at eight, they should be able to have everything moved by noon."

"That would be great. Then it's just merchandising the place and finding a more practical spot for all of those boxes." Picking up her burger, she motioned toward the parlor. "I definitely don't want them lining the walls in the bedroom again." She took a bite.

"What if I added some shelves in the closet?"

Once she'd finished chewing, she said, "You mean where there used to be more boxes?"

"Shelves would make better use of the space."

"True. Do you have time?"

"Sure. It won't take long. Worst case, I'll do it Thursday."

"Sounds like I'd better tell Irma she can move in Friday then."

"What were you thinking before?"

She picked up a fry. "I was hoping for Thursday, but I think I'm going to need the extra time to get everything situated the way I envision it."

"Friday it is, then." He popped a fry into his mouth. "And then you and I could go on a date Friday night to celebrate."

She felt her eyes widen. "A date?"

He grinned. "Yeah. A nice, leisurely dinner somewhere, just the two of us."

Shoving the fry in her mouth, she said, "What about Sarah-Jane?"

"I'm sure Rae will watch her."

With the air-conditioning whirring in the background, Laurel stared at her burger. She hadn't been on a date in...well, the last date she'd had, if one could call it that, was with Wes in Las Vegas. They'd had sushi and ice cream, then walked the strip for hours, talking. She'd never forget how special Wes had made her feel. He was the only guy she'd ever wanted to give her heart to. And now she found herself battling that same urge again.

But Wes was leaving in only five days.

"Dah!" Sarah-Jane reached for another piece of chicken.

Wes's mouth fell open. "Did you hear that? She just said *daddy*."

Laurel cast him an incredulous look. "Oh, come on, that didn't sound anything like daddy."

"Dah!" Sarah-Jane grinned at Wes, scrunching her nose.

"See." He looked as though he might burst at the seams. Touching his forehead to his daughter's he said, "You did say daddy, didn't you?"

She looked at Laurel then. "Mah!"

"I'm right here, baby."

Sarah-Jane turned to Wes then. "Dah."

This time the word came out more deliberate and sweeter, like a term of endearment, and sent a strange sensation weaving its way through Laurel. Something giddy and exciting filled her, much the way she'd felt when Wes had held her hand that night two years ago. It made her wonder what things might be like if they were a real family. If Wes loved her and she loved him.

Smiling, she captured his attention. "The nearest sushi place is about an hour from Bliss."

His eyes seemed almost riveted to hers. "Sounds perfect to me."

Chapter Sixteen

Wednesday and Thursday passed in a blur as a flurry of activity descended on Irma's. The major work was finally over, and it was time to make the grand old Victorian a home again. Fortunately, plenty of volunteers had shown up, enough that Wes and Laurel had been able to call it a day early Thursday and take Sarah-Jane to the park before throwing some chicken on the grill back at Laurel's. Wes enjoyed those times together, just the three of them. And now that he'd gotten used to them, it was going to make leaving even harder.

At least they still had the weekend, just as soon as they got Irma settled back in.

He stood on Irma's porch with Laurel and Irma, overlooking a yard filled with people who'd pitched in to make this repair go as quickly and smoothly as possible, including Pastor Kleinschmidt and his wife, Paisley, the insurance fellow, the exterminator, and numerous others from the church and community. Wes was in awe of the way the people of Bliss had rallied to help one of their own.

While Wes held Sarah-Jane, Laurel slipped an arm around Irma's shoulders.

"Are you ready to come back home?"

"Oh, I'm more than ready, Laurel." Irma quickly turned her attention to Joyce, who stood on the top step, holding on to the wooden rail. "No offense, Joyce. But as Dorothy said in *The Wizard of Oz*, 'There's no place like home.'"

Laurel moved to the door and took hold of the handle. "In that case, Irma, the place is all yours." Wearing a big smile, she pushed the door open wide.

Wes followed them inside with Sarah-Jane. The once-musty smell of the house had been replaced with the fragrance of fresh paint and something sweet and floral Laurel had plugged into outlets in some of the rooms. "Just wait till you see your brand-new bedroom."

Still in the entry hall, near the base of the stairway, Irma turned to her right and stared through the doorway of her bedroom, her eyes widening as one hand went to her mouth. "This is *my* bedroom?" She stepped tentatively into the space. "It's so beautiful and bright." Her gaze shifted to the corner. "Is that my wedding dress?"

"Yes, ma'am," said Laurel. "It was too pretty to be tucked away in some box."

Reaching for Laurel's hand, Irma grinned. "I never imagined it could look this way. The transformation is like those you see on TV." She hugged Laurel then. "Thank you so much."

"You're welcome." Laurel set the woman away from her. "Paisley and Drenda helped me, along with some other ladies."

"Well, it is just beautiful." Irma chuckled. "Makes me want to take a nap."

"No naps yet." Wes started toward the door. "We have more to show you." He led them into the family room. "I'd never seen a family room with a bathtub in it before—" he turned "—but I think I like this much better."

"This looks like a brand-new room." Irma spun in slow circles.

"All we did was add some fresh paint and move the furniture around a little." Laurel looked at the woman. "I hope you don't mind."

"Mind? I might have to hire you to do the rest of the house."

Wes leaned toward Irma. "Would you like to see what we did with your bathroom?"

"Oh, yes, please."

Laurel helped her up the stairs, then stopped just outside the bathroom door before turning on the light.

Mouth agape, Irma scanned the space. "I was worried the tile might make the room too modern for the house, but this floor looks as though it could have always been here. This is a perfect Victorian bathroom." She looked from Laurel to Wes. "I can't believe the two of you did all of this. You should consider starting a business."

"We had lots of help," Laurel was quick to say. "Which reminds me, we should probably let everyone else in so they can look around."

Things turned into a party then. Paisley and Drenda served up cake and punch on the sideboard in the dining room while people milled about, taking in not only the restoration, but the historic home itself.

Sitting at the dining room table, sharing a piece of cake with Sarah-Jane, Wes experienced a sense of satisfaction he hadn't felt since leaving the military. Was this how he'd feel about his work in Iraq? He'd be helping others, after all, though his heart would definitely be somewhere else.

He snuggled Sarah-Jane closer, then offered her another bite that she readily accepted.

"Mind if I join you?"

Wes looked up to see the pastor easing into the next chair. "Not at all."

"Wes, what you did here is pretty amazing." The man dug his fork into his slice of chocolate cake. "And in just a little over two weeks."

"A job can move much quicker when things fall into place." Like the exterminator and the plumber. "Whenever anyone heard the work was for Irma, they dropped what they were doing and came right here."

"Everybody loves Irma. But you still did the bulk of the work yourself. And this was quite a feat." The pastor set his fork down. "You know, I'm on the board of an organization that aids with rebuilding and disaster efforts right here in Texas. If you decide to come back to the area after Iraq, I'd like to talk with you about it. We could use someone with your skills to help head things up."

An opportunity to do what he loved right here near Laurel and Sarah-Jane? "Yeah, I'd love to know more." His phone buzzed in his pocket just then. Pulling it out, he glanced at the screen. It was Eddie, the man who'd been Wes's spiritual mentor even before he went to work for Servant's Heart. "Excuse me, Pastor. I need to take this."

Standing, he tapped the screen and put the phone to his ear. "Hey, Eddie."

"Are you available to talk for a minute?"

"Yeah, hold on just a second."

Laurel walked into the room just then and offered to take Sarah-Jane.

"Thanks." He smiled at her before heading toward the door. Outside, he moved around the side of the house. "Sorry about that. What's up?"

"We just realized that there was a mistake on your paperwork. The info they sent you has you starting training here in North Carolina on the fifteenth. It should have said the thirteenth."

Wes's heart sank. "That's only three days from now."

"I know. I wish we'd caught this sooner. I know this is a lot to ask, and we'll work around it if you can't, but is there any way you could be here to start your training on Monday?"

That meant he'd have to leave tomorrow, or early Sunday at the latest, but that would mean driving for eighteen hours straight. He'd done worse in the military, but what about Laurel and Sarah-Jane? He and Laurel had a date tonight.

"I'm not quite sure, Eddie. There are some loose ends I'd need to tie up first, but I'll certainly try."

"At this point, that's all we can ask, Wes. Just holler at me when you know for sure."

"I'll do that." Ending the call, he stared up at the sprawling branches of an old live oak. *God, I'm not ready to say goodbye to Laurel and Sarah-Jane yet.* He'd already been lamenting the fact that his time with them was about to end. How was he going to tell Laurel?

Laurel had probably only had a handful of dates in her life. Throw in the fact that Wes was the father of her child *and* that her feelings for him were already veering out of the friendship lane, and she was doubly nervous about their dinner tonight. She just hoped she could cast those nerves aside long enough to actually enjoy herself.

Glancing across the cab of Wes's pickup, she couldn't help noticing that Wes looked nervous, too. Something she found rather sweet, not to mention comforting. Though they'd talked during most of their journey, there were times when she'd catch him with his elbow perched on the door and chewing on his thumb.

At the strip center where the restaurant was located, Wes parked his truck, then came around to her side and offered his hand to help her out.

"Thank you." Considering she was wearing a dress, albeit a casual one, she appreciated the gesture. However, the moment her hand touched his, a sharp jolt of awareness shot through her.

"Have I told you how nice you look tonight?" He closed the door behind her without ever releasing her hand.

"Twice." She tucked her hair behind her ear, trying to rein in her suddenly out-of-control emotions.

"That's all?" Continuing toward the restaurant, he added, "I need to step up my game."

"For what it's worth, you look very nice, too." She swept an appreciative gaze over him as he opened the door to the restaurant. He wore a light blue button-down, open at the top, under a navy blazer with dark-wash jeans. The combination of blues made his eyes even more gorgeous than usual.

"Sushi bar or booth?" Behind a narrow podium, the hostess smiled as they entered.

"Booth?" Eyebrows raised, Wes deferred to Laurel. "Fine by me."

As they followed the twentysomething young lady across the stained-concrete floor, Wes placed a hand against the small of Laurel's back, a simple act that made her feel protected—cherished, even. Something she'd experienced only once before, and it had been Wes who'd made her feel that way then, too.

After waters were delivered and they'd ordered a California roll and some salmon sashimi, Wes rested his forearms on the wooden tabletop. "Okay, I may have told you all of this before, but I just want to make sure I don't forget."

Strange, he didn't usually talk so fast.

"I've set up a payment to your checking account each month for Sarah-Jane, and I've named you as my beneficiary both with Servant's Heart and my life insurance, should something happen."

Nothing like throwing a wet blanket on things. "Wes, I thought this was supposed to be a celebration."

"It is."

She rested her crossed arms on her side of the table and leaned closer. "Things like 'beneficiary' and 'should something happen' are not conducive to a party atmosphere."

"Yeah." Lowering his head, he let out a sigh. "I guess not."

Tilting her head, she eyed him suspiciously. "Is something bothering you?" Perhaps his impending departure was starting to get to him. She certainly didn't want to think about it.

"I'm sorry, Laurel. It has nothing to do with you, though."

With her elbow still on the table, she cradled her neck in her hand. "Okay, so what's wrong?" Wes had helped her talk through her feelings about her father. He'd held her when she cried. She welcomed the chance to support him in return.

He took a sip of his water. A delay tactic if she'd ever seen one. Something was definitely up.

"That phone call I received while we were at Irma's this morning. It was from Servant's Heart. Seems someone messed up. I'm supposed to start my training Monday, not Wednesday, as stated on my paperwork."

Her insides tightened. "But you're not leaving until Monday."

"They've asked me to try to make it to North Carolina by Monday."

Indignation sparked inside her. "How can they do that, though? The mistake was theirs, not yours."

"I know. But that doesn't mean they can't ask."

Laurel watched the man across from her. Wes was a man of his word, committed to whatever he did. "And you feel as though you should try to accommodate them."

He dragged a hand through his hair. "I don't want to go any earlier than I'd originally planned. The thought of leaving you and Sarah-Jane is already eating me alive."

In which case, she was probably only adding to his misery. "Are you leaving tomorrow, then?"

"No. I want more time with Sarah-Jane." Reaching across the table, he grabbed Laurel's hand. "And you." His determined gaze bore into hers, making a lump the size of Texas lodge in her throat.

"California roll." The waiter set the first plate on

the table as Wes let go of Laurel's hand. "And salmon sashimi." After depositing the plate, he looked from Laurel to Wes. "Anything else?"

Wes forced a smile. "Not right now, thank you."

Watching Wes, Laurel removed her chopsticks from their paper sleeve, her appetite waning. "What are your plans, then?"

He moved his napkin to his lap. "To spend tomorrow with you and Sarah-Jane, then head out first thing Sunday morning."

Pinching a slice of the California roll between her chopsticks, she looked at him. "How long of a drive is it?"

"Eighteen hours. Give or take."

She dropped the roll and the sticks on her plate. "Wes, you can't drive that straight through. That's insane."

"I'll take breaks."

"That doesn't take the place of sleep."

"Laurel, I was in the military, remember? There were times I was up forty-eight hours straight."

"Yes. But you were probably in a war zone, surrounded by the enemy or something."

He laughed.

"What?"

"You have an active imagination."

"Only because I care about you."

"That's good to know. Because I care about you, too. So why don't we change the subject and try to enjoy ourselves. Like you said, this is supposed to be a celebration, after all. And I can't think of anything better to celebrate than being with you."

Laurel wasn't sure she knew what a swoon was or

if one could do it sitting down, but looking into Wes's amazing blue eyes right now, she was pretty sure she was swooning.

They changed the topic and spent the rest of their meal discussing Sarah-Jane and how well things had come together at Irma's. Not to mention that crazy dinner they'd shared with Joyce and Irma. By the time they left the restaurant, they were laughing and holding hands once again.

"Look." Wes pointed toward the western horizon as they reached his truck.

Shades of pink and orange colored the sky. "What a beautiful sunset."

"Mmm-hmm."

When she looked at Wes, he was staring at her.

"But it pales in comparison to you."

Her heart beat a staccato in her chest as his hand cupped her cheek. She swallowed hard as his eyes searched hers. Was he going to—?

Before she could finish her thought—wish, perhaps—his lips touched hers. Tenderly, yet thoroughly, he kissed her. Right there in the parking lot for all the world to see. And all she could think about was how she was falling for this man. How he made her want things she never dared to dream of before. How— Her phone rang.

Reluctantly tearing herself away from Wes, she located the phone in her purse and pulled it out to look at the screen. "It's my father." She swiped the screen. "Hello."

"Laurel, honey." A ragged breath came through the line. "I'm sorry, but I'm afraid I'm not going to make it out there tonight like I was hoping."

"Oh." Disappointment pricked at her. "Do you know when you might make it back?"

"No, I don't. Things have gotten a little crazy here, and I just…" His voice trailed off. "I'll keep you posted, though."

The same heart that had been soaring moments ago went into a tailspin. The man could make all the promises he wanted, but Laurel knew the truth. Her father wasn't coming back. Not today, not ever.

She eyed the man beside her. Wes was leaving, too. What if he decided not to come back? Even if he did, would it be for Sarah-Jane or would he want Laurel, too?

Blowing out a breath, she tucked her phone back in her purse, wondering if that was a risk she was willing to take.

Chapter Seventeen

Wes had had such high hopes for this evening. And everything had been going so well until Laurel got that call from Jimmy. Naturally, she tried to act as if his delayed return didn't bother her, but Wes knew better. Their chatter wasn't near as lively as it had been on the way to the restaurant. He did his best to keep it going as they made the drive home, but then Laurel would grow quiet and simply stare out her window.

When he pulled his truck into her drive less than an hour after they'd left the restaurant, he killed the engine before helping Laurel out of the vehicle.

"Thanks." This time, she promptly let go of his hand and started toward the porch.

"Y'all are back early." Rae was sitting on the living room floor, playing with a pajama-clad Sarah-Jane. "I wasn't expecting you for another couple of hours."

Moving around the sofa, Laurel smiled at the two of them. The first smile Wes had seen since her father called. "That would explain why someone is up past her bedtime."

"We've been having a great time." Rae looked up at

them. "We ate macaroni and cheese, we sang, we danced. 'Baby Shark' makes for a very good workout, you know."

"I can imagine," said Laurel. "Except now it's going to be stuck in your head for who knows how long."

"Yeah, you're probably right." Rae stood as Sarah-Jane spotted Wes.

The child pushed to her feet and toddled toward him as fast as her wobbly legs would allow. And Wes's heart swelled faster than the Grinch's when he discovered the true meaning of Christmas.

He scooped his daughter into his arms and inhaled the sweet smell of baby shampoo. That was one of many simple pleasures he was going to miss when he left. Stepping over toys, he carried her to the glider near the fireplace and sat down while Laurel and Rae resumed their discussion of the events at Irma's this morning.

Once he set the chair into motion, Sarah-Jane didn't seem to mind. Instead of trying to get down, she yawned and snuggled against him.

"Wes doesn't even live here—" his sister shot him a glance "—and I've already had people inquiring about how long he's going to be in town because they've got projects they'd like him to tackle."

"How would they even know?" He eyed Rae.

"Small town," said Laurel. "Word gets around fast, and reputations are everything."

"In that case, Rae, you can tell them I'm scheduling for next summer."

"Well, considering that Mason Krebbs is about their only option, I could probably have you booked up in no time."

"It's definitely something I'll keep in mind." Though it wouldn't be service oriented, like he preferred. But he could talk to the pastor about the organization he'd mentioned.

Laurel looked at Wes with a half smile, half pout. "Looks like someone was more tuckered out than she thought."

He lowered his gaze to see a sleeping Sarah-Jane.

"I can take her." Laurel started toward him.

"That's okay." He snuggled his daughter closer. "I'd like to hold her awhile longer."

"I have a feeling I'll conk out pretty quick once I get still, too." Rae retrieved her purse from the counter. "You two enjoy the rest of your evening." She hugged Laurel before leaving.

After closing the door, Laurel crossed the room to come alongside Wes. She stroked Sarah-Jane's head. "So precious."

He couldn't stop looking at his daughter. "Yes, she is. Leaving her is going to be the hardest thing I've ever done." Turning his attention to Laurel, he added, "It's tearing me up just thinking about it."

"I guess we'll have to get those video chats going as soon as we can."

"I'm not very computer savvy, so I might need a tutorial."

"It's not that bad. We'll go over things tomorrow." Her focus returned to Sarah-Jane. "I should probably put her in bed now."

"Would you mind if I did it?"

She blinked twice. "No, not at all."

Standing along with him, Laurel remained in the living room while he carried his daughter down the hall to her room.

Before laying her in her crib, he placed his mouth

near her ear and whispered, "I love you, Sarah-Jane. Don't you ever doubt that." He kissed her soft cheek. "Sleep well, sweetheart."

As he laid her down, he marveled at the way she rolled onto her side, her hands coming together as though she were praying.

His eyes burned. *God, You've granted me such precious gifts in Laurel and Sarah-Jane. And now I have to walk away. I know it's temporary, but I'm going to need Your help to get me through this next year.*

Moving into the hall, he pulled the door to before returning to the main part of the house, where he saw Laurel in the kitchen, cradling a mug of something steamy. She looked as though she'd been crying. Was she still upset about that phone call from her father? Or was it something more?

"She's out like a light," he said as he entered the room.

"I'm sure Rae wore her out." She set her cup on the counter. "Are you going to head out?"

Approaching the kitchen, his heart tightened. Did she want him to go? "I was hoping to spend a little more time with you."

After a deep breath, she nodded. "I fixed myself some herbal tea. Can I get you something?"

Yeah, the Laurel he'd had a wonderful time with at the restaurant. "No, I'm good." Or more like disappointed. Nervous.

With the peninsula between them, he said, "About your father."

Her sad eyes met his.

"Saying goodbye to you was as tough on him as it was on you."

She clasped her mug so tightly, her knuckles were white. "How do you know that?"

"Did you not see the pain in his eyes? But he has a business to run. Things happen. I'm sure he'll be back just as soon as he can."

She removed the tea bag from the steaming cup and tossed it into the trash. "You're probably right." Whisking past him, she moved to the table and pulled out a chair.

Not exactly what he'd had in mind. The sofa was definitely cozier, but he could let it go for now.

"Did you hear what Irma said today? About hiring me—us—to redo the rest of her house." A nervous chuckle escaped her pretty lips.

"She also said that we should consider starting a business." He watched Laurel, hoping his next statement would help him get a better read on her. "What would you think about that?"

"I think that would be impossible since you're going to Iraq." Cradling her mug, she took a sip.

"What about when I get back?"

She set her cup on the table. "Does that mean you're planning to come back to Bliss?"

He wanted to think he saw a glimmer of hope in her eyes. "Absolutely. Sarah-Jane is my daughter, and I plan to be a father to her. The only way I can truly do that is to be here for her."

Laurel gave a curt nod. "She'll like that."

"It's more than just that, though."

"Oh?"

"Laurel, spending time with you these past few weeks, seeing how well we work together… What I'm trying to say is that I care about you. You're important to me. And I was hoping that, maybe when I get back, we could talk about giving our daughter the kind of family she deserves. You know, a mother *and* a father. Together."

Her eyes searched his for the longest time until he finally said, "Tell me what you're thinking, Laurel."

Standing, she crossed to the kitchen. "I'm sorry, Wes. Sarah-Jane and I are not some sort of package deal where you can get two for the price of one. Yes, I want Sarah-Jane to have an ongoing relationship with you. But you and me?" She wagged a finger between them. "That's not going to happen."

Wes felt as though he'd been punched in the gut. Staring blankly at the table, he wasn't sure what to say or do. Should he stay and try to plead his case? Or should he just leave?

"I think you should go," Laurel said, giving him the answer he hadn't wanted or even expected.

Just a couple of hours ago, things were going so well. Laurel had been in his arms and seemingly wanted to be there. Now...

Was it the phone call from her father that had shifted things? Had she convinced herself that Wes wasn't coming back, even though he'd told her he was?

Shoving his chair away from the table, he stood, his heart aching as much as it had when he'd learned of his parents' deaths. He paused in front of her on his way to the door. "Good night, Laurel."

She looked away, and Wes found himself wondering what he was going to do now.

Laurel woke up on the couch the next morning, feeling as though her eyes were filled with grit. From the monitor on the side table behind her, she could hear her daughter happily jabbering—the same way she'd heard Wes telling Sarah-Jane that he loved her.

If only he loved Laurel, too, last night could have turned out so much different. Instead, Wes had just assumed that since he was Sarah-Jane's father, Laurel would automatically agree to marry him.

The thought made her heart ache anew. Wes might care about her, but she wasn't important enough to love.

"Mah!" Sarah-Jane's voice grew louder, and Laurel smiled.

There was one person who loved her, though. One precious little girl that Laurel wouldn't trade for the world.

Still wearing her dress from last night, she stood and stretched before continuing down the hall to Sarah-Jane's room. "Good morning, sunshine."

Sarah-Jane's smile was big as she bounced up and down, holding on to the side of the crib.

"Looks like you've got plenty of energy today." Too bad Laurel couldn't say the same. She'd spent much of the night either crying or chastising herself for doing so until she finally fell asleep in the living room. Even now it frustrated her. Wes was not worth losing sleep over. Yet no matter how many times she told herself that, things kept shooting through her head, reminding her to the contrary.

After changing Sarah-Jane's diaper, Laurel set her daughter on the floor and followed her down the hall. Her walking was getting better, and she was finally reaching the point where she preferred walking over crawling.

About the time they made it to the kitchen, there was a knock at the door, and Laurel's whole being tensed. What if it was Wes? This was his last day in Bliss, after all, and he'd said he wanted to spend the day with Sarah-Jane. Okay, so he'd included Laurel in that, too, but now she knew she was nothing but extra baggage.

She sucked in a breath and moved to the door, praying her eyes weren't too puffy. The last thing she wanted was for Wes to think she'd been crying over him. Even if it was the truth.

When she opened the door, though, it wasn't Wes standing there, but her father.

Feeling more than a little befuddled, she said, "What—? I thought—"

"Soon as I hung up with you, I realized that if I waited until everything was under control, I might never make it back here. Laurel, you're more important to me than any ol' business. So I left instructions with my crew, hopped in my truck and drove until I got to Bliss."

She simply stood there with her mouth hanging open. "But what about your heart? Don't you know you need your rest?"

"I called the Bliss Inn on my way out of Midland so they'd have a room waiting for me when I got in."

"Which was?"

"Somewhere around two. So yes, I got some sleep. But I couldn't wait to see you."

Tears filled Laurel's eyes, spilling onto her cheeks.

"Oh, Laurel." He stepped inside, the aromas of coffee and soap enveloping her right along with his arms.

For the first time in her life—that she could remember, anyway—she hugged him back with all of her might. These past few weeks had been such an emotional roller coaster, and now everything had finally caught up to her, including one freshly broken heart. "God must have known I needed a daddy today." The words were muffled against his chest.

Just then, she felt Sarah-Jane at her leg. She pulled away to see unshed tears in her father's eyes, too.

She picked up her daughter. "Do you remember your pawpaw?"

Sarah-Jane laid her head against Laurel's shoulder.

Jimmy smoothed a hand across her back. "That's all right. We'll have time to get to know each other." His eyes moved to Laurel. "Now what did you mean when you said you needed a daddy?"

Her bottom lip pooched out as fresh tears welled. "I'll tell you over coffee."

A short time later, she and her father sat across from each other at the table, each nursing a cup of fresh brew, while Sarah-Jane nibbled on a banana in her high chair. And Laurel opened up about last night.

"We went on a date, and it was probably the best time I've had since…well, since the last time Wes and I went out." Even Wes's kiss had held such promise. "Then when he was putting Sarah-Jane to bed, I heard him on the monitor, telling her how much he loved her."

"Is that a bad thing?"

"No. But he doesn't love me."

Her father winced. "He said that?"

"His exact words were that he cares about me and I'm important to him. Then he went on to suggest that when he gets back next year, he and I should 'talk about giving our daughter the kind of family she deserves.' With 'a mother *and* a father.' As if that was the only reason we should be together."

"So you think he's considering a loveless marriage for the sake of Sarah-Jane?"

"That's what it sounded like to me. I mean, there was no mention of love or wanting to be with me. Only Sarah-Jane."

"Laurel, have you told Wes how you feel about him?"

"I told him I cared about him."

"I'd venture to say you're in love with him."

Her shoulders sagged. "I am. But I'm not going to tell him that. If he told me first, that would be one thing, but—"

"Have you stopped to think that maybe he's just as afraid to tell you as you are to tell him?"

"Whose side are you on?"

"Yours. Always. That's why I don't want you to throw away something precious the way I did. I didn't come back for you because I was afraid your mother had found someone else and would send me packing. It wasn't until I had nothing to lose that I finally found you, and things turned out better than I ever imagined." He stared into his now empty cup. "Laurel, I'd hate to see you let fear keep you from your dreams, especially since I'm fairly certain Wes loves you, too."

Tilting her head left and right, trying to work the kinks out of her neck, she said, "It's Sarah-Jane he loves. Not me."

"Are you sure? Or are you just afraid to find out? I've seen the way he looks at you, the way he protected you when I showed up." Her father eyed her across the table. "It's not all about Sarah-Jane. It's about you."

I've never forgotten you, Laurel. Wes had said that the day he asked her about Sarah-Jane's name. Could it be true? Could she have lingered in Wes's mind the way he had hers?

"Let me give you something else to think about."

She looked at her father. "What's that?"

"Do you want Wes to leave thinking that you don't love him?"

"No." She tried to focus on her daughter so she wouldn't cry. "But I'm scared."

"Can't be any worse than what happened last night."

The man had a point.

God, it is so not like me to do something like that. Should I?

"I'd be happy to watch my granddaughter if you'd like to pay him a visit."

It sounded like she had her answer.

A giddy, nauseous feeling began to swell in her belly. "Okay, I'll do it."

After scrubbing her face, pulling her hair into a ponytail and donning some yoga pants and a cute tunic, she thanked her father and headed to Rae's.

Just about every parking spot was taken as people filed in for a leisurely Saturday breakfast, but she managed to snag the last one. Then, with a fortifying breath, she willed herself through the doors of the Fresh Start Café and marched straight to the back and the stairs that led to Rae's apartment.

"Laurel?"

She turned at the sound of Rae's voice.

Coffeepot in hand, her friend continued toward her. "What's up?"

"I need to talk to Wes."

Rae's expression went blank. "I guess you haven't talked to him."

"Not since last night."

"He left for North Carolina before sunrise. He's gone, Laurel."

Chapter Eighteen

Wes walked across the parking lot of the Servant's Heart headquarters Monday morning, feeling as though he'd had the life sucked out of him. While the eighteen-hour drive had been uneventful, he was a mess. His insides hadn't been this knotted up in years. While leaving Sarah-Jane had been challenging enough, hearing Laurel say there was no future for them had cut him to the quick. What had changed her mind? Or had he read her wrong all along?

For the thousandth time, he thought about their kiss. From where he stood, she'd been all in on it…until her phone rang, anyway. Could that have had something to do with her pushing him away? Her conversation with Jimmy had definitely dampened her mood. Could that call have caused her feelings of rejection to resurface?

Except Wes hadn't rejected her. He'd told her that he cared about her and that he wanted them to be together. The only thing he hadn't done was tell her he loved her. Yet instead of going back and confessing his true feelings, he'd hightailed it out of Bliss early the next morning without so much as a goodbye to Laurel or Sarah-Jane. A fact that had him kicking himself halfway across the country. Would it have made a difference, though?

He dragged a hand through his hair. It wasn't like he was adept at understanding women. So when one finally broke through the wall he'd built and actually captured his heart, it figured that he'd blow it.

Passing through the double glass doors of the large, relatively modern office building, into the reception area, he hoped he looked better than he felt. Because he felt as though he'd been run over by a tank.

A young woman smiled as he approached the reception desk. "How can I help you?"

"I'm here to meet with Eddie Perkins."

She took Wes's name then told him to take a seat while she let Eddie know he was there.

Perhaps it was good he'd be seeing his old friend today. He and Eddie had always been close and Wes appreciated his friend's perspective on things. Once Wes told him all that had transpired in the past few weeks, his friend was certain to have some sage advice.

Easing into a padded chair, Wes stared blankly out of the floor-to-ceiling windows, wondering what Laurel and Sarah-Jane were doing. Probably finishing up breakfast. They were an hour behind him, after all. How he longed to see his baby girl. But what would that look like now? Laurel would be a part of any video chat. Sitting on the other side of the screen, staring at her beautiful face, knowing she would never be his. How awkward was that going to be?

Before Wes had time to contemplate the magazines on the table beside him, Eddie came around the corner.

"Wes." Arms wide, he approached as Wes stood.

"Good to see you," Wes said as the two briefly hugged.

"You, too." Releasing him, Eddie studied Wes. "You're looking kinda rough, though. You must have really jumped through some hoops to get here."

Wes rubbed the back of his neck. "I'm not gonna kid you. It's been a rough couple of days."

"Let's go to my office so we can talk."

Wes followed his friend across the tiled lobby, down a carpeted hallway and into a rather generic office, save for the family and military photos that lined one wall.

Eddie motioned for Wes to take one of two chairs in front of the desk, while Eddie continued to his office chair. "So how have you been? What have you been up to?"

Pondering all that had transpired in the last three weeks, Wes shook his head. "Well, for starters, I've just recently learned that I have a daughter. I don't know if that's going to be a problem for the organization or not, the fact that I wasn't married to her mother."

Forearms resting on his desk, Eddie studied him. "No wonder you're so messed up."

"Saying goodbye to that little girl was one of the toughest things I've ever done, especially since I just met her."

"How old is she?"

"Just turned fifteen months."

"Oh, so she's little."

"Yeah. Cute as a bug, too." He pulled his phone from his pocket, brought up a picture and showed it to Eddie. "Her name is Sarah-Jane."

Eddie leaned in to look at the screen. "What a doll. She's got your eyes."

A sense of pride swept through him. "I got to see her

take her first steps." That was also the first time Laurel had referred to him as *daddy*.

"Where does her mother fit into this picture?"

"I'm not sure." Wes leaned back in the chair. "Laurel is the only woman I've ever been drawn to. And while I've always said I don't deserve a family, now I want it so bad I can taste it."

"Are you saying you love Sarah-Jane's mother?"

He thought about the way he felt when he was with Laurel. And how horrible he'd felt since he'd left. "I think so. Yes."

"Any idea how she feels about you?"

"That's what's got me so confused." Resting his elbows on his knees, he went over the ups and downs of their relationship, before sharing the events of Friday night.

"Wes, do you think Laurel is worth fighting for?"

"Without a doubt."

Eddie leaned back in his own chair, clasping his hands behind his head as he contemplated everything Wes had shared. A move Wes recognized from their time together in the military.

"To answer your first question," Eddie began, "I don't think you fathering this child will be a problem for the organization. We've all sinned. If not, we wouldn't need Jesus. What I'm wondering, though, is if this job is still a good fit for you. Your life has changed a lot and rather suddenly. You have a little girl who needs her father. So, perhaps, this position isn't the best fit for you anymore."

"But I made a commitment."

Straightening, he turned his chair, so he was looking straight at Wes. "And what about your commitment to your daughter?" Hands clasped tightly, his gaze bore into Wes's. "Being a father is the greatest gift you could be given."

His friend's intensity had Wes sitting taller. "I'm aware of that, sir. Trust me, I don't take this lightly."

"And what about her mother? Are you just going to let her slip through your hands? Or are you ready to fight for that family, I believe, God wants you to have?"

Wes had been gone for a week, and Laurel still missed him. Countless times she'd reached for her phone, determined to call him and tell him that she loved him. Yet each and every time she'd stopped herself. The man was preparing to go overseas, and she didn't want anything to distract him from his mission.

Besides, he hadn't called her, either—well, Sarah-Jane, anyway. Laurel knew he must be missing his daughter. He was probably just busy with his training.

With Irma's house complete, and Wes and her father gone, Laurel had tried to return to her usual routine. It was nice to make her morning trips for coffee again but, other than that, things just felt…different.

Her life had changed so drastically in the last few weeks. Things she'd once only dreamed of—a father, falling in love—had, by the grace of God, found their way into her life. And while neither had come without trepidation, she wouldn't trade them for the world.

She and her father had spoken every day since his return to Midland on Tuesday. Not only had they made a promise to be open about their feelings, he was worried about her. And Laurel couldn't help thinking how good it felt to have someone, family, who cared.

She'd also spent a lot of time thinking about her

grandmother this week. The woman had truly loved Laurel, in her own misguided way. And without Grandmama Corwin, Laurel never would have found her way to Bliss, where her life had taken on so much more meaning.

If only Wes were here. Apparently the old adage "absence makes the heart grow fonder" was true, because there wasn't a moment that had gone by that she didn't think about him.

"Mah."

Standing in the kitchen, Laurel looked down at her daughter, who was trying in vain to open the cabinet door.

"I knew those child locks would come in handy someday." She knelt beside Sarah-Jane. "Sorry, baby. There are things in there that could hurt you."

Sarah-Jane smiled and began to bounce.

"Let me finish restocking your diaper bag and then we'll go to the farmers market, okay?" Standing again, she snagged a couple of snacks from the pantry, carefully hiding them from those watchful blue eyes that seemed to have grown keenly aware of the portal that contained a certain little person's favorite treats.

After adding them to her bag, she snatched it up and started for the front door to put it in the stroller before loading Sarah-Jane.

"I'll be right back, baby." She moved around the peninsula, continuing into the living room. But when she opened the door, her heart skidded to a stop.

"Wes?" Standing there, dumbfounded, she found herself clinging to the knob as a thrill sprang to life inside her, though angst and doubt quickly tried to overtake it. "What are you doing here?" Well, that was a stupid question. "I mean, let me get Sarah-Jane." She started to turn.

"I'm not here because of Sarah-Jane."

A lump formed in her throat as she faced him again.

"I'm here because of you, Laurel. You captured my heart the moment I saw you at that pool two years ago, and no matter how hard I've tried to dismiss or forget you, I can't."

She had to be dreaming. Wes was in North Carolina.

She squeezed her eyes shut. But when she opened them, he was still there on her porch, hands dangling from the pockets of his faded jeans.

"Dah!"

Laurel turned at the sound of her daughter's voice. "You heard your daddy, didn't you?"

Spotting her father, Sarah-Jane's pace quickened. Arms in the air, she grinned as she beelined toward him. Until she lost her balance.

"Uh-oh." Wes stepped inside, scooping Sarah-Jane into his arms before she hit the floor. "Got a little too much forward thrust going on there."

"She's excited to see you." Truth be known, Laurel was, too. She watched as her daughter laid her head against Wes's shoulder.

Wes patted her back, his attention returning to Laurel. "That night we had dinner with Irma and Joyce, I told you my dream of finding the perfect partner died along with my parents. But since spending time with you, that dream has been resurrected."

Tears pricked the backs of her eyes. Could this really be happening? Was Wes really saying these words to her?

"I'm back in Bliss for good, Laurel, in hopes that I

can win your heart. I love you, and I'd like nothing more than for us to be a family. You, me and Sarah-Jane."

Emotions threatened to overtake her. She'd never heard such words directed at her. And the amount of joy vibrating through her being was almost more than she could stand.

With her heart racing, she stared at this man she loved more than anything. "But what if I want more babies?"

His grin went from hesitant to certain. "Then I'm in for that, too. Whatever God has in store for us." He slipped an arm around her waist and pulled her close. "So long as I get to share every moment of it with you."

Placing her hand over his heart, she felt it pounding every bit as wildly as her own. She peered up at him. "My heart already belongs to you, Wes. I love you, too."

He lowered his head and kissed her as thoroughly as he could with Sarah-Jane in his arms. When they parted, he said, "You hear that, Sarah-Jane? We're going to be a family." He tossed their daughter in the air before setting her on the floor. Straightening, he cupped Laurel's cheeks in his hands and stared into her eyes. "You are the greatest gift I've ever been given. Will you marry me?"

With happy tears streaming down her cheeks and her heart overflowing with joy, she smiled bigger than ever before. "In a heartbeat."

Epilogue

"What do you think, Sarah-Jane?" Standing in the glow of hundreds of tiny white lights, Laurel smiled at the wide-eyed child tucked in her father's arms. "Our first Christmas tree as a family."

"And in our new house," Wes was quick to add.

Laurel looked around the spacious room with vaulted ceilings. "When we came here back in April for dinner with Joyce and Irma, I never would have guessed I'd be living here."

"You mean that *we'd* be living here."

Deciding she wanted to be near her children in Dallas, Joyce had come to Laurel and Wes even before their September wedding and offered them her house, saying, "It's the perfect home for a family."

Of course, as soon as Wes heard it was on an acre and half and there was already an outbuilding he could use as a shop, he was sold. Then he learned Joyce had offered it to them at well below market value. After updating the kitchen and bathrooms, not to mention going through gallons of greige paint to cover that dark wood paneling, the home had turned out to be perfect for them. An office plus four bedrooms meant they had room to grow.

"All that's missing now," said Wes, "are the ornaments."

As if on cue, the doorbell rang.

Laurel feigned a gasp. "Who's here, Sarah-Jane?"

The three of them made their way to the door. Laurel and Wes knew that no tree-trimming party would be complete without the rest of their family.

"Merry Christmas!" Rae, Paisley and Christa cheered collectively as Laurel opened the door.

"Merry Christmas to you." Laurel hugged each of them as they entered.

Rae promptly kissed her niece while a Santa hat–clad Christa held up two bottles of sparkling cider.

"Where should I put these?"

"The refrigerator is good for now." Laurel started to close the door.

"Wait for me."

She yanked it back open. "Hey, Dad."

Almost three months ago, he'd walked her down the aisle, making two of Laurel's dreams come true at one time. He'd also sold his business in Midland and moved to Bliss shortly after that and was now living in Laurel's old house, where she could keep him under a watchful eye. Fortunately, his congestive heart failure was in the early stages, and getting out from under the stress of his business had greatly improved his blood pressure. Now all she could do was monitor his diet and pray that God would grant them as much time together as possible.

"Looks like it's time to get this party started." Wes set Sarah-Jane on the floor and followed her as she ran back into the family room.

"Would you like to eat these now or later?" Beside Laurel, Paisley motioned to the beautiful tray of cookies she'd brought.

"Now. Definitely."

They all moved into the family room, where Sarah-Jane stared up at the illuminated tree.

"Before we get started—" Laurel grabbed a sparkling bag from the kitchen counter "—I have something for each of you." One by one, she handed each of their guests a wrapped bundle. "I wanted every member of our family to have an ornament on our tree."

"Can we open them?" Anticipation filled Rae's voice.

"Of course." Laurel had chosen ornaments suited to each person. Rae's was a glittering cup of coffee, Christa's a shimmering tool belt. Paisley received a stylishly dressed baker holding a plate of cookies, while Jimmy's was an oil derrick.

"This is perfect." Her father chuckled as he held it up for inspection.

Reaching into the bag, Laurel pulled out one final box. "And I have one more for Sarah-Jane." She handed it to her daughter, who was now sitting in her daddy's lap on the floor. "Why don't you help her, Wes?"

"All right. Let's see what we got, Sarah-Jane." He tore one end open, allowing his daughter to take over from there.

Anticipation rose inside Laurel.

Finally, he pulled out the ornament with two teddy bears sitting atop a rocking horse. "Look at that, sweetheart." He held it up for her to see. "It says Big Sister."

Notes of "White Christmas" played softly in the background as everyone except for Wes fell quiet.

"What do you think about that, Sarah-Jane? Shall we put it on the tree?"

Laurel held her breath, trying not to laugh. She glanced at her father, Rae, Christa and Paisley, who were all doing the same. Obviously Laurel's little hint was lost on her husband.

Helping Sarah-Jane hang her ornament, he said, "See there, someday you're going to be a big sist—" Slowly he turned to face Laurel. "Wait. Does this mean...?"

Laurel nodded. "You've got until July to get the nursery ready."

A nanosecond later, he swooped her up in his arms and kissed her.

"Now this calls for a celebration," she heard Paisley say. "Christa, pop the top on that sparkling cider."

When Wes finally allowed Laurel's feet to again touch the ground, he cupped her cheek and stared at her with an intensity that made her heart race. "I love you so much."

"I love you, too."

Moments later, Rae lifted her glass. "A toast to my brother and my best friends."

Surrounded by all the people she loved, Laurel's heart overflowed. God had been so gracious to her. He'd heard the prayers of a lonely heart and given her the family she'd always longed for. And that was the greatest gift she'd ever been given.

* * * * *

A BABY FOR THE RANCHER

Margaret Daley

To the other five authors in this continuity series.
It was fun working with you all.

If we confess our sins, he is faithful and just
to forgive us our sins, and to cleanse us
from all unrighteousness.
—*1 John* 1:9

Chapter One

Sheriff Lucy Benson carefully replaced the receiver in its cradle, in spite of her urge to slam it down. Frustration churned her stomach into a huge knot. *Where is Betsy McKay?* None of her law-enforcement contacts in Texas had panned out. She'd been sure that Betsy was in Austin or San Antonio, the two largest cities closest to Little Horn in the Texas Hill Country.

Lucy rose from behind her desk at the sheriff's office. She grabbed her cowboy hat from the peg on the wall, set it on her head and decided to go for a walk. She needed to work off some of this aggravation plaguing her ever since the series of robberies had started months ago in her county. She still hadn't been able to bring in the Robin Hoods, as the robbers had been dubbed since many gifts given to the poor in the area had mysteriously started not long after the cattle rustling and stealing of equipment began.

Stepping outside to a beautiful March afternoon, she paused on the sidewalk and relished the clear blue sky, the air with only a hint of a chill. They needed rain, but for the moment she savored the bright sunshine as a sign of good things to come.

She was closer to figuring out who the Robin Hoods were. They were most likely teenagers who were familiar with the area and ranch life. Of course, that described all the teenagers surrounding Little Horn. But there also seemed to be a connection to Betsy McKay. The ranches like Byron McKay's were the main targets. The owners of each place hit by the Robin Hoods hadn't helped Mac McKay when he needed it. Could this be mere coincidence? Mac's death, caused by his heavy drinking, had sent Betsy, his daughter, fleeing Little Horn her senior year in high school.

The Lone Star Cowboy League, a service organization formed to help its ranchers, could have stepped up and helped more, although Mac hadn't been a member. But even more, Byron McKay, the richest rancher in the area and Mac's cousin, should have helped Mac when he went to Byron for assistance.

Lucy headed toward Maggie's Coffee Shop to grab a cup of coffee, and then she had to come up with another way to find Betsy. As she neared the drugstore, the door swung open and Ben Stillwater emerged with a sack. His Stetson sat low on his forehead, and he wore sunglasses, hiding his dark brown eyes that in the past had always held a teasing twinkle in them.

But that was before he had been in a coma for weeks and struggled to recover from his riding accident. The few times she'd seen him lately, his somber gaze had held none of his carefree, usual humor. He had a lot to deal with.

Ben stopped and looked at her, a smile slowly tilting

his mouth up as he tipped the brim of his black hat toward her. "It's nice to see you, Lucy. How's it going?"

"I'm surprised to see you in town."

"Why?" The dimples in his cheeks appeared as his grin deepened.

"You just got out of the hospital."

"Days ago. I'm not letting my accident stop me any more than necessary. I'm resuming my duties at the ranch. Well, at least part of them. I know that my foreman and my brother have done a nice job in my—absence. But I'm home now, and you know me—I can't sit around twiddling my thumbs all day."

For a few seconds, Lucy glimpsed the man Ben had once been, the guy who played hard and wouldn't stay long with any woman. He'd never been able to make a long-term commitment. How long would it take before he reverted to his old ways? Yes, he had been a good rancher and put in a lot of work at his large spread, but still, he had never been serious about much of anything except his ranch. And helping teens. "How's the Future Ranchers Program at your place going with your absence?"

"Zed and Grady have kept it going. I'd been working a lot with Maddy Coles, Lynne James and Christie Markham before the accident, so they knew what to do."

Maddy had been Betsy McKay's best friend while she'd lived here. Did she know where Betsy was and wouldn't say? "What are you doing in town?"

"Picking up my prescriptions. I had to get out of the house. I hate inactivity even if I have to work through some pain. I'm going stir-crazy, and I promised Grandma that I wouldn't go back to work until I'm home a week." Again those dimples appeared in his cheeks. "What was I thinking? Only thirty-six hours, then I'm a free man."

"How's Cody doing?" She still couldn't believe that Ben was a father, although the DNA test that had come back could only state Cody was a Stillwater, a son either of Grady or Ben, identical twins. The eight-month-old was staying at the Stillwater Ranch, and Ben seemed to accept the fact he was the boy's dad since Grady had said the child couldn't be his. She'd always thought of Ben as a playboy, happiest with no ties to hold him down, but a baby could certainly do that.

Ben removed his sunglasses, his dark brown eyes serious. "A little man on the go. I think he knows the house better than I do."

She'd wanted to ask him about the letter, addressed to Ben, that she'd given Grady to give him. She'd found it in the wreck outside town where a young woman had died. Was she Cody's mother? What did it say? The words were on the tip of her tongue to ask him when she spied Byron heading for her.

Ben glanced at the tall man with a large stomach and wavy strawberry blond hair coming toward them. "He looks like he's on a mission."

"Yeah, I'm sure he is."

"Do you want me to stay?" Ben put his sunglasses on.

"No, he's my problem. You don't need the stress." The less others heard Byron's tirade the better she would feel. If she could escape, she would.

"But—"

"I mean it. Listening to him is, sadly, part of my job. Take care."

Ben tipped his hat and strode toward his truck, pausing a moment to speak with Byron, who frowned and continued his trek toward her.

"Sheriff." Byron planted himself in Lucy's path. "What kind of progress have you made on the thefts occurring?"

"I have a few leads I'm following."

"Like what?" he demanded in a deep, loud voice.

Lucy glanced around, wishing this conversation could take place in her office, not on the main street of Little Horn. "I have a possible lead on where the cattle are being sold. Without brands, it's harder to track the stolen cows." The rustlers had stolen new cattle that hadn't been branded yet.

"Yeah, we all know the thieves know what's going on here. Maybe when you find them, we should elect one of them sheriff next year when you're up for reelection."

Heat singed her cheeks as a couple slowed their step on the sidewalk to listen to the conversation. "That would be a brilliant idea. Put the crooks in charge."

"Sarcasm doesn't become you. I help pay your salary, and I want to see this settled. Now."

The drugstore door opened, and Lucy looked to see who else would witness Byron's dressing-down. His twins, Gareth and Winston, came to a stop a few feet from their father. Winston's eyebrows slashed down while Gareth's expression hardened.

Holding up a sack, Winston moved forward. "Dad, we've got what we need for the school project. Ready to go?"

A tic twitched in Gareth's cheek, his gaze drilling into his father.

The twins weren't happy with Byron. Lucy couldn't blame them. He'd been going around town, ready to launch into a spiel with anyone who would listen about what should be done to the rustlers and why she wasn't doing her job. His ranch had been hit the hardest.

Her gaze swept from one twin to the other. Maybe the boys knew where Betsy was. She needed to talk to them without their father. Anytime the conversation turned to Mac or Betsy, Byron went off on one of his heated outbursts.

Byron nodded at his sons, then turned to her and said, "Think about when you run for sheriff next year. Do you want me as a supporter or an enemy?"

"Dad, we've got a lot of work to do tonight," Gareth said in an angry tone, then marched toward Byron's vehicle across the street.

Lucy watched Winston and Byron follow a few yards behind Gareth; the middle-aged man was still ranting about the situation to Winston, whose shoulders slumped more with each step he took. Did those twins have a chance with Byron as their father? They were popular, but stories of them bullying had circulated; unfortunately, nothing she could pursue. It wouldn't surprise her because Byron was the biggest bully in the county.

With long strides Lucy headed again for Maggie's Coffee Shop. She needed a double shot of caffeine because she would be spending hours tonight going over all the evidence to see if she'd missed anything.

Ben Stillwater sank into the chair on the back porch of his house at his ranch near Little Horn. He cupped his mug and brought it to his lips. The warm coffee chased away a chill in his body caused by the wind. To the east the sun had risen enough that its brightness erased the streaks of orange and pink from half an hour ago.

Ben released a long breath—his first day back to work after his riding accident that had led to a stroke caused by a head injury at the end of October. He had gone into a coma, then when he had woken up, he'd faced a long road with rehabilitation. The accident seemed an eternity ago. He'd just discovered a baby on his doorstep, and he'd been on his way to Carson Thorn's house to figure out what to do when his world had changed. He couldn't believe months had been taken from him. An emptiness settled in his gut. He wasn't the same man.

So much has changed.

I have a son. Cody.

But who is Cody's mother?

He was ashamed he didn't know for sure. His life before the injury had been reckless, with him always looking for fun. Was the Lord giving him a second chance?

When he had come out of the coma, he didn't remember what had prompted him to go see his neighbor that day of the accident, a trip he'd never completed because his horse had thrown him and he'd hit his head on a rock. But lately he'd begun to recall the details. Finding the baby on his front doorstep. Holding the crying child. Reading the note pinned to the blue blanket with Cody's name on it. *Your baby, your turn.*

Grandma Mamie had told him in the hospital the DNA test had come back saying Cody was a Stillwater, which meant either he was the father or his twin brother, Grady, was, and Grady knew the baby wasn't his. The news had stunned him.

That leaves me. I'm a father.

He'd known it when Grady and Grandma had brought Cody to the hospital to meet him. In his gut he'd felt a connection to the baby.

Grady had gone into town, but the second he was back they needed to talk finally. One last time he had to make sure his twin brother wasn't Cody's father before Ben became so emotionally attached to the baby he couldn't let him go. And if Grady wasn't Cody's father, then that brought Ben back to the question: Who was Cody's mother? He should know that.

He sipped his coffee and thought back to seventeen months ago. He'd been wild before his riding accident. He'd worked hard, and he'd played hard. Not anymore. He had a little baby to think of. Lying in that hospital, piecing his life back together, he'd come to the conclusion he couldn't continue as he had before, especially because of Cody.

The back door creaked open, and Ben glanced toward it. Grady emerged onto the porch with a mug in his hand. Although they were identical twins, when Ben had stared at himself in the mirror before he'd shaved this morning, he'd seen a pasty-white complexion that had lost all its tan since he was in the hospital. His features were leaner, almost gaunt. A shadow of the man moving toward him with a serious expression, his dark brown eyes full of concern.

"I'm not sure I want to ask what's wrong," Ben said as Grady folded his long body into the chair across from him.

"Grandma said you were talking to her about Cody and his parentage. Are you having doubts you're Cody's father?"

"Are you?"

"No," Grady said in a forceful tone.

"I didn't really think it was your child."

"Why do you say that?"

"Because you're the serious twin. You're the one who does the right thing. I'm the rogue of the family. Everyone knows that. I was wondering more about who is Cody's mother. Sadly I don't know for sure. There's more than one woman it could be." Ben shrugged, then set his mug on the wicker end table near him. "Grandma said you had a letter for me."

Grady frowned. "She wasn't supposed to say anything. I was."

"I think y'all have waited long enough. I've been awake for weeks."

"Trying to recuperate from a stroke and head trauma. I didn't want to add to the problems you were facing with rehabilitation."

"I'm not fragile. I won't break, and I don't need protecting."

His twin started laughing. "You must be getting better. You're getting feisty and difficult." Grady reached into his back pocket and pulled out an envelope with Ben's name on it. "This is for you."

"Where did you get it?"

"The sheriff gave it to me for you."

"Lucy Benson? Where did she find it?" Why didn't she say anything to him the other day when they met in town? He intended to ask her that when he saw her.

"She found it on the front seat of a car involved in a wreck. The driver, Alana Peterson, died. There were also several bags with baby items in them on the floor."

Cody's mother was Alana? Ben had liked her and had had a lot of fun with her, but there had never been anything serious enough to lead to a marriage. He had a lot of mistakes to answer for. "When did this happen?"

"A week ago."

"You're just now getting around to it?"

"Yes." Handing the letter to Ben, Grady pinned his dark eyes on him and didn't look away.

Ben snatched it from his grasp but didn't open the envelope. If this was from Cody's mother, he would read it in private.

"Aren't you going to open it?"

"Later," Ben said while gritting his teeth.

"I know this is a lot to take in after all that has happened—is happening—but Chloe won't always be able to watch Cody."

"I figured when you two married she wouldn't be Cody's nanny for long. Y'all have your own life."

"She can for now, but she'll be having her own baby soon, and she wants to open a clinic. I want to see that dream come true for her," Grady said in reference to his fiancée, who was pregnant with her ex-husband's baby.

"She should have that clinic. She's been a great physical therapist to work with. I can't avoid doing my exercises each day here at home since she lives here. And I know you'll be a good father to her child."

"The ranch is going to be different with little ones running around."

"And not always the safest place for curious toddlers." Ben rose, stuffed the letter into his pocket and picked up his mug. "I've got a lot to consider. I'm meeting Zed at the barn." He started for the back door.

"I know we've had our problems in the past, but you've done well with the ranch."

Ben glanced at his twin and smiled. "Thanks. That means a lot coming from you."

As he entered the kitchen, he finished the last swallow of coffee and put his cup by the pot. He'd probably have more later, but he was eager right now to see the foreman. Zed had kept the ranch running while he'd been in the hospital. He headed for the front room where Grandma, Chloe and Cody were to see them before he went to the barn.

As he crossed the foyer, the doorbell rang. He detoured and answered the door, surprised to see Sheriff Lucy Benson. "What brings you out here? Did you catch the thieves?"

"Not yet, but I will. That's the reason I'm here." Lucy's furrowed forehead, intense green eyes and firm mouth shouted her seriousness.

Before his riding accident, a series of robberies had occurred, with cattle and ranch equipment and other items being stolen. When he came out of his coma, he discovered they were still occurring. The ranchers had been riled then, and now they were even more so, putting pressure on the sheriff to find the thieves with Byron leading them. "Sure, what can I do to help? Take on Byron for you?" He'd wanted to stay Wednesday afternoon, but Lucy liked to fight her own battles. She'd always been very independent and determined.

"Let's talk outside." Dressed in her tan uniform and cowboy hat, Lucy pushed the screen door wide to let Ben join her on the porch. As usual she was all business.

What would she be like off duty? Ben stepped to the side and waited for her to turn toward him, pushing that question from his mind. She'd always been off-limits to him. She'd made that clear when they were teenagers. "Is this concerning the thefts?" He stuffed his hands into his front pockets and encountered the letter Grady gave him.

"I don't know if anyone has informed you that your ranch is one of the few big ones that hasn't been robbed yet."

He nodded, slipping his hands free. "Grady told me." He should ask Lucy about the letter, but all he wanted to do was forget he still needed to read it.

"I think somehow the robbers are connected to Maddy Coles or Betsy McKay, maybe both."

"I've been out of the loop. Why do you think that? Maddy is a great worker, and Betsy has been gone for almost a year, so how could she be involved?"

"After analyzing the ranches hit against the ones not robbed, I found a connection. Betsy McKay. People who were kind to her were spared. Then I took a look at who received gifts. Maddy did, including an iPod in her favorite color. That was a very personal gift, not the usual gift of animals or equipment the ranchers in need received from these Robin Hoods."

There was a definite divide among the people in the area because some of the poorer ranches were receiving help where they needed it, or at least they had until Lucy had started confiscating the nonanimal gifts. "It could be a secret admirer that gave Maddy the iPod."

"That's an expensive gift."

"Why are you focusing on Maddy? Others received gifts. Expensive ones."

"Maddy and Betsy were best friends. The ranchers who didn't help Betsy's father when he needed it were hit the hardest. Byron McKay, Mac's cousin, has been robbed more than anyone, and I think it might be because he refused to help his own family when Mac asked. Meanwhile, nothing has happened at this large ranch, one of the few left untouched."

"I can't see Maddy being involved in the robberies. Is that what you're thinking?"

Lucy took off her hat and ran her fingers through her short blond hair. "I didn't say she was. I said that there's a connection. The thieves have taken an interest in her. Why?"

"Do you think that Maddy working here is why we haven't been robbed?"

"It's a possibility. I have to look at this from every angle."

He wanted to help her. He imagined she wasn't happy with herself that these robberies had been going on for so long, especially with Byron spouting off to anyone who'd listen that Lucy wasn't doing her job. "What do you want to do?"

"What is Maddy's work schedule?"

"During the school year, she's out here after classes are over, for three hours. Then she comes for a full day on Saturday. The other interns, Lynne and Christie, have the same hours. They come and leave together. Before I was in the hospital, I often supervised them. I want this program to be a success."

For the first time, Lucy cracked a grin. "Yeah, I understand the intern program is your pet project."

Her smile transformed her pretty features and gave Ben a glimpse of her softer side. He'd been attracted to her in the past, but she'd made it clear she had no room for him in her life. Not that he could blame her. He'd never been serious about a relationship, and Lucy was definitely a woman who would want only a long-term one. He'd kept his distance.

"I'd like to hang around when they're here," she said now. "Maybe get to know Maddy better. I need to discover the connection between Maddy and the thieves. I might overhear something that will help."

"Won't the interns think it's strange all of a sudden to see you here?" Not that he wouldn't mind seeing more of the sheriff. He wasn't the same man he was before his injury. He had a son to think about.

"That's why I wanted to talk with you. I need a reason."

"We could pretend we're dating."

A blush tinted Lucy's cheeks. "Out of the blue? No one would believe that. Your reputation precedes you."

"I'm not that guy anymore."

One of her eyebrows hiked up. "Since when?"

"I could have died. That makes a man pause and take a good hard look at his life." He smiled. "It's not that far-fetched. I'm single. You're single."

"How about friends?"

"Getting to know each other?"

"I know you. That's the problem. When are you serious about anything?"

"I'm serious about my son, my family, the ranch and the intern program." He took a step toward her.

She moved back. "We don't have to say we're dating. You can be helping me learn about taking care of a horse. I might get one later."

"You've never had a horse?"

"My family didn't have a lot of money for that kind of stuff. You know that."

"Yeah. It seems I remember you occasionally would

go for a ride with Grady and me when we were teenagers. Have you ridden besides then?"

Already tall, almost six feet, Lucy straightened even more. "I've ridden. I had other friends who had horses besides you."

"Good to know you consider me a friend. Come tomorrow. It's Saturday. We'll go riding, and I'll show you what you need to do afterward with that horse, just in case you don't remember. That ought to give you a reason to hang around. Then we'll go from there. Okay?"

Her eyes gleamed as she gave him a nod. "I appreciate the help. If I don't catch these thieves soon, I'm going to have a lot of ranchers mad at me."

"Not me." He winked.

Her blush deepened. "That's because you haven't been robbed."

"True, but we could be."

"We haven't had any thefts in a month."

"See, you must be doing something right."

"I'm taking the nonanimal gifts away and keeping them as evidence for when I catch the thieves. I guess the Robin Hoods aren't too thrilled with that." Lucy finger combed her hair, then set her cowboy hat on her head.

"If they can't give to the poor, they aren't stealing from the rich?"

She started toward her sheriff's SUV. "It's that or something else, but I'm still going to find out who's behind this and bring them in. Just because it has stopped doesn't mean I'll stop pursuing them."

"Nor Byron McKay." Ben descended the porch steps. "I wouldn't expect anything less from you. I personally think you do a good job as the sheriff." Ben followed and hurried to open her driver's door.

Lucy chuckled. "You haven't lost any of that charm you're known for."

"My mama taught me manners, and since my grandmother is peeking out the front window, I need to make sure I keep those skills intact or…" Ben shrugged. "I'll incur Grandma's wrath."

"Smart man." Lucy slid behind the steering wheel. "What time tomorrow?"

"How about ten?"

"See you then." She gave him another smile, then started her car.

It will be interesting to see what she's like when she isn't being the sheriff.

Chapter Two

As she drove away, Ben kept his back to the house. He imagined his grandmother was still spying on him even though Lucy had left. Grandma Mamie had fretted over him ever since he'd come home from the hospital. If he had his hat that he liked to wear while he was working in the sun, he'd go on and walk to the barn to see Zed, who had stepped up into the foreman position when he was injured. But his Stetson was still on the peg in the hallway, which meant he would probably have to answer questions about Lucy's visit. Who was he kidding? Even if he didn't get his hat, his grandmother would interrogate him about Lucy's visit. He might as well get it over with.

As he strolled toward the front porch, he surveyed the pastures near the house. Several contained the horses they used on the ranch while one held their prized bull. They'd brought most of the cattle closer since the thefts started, but the barn and bunkhouse, where some of the cowhands lived, partially blocked the view.

As he entered his home, he spied Mamie in the doorway to the living room, holding Cody. Watching his son wiggle in his grandmother's embrace, Ben fought to suppress the laugh. Cody was going to be a handful. Already in the short time *his* son had lived with him, he was getting into everything he could reach when he crawled and used the furniture to stand up.

"I declare, this boy reminds me of you more each day. He doesn't like to stay still." Mamie thrust Cody into Ben's arms. "We're gonna be in serious trouble when he starts walking."

Ben swung him around, his laughter mingling with Cody's. "But he's got your stubbornness, Grandma."

She grinned. "That's true."

Ben peeked into the living room. "Where's Chloe?"

"She went to talk to Grady out back. I think they're trying to decide when to get married now that you're okay."

Ben kissed Cody's cheek, then held him against his chest, but the eight-month-old started wiggling again. "Okay, little man. You can get down until you get into trouble."

"Are you going to meet with Zed?"

Ben kept an eye on Cody as he crawled into the living room, heading straight for the coffee table and the few toys on the floor nearby. "Yes. With Cody living with us, I've decided to keep Zed in the position of foreman. He's been here the longest and has a lot of experience."

"I like that. He started out when your dad first ran the ranch."

The mention of his father made Ben clamp his teeth together before he said something he'd regret. His father had died a few years ago, but Ben could still hear the disapproval in his voice. Reuben Stillwater had been by the book, disciplined and serious like Grady, whereas Ben had taken after his mother. She'd divorced Dad when Ben was fifteen, and he'd become the focus of his father's anger. They'd always butted heads, but it had become worse, especially when she'd remarried after Ben turned seventeen. But while Grady had left the ranch to serve his country, Ben had stuck it out, trying to please his dad but never quite succeeding.

"He'd be proud of you, Ben. You've run this ranch well and increased the number of cattle we have, as well as the horses you're training for the rodeo. You even took his place on the Lone Star Cowboy League. Look at the intern program. That was all you."

"But whatever I did was never enough for him. At least I know how not to be a father."

"Remember, kids need boundaries, too."

"But love would have helped." And in the end his mother had left not only his father but him. She had been too busy having fun with her new husband until finally a skiing accident in the Alps had taken her life.

Grandma Mamie frowned, the wrinkles in her face deepening. "He loved you in his own way. He just wasn't a demonstrative man."

He wouldn't make that mistake with his son. Cody would know Ben loved him. "I need to get to the barn." Ben peered around his grandmother to make sure Cody was still playing with his toys. Then he clasped Grandma's arms and kissed her on the cheek. "But I'm glad I always had you, especially after Mom left." That day would always be carved with regret in his mind.

"I'm not surprised she left." A touch of bitterness laced Mamie's voice.

"She hated ranch life. She was happier traveling and

having fun with no worries." And forgetting about her two sons.

"That's true. When she married your dad, she never thought she would be stuck here all the time. Do you ever want to travel and see the world?"

Ben stepped to the peg and plucked off his cowboy hat. After setting it on his head, he turned toward his grandmother. "No, I love the ranch."

"It seems to me you have more of your dad in you than you realize, and Grady has more of his mother in him. He's the one who traveled and saw the world."

Ben needed this conversation to end. He strode to Cody, picked him up and gave him a hug. His heart swelled as he inhaled his son's baby scent and heard his giggles. Then he passed Cody to Mamie and headed for the front door.

"Have you read the letter yet?"

"No."

"Why not? Aren't you curious what Cody's mother had to say?"

"We don't know that for sure." *Alana Peterson.* He rolled the name of the woman in the wreck—Cody's mother—around in his mind.

"Then, why else did she write a letter addressed to you and have all those baby items in her car? Read the letter and find out."

He opened the door and glanced back at Grandma holding a content Cody. "I'm afraid to read it."

"You aren't afraid of anything. You'll try everything at least once."

"Not anymore. I'm a father now." He would not abandon his son like his mother had, or for that matter like his father, who had been there for him physically, but not emotionally. "I know he has you and Grady, but I want Cody and me to have a strong relationship. I want him to know I love him."

"Your dad loved you."

"He had a funny way of showing it. I'm not the same man I was the day I found Cody on our doorstep." And he did have fears, even if he didn't let on to others. He didn't want to end up like his father, bitter and alone, or like his mother, rootless and aimless. His examples of being a parent weren't the best, and he prayed he didn't end up like one of them.

Ben left the house and headed for the barn, his hand slipping into his pocket where the letter was. Mamie was right. He couldn't keep putting off reading what Alana had to tell him. He made a detour toward the corral near the barn and watched a stallion prancing around, showing off to the mares in the field nearby.

He leaned back against the railing and slowly removed the letter. He'd made a lot of mistakes in the past, and this short fling with Alana was one of them. He couldn't continue casually dating, never settling down. His son needed a mother, stability.

He opened the single sheet and read, his teeth grinding together. With a tight throat, Ben stared at Alana's words written in a neat handwriting.

"I tried being a mother. I just wasn't any good at it. I just want to have fun. You should understand that and not condemn me. I did some checking. I know your grandmother will help you. I have no one."

Those sentences jumped out at Ben. *How about me? I would have helped if you'd have let me know about Cody.*

Ben crushed the paper into a ball, then stuffed it into

his front pocket of his jeans. He remembered how he'd been before the accident, and he could see why Alana would say that. He'd always gone into a relationship with a woman knowing it was only temporary and casual. He didn't want to be responsible for another person's feelings. He'd already disappointed his father after trying for years to be the son he wanted. His mother, the one parent who he'd thought loved him unconditionally and accepted him for who he was, had left him, rarely contacting him because she was too busy building a new life with a new husband. And now she was dead and he had no chance of having a relationship with her.

He looked at the house, where his son was. He didn't deserve him, but maybe he could learn to be a good father, give him what he hadn't had with his own dad.

But not by living the way he had before. That was no life for a child. He needed at the very least a good nanny, or maybe it was time for him to get serious and settle down. Maybe in the future even marry. He had to change. He couldn't keep going down the same road. It led nowhere.

Where do I start? He felt lost and out of his depth. Then he remembered one of Grandma Mamie's favorite Bible stories about the prodigal son who finally came home, broken and humble. His father had greeted him with love and celebrated his return. Maybe it wasn't too late for him to reconnect with the Lord.

Lucy stopped by her small white house not far from Main Street to change from her uniform into more appropriate clothes to go riding with Ben this morning. She must be getting desperate to ask him if she could hang out at the barn when Maddy was working. But in her gut, she knew the girl and Betsy were somehow connected to the thieves. She needed results, and soon.

As a police officer in San Antonio for a few years before returning to Little Horn, she'd been a valuable member of several important cases. She wasn't alone in her frustration. The members of the Rustling Investigation Team of the Lone Star Cowboy League were aggravated, too. Their speculations of who the thieves might be weren't enough without hard evidence. In the past few months there had been enough accusations flung at certain people without any proof. That had divided her hometown. She didn't want to see that anymore. She needed hard evidence before arresting anyone, especially teenagers.

After changing into jeans, boots and a blue T-shirt, she headed to her personal car, put her gun in the glove compartment and drove to the Stillwater Ranch, bordered on one side by Carson Thorn's huge spread. She and Carson, as the president of the Lone Star Cowboy League, had been working closely to find the Robin Hoods. She always appreciated his counsel and was glad he finally was engaged to his high school girlfriend, Ruby.

Lucy parked next to the barn where other vehicles were, drew in a composing breath and climbed from her eight-year-old Mustang, purchased the first year she'd been a police officer in San Antonio. She'd always wanted to follow in her father's footsteps. She'd thought the action in a big city would prepare her for anything in the county when her dad retired from being the sheriff. But her hometown and rural county were very different from San Antonio.

As she walked into the long barn through the double

doors off the yard, two female voices came from one of the stalls on the right. Lucy spied a cowhand, not Ben, at the other end. She made her way to the girls cleaning out a stall.

Lucy stopped in the entrance, the scent of manure and hay overpowering. "Hi, Maddy. Christie. Do you know where Ben is?"

Maddy smiled. "He went up to the house but said to tell you he'd be right back." The two teenagers exchanged looks before Maddy added, "He mentioned y'all were going riding."

From the gleam in their eyes, Lucy wondered if Ben had implied something more about her presence here today. "Yeah, it's been a while since I've ridden. I don't want to get rusty."

"I can't see you forgetting how to ride. Remember you used to come out here when your dad visited mine, and we usually ended up riding."

Ben's deep baritone voice shivered up Lucy's spine. She glanced over her shoulder as he approached her. His cowboy hat, pulled down low, shadowed his dark brown eyes, but she knew there was a twinkle in them from the grin on his face and two dimples in his cheeks. He used to love to tease her when they were in high school. But then he'd flirted with all the girls. He would date, then move on, nothing long-term.

He paused right behind her—too close for her peace of mind. She held her ground. He'd reminded her that at one time they'd been friends, and he was giving her a chance to be here at the ranch and hopefully help her to get to know Maddy better.

Lucy slid her hand into her front pocket. "I remember, especially that time the bull got loose and nearly trampled me."

"I saved you."

"But you didn't latch the gate properly, and that's why the bull got out in the first place."

"It must be your dazzling smile that made me forget to check the handle was secured."

Lucy balled her hand in her pocket and forced a sweet smile. "I hope you've replaced that latch by now." The bull could be dangerous, but she decided Ben was more, especially when he grinned and focused his full attention on her.

"Right after you left. Is that why you never came back to ride?"

"It was traumatic, but I was leaving for college in San Antonio the next week and didn't have time."

"If it'll make you feel better, we don't have that bull anymore. But Fernando is probably twice as mean, so stay clear of him."

Behind her, whispers drifted to her, then one of the girls giggled. She was not going to blush. Instead, she jammed her other hand into her jeans pocket and curled it into a fist. "Thanks for the warning."

"Our horses are saddled and out the back door. I need to see Zed for a few minutes, then we'll leave. Maddy and Christie, why don't you show Miss Benson around since it's been a while. We've expanded the barn since you were a teenager."

Lucy wanted to hug Ben and stomp on his foot. He could be so aggravating and accommodating at the same time. He was giving her time to establish a rapport with Maddy. "That would be nice."

The tour was brief, consisting of a walk-through of

the barn with a hand wave toward the tack room near the front entrance and Zed's office closer to the back one. Most of the horses were in their corrals. When Lucy stepped outside with Maddy and Christie, she noticed two horses saddled and tied to the fence. Maddy pointed out the various paddocks and pastures nearby besides explaining which animals were usually in them.

"Do you all enjoy working here?" Lucy asked, hoping the girls would forget she was the sheriff in time. "I once thought I might train horses, but then I was only ten and soon decided I wanted to be a nurse until I realized I would have to give people shots. I hated shots. I couldn't see myself doing that." It hadn't taken her long to realize she'd really wanted to follow in her father's footsteps, and now she was.

"I want to train horses, and Saul has been working with me and showing me what he does as a trainer since Ben's accident. Before that, Ben was training me." The wind caught Maddy's ponytail and it danced about her head.

Christie shrugged. "I get school credit working here. Dad wanted me to learn about ranching, so I signed up for the work program. Since I can't participate in Future Ranchers at our own place, this is a good choice. Ben is a great boss."

"Yeah, we hated what happened to him." Maddy glanced behind her. "I've fallen off a horse, but thankfully I didn't hit my head on a rock like he did."

"Me, too. I broke my arm when I was twelve," Christie said.

"Isn't there a third girl who works here?" Lucy asked as Ben walked toward her.

Maddy brushed stray strands of her hair, caught in

the wind, from her face. "Lynne is out working with Emilio and Josh mending fences."

Ben joined them. "After lunch, y'all will go out there with Lynne. Thanks for showing Lucy around."

The mention of lunch made Lucy's stomach rumble. She should have eaten her usual big breakfast, but she'd spent the morning catching up on paperwork, which was still not finished, and only managed to eat a hard-boiled egg and drink two cups of coffee.

When the teens strolled toward the barn, Ben swept his arm toward the two horses tied to a fence railing. "Ready?"

Something in his voice, a catch on that one word, caused her to look at him more carefully. "Are you all right?"

"I just realized this is the first time I've been able to ride since my accident. It's not as if I haven't been thrown from a horse before. I rode broncos in the rodeo, and I came close to really being injured several times."

His confession took her by surprise. He'd never shown her a vulnerable side before. In fact, she'd thought he'd never been bothered by much. "I once was pinned down in a shoot-out in San Antonio. I didn't think I was going to get out of there. I was out of ammo, and all I could do was pray to God."

"He answered your prayer?"

"Yes. It wasn't a minute later before the gang realized I didn't have any more bullets, but backup arrived."

"I think what's different about this time is that I have a son now to think about. With his mother dead, I'm his family."

"How's Cody? Chloe has kept me informed about him."

A grin lit his face, forming those two dynamite dimples in his cheeks and putting a gleam in his dark eyes. "Into everything. I walked early. I would be surprised if he doesn't in the next month or so."

Ben had a great smile, and when it was coupled with his charm, she could see why women were attracted to him. "And you were probably climbing everywhere."

Ben chuckled. "Yep. When I was eighteen months, my mom once found me on top of her tall dresser. I used the drawers as steps."

The familiar sound of his laugh warmed Lucy. When she'd seen him in the hospital the first time, she'd wondered if she would ever hear that again. "Do you remember doing it?"

"Nah. Mamie has told me a couple of times this week when warning me about Cody." He started toward the smaller horse. "I'll give you a leg up."

Lucy lifted her left foot into his connected hands, getting a whiff of his lime-scented aftershave as he helped her mount. Her heartbeat kicked up a notch, only because she hadn't gone riding in a while. It had nothing to do with the man accompanying her. They were just friends.

When Ben sat on his black stallion, he paused and looked around.

Beneath the shadow of his hat, Lucy glimpsed a neutral expression. She couldn't read anything in it, which was unusual for Ben. "Are you okay?"

Then he grinned. "Just deciding where to ride. I thought about heading toward Carson's ranch, but Thunder was the horse that threw me, so going that way might not be the best choice for my first time in the saddle in months."

"How did your accident happen?"

"I was preoccupied about finding Cody at the ranch and didn't see the snake until it was too late. Unfortunately Thunder saw it and reacted. I'm just glad the rattler didn't bite me when I was on the ground unconscious."

"God was looking out for you."

"You think? Lately I've been wondering if the Lord was giving me a wake-up call. I know I attended church with the family, but to be honest, I've never been that serious. I needed to be shaken up. I have a child now." He pulled his rein to the right and started toward the dirt road in front of the barn.

"You're serious about changing?" Lucy had known Ben forever and only saw him as the charming ladies' man that he'd been for the past fifteen years.

"I'm working on it. When I woke up in the hospital, I knew that I had been given a second chance, and this time I don't want to blow it."

Lucy had seen others say they were going to change, but they never did. It wasn't an easy thing to do. Habits were hard to break—and human nature even harder.

"Chloe told me riding would be good for me. Help me get stronger. I feel like a weakling and, you know," he added, swinging his attention to Lucy, "we macho men don't like to be weak." Then he winked at her.

Laughter bubbled to the surface. "You're incorrigible."

The dimples deepened as he touched his brim and nodded once. "I aim to please. I'm feeling cautious today. Let's go toward Tyler's ranch."

She rode next to Ben along the road passing by the older original barn. He stopped in front of it. "I'm thinking of hosting a young cowboy/cowgirl camp here this summer and using this barn. It's still in good shape but a distance from the house, so not used as much."

"Didn't your granddaddy move everything to the new location?"

"Yeah. Grandma Mamie still comes once a month to weed the garden she had at the old house. Zed, who lives here, is thrilled she does. As tough as he tries to be, he loves the flowers that bloom in the garden. He told me once coming home after a long day and seeing those bright colors always lifted his spirits."

"Maybe Mamie would come over and plant a garden like that for me. Of course, she'd probably have to take care of it. I barely have time for housework, let alone yard work."

"Zed and you aren't the only ones who love bright colors. Cody almost got hold of the flowers in a vase on an end table. Thankfully I managed to grab him in time." Ben urged his horse to move forward.

Lucy fell in beside Ben on the road. "Your son is named after your grandfather. That couldn't be a coincidence. Are you Cody's father? Is that what the letter I gave Grady from Alana was about?"

All evidence of a smile disappeared. "Yes."

"I'm sorry Cody's mother died in the car accident. Was she coming back for him?"

Ben's mouth turned down, his posture ramrod straight. "No, she didn't want Cody. I'm just glad she left him at our ranch and not somewhere else."

Tension poured off Ben for a long moment, and Lucy wished she hadn't brought up the subject of Cody's mother. She knew that Ben's mother had walked away from her marriage and sons. She rarely had come to see them before she died. Was Ben thinking about the correlation?

She wanted to change the subject. Never before had she and Ben had deep conversations, and all of sudden they were talking about the past. "How far along are you with plans for the camp?"

"Before my accident, I'd been talking with Carson about it. I wanted the Lone Star Cowboy League to sponsor the camp as an outreach project. Last week before I came home, I told him I was still interested in doing it. We'll be getting together about it soon, since the camp could start in June, if we have the time to do it that fast. There will be a lot to do in three months. It'll be something my son will enjoy when he gets older."

She slanted a look at Ben as he headed across a field behind the old barn. She'd never thought of Ben as father material. This side of him was interesting, but would it last? Like a hummingbird, he'd flit from one flower to the next, never staying long.

Chapter Three

Sitting around the large table in the kitchen, Lucy still felt shell-shocked. She hadn't intended to stay longer than necessary for her job. The horse ride had been over an hour when she'd thought it would last maybe thirty minutes. And now she was eating lunch with the family. How had she let Ben talk her into staying? He was lethal when he turned his full-fledged smile on her. But in her defense, she'd been starving, and riding the mare had only increased her hunger.

Yes, that's it. Not Ben's charm.

But then she looked across the table at Ben. A hard knot in her stomach unraveled. He was feeding Cody, who sat next to Ben in his high chair, and she had a front-row seat to watch. His baby giggled, grabbed for the spoon and flung some sweet potatoes into Ben's face.

Lucy pressed her lips together to keep from laughing. She couldn't hold it in and joined the rest at the table while Ben patiently took his napkin and wiped it off his cheek.

"Good aim, son. I guess you aren't hungry anymore."

"I always say when a child starts playing with their food, they're finished." Mamie grabbed the plate while Ben went for the spoon in Cody's hand.

But the baby was too quick, and the utensil sailed halfway across the table, landing in the middle of the pasta salad.

Ben moved the high chair back a little so Cody couldn't get hold of anything else to throw, then took a bite of his turkey sandwich.

Lucy turned to Chloe. "See what you get to look forward to. Food fights."

Chloe chuckled. "Cody is definitely preparing me for my own child."

"When are you due?" Lucy took a swallow of her sweetened tea.

"Three months and counting. That's why," Chloe said, glancing at her fiancé, Grady, "we've decided on a small wedding this month with family and close friends. I don't want to be a whale waddling down the aisle."

"Never, not you." Grady leaned toward her and gave her a quick peck on her cheek.

"Just let me know when to show up," Ben said, accompanied by a wail from Cody.

But as he turned toward his son, Mamie stood and took the crying child out of his high chair. "He usually takes a nap after lunch. Almost like clockwork. I was afraid he wouldn't last since we held lunch. I'll be right back."

"Grandma, I can take him to his room." Ben started to rise.

His grandmother waved him down. "Nonsense. You have a guest here." Then she scurried unusually fast for a seventy-eight-year-old woman.

Ben watched them leave, then faced the three remaining at the table. "I know everyone has tried to fill me in on what I've missed while I was in a coma and the hospital. Besides the crime spree with the Robin Hoods, anything else you've forgotten to tell me other than the letter you gave me *finally* yesterday morning?" He stared at his brother.

"I'm pleading ignorance." His mouth twitching, Grady took a sip of his drink. "I was gone for two months of that. You'll have to depend on Chloe and Lucy to tell you."

Everyone peered at Lucy. She held up her hand. "Why are you looking at me?"

"You're the sheriff, and you know everything," Ben said with a grin.

No, she didn't. What had been in that letter from Cody's mother? "Other than six months of robberies and now nothing, that's it. It's been pretty quiet, thankfully."

"Carson finally proposed to Ruby. They are engaged, and it was about time. I thought they would marry in high school." Chloe reached for the pasta salad and took the spoon from it before dishing up more on her plate. "You know the saying. I'm eating for two."

"And Eva and Tyler got married. I'm glad our cousin and Tyler are together." Grady stood and took his plate to the sink.

"Yes, and I hope they'll adopt a baby," Mamie said as she came back into the kitchen. "Eva was really good with Cody and would make a great mother."

Lucy finished the last bite of her sandwich. "I guess the biggest surprise was Amelia and Texas Ranger Finn Brannigan. I never saw her falling for another Texas Ranger. Funny how things work out."

"You should never say never. I've found it comes back to bite you." Ben retrieved a wet dishcloth and wiped down the high chair. "I never saw myself as a father, and I wake up from a coma to find the baby left on our doorstep is my son."

Lucy almost asked Ben why he didn't think he'd ever be a dad, but she didn't. She knew about the shaky relationship he'd had with his own father, but from what little she'd seen today, Ben was trying hard to be a good one.

"Another surprise was Clint falling in love with Olivia. He'll be an instant dad to triplets when they marry in June." Grady refilled his iced tea.

Just weeks ago Clint's father's remains were found in the Deep Gulch Mountains, where he'd met an accident years ago. Clint hadn't been abandoned like he'd thought. "The nice thing is Clint now has closure about his dad leaving him when he was a child. I think he'll be able to relate to Olivia's boys."

"Lucy, what happens if you can't find out who's stealing from the ranchers?" Ben retook his seat across from her.

"I'm going to." She was up for reelection next year, and if she didn't find the persons responsible, Byron McKay would probably put all his money and community presence behind getting a new sheriff.

"The Rustling Investigation Team thinks it could be teenagers," Grady said, covering Chloe's hand resting on the table.

Ben threw Lucy a look. "Is that really why you want to hang around the barn? I thought it was my irresistible charm."

"Like I *already* told you, Betsy McKay is connected

somehow, and Maddy was her best friend. I've talked with her as the sheriff before today, but she was wary. I didn't feel that way earlier." She was not going to let Ben get to her.

Chloe's forehead creased. "You think Maddy and Betsy are robbing the ranchers?"

"We've tried to find Betsy but haven't been able to locate her. But no, not Maddy. I did some checking, and she has an alibi for one of the robberies. She was at a sleepover with four other girls. She may know something and not realize it." From what she'd seen and heard about the foster child, she was a good kid.

"So this is why you asked the league for a list of members with teenagers," Grady said.

All eyes turned to Lucy, and for a brief moment she felt like a suspect being interrogated. "Yes. As we have surmised, the Robin Hoods are probably two or more teenagers, most likely boys based on the equipment they took. The thieves would have to be strong. Neither Maddy nor Betsy fit that profile. The Robin Hoods would have to be comfortable around cattle and horses to take them without anyone knowing. They would also have to be able to drive a trailer and be familiar with the area around here."

"That describes most of the teenage boys in the vicinity. I see why you want that list." Ben shifted his attention to his twin. "I understand Tyler is going on his honeymoon soon. I'd like to take his place on the Rustling Investigation Team. We need to find whoever is doing this."

Grady shook his head. "You've only been home awhile, Ben. You're just getting your strength back."

Ben drilled a hard gaze into his brother. "I know

what I'm capable of. Do I have to go to Carson about this?"

"No." Grady glanced toward Lucy. "If you want to take Tyler's place, then do, but don't forget you were in the hospital for a long time. You don't have to do everything the minute you are released. I was going to sit in for Tyler, but you can instead. I have to go to the VA in San Antonio for a couple of days next week. The team is meeting Wednesday night. Lucy, is that okay with you?"

"Sure." Oh, great. More time she'd be spending with Ben. She placed her napkin on the table. "Thank you for inviting me to lunch, but I have paperwork to finish at the office, so I'd better leave."

Ben's grandmother grinned. "I'm so glad you could join us. Don't be a stranger."

"I'll walk you to your car." Ben rose at the same time Lucy did. She shouldn't be surprised he'd said that because Ben was always a gentleman.

Outside, Lucy set her cowboy hat on her head and slipped on her sunglasses. Ben strolled next to her without his Stetson. When he paused next to her car, he squinted, the wind catching his sandy-brown hair that touched the collar of his plaid shirt.

He took her hand. Lucy started to pull it away when she spied Maddy and Christie standing just inside the barn doors looking at them.

"I thought we decided *not* to play that game," she whispered while giving him a sweet smile.

"We're not playing any games. You are a friend, aren't you?"

She nodded.

"I'm thanking you for a nice ride this morning. I didn't think about falling from my horse once while on Thunder. It must be the company I was keeping. Will I see you before Wednesday night?" The volume of his voice rose enough that the girls probably heard the question.

"At church tomorrow?"

"I'll be there. But I thought you'd want to go on another ride before the sun sets after work next week."

"How about next Wednesday? I'll come early, maybe go for a ride, then go to the meeting?" The things she did to get to the bottom of this investigation.

"Sounds like a date." He quirked a grin and squeezed her hand before releasing it and opening her driver's-side door.

As she drove away from the ranch, she glimpsed Ben saying something to the two teenage girls, then heading back to the main house. Tall, he walked with confidence, but he'd lost weight while in the coma. But that wasn't the only thing that was different from before. There was something in Ben's bearing that had changed. Maybe because he was a father now.

Lucy entered Maggie's Coffee Shop and spied the owner behind the cash register. Maggie Howard had been a few years ahead of her in school and had always been a kind and generous woman. Lucy smiled and waved at the petite redhead, then scanned the café for Chloe. Lucy saw her and made her way toward one of her best friends. Although Lucy's job as sheriff took her all over the county, Little Horn would always be her home and base. She'd discovered when she lived more than six years in San Antonio that she was a small-town girl at heart.

"I'm glad you could meet me for lunch," Chloe said to Lucy as she sat down.

"It sounded important."

"We finally decided last night what we want for our wedding. Pastor Mathers will marry us at church, and then we'll go back to the ranch for a small gathering of family and friends."

Lucy knew about all the problems Chloe had had in her first marriage and her ex-husband's unfaithful behavior, and was thrilled her friend had found someone who would be a good dad for her unborn baby. When Chloe's ex-husband had heard he would be a father, he'd wanted nothing to do with the child. "When is it?"

"In ten days on Friday evening. The wedding will be at six and the dinner at the ranch at seven."

"I hope I'm invited, or I'm going to crash your wedding."

"Of course, you are. I want you to be my maid of honor. The only people at the church will be Mamie, Ben as best man and you."

The waitress stopped at the table to take their orders. After she left, Lucy leaned forward and asked, "What can I do to help?"

"The beauty of a small wedding is there won't be much to do. The cook at the Stillwater Ranch and Mamie are going to plan the dinner. So all you have to do is show up at the church." When the waitress set their drinks on the table, Chloe paused, then said, "Are you dating anyone?"

Lucy dropped her jaw, then snapped it closed. "Why?"

"Just wondering. The last time we talked about men I was going through a divorce and you weren't dating anyone, but you've been at the ranch a lot lately. Interested in Ben?"

"It's police business." Lucy sighed. "Are you going to be one of those women who because she's deliriously happy thinks everyone around her should be in a relationship?"

"What's wrong with that? I want my friends to be happy."

"You forget I tried a serious relationship in San Antonio. Jesse didn't work out." That was putting it mildly. She and Jesse had been talking about getting married until she'd stumbled across a woman he was dating in Austin when he went there for work. Then to make it worse, he had begun taking out another lady in San Antonio while professing the whole time he was in love with Lucy. "The men I've seen and dated have a commitment phobia. I'm usually around two kinds of men—law-enforcement officers and criminals. Neither have I found to be good husband material."

"Your father has been married to your mom for thirty-eight years. Every time I've seen them when they visit you, they're still in love as though they are newlyweds."

"My dad is the exception." He was nothing like Jesse, the FBI agent in San Antonio who'd stolen her heart and stomped on it. But besides Jesse, she'd also seen fellow officers on the San Antonio police force she'd worked with either drink excessively or date excessively. When they did marry, the marriages usually didn't last. She didn't want that for herself.

"Do you find it hard to follow him as sheriff?"

"Lately I've felt I'm letting people down."

Chloe waved her hand. "Stop right there. That's

Byron McKay talking. He's never happy about anything."

"He has been hit hard by the cattle rustlers I can't seem to find."

"That isn't your only case. You take care of everyone in the county. Remember the robbery in the next town? You caught the guy within twelve hours. And when that toddler went missing six months ago? You found the two-year-old within hours."

Lucy chuckled. "Okay, you've made your point. But reelection is next year, and I want to continue my dad's legacy."

"You are."

Abigail set the plate with a chef salad in front of Lucy, then gave Chloe her order. "Can I get y'all anything else?"

"No, this looks delicious." Chloe dug into her hamburger immediately. "Mmm, and I wasn't wrong."

Abigail grinned. "I'll tell Maggie. She loves to hear her customers are satisfied." The waitress left, hurrying toward the kitchen, her long black ponytail bouncing with her strides.

Lucy glanced around. Every table was occupied, which was usual at this time of day. When the door opened, she caught sight of Ben entering. He scanned the coffee shop.

"Ben!" Chloe held her arm up. "You can join us."

Lucy chewed her bottom lip as Ben threaded his way through the crowded café. She always looked forward to her girl time with Chloe, but she couldn't blame her for signaling that Ben should sit with them. Chloe would be his sister-in-law in ten days, not to mention she was taking care of his son.

Ben removed his hat and set it in a vacant chair and then took the last one at the table for four. "I keep forgetting this isn't a good time to come to Maggie's, but I thought I would grab something to eat before heading to see Pastor Mathers."

"You've been out of action for a while. That's understandable." Chloe popped a french fry into her mouth.

Ben peered at Lucy, his gaze penetratingly warm. "You're still coming to the barn before we go to the meeting tonight?"

She nodded and speared some of her lettuce, trying to ignore the quickening of her heartbeat at his perusal. "I want to spend time with Maddy, Lynne and Christie. I find when teenage girls get together they gossip. I might overhear something that will help me." That was the easiest way for her to get a glimpse of what was going on with the teenagers in Little Horn. She still felt two or more were involved in the thefts. At twenty-eight, Lucy was the youngest sheriff to date for the county, but she would stand out at school, so her undercover work had to be somewhere else.

After Abigail took Ben's order, Chloe retrieved a couple of five-dollar bills from her wallet. "This is for my lunch. Cody will be getting up from his nap, and I need to be there. I've been gone all morning to the doctor."

Ben pushed the money toward Chloe. "Keep it. My treat. Is the baby okay?"

"Right on target. In three months, she should be here."

"Grady is excited and can't wait." Ben took his mug of coffee from Abigail and drank a long sip. "I'll be back after I meet with Pastor Mathers."

Chloe stood. "Are you going to be at the barn, then?"

"Yes, but I can always be reached by cell. Thanks, Chloe, for staying on as Cody's nanny. It's hard being a single parent, and I've only dealt with it for a brief time."

"I love being with Cody. It's good experience." Chloe headed for the exit.

Ben turned his full attention on Lucy. She felt he was assessing her in a new light. "Did you enjoy Pastor Mathers's sermon on Sunday?" she asked, hoping to divert his focus.

"It's made me think about what's my purpose. I never really thought about it other than taking care of the ranch. But we're more than our job."

Lucy couldn't really say that. "My work is my life. It requires long hours and being willing to go out to a crime scene in the middle of the night."

"Do you have to do that often?"

"Lately, more than usual. If a serious problem arises, I need to be available."

"Twenty-four/seven?"

She nodded and focused on eating while Abigail delivered a roast-beef sandwich to Ben. "I want to be involved. That's the way my father was. By the time he retired, he knew most of the people in the county. That fact helped him numerous times besides knowing the terrain. I think some of the stolen cattle are being kept somewhere nearby, but I don't have the manpower to cover every square inch."

When her cell phone rang, she snatched it off the table. "Sheriff Benson."

"There's a robbery in Grafton. 214 Second Street. The feed store," the dispatcher said.

"I'm on my way." Lucy rose as she withdrew her wallet.

Ben shook his head. "My treat. See you tonight. If you can't come to the ranch beforehand, let me know, and I'll meet you at the Lone Star Cowboy League center."

"Thanks." As Lucy left the coffee shop, she glanced over her shoulder, and her gaze instantly connected with Ben's. Again her heartbeat picked up speed, and she hastened outside before she did something crazy like blush.

Ben entered Little Horn Community Christian Church and hurried toward Pastor Mathers's office. When he'd called Ben to set up this meeting, Ben had wondered why. He almost felt like a child being called to the principal's office, but he and his family had attended this church for years. He might have doubts about his faith, but the pastor had come to the hospital every week and prayed for him. Grandma Mamie had been certain he'd regained consciousness and recovered faster than the doctors thought possible due to all the prayers being sent up in his behalf, led by her and Pastor Mathers.

Ben spied the pastor in his inner office. The man waved to him to come straight inside.

"I'm so glad we have a chance to talk." Pastor Mathers skirted his desk and stretched out his arm.

Ben shook his hand, then sat where the man indicated on a comfortable-looking brown couch against a wall. "I enjoyed your sermon Sunday."

Pastor Mathers took his seat at the opposite end of the sofa. "I was glad to see you at church. It's been months. I know how concerned your grandmother was, but our prayers were answered."

It took all Ben's willpower not to squirm on the leather cushion. He'd never felt comfortable talking about his feelings, and he certainly didn't know his purpose in life. "Is there something you needed to see me about?"

"Yes. This year is the Stillwater Ranch's turn to hold the children's annual Easter-egg hunt and celebration. I told your grandmother we could skip your ranch this year because of your injury, but she wants to do her part. I know you're still in physical therapy and with having been away from the ranch for months, you have a lot to catch up on, so I thought I would ask what you think. I don't want to put too much on you. The community will understand if you pass. In fact, Carson offered his place so don't feel you have to."

"Are you kidding? It's a big, fun celebration for the kids. I love helping with that event even when it's not at my ranch, and now that Grady is home there will be two of us." He and his brother hadn't really talked about if Grady was staying in Little Horn or not, but Ben hoped so. Right before Grady had left for his last overseas assignment, they had gotten into a huge argument, to the point he was surprised to see Grady when he woke up from his coma. Their relationship was still strained, but there was hope it would heal. He'd been thrilled when Grady had asked him to be the best man at his wedding this morning.

"If you're sure, then I'll add you to the planning committee. Their first meeting was in January. I know every year you've helped with any extra activities like races. It's always been a highlight, but I didn't know what kind of restrictions your doctor has put on you."

He remembered his neurologist had told him under no circumstances was he to participate in any bronco competition or a similarly dangerous activity that would cause him to be thrown from a horse repeatedly. If he hit his head like he had, he probably wouldn't recover. "I won't be doing anything risky. I have a son to think of now. No more things like riding a bronco in a rodeo."

As he said that to Pastor Mathers, Ben was beginning to understand how Grady felt with his war injury. For years they had never had much in common except a last name, but maybe at least his head trauma would bridge the gulf between him and Grady.

Pastor Mathers nodded. "I understand. I know how much you've enjoyed working with children, so I believe you'll be a wonderful father."

Ben was glad the pastor thought that, because he felt as if he'd been thrown into deep water without the ability to swim. But the one thing he knew was that Cody was quickly becoming the center of his life. All his son had had to do was smile at him that first day Mamie and Grady had brought him to the hospital for Ben to see and hold him.

"Maybe next year you can think about being a helper with the youth group."

"Me?"

"Sure. I think you'd be perfect."

How? His attendance at church was sketchy, and he wouldn't call himself an overly religious man. "I'll think about it."

"No decision needed until August, but there will be at least one vacancy at that time."

Ben left the church, his mind in turmoil with thoughts racing through it. Ever since he'd started having the teenagers at the ranch in the intern program, he'd been looking for other ways to help the young people in the community. He wanted to give them chances he really hadn't had. And now the pastor was asking him to help with the youth leader. Him! He wasn't the most likely candidate, and the request had stunned him.

Ben drove through the main gate at Stillwater Ranch, still trying to decide what he should do. He couldn't accept it if he wasn't the best person for the job. *God, what are You telling me?*

After he parked near the house, he went inside to check on Cody before going to the barn. The urge to hold his son swept over him. He'd never thought of himself as father material, but in this case he didn't have a choice, and he wouldn't do a job unless he could do it well.

He entered the house through the kitchen and headed toward the front room, where most of the family congregated. The large window afforded a beautiful view of the family's horses in a pasture, the bluebonnets starting to bloom and poke their heads up through the sea of green grass.

Cody's giggles floated to Ben. He hurried his step. When he paused at the entrance into the room, he honed in on his son grasping the cushion of the ottoman. Then he began pulling himself up. When he stood, Cody let go of the cushion but didn't take a step.

"When did he start doing this?" Ben asked Chloe, who sat in the chair with the ottoman.

"I'm as surprised as you are. He's always holding on when he stands."

Cody gripped the edge and then with one hand tried to reach for a ball he loved to play with. He wobbled, then plopped back onto the floor. Ben moved closer to watch his son again drag himself to a standing position and try to grab the ball—just out of his reach. Cody stood on his tiptoes and his chubby fingers grazed the red plastic toy. It rolled away. Finally he burst out crying and fell down.

Ben scooped Cody into his arms and rocked him. "You're okay. Before long you'll be climbing up on that ottoman."

Cody slowly calmed down and looked at Ben, touching his face. Ben kissed his fingers, then swung him high. His son's laughter resonated through the house.

"I wish I could stay and play, but your daddy needs to get to work. See you later, little man."

Ben sat him on the floor by his toys, plucked the red ball off the ottoman and rolled it to Cody.

"Is Grandma here?" he asked as he straightened.

"She's taking a nap."

"Is she sick?"

"Just a little tired. Cody apparently didn't stay down for his nap as long as he usually does."

"Thanks, Chloe. I'll be at the barn."

As he walked across the yard, he realized he had to find at the least someone to take Chloe's place. It wasn't fair to Mamie to think she could take over full-time when Chloe wasn't available. Maybe even a woman he was interested in. He needed to look beyond just a nanny for his son. Cody needed stability. He'd been shuffled around enough. He'd checked and found that Alana had left Cody with her aunt for a month before dropping him off at the ranch.

When he stepped through the double barn doors, no one was around. Zed should be back soon with the interns and cowhands. They were rotating the cattle to another pasture. A noise at the other end turned his attention in that direction. Suddenly a hunched figure, wearing baggy sweats and a hoodie, raced out of Zed's office midway down the long center aisle toward the back door.

"Can I help you?"

The person increased his speed and darted outside.

Ben rushed after the trespasser. Was this one of the thieves? Had he taken anything? Ben reached the yard behind the barn and glimpsed the guy climbing over a fence. Ben went after him, his breathing labored, his muscles protesting the exertion. As he scaled the fence, the person put more distance between them.

Perched on the top railing, Ben realized the futility of trying to pursue the intruder. He hadn't regained his full strength. Something that would have been easy six months ago wasn't anymore. After catching his breath, he retraced his steps toward the barn, wondering why that person had been in Zed's office. Had the thieves started robbing again?

Chapter Four

Ben entered his barn, his body protesting his mad dash after the intruder. Still winded, he inhaled deep breaths and came to a stop as Lucy appeared in the doorway at the other end. A smile brightened her face when she looked at him and headed toward him.

As she drew closer, tiny lines crinkled her forehead. "Is something wrong?"

"I'm not sure." He slid a glance at Zed's office. "There was someone in here. When I came in, he walked out of there, saw me and raced out the back. I'd say that's a big red flag."

"Did you recognize him?" Lucy moved toward the office. "Did he have anything in his hands?"

"He wasn't carrying anything. He was dressed in a dark hoodie, and about all I could say was the guy was slim and about five feet eight inches."

"But you think it was a male?"

"Yes." Ben removed his Stetson and ran his fingers through his hair, finally beginning to breathe normally. "At least by the way he walked and his body build." He followed Lucy into the room, which had a desk and chair. His gaze fell on the chart of the layout of his ranch that took up almost one wall.

Lucy stood near the desk, examining the contents on top. "Do you see anything out of place?"

"You'll have to check with Zed for sure, but the computer, printer, phone and my rodeo championship trophy are all here." He crossed to the computer and switched it on. "You have to enter an access code." After typing it in, he checked a couple of folders. "I'll have Zed go through it more thoroughly, but I don't think the intruder messed with it."

"Okay, then why in the world did someone come in here for nothing and risk getting caught?"

Ben turned his attention from the focal point, the desk, and surveyed the rest of the office. After he tried the file cabinet, he said, "It's still locked. Zed keeps it that way when he isn't in here." As he continued his inspection, his gaze latched on to the three teenage girls' belongings on the floor behind the door.

A stack of all the Harry Potter books in the series were tied together with a red ribbon, and on top of them was a silver music box with Maddy's name engraved on it. He gestured at the gifts. "I can't image Maddy bringing these in here. She would leave them in the car with her backpack."

"Do you think the intruder left them?" Lucy leaned down and lifted the lid on the music box with a pencil. Her eyes widened.

Ben stepped nearer, getting a whiff of Lucy's light flowery scent as he stared at the silver necklace with a horse charm dangling from it. "Whoever gave this to Maddy, he has good and expensive taste. None of these presents are cheap."

Lucy turned her head and peered up at him, so close he glimpsed the light sprinkle of freckles on her pert nose. She opened her mouth to say something, but no words came out. Instead, their gazes embraced and held.

Voices out in the barn disrupted the moment, and Ben quickly straightened. Lucy stood, a rosy hue on her cheeks, and put some distance between them.

"Let's see what Maddy does when she sees the items." Lucy sat in a chair while Ben lounged back against the desk, his hands gripping its edge.

"Hi, boss," Zed said as he entered the office. "We just finished moving some cattle to a new pasture."

"Did Maddy, Lynne and Christie help y'all?"

Zed nodded. "I'm gonna hate to see them go at the end of the school year."

"Me, too. I'm thinking of hiring a couple of teens for the summer months."

Zed looked at Lucy. "Are you two still going riding?"

With a glance at the clock on the wall, Ben shook his head. "I guess we both got delayed. We have to be at a meeting in an hour." Shifting to Lucy, he grinned. "Can we have a rain check on that ride?"

"Sure."

Lynne knocked on the open door. "I need to get something from my jacket."

Ben swept his arm toward the area.

As the teenager stuck her hand into her coat pocket, her attention fastened on to the gifts on the floor. She bent over to read the engraved name, then popped back up and hurried from the office. "Maddy, you need to see what you got in here."

Ben exchanged looks with Lucy while Zed asked, "Where did those come from?"

Ben shrugged. "Maybe Maddy knows."

"I know what?" The girl paused in the entrance, her view blocked by the door.

"About these gifts." Ben pointed toward them.

She spied them and squealed, stooping by the books and picking up the music box. When she opened it, her jaw dropped. "Who would do this?"

Lynne and Christie leaned around the door. "You've got a secret admirer, Maddy. Probably the same one who gave you the iPod," Christie said and whistled.

Maddy blushed. "Ben, can I put these in the car?"

"Yes. You don't have any idea who gave you these beautiful gifts?"

"No, sir. But I love them, especially the necklace. I don't have a lot of jewelry." Maddy rose with the books and music box and hurried out of the office with her two friends right behind her.

Lucy walked to the doorway and peered at the girls leaving out the front of the barn, giggling and whispering.

Ben came up behind her. "What do you think?"

"She seems genuinely surprised, but do you really think she doesn't know who is giving her the presents?"

"Yes. In all my dealings with her, she has been very straightforward."

"What happened here, boss?"

Ben pivoted toward Zed. "I chased an intruder out the back of the barn. I didn't see who it was, but he came out of your office. I think he left these gifts."

Zed's bushy eyebrows shot up. "Well, I'll be."

"Has Maddy said anything about a boyfriend?" Lucy moved into the office as the sound of the girls returning floated on the air.

"No, but then I don't think they would be gossiping when I'm around." Zed tossed his hat on a peg and sat behind his desk. "Just a reminder, the girls are only staying another half an hour. They have their monthly Future Farmers of America meeting tonight."

"I'd forgotten about that." Ben drew Lucy out of the office and took her hand, then strolled out the back. "I want to show you where the intruder fled."

Lucy peered over her shoulder at the three teenagers parting and each disappearing into a separate stall. When they were around the corner and out of sight of anyone in the barn, she tugged her hand free from his. "The show is over."

"What show?" he asked, pressing his lips together to keep a straight face while Lucy tried to control the flush staining her cheeks.

"You keep insisting on acting as if we're a couple."

"Me?" He pointed to his chest, then chuckled. "Lucy, it's the most logical reason for you to be coming to the ranch and hanging out with me at the barn."

Releasing a long breath, she shook her head. "You're certainly persistent. I'm going to have to find someone for you to become interested in."

"How about you come tomorrow afternoon? We can go for a ride, then have dinner."

She opened her mouth.

He knew she was going to say no, so he hurriedly added, "Once a month Grandma has the girls come up to the house after work and have dinner with us. She doesn't believe they eat enough. I think she's trying to put some pounds on their bones. It's always the day after the FFA meeting."

"How does your grandmother do everything? She's always got something going either here, in town or at church."

"Talking about church, as you know I met with Pastor Mathers today. It's Stillwater Ranch's turn for the big Easter-egg hunt."

"So you told him you'd host it this year?"

"Yes. I always enjoy it. I think I'm a kid at heart."

She laughed. "You won't get an argument from me. So I guess you're coming to the next meeting at church about the Easter-egg hunt?"

"Yep. Why?"

"Because I'm chairing it this year."

He stared at her. "Where do *you* find the time to do everything?"

"Good question. I don't sleep." One corner of her mouth lifted. "No, seriously, I like to stay busy."

"Well, so do I, but I also find time to play. Lately, it's been me playing with Cody."

"He's a cutie. What are you going to do when Chloe has her baby?"

"I don't know. I'm working on it. But let's get back to the question of coming for a ride and dinner tomorrow night. Are you coming?"

"First, I wasn't the one who sidetracked the earlier topic. You were. Second…"

When she paused for a few seconds, he hurriedly said, "It'll help keep up the charade we're a couple in the girls' eyes."

She frowned, looked toward the barn, then at him again. "*Charade* is a good description of what this is because we are *not* a couple."

He loved to rattle her. "It's still the best way for you to hang around here. So should I tell Grandma we have another one for dinner tomorrow?"

"Yes, now show me where the intruder went. Since it's been so dry, I doubt there are footprints, but maybe the tide is turning on this investigation and we'll get fingerprints."

Ben started for the fence. He wanted the Robin Hoods found like everyone else, but it sure was fun having Lucy hanging around his ranch.

At seven o'clock, Lucy pulled out of the parking space in front of the Lone Star Cowboy League building. "Since you're replacing Tyler on the Rustling Investigation Team, at least tonight was a good time to get you caught up on what has been happening since the end of October."

Ben angled toward her. "The only promising lead is where the cattle possibly are being sold, if not in Texas."

"Yes, the Oklahoma State Police are working on it from their end. I've also contacted New Mexico."

"If they are being sold in Oklahoma or New Mexico, then how could it be a couple of teenagers? If they were gone several times to sell the cattle, they would have to be away for at least a day. I could see it once, but to move the number of cattle they have stolen, it would be four or five times. Wouldn't their parents realize something is going on?"

"Kids can get creative. Some parents would, but others don't keep track of their teenagers like they should."

"What if the teenagers are working with someone else to sell the stolen cattle? Maybe they aren't leaving but that person is."

"Once we find the place we think the cattle are going, we'll be able to figure out if there are more people than the Robin Hoods involved. But having a middleman makes sense. You think that person could be from around here?"

"Maybe. Maybe not. Let's grab some hamburgers before going home." Ben pointed at the Hamburger Hut at the end of Main Street.

Lucy slanted a glance at him. During the meeting, Tom Horton and Amanda Jones, other members of the team, had been giving Ben and her quizzical looks. But then she couldn't blame them. Ben sat close to her and even once had put his hand on the back of her chair. "Frankly, I'm surprised Amanda didn't ask me after the meeting if you and I were dating with all the attention you gave me. Is this dinner in public to continue your rouse we're a couple?"

"We aren't even getting out of the car. They serve us curbside. But no, I'm starving and trying to put some weight back on."

Lucy chuckled. "That's not a bad problem to have. Not having to worry about what and how much you eat."

"The key to the diet is being in the hospital and rehab for months, not even doing half of what you're used to."

Although Ben's tone was light, teasing, Lucy parked at Hamburger Hut and shifted around. "Dieting is never easy, but that isn't the way I would want to lose weight. How are you doing? Really?"

"I wish I had the energy I had six months ago. I'm glad Grady is still at the ranch to help me otherwise..." He sighed. "I'm not sure what I would do."

"You're doing quite a bit."

"Yeah, with the help of an afternoon nap. A couple

of days ago Zed found me napping in the hay. I didn't even have the energy to go back to the house and lie down. If nothing else, my accident showed me not to take anything for granted. You'll never know when it will be taken away."

The wistfulness in his voice touched Lucy. He was right, and it took incidents like what happened to Ben to reinforce that. "Good advice."

"Hey, don't sound so surprised. Occasionally, I can be serious."

"What do you want to order?" Lucy asked as she studied the menu and decided on her usual.

"The hamburger platter special with a vanilla milk shake and water."

Lucy placed their orders, then relaxed against the seat for the first time that day. "I like their platter special, too. I wish I could have the milk shake, but iced tea will have to do. What time do you want me to come tomorrow?"

"The interns work from three to six, so anytime you can after three. We'll eat shortly after six."

"Four." Which meant she would go to the station early. She wouldn't want Byron McKay to accuse her of slacking off on her duties.

"I'll have Maddy show you how to saddle your horse."

"I've done it before."

"Let's call this a refresher course."

She smiled. "I appreciate your help in getting some time with Maddy."

"I want this settled as soon as possible. I heard in town today some ugly rumors flying around about

Byron challenging you as sheriff. Obviously he's come out vocally against your right to be sheriff."

She squeezed her hands into fists. "I don't think he wants to be sheriff, but he does want to control the person who is."

"All the more reason to vote for you."

Ben's stamp of approval strangely eased her tension at the mention of the man trying to make her life difficult. "Thanks."

"Look, that's Maddy with Lynne and Christie. Their FFA meeting must be over with."

Lucy examined Ben's innocent expression, except for a mischievous gleam dancing in his eyes. "What a coincidence. When did you hear they were going to be here tonight?"

"Am I that obvious?"

"Actually it's quite sweet, but—"

"Our food is here," Ben interrupted her and removed his wallet. "I'm paying for this."

"Bribing the sheriff?"

"You're off duty."

"I'm always on duty. At least several times a month my sleep is disrupted because of a call I need to deal with. Some folks think only the sheriff should take care of their problem."

"Like Byron McKay."

She chuckled. "That's putting it mildly. He's at the top of the list."

"My sleep was disrupted last night. Cody is getting a tooth and was not a happy camper. He didn't want anyone else sleeping since he wasn't."

"What did you do?"

"Rubbed a numbing gel on the area, then rocked him until he fell asleep. We moved him upstairs to give Grandma a break and me experience taking care of him. I'm learning all kinds of stuff from Mamie and Chloe. I'm gonna be an expert by the time he's eighteen."

"That sounds as though you're preparing for more children." She'd never thought of Ben as a father. He never stayed with a woman long enough.

"I'm not opposed to the idea. Cody is quickly becoming the center of my life."

If she hadn't seen him with his son the other day, she wouldn't have believed a word he said. This change in Ben had taken her by surprise, but it shouldn't have if she considered his interest in young people and the intern program.

"I already know what not to do."

"You do?"

"Let just say the last years with my dad were a good lesson in what not to do. He barely tolerated me. He'd have kicked me off the ranch if Grady hadn't left to serve his country. He figured I was better than nothing."

"How are you and Grady getting along?" They were opposites. Grady had always been the serious one, disciplined and in control.

"I'm glad he came back. The ranch needed him."

"But not you?"

"When he left the last time he came home, I was glad he was gone. He was always on my case. This time is different. For one, it's time we become brothers in the true sense of the word. We weren't always at such odds. When we were younger, we got along."

"What happened?"

Ben shrugged. "We grew apart. My interests became different."

"Girls?"

"Not totally." He cocked his head to the side. "I think it really began when my father seemed to favor Grady over me. If we were working on a project, he got the compliment. I was an afterthought."

She glimpsed the waitress bringing their tray of food. After Lucy passed Ben his dinner, he leaned over and handed the young girl the money to pay. His arm brushed against hers, and his scent, not unpleasant but outdoorsy, swirled around her.

When the waitress left and he sat back, Lucy realized she'd been holding her breath and finally exhaled. "I'm glad you and Grady are getting reacquainted. He hated seeing you like that in the hospital." And so had she. For a while she'd wondered if he would ever recover consciousness, and the thought of not seeing Ben's teasing smile again had bothered her more than she realized. "What are you going to do when Chloe has her baby?"

"That's a good question. At the very least I need a nanny. I won't leave Cody for Mamie to handle all the time by herself. Don't tell her that. She would protest. But what Cody really needs is a mother."

"You, settle down with one woman?"

"That's not an impossibility if I find the right person."

"What are you looking for?"

"Someone who loves children, has a good sense of humor, knows what she wants and…"

She waited half a minute before saying, "And what?"

"There is a connection between us—chemistry. Any suggestions on how to find a mother for Cody?"

In that moment, his gaze locked with hers, robbing her of any response. A lump swelled into her throat, taking her by surprise. She wanted the best for Cody—and Ben. "Let me think on it. Cody is a special kid. You'll only want the best for him."

His eyes gleamed. "Of course. He's a Stillwater." He took a long sip of his milk shake, watching her the whole time.

Goose bumps ran up her arms, and she focused on eating her juicy hamburger, savoring its delicious taste while ignoring the man so close to her in the sheriff's SUV.

"Looks as if the girls are leaving," Ben said while returning Maddy's wave.

"If she didn't know we were here before, she does now."

"Let them think what they want, especially if it helps you with solving the robberies."

"I'm going to check around about the music box and the necklace. They look expensive, so I might be able to find where they were bought."

"Not if they were bought online."

Lucy peered at Ben. "You think like a police officer. True, but it's worth looking into."

"While you do that, I can look on the internet and see if I can find a place that sells either one."

"I should do that."

"I want to help. Anything to get Byron off his high horse. It's okay to ask for help, and remember, I'm now part of the Rustling Investigation Team."

"As if you don't have enough to do."

"I could say the same thing to you."

She nodded once. "Touché." After washing down

her last bite of food with the iced tea, Lucy balled the wrapping paper and stuffed it into the sack. "Ready. I'm one short at the station, so I imagine tomorrow will be busy."

"I understand you're going to be the maid of honor for Chloe."

Lucy grinned. "I'm so happy for her. She deserves a good man after that husband she had. I can't believe a guy leaving because his wife was pregnant with his child."

"Seeing her with Cody, I can tell Chloe is going to be a great mother."

She needed to find someone like Chloe for Ben. In the next few days she would take a look at the single females in Little Horn. If not, in the towns nearby.

"Will Eva and Tyler be back for the wedding?" Lucy turned onto the highway heading out of town.

"Yes, the day before."

"Good. Eva was rooting for Grady and Chloe."

"There seem to be a lot of happy couples recently."

"Yeah," she murmured, wondering if Jesse and she had worked out in San Antonio where she would be today. She liked her life in Little Horn, in spite of Byron being on her case, and was glad she discovered Jesse's tendency to be unfaithful. Never again. One Don Juan in her life was enough.

Suddenly a movement up ahead caught her attention, and she straightened, leaning forward to see better. "What are they doing?"

In her headlights, two figures, dressed in dark hoodies, were illuminated on the side of the road, holding up something between them. They froze for a few seconds in the bright glare, then dropped the sign, whirled around and raced into the field beside the road.

As she came to a stop on the shoulder where the two people had been, she reached for her flashlight. "Was that the town sign they were holding?"

Chapter Five

"It looked like it." Ben gripped the handle of Lucy's sheriff's SUV, ready to get out.

"Those two are long gone by now, but I want to check the area out." After she retrieved her weapon from the glove compartment, practically leaning across Ben, she climbed from the car and strapped on her gun belt.

Trying to ignore the jump in his pulse rate created by her nearness, Ben exited the car and started for where the two people had been. "I'm coming with you." She was the one wearing the firearm, not him, but something deep inside him wouldn't let him sit in the car and wait for her to investigate. What if the guys were watching from the brush? What if they tried to harm her? He wouldn't let that happen.

"If it would do any good, I'd tell you to wait in the car." Lucy went through the overgrown grass and weeds, coming to a stop a few feet in front of Ben. She shone her flashlight at the ground. "This is the sign stolen months ago."

Ben skirted her and bent over to pick up the metal plaque proclaiming, Welcome to Little Horn, Texas.

"Don't. Leave it. I want to run fingerprints on the sign."

"Now?" Ben straightened and faced her.

"No. I'll be right back." Lucy trudged to her vehicle and opened the rear hatch, then the back doors. A half a minute later she returned and handed him a pair of latex gloves. "I need your help carrying the sign to my SUV. I put the backseat down so we can get this inside."

"Sure." He snapped on the gloves and lifted one end while being careful not to touch any more of the sign than was necessary to carry it. "Everything happened so quickly, but it looked as though the two guys had on gloves."

"They did. I'm hoping they haven't been that careful in the past."

Ben stopped at one side of the rear bumper. "Won't there be tons of prints on the sign?"

"I know this is a long shot, but I can't ignore this piece of evidence. The new welcome sign has been up for several years, and I've doubt many have touched it since the initial installation."

After they slid the piece of evidence into the back, Lucy shut the rear hatch and started back to the area.

"What are you doing?" Ben followed her.

"I'm going to check the ground for any evidence in case one of them left something behind. Once they left a watch at a crime scene and one came back to get it. We almost had him, but he got away. My life would be much easier if I had."

"I wonder why they brought it back." Ben stood back from the area while Lucy shone her light on the tramped grass.

"This is one of the reasons I think the Robin Hoods

are teenagers. Anyone interested in making money by stealing cattle and equipment wouldn't have bothered taking the sign. But these robbers are making a statement. They are angry."

"Then, why return the sign?"

Lucy took one last look, then joined Ben at the edge. "I don't think their anger is directed at the whole town, and this sign belongs to everyone. I think they've finally realized that."

"It makes sense. Hopefully they realize stealing is wrong and want to make amends." Ben walked beside her to the car. "I'll keep an ear out with the girls at the ranch. You can't always be there when they are, but I can try to be. I might be able to overhear something." Reaching around her, he grasped the driver's-side door and opened it for her.

"The day I can bring these guys in can't come fast enough for me." She slid behind the steering wheel.

"We'll have to celebrate when that day comes." Ben leaned down, her fresh, clean scent wafting to him. In the dim interior light, her crystalline green eyes transfixed him and held him rooted to the spot.

"I'd like that." A smile transformed her mouth from a thoughtful look to a radiant one.

She was beautiful, but even more than that he liked her caring and integrity. He pulled back and shut the door, then rounded the cruiser to sit on his side.

As she drove through the gates of the Stillwater Ranch, Ben relaxed back against the seat. "I hope you'll come in. Mamie usually has a pot of decaf coffee on at this time. She makes the best coffee."

"I know. I've had it before. Do you think Chloe will be there? I'd like to talk to her about the wedding next week. I want to make sure I do everything I need to as a maid of honor. This is my first time being one."

"She should be. I wonder if I need to throw Grady a bachelor party."

"I get the impression they want it low-key, but it's a good question to ask them." Lucy pulled up in front of the large, sprawling white Western-style Colonial house. "I've always thought your home fit your ranch, whereas Byron's flashy mansion doesn't really fit in Little Horn."

"Byron does everything with grandeur."

"Even when he's a pain."

Laughing, Ben unlocked the front door and stepped to the side to allow Lucy to enter first. In the foyer, he poked his head into the living room, saw Grandma reading her Bible and waited until she glanced up. "Where's Cody?"

"Asleep."

"That's early."

"He didn't nap well again today, so he was tired earlier than usual." His grandmother closed her Bible and put it on the end table next to her on the couch, smiling when Lucy came into view. "It's good to see you again. How did the meeting go?"

Lucy stopped beside Ben. "With no new robberies, we went over what's being done to find the Robin Hoods. But on the way here, we," she said with a pause, slanting a look at Ben, "saw two guys trying to put the town's welcome sign back in place."

Mamie's eyes grew round. "You caught the Robin Hoods?"

Lucy shook her head. "But I have the sign and will put it back up tomorrow."

"Good." Mamie pushed to her feet, her shoulders sagging as though she was fatigued. "There's fresh coffee in the kitchen. I'm going to follow Cody to bed early tonight."

"Grandma, where are Grady and Chloe?"

She walked toward the hallway, paused and turned toward them. "Out on the back porch, discussing their wedding plans. Good night, y'all." Then she continued toward her downstairs bedroom in the back.

Ben watched her and wanted to help her, but when he had tried a few days ago to talk to her about slowing down, she'd lashed into him, informing him she was just fine. He leaned toward Lucy's ear. "I want her to do less, but she refuses."

"That sounds like her. She told me she is as young as she thinks she is."

"Let's get coffee, then go out back." He took her hand and tugged her toward the kitchen. When she didn't move, he glanced back at Lucy.

She stared at their clasped hands, then up at him, her forehead creased, her green eyes dark.

"We're friends, Lucy. That's all." He released his grasp and pivoted toward the hallway that led to the kitchen. It was clear that was all Lucy wanted, and that bothered him.

Lucy sat in a comfortable, cushioned chair on the back porch at Stillwater Ranch and listened to Grady and Ben talking about pranks they pulled on each other growing up. Laughter surrounded her, and she even joined in, but she couldn't shake the sensations that had flooded her when Ben had taken her hand in the hallway.

For a split second, a connection had sprung up between them that had nothing to do with being friends. It had come out of nowhere, and she didn't know why. She'd known Ben all of her life and had seen him often except for those years she'd spent in San Antonio. Was he really different since he'd woken up from the coma?

Chloe turned to Lucy and said in a low voice, "These past weeks, it's as if Ben and Grady are reacquainting themselves."

"As teens they became more adversaries than brothers. I'm glad to see them like this."

"Maybe it takes near-death experiences for a person to see what's important."

Lucy slanted a glance at the brothers. "Who are you talking about, Ben or Grady?"

"Both, in a way. The war changed Grady."

"What are y'all whispering about over there?" Ben asked in a teasing voice.

"Our own childhood escapades. You two aren't the only ones. Chloe and I were friends growing up."

Ben chuckled and looked at his twin brother. "I believe we've been ignoring the womenfolk."

"Womenfolk!" Chloe burst out laughing.

Again Lucy responded to the humor in Ben's expression. When they were growing up, he'd often thrown caution to the wind and dived into something he wanted to do without considering the risks. Sometimes she wished she had that ability. "Yes, you have been ignoring us. I can't stay long. I have an early day tomorrow. This conversation is supposed to be about the wedding. I know, Chloe, you told me not to worry. Just show up at the church Friday afternoon. But surely I can do something for you and Grady."

Chloe shook her head. "There isn't any time. We did it this way because we didn't want a fuss made."

"How about I have a luncheon for you on Thursday at my house? A few friends. Nothing fancy, since I'll be making it." Lucy took a sip of her coffee.

"Well, in that case, Grady, we should have a little gathering with a few friends," Ben chimed in. "I can't let Lucy outdo me in the department of maid of honor/best man."

"This isn't a contest, Ben." Lucy set her empty mug on the table nearby.

"The dinner here after the wedding is all we want." Grady said as he and Chloe both stood at the same time. He took Chloe's hand. "It's been a long day for Chloe. I'm gonna escort her to her bedroom, then check with Zed at the barn about the cattle rotation."

Chloe nodded. "If you want to do something, I'll let you give me a baby shower closer to the due date. Okay, Lucy?"

"Short of hog-tying you and kidnapping you to come to the luncheon, I have to accept your wishes." Lucy grinned. "Mainly I want you to know I'm here if you need me. Just ask."

As Grady slung his arm over Chloe's shoulder and started for the back door, his fiancée replied, "I will."

When they disappeared into the house, Lucy remembered the glow of love on her friend's face. Chloe stayed at the ranch because of Cody and slept in her own room connected to the baby's. Lucy wished she could find a love like Chloe and Grady had, but she couldn't seem to get past Jesse's betrayal. She wasn't the risk taker Ben was.

"We could always throw a surprise party for each of

them. For it to work we would have to do it at the same time." Ben slouched back in his chair, his elbows on the arms and his hands clasped in front of him.

"And lose my best friend? No way."

"Yeah, Grady wouldn't be too happy with me, either. We're starting to work out our past differences. That might add fuel to the fire."

"It was nice hearing you all talk about the good times."

"It's been a long while since we did."

"It's time to put the past where it belongs. In the past."

A twinkle in his dark brown eyes followed with a half grin preceded him saying, "In your infinite wisdom, you're correct."

"All I ask is for you to remember just what you said when you start to argue with me." She rose. "I need to leave. Finding the town sign adds another task to my long list for tomorrow."

"Let me know when you're going to put it back up. I think the area around it needs to be tended. That would be a good task for my three interns. Of course, I'd want your input in how to do it. Maybe you can help or supervise us."

"Ben Stillwater, you are a good man to have on a team. I appreciate the offer and accept. I was thinking about it when tramping through the tall grass and weeds this evening. If we let it go too long, then no one will be able to see the sign."

"I could give you the cliché line about brilliant minds thinking alike, but I won't. I was thinking if Maddy is the reason our ranch hasn't been hit, then having her work on the sign-beautification project might keep it safe this time." He stood, grabbing his mug, then reaching for hers…at the same time she did.

Their fingers touched. Their gazes embraced. All thoughts fled Lucy's mind. A lock of his sandy-brown hair fell over one eye. The urge to brush it back inundated her and sobered her to the effect he had on her. She had to find him someone who would be a good wife and mother. Then everything would get back to normal between them. It was clearly not going to be her, a tomboyish, work-dedicated sheriff.

She snatched the mug and brought it up to her chest as though it was a barrier between them. "I'd better go."

She marched toward the back door and hurried inside, needing to put some space between them. Fast. She'd promised herself as a teenager she would never fall for his charm. She'd seen him break one girl's heart after another. Not hers.

After putting the mug in the sink, she pivoted to head into the hallway and ran right into Ben.

He stepped back—thankfully—and set his cup next to hers. "I'll walk you to your car."

"You don't need to. Remember you're recovering from a serious accident."

"Please, don't remind me. I'm trying to put that incident in my past." One corner of his mouth quirked.

"Good. I'm glad you're learning how." She sidestepped him and strode toward the hallway. Now if only she could learn to put her past behind her. She hated the idea that Jesse's betrayal still affected her. But it did.

He moved ahead of her and opened the front door.

As she passed him, she said, "I'm going to have to compliment Mamie on raising such a gentleman."

His chuckles filled the night air and sent ripples of

awareness of the man walking beside her to her car. Again he opened her driver's-side door.

"You know, a gal could get used to this," she said as she slipped into her sheriff's SUV, rolling down her window. "Good night, and thanks for coming up with ways for me to get closer to Maddy."

He leaned against the car, his elbows on the open window. "You're welcome. Anything to help a friend."

When she started the engine, he pushed back and stayed there as she drove away. She took one last glimpse of him as she drove around the curve toward the main gates of the ranch.

The whole way to town, her mind raced with possible women for him to date. What about Ingrid Edwards? She was husband hunting, declaring she wanted to be married by twenty-six, which wasn't too far away. No, she was too needy. Jenna Thorn might be a possibility. Ben knew her because she was Carson's sister. No, she didn't have her life together.

By the time she reached her small house in Little Horn, her thoughts swirled with eligible women in the area. She let herself in and put her purse on the counter in the kitchen, decorated in tones of green and burgundy—her mom's touches. When her parents left to travel throughout the United States, she'd moved into her childhood home and she still hadn't made any changes to it. One day she hoped they'd be returning to Little Horn. Then she would find her own place to live.

Suddenly a name popped into her head for Ben: Paula Morris, the only Realtor in town. She would be a good candidate for Ben. She was pretty, sensible and nice. Perfect.

* * *

Lucy rode on Daisy Mae, a pinto mare, beside Ben the next day across the pasture near the barn. "I met with Paula Morris today about looking for a place for me to live in the area, hopefully in Little Horn."

"Are your parents coming back to town to live?" Ben slowed his stallion to a walk.

"They haven't said anything, but every time I talk to Mom, it sounds as though she misses home. I've been saving up to buy my own place for the day they do return for longer than a visit." Lucy slid a glance at Ben. "Paula knows this area inside and out. There isn't anything right now, but she'll let me know when something does come up."

"You're thinking of moving to another town in the county?"

"I might have to. Of course, if I don't get reelected, I might have to look for another job, too."

Ben's jawline hardened. "I'm not gonna let Byron get his way. You'll be reelected."

"You want to be head of my reelection campaign?"

"Me?" He stopped Thunder and looked at her. "Are you kidding?"

She brought Daisy Mae to a halt and twisted around so she faced Ben. "You know this county well, and whenever you do something you go all out. I couldn't ask for a better campaign manager."

He tipped his black Stetson. "Well, thank you, ma'am. I just might do it, but it's not for another year. I try not to plan too far in the future. I've learned it can change in a blink of an eye."

"True. Speaking of Paula, you two would make a nice couple."

One of his eyebrows rose beneath his hat. "When were we speaking of Paula and dating? You mentioned looking for a place to live." His mouth pinched together. "Or was that a way to bring up Paula?"

"Yes. I've been giving it a lot of thought since you talked about finding a nanny or wife soon. You've been out of circulation for months. Paula wouldn't be the nanny, but she isn't dating anyone now. She's pretty..."

Ben urged his stallion into a gallop, leaving Lucy to watch his back. Obviously Paula didn't fit his idea of a date. Okay. She would come up with someone else.

She nudged her mare into a gallop and arrived at the barn a couple of minutes behind Ben.

He'd handed his reins to Christie to take care of Thunder while he said to Maddy, "Show Lucy how to care for her mount when she comes back from a hard ride."

"Will do." Maddy waited by Daisy Mae while Lucy dismounted, then the teenage girl handed Lucy the reins. "We'll do what we did earlier in reverse." She ran her hand over the mare's neck. "She's sweating, so we'll cool her off after that."

"She's a good horse for me. She seems to know what she needs to do with little prompting from me. Do you ride much, Maddy?"

"I have since I started working here. Ben lets us ride several times a week. He said that's part of learning ranching—becoming an extension of your horse. That's my favorite part of the job." Maddy removed the saddle and the blanket under it and put them on a rack.

"I see you're wearing the necklace your secret admirer gave you. Do you know who he is?"

Maddy blushed. "No."

"Who would you like it to be?"

Christie walked by with Thunder and said, "Gareth McKay, if she was smart."

"Christie!" Maddy's cheeks reddened even more.

"You know he has a serious crush on you. All you'd have to do is show him you're interested and he'd ask you out."

Maddy took the reins from Lucy. "Ignore her. She doesn't know anything. Gareth would never be interested in me."

"Why?"

"He's the son of the wealthiest man in the county. I know his father would never allow it. Gareth's father wouldn't even have anything to do with Betsy, his cousin."

"Ah, so you like Gareth."

The teenager turned away, her shoulders slumped. "I'll take it from here. All we're gonna do is walk the horses until they are cooled down, then I'll turn Daisy Mae out in the pasture."

Lucy caught up with her walking toward the rear door. "Maddy, you have a lot to offer a person. You're a hard worker, and according to Ben, you're a natural with the animals."

"But I'm in foster care. I have no family." Her eyes widened. "Don't get me wrong. My foster parents are good to me, but when I become eighteen and graduate from high school, I'm on my own."

"What do you want to do?"

"Ultimately I want to be a vet and work with big

animals, but the money…" Maddy cleared her throat. "Since I can't do that, training horses would be a good job."

"You've got another year. There are loans and scholarships out there you might be able to apply for."

Her eyes glistening, Maddy looked at her. "My grades are all right, As and Bs, but the competition for those scholarships is stiff."

Lucy gave Maddy a hug. "Keep doing the kind of work you do here, and you'll have people to champion your cause."

Maddy pulled back, swiping at a tear that rolled down her cheek. "I try not to think about the future, but sometimes I do and I always get discouraged. For several years I've known this is what I'm supposed to do with my life."

"God has a plan for you. He'll provide a way." Lucy's throat thickened. The young girl touched her heart. If she could help Maddy, she would.

"I know. That's what Pastor Mathers says. I reckon he knows what he's talking about."

"A wise man. I'll see you at dinner."

Maddy continued her trek toward the rear of the barn. Lucy watched the girl, her shoulders squaring, her head held up.

"What were y'all talking about?" Ben whispered behind her.

She jerked, surprised by his presence. She'd been so wrapped up in Maddy she hadn't realized he was nearby. "She wants to be a vet and doesn't see how she'll be able to do that."

"When the time comes, the Lone Star Cowboy League might be able to help her like they did for Tyler when he wanted to be a doctor. We've been talking about doing it on a regular basis for a youth around here who can't afford college otherwise."

A smile spread through her. "Right. That's one possibility. She certainly has the need and she's a good kid."

"Did she say anything to help your case?"

"She likes Gareth. Not sure if he returns the feelings or not, but I'm going to check around. Gareth McKay has the money to buy those gifts for Maddy, and he has a tie to Betsy."

"Let's go to the house. The girls know to come up to the house a little before six." He ambled toward the front entrance. "Are you thinking the Robin Hoods are Gareth and his twin, Winston?"

She glanced at her watch, surprised to see it was five forty already. When she was with Ben, time seemed to race by. "They fit the body type we saw last night, they know about ranches and cattle and have access to equipment to move the cattle."

"You'll need more than speculation before you confront Byron and his sons."

"I know, and I could be wrong. The twins are connected to Betsy, and now Gareth with Maddy. I should hear from the New Mexico State Police about the man they caught moving stolen cattle near the Texas border. And I'm still making inquiries about the music box and necklace. So far nothing in the immediate area. Did you find anything online?"

"No, but there are tons of places on the internet that would sell something like that. I doubt I'll find half of them."

"I know it's a long shot, but that's how some cases are solved. A lot of legwork, or in your case, finger work."

"How are you doing with the physical places?"

"In this county, I'm visiting the stores and taking a picture of the items to see if they sell them."

"What if it's somewhere like Austin or even San Antonio?" Ben placed his hand at the small of her back as they mounted the stairs to the front porch.

"I'm going to fax the picture and inquiry. My dispatcher/receptionist is making a list of ones in the Austin area for me. I'm hoping it doesn't go that far away, though." The feel of his light touch zipped up her spine and reminded her of when he took her hand last night. She hadn't expected it and had been surprised by it.

"Then you have Fort Worth and Dallas north of us."

She moaned. "Don't remind me. This is the drudgery part of being a police officer."

"Not stakeouts?" He opened the front door.

"With a stakeout there's the anticipation you'll discover something important to crack your case."

In the hallway he faced her. "You really enjoy what you do."

Although not a question, she nodded. "Ever since I went to work with Dad one day when I was twelve, I've wanted to be a police officer. You never know what to expect."

"I can see the enthusiasm on your face when you talk about your job. That's the way I feel about running this ranch."

"You used to accuse me of being an open book. I probably would never be good at undercover work." The sounds of giggles coming from the living room drew her attention.

"That's Cody. In a short time I've learned his laughter and can tell what a few of his cries mean. Well,

Grandma helped me with that one." Ben swept his arm toward the living room.

When he entered behind Lucy, Cody saw him and began crawling to him. Ben met him halfway, scooped up his son and swung him around. The baby's laughter echoed through the room. "This has become our routine when I see him." Ben stopped turning and held his son.

Lucy looked around the pair and said, "It's nice to see you, Mamie." She took in a deep breath of the aroma floating from the kitchen. "Thanks for the dinner invitation. It smells wonderful."

The older woman rose slowly. "Now that y'all are here to watch Cody, I'm going to help Martha Rose set the table and put the food on."

"Can I help, too?"

"No, you're a guest. Enjoy Cody."

After Mamie left, his son's small hand reached up and grabbed the brim of Ben's cowboy hat, then yanked on it. The Stetson tumbled off his head with a little encouragement from him. It hit the floor between Ben and Lucy.

He put Cody down by the black hat. "Watch this," he said and stepped back by Lucy.

Cody sat up next to it and dragged the Stetson to him. He lifted it but couldn't get his head under it. Finally Ben plopped it on his son's head and tilted it back so Cody could see out the front.

"I'm definitely getting you a hat, little man, and then cowboy boots when you start walking." He ruffled his son's dark hair and took his Stetson to hang on the peg in the hallway.

Lucy knelt near Cody, seeing his face screwing up for a protest. She swept him into her arms and stood.

"Look at all the toys you have." She moved to a few scattered ones on the floor in front of the coffee table. "I haven't stacked rings in a *long* time. Can you show me how?" She handed him the red doughnut-shaped toy.

It went into Cody's mouth, and he gnawed on it.

Ben squatted next to Lucy. "He's teething and loves to chew on anything he can get into his mouth. I used to let him have my hat longer until he began trying to eat the brim."

While Ben interacted with his son, Lucy sat cross-legged next to them and enjoyed the scene. Ben was good with Cody, as if he instinctively knew what to do. He hadn't been involved in his child's life for long, but a person wouldn't know it. He was born to be a father, in spite of the strained relationship with his own dad.

When Ben lay on the floor and Cody crawled onto his chest, Lucy marveled at the sight. Ben had told her he was a changed man. Maybe he was after all.

Chapter Six

The sound of cries penetrated Ben's sleep, yanking him awake. He sat up straight, his heartbeat kicking up a notch. Cody was awake.

Ben slipped out of bed, glancing at the clock on the bedside table. Four in the morning. The cries increased, and he hurried his pace to Cody's bedroom down the hall. When he came into his room, his son stood up in his crib, his face beet red as he worked himself into a rage.

Ben shut the door and rushed to pick up Cody. "Shh. I'm here. You'll be okay."

He sat in the rocking chair and started going back and forth. His son's screams blasted his ears. Ben checked to see if Cody was wet. No. He shouldn't be hungry yet. It must be his teeth. After he applied the numbing gel in the area where a tooth was coming in, he rocked his son, humming a lullaby Grandma Mamie used sometimes.

In the dim glow of the night-light, Cody's eyes began to slide close, only to snap open, then do it all over again. "Shh. Don't fight it, son," Ben said in a singsong voice.

As his child fell asleep, Ben leaned back and closed

his eyes, relishing the soft bundle in his arms. Love and a fierce protective instinct assailed him. If he'd known this was what being a father felt like, he would have seriously considered settling down years ago. Looking back over his life, he realized his behavior had started because his own father had criticized everything he did. His rebellion had become a contest between them. He didn't want that for Cody and him.

Lord, I know I haven't been the best son to You or my father. Show me what I need to do to make this right. I want to have the kind of relationship Lucy has with her dad.

He could remember seeing Lucy as a deputy sheriff working for her father. They had been a team. He couldn't recall his dad and him ever having been like that.

When Cody was sound asleep, Ben slowly rose and placed him gently in the crib. He kissed the tips of two fingers and lightly touched his son's cheek. His heart swelled at the sight of Cody at peace and content. He wished he was. His life was unsettled—had been for years, if he was truthful with himself.

After leaving his son's room, Ben headed downstairs. It was after five. No sense trying to go back to sleep. He was usually up by six or six thirty anyway. In the kitchen, he made a pot of coffee that could tide him over until his grandmother got up. His brew wasn't nearly as good as hers.

As it perked, he lounged against the counter, his legs crossed and arms folded. He stared at the tile floor. A lot had happened in town but also here at the ranch. He still wanted to go forward with a summer camp for kids— for Cody. If he started small this summer, he could expand in the years to follow if it worked.

"What great world affairs are you contemplating?" Grady asked from the doorway.

Ben glanced at him. "A summer camp. We have that old barn we could use with some renovations."

"For who?"

"Kids."

Grady laughed. "I kinda figured that one out."

Ben pushed off the counter and crossed to the coffeepot. "Want some?"

"Sure."

While Ben filled two mugs, he said, "I'm still trying to figure it all out. I started last fall in hopes of having something for this summer. Since my accident delayed that, I thought about having one week this year, maybe in conjunction with the church. If it went well, then I would expand it for the following year."

"That's a mighty tall order."

"When I first got home from the hospital, I kept thinking I could pull it off for this summer. Have the camp in June and July." Ben cocked a grin. "Since then common sense has taken hold. I can't do it all in that short amount of time, especially the way I want it to be, but one week is doable and a good start to see how it would go."

"One week would still be a lot of extra work."

"I can do it, especially if you're back to stay. It would allow me more time to devote to planning the summer camp."

Grady sat at the table, his eyebrows slashing down. "I never figured you for something like this."

"Why, because I was a woman-chasing man?"

"Frankly, yes." Grady took a drink of his coffee.

"That's not me anymore. I have Cody to think of. If you're not staying, I'll do it anyway. It will start on a small scale. The children can learn everything about the ranch. The intern program through the school would be a great place to hire counselors. Our place is doing well, and I want to give back some."

"Is this a free camp?"

Grady had always been the practical one growing up, and Ben had learned that necessity as he ran the ranch, but he still liked to dream. "Not exactly, but there would be a sliding scale depending on the parents' ability to pay. So, yes, there would be some that would attend free." As he talked about his vision to help the community, excitement built in him. His accident might have delayed the project, but it didn't mean he had to abandon it.

"Who else knows about this?"

"Grandma, Lucy and Carson. I actually got the idea from one of the interns in the high school program. The teen grew up in town and hadn't been exposed to a lot of ranch life earlier. Carson said he would be interested in the Lone Star Cowboy League being a part of it." Ben sipped his coffee, studying his brother's expression. He should know him better, but for years he'd served in the army and been gone. Grady's experience in the war zone had affected him, even changed him, but Ben realized one incident could do that. They had that in common.

A slow grin spread across his twin's face. "I like it."

Ben relaxed back against the chair. "Good. I'm going to talk with Pastor Mathers and see if we can hold the Vacation Bible School here this summer as a start. After that, I'll know how to proceed forward, but I'm glad I have your backing."

"And help."

Those two words meant a lot to Ben. He hoped that he and his brother could mend their relationship. This could be a start.

On Sunday before and during the service at Little Horn Community Christian Church, Lucy had scanned the young women, trying to come up with another candidate for Ben either as a nanny or a possible wife. Her gaze fell on Abigail Bardera, who worked at Maggie's Coffee Shop as a waitress. She was friendly, polite even to demanding customers like Byron; she was also attractive and not dating anyone.

As the crowd filed out of the pews, Lucy stood and made her way toward the exit. Now all she had to figure out was how to casually bring up Abigail to Ben, at least better than when she did Paula.

"Your problem can't be that bad," Ben whispered behind her.

She glanced over her shoulder. "Where did you come from?"

"From the front pew where Mamie wanted to sit."

"Oh, I thought you had already left."

"I had, but Mamie had left her Bible in the pew and I came back to pick it up." He stepped beside her, holding up the black book.

As they shuffled forward in the line waiting to shake hands with Pastor Mathers, Lucy asked, "Where's Cody?"

"In the nursery. How would you like to have a picnic with Cody and me? I wanted to start showing my son the ranch."

"I don't know. I…" She couldn't think of a reason not to, and it would be nice to take some time off from thinking about the Robin Hoods.

"Are you working today?"

"No—well, sort of. I have laundry to do and some chores around the house."

"Surely you'd rather go riding with Cody and me."

She fastened her gaze onto his dimples. When he turned them on her, it was hard to resist him. "Actually, anything would be better than housework."

He chuckled. "I'm not sure if that was an insult or not."

She grinned. "It wasn't meant to be. When are you going?"

"When I get home. I can have Martha Rose make us something for lunch. We can have a picnic. The weather is great. We should be outside on a day like this. You've been working too hard. You need to play some, too."

"I thought you said you were changing."

"I am, but I'll always relax and take time to enjoy life. Even the Lord took a day of rest. You're much too serious."

"And you aren't," she said without thinking. She wanted to take those words back because she had seen a change in Ben. But would it last?

"I have my moments," Ben whispered into her ear.

She slowly moved forward, thinking way too much about Ben's breath tickling her neck. When it was her turn to talk to Pastor Mathers, for a few seconds her mind went blank.

The pastor shook her hand, yanking her out of her fixation on Ben beside her. "I enjoyed your sermon today on forgiveness."

"I just hope some members of the congregation were listening with all that has been going on these past six months."

"Emotions have been running high. When we find the Robin Hoods, I wouldn't want to be in their shoes. Good day." Lucy moved forward and paused to wait for Ben.

"I need to see you this week about Vacation Bible School this summer. I have a proposition for you," Ben said after greeting the pastor.

"Why don't we talk before or after the meeting with the Easter-egg hunt committee?" Pastor Mathers looked at Lucy. "We are still meeting Tuesday night at the church, aren't we?"

"Yes, most of the planning has been done, but we still have a few items to discuss."

"Good. Ben, I'll talk to you then. The meeting is at six. Is five thirty okay?"

"That's fine with me. I can't believe Easter is only weeks away." Ben nodded his head at the pastor, then joined Lucy.

"I need to go home and change. I'll meet you at the ranch in half an hour. Is that okay?"

"I'll be at the barn." He headed for the nursery.

As Lucy started for her car, she nearly collided with Byron. She glanced away to see where his sons and wife were. They weren't around. "Excuse me."

Byron moved into her path. "How's the investigation going?"

"We're following some promising leads. You'll be one of the first to know when we catch the robbers."

"How come your friend, Ben, hasn't been hit? Have you ever asked yourself that? Maybe it's one of his hired hands or..." Snapping his mouth closed, Byron peered beyond Lucy.

"I couldn't help but overhear your question to the

sheriff." Ben held his son in his arms. "You'll have to ask the Robin Hoods when they're found." He handed Cody to Lucy, then crowded into Byron's personal space. "Don't you start accusing anyone connected with the Stillwater Ranch. I won't take it like others have."

The bluster in Byron faded, but his face reddened as he looked around at the people nearby. "It's a question we need to ask of anyone who hasn't been hit by the robbers."

"A better question is why were you hit a number of times. I believe from what I've heard since I woke up from my coma, you've been a victim of the Robin Hoods more than anyone else. Why? What makes you so special?"

Byron glared at Ben, opened his mouth but only ended up snorting before he stepped around Ben and hurried toward the meeting hall.

Lucy panned the faces of the congregation around them. Smiles graced the people's expressions.

Tom Horton came forward and clapped Ben on the shoulder. "Welcome back. We've missed your candor."

To the side and behind Ben stood the twins, Winston and Gareth, gaping at the scene. Lucy peered over her shoulder to see if Byron was around. He wasn't.

She started for the teenage boys but behind her, Byron called, "Winston. Gareth. Your mother is wondering where you are."

The twins plodded toward their father in the doorway into the meeting hall.

She sighed.

Ben appeared in front of her. "Sorry about that. I couldn't let him start in on you at church or on anyone working at my ranch."

"I can take care of myself, but thanks for thinking of me. I'll see you in half an hour."

As Lucy drove home to change into jeans and a T-shirt, her hands gripped the steering wheel so tight they ached. In her driveway, she released her tight grasp and wiggled her fingers. Byron was like a burr under a saddle blanket. When she approached him about interviewing his two sons, she had to have enough evidence to make a case against them or he would make her life miserable until time for reelection. It would be a *long* year for her.

It took ten minutes to change her clothes and jump into her Mustang to head to the Stillwater Ranch. She arrived a few moments ahead of schedule and decided to park at the house until she glimpsed Ben exiting the barn with Cody in his arms. When Ben waved, Lucy put her Mustang in Reverse and headed to the barn.

He opened the door to her vehicle with a big grin on his face. "That's what I love about you, Lucy Benson. You don't keep a man waiting. You're always on time—or before."

She climbed from her car, saw Cody's smile directed at her and held her arms out for the baby. "Cody, I wouldn't dare be late to meet you. Now, your daddy, on the other hand, is a whole different story."

"Waiting for you isn't a big chore," Ben said, then winked and walked toward the barn.

She trailed behind him. "That's because you don't have to. Remember what you said."

At the entrance, he swept around and plucked Cody from her arms. "I'll let you saddle your horse first, then you can hold him while I take care of Thunder."

"What! You aren't going to do both?"

The dimples in his cheeks deepened. "Nope. I need to see if you learned anything from what Maddy showed you the other day."

She narrowed her eyes and proceeded to where he had Daisy Mae tied. Without a word she did everything correctly, even adjusting her stirrups to where they should be for her. Then she whirled about with her hand on her waist. "I'm not a total novice. I used to ride when I was younger. Remember? Here at your ranch?"

"Ah, yes. How could I forget those races you lost to me?"

She pursed her lips and marched to him, took Cody and kept going toward the rear exit. The baby played with her hair. When he stuck some strands in his mouth, she laughed and gently tugged them free.

"I'm glad my son can make you laugh. I need to take lessons from him."

"I won't be laughing if you put my hair in your mouth."

Forty-five minutes later, Ben laid Cody on the blanket, spread out under a large pine tree that blocked the sun. "I loved hearing his giggles as he rode with me. He's going to be a natural rider."

"Thunder was great letting him pat him over and over. I can't believe Cody fell asleep." Lucy settled next to the baby on one side while Ben did on the other.

"It's kinda like a rocking chair. He usually doesn't sleep for another hour, but he was up some last night because of his tooth coming in. I'll be glad when it's in."

"Then it'll start over with the next tooth."

"Please don't remind me." Ben lounged back, propping himself on his elbows.

"You'll do fine. From what I've seen, you've jumped in with both feet into this daddy gig."

"When I do something, that's the way I am. Why do it halfway?"

"All or nothing. Interesting."

Ben wasn't sure what she meant by that comment. Interesting how? But he held back asking Lucy. Since he'd woken up from his coma and left the hospital, his relationship with Lucy had shifted. He wasn't sure quite what was going on, but like riding a bronco, he was holding on tight and seeing where it was going. "Grady and I talked this morning. I told him about my summer camp I wanted to do, and he actually supported the idea. I think that is a first, at least in a long time."

"He was mighty worried about you while you were in the hospital. Just be careful. You've got a lot on your plate. Don't overload it."

"I've been out of the loop for months. All I did was sleep. I'm ready to tackle life again." Ben stared up at the pine needles above him, looking at a bright red cardinal on a branch. "I think the Lord gave me Cody for a reason."

"What reason?"

"I'm not sure yet. I was already planning a summer camp and getting involved in the intern program at the high school. When I pick up Cody, I feel at peace. I really never thought of myself as a father, especially with the bad relationship I had with my own. Grady seemed more likely to carry on the Stillwater name." Thoughts he'd been mulling over for weeks since he'd known about Cody being a Stillwater came rushing out, surprising him. Why was he sharing this with Lucy?

"I never had any brothers or sisters. My parents were

great, but I wanted siblings. They did, too, but Mom couldn't have any more children."

"I don't want Cody to be an only child. I know he'll have a cousin soon when Chloe gives birth, but it's not the same thing." Finally he looked at Lucy sitting cross-legged on the blanket facing him with a sleeping Cody in between. A blank expression hid her feelings. He wanted to know how she felt about having children, but ground his teeth to keep that question to himself.

She pushed herself to her feet. "I need to stretch my legs, especially after sitting in church, then on Daisy Mae."

"Not a bad idea. If I sit too much longer, I might go to sleep like Cody."

She gazed at his son. "It's always nice to see a baby sleeping so peacefully. Their only worries are when are they going to be fed and changed. Those were definitely simpler days, with no Byron around to bug me every day about the investigation."

"He is used to having things taken care of immediately when he wants something done."

"Believe me, I would if I could, but since I'm leaning more and more to Winston and Gareth, I need to have the evidence before I confront them. It would be nice if I didn't have to have Byron in the room when I interview them."

"Why would they rob their own ranch? To take any suspicion off them?"

"Maybe. I still think it's about Betsy. And if Gareth is Maddy's secret admirer, can you imagine his father's reaction to that?"

Ben paused near the stream, turning to keep an eye on Cody still sleeping. "I remember Carson's father's reaction when he dated Ruby. His actions were what separated the two and made Ruby leave town. Thankfully they're together, but it took years before that happened. Like Ruby, Maddy is a good kid, and I think Gareth would be much better off dating her rather than some other girls."

"You're already starting to sound like a father. Remember that when Cody is Gareth's age."

Ben exaggerated a shiver. "I shudder to think about Cody being a teenager. Those days weren't that long ago for me. Looking back, I see where I didn't make it easy for my father and me to have a relationship. It wasn't all his fault. I couldn't have said that this time last year."

Lucy touched his arm. "A lot has happened to you since then."

"Yeah, like I missed part of it." He stepped closer, her fragrance mingling with the scents of nature surrounding them. "It's been good talking to you. I'm not there with Grady yet. As young boys, we were close. I'd like that back. I'm discovering how important home and family are."

"I miss my parents." She dropped her arm to her side.

He missed the connection. "Are they going to come back to Little Horn to stay one day?"

"I hope. We do have a close relationship, and conducting it long distance isn't the same thing as face-to-face."

He cocked a smile. "Even with video calling."

"Not even with that."

Inching forward, Ben clasped her shoulders. When she didn't shrug away, he inhaled a deep breath of relief. There was something about Lucy that drew him. He wanted to explore these feelings, but Lucy only saw him as the man he used to be. "If you want, we can eat before Cody wakes up. I brought finger foods for him."

"What did Martha Rose fix for us?"

"Leftover fried chicken from yesterday, and as usual it was delicious. Some coleslaw and potato salad. Iced tea to drink."

"Sounds great," she murmured but didn't take a step toward the blanket.

And Ben was in no hurry to, either. "Your muscles are tight."

She nodded. "That's where my stress settles."

His gaze seized by hers, he kneaded her shoulders. He wanted to kiss her. He had for years, ever since she'd slapped him as a thirteen-year-old when he'd tried.

His hands stilled, then slipped to her face, framing it, her warm cheeks beneath his fingers, drawing him closer. Her mouth beckoned him. He slanted his head and slowly closed the distance between them and settled his lips over hers. The sensations bombarding him surprised him and yet didn't. He'd known kissing Lucy would be everything he dreamed as a teenager.

Cries pierced the air, shattering the brief moment.

Lucy pedaled backward, her eyes large, tiny lines grooving her forehead.

As much as he wanted to pursue what just happened between them, his son had awakened and didn't know where he was. He hurried toward Cody and scooped him up. "I'm right here, little man. I won't leave you."

Chapter Seven

With a sigh, Lucy eased into the chair at the head of the conference table at church. No one else had arrived yet for the meeting about the Easter-egg hunt, which was only ten days away. Today had been another long day, mostly spent between Bakersville and Blue Creek, towns on opposite sides of the county. One had been a good lead on an abandoned cattle trailer, but what she'd found couldn't have been used for anything in the past few years. With all the holes in its floor, nobody would have been able to transport the number of cattle stolen anywhere.

Amelia Klondike, soon to marry Finn Brannigan, appeared in the entrance with a bright smile on her face. "Good. No one else is here. We have time to talk." Her good friend for years sat down next to Lucy. "What's this I'm hearing about you and Ben being an item, seen together a number of times since he left the hospital?"

Lucy lifted one shoulder in a shrug. "I don't listen to the gossip, so I can't answer that question."

"Don't play innocent with me. Your cheeks are getting red, a sure sign something is going on between you two."

"We are friends." But even as she said that, Lucy knew it was more than that. When he'd kissed her on Sunday at the stream, she felt connected to Ben beyond friendship. He spoke to a need she thought she'd buried after Jesse. "How are the wedding plans coming along?"

Amelia shook her head and sank against the back of the cushioned chair. "I'm not going to tell you a thing if you don't share with me."

Lucy heard the outside door open and bent toward the curly-haired blonde beauty. "Ben and I are friends. Like you and I are."

Amelia burst out laughing as Pastor Mathers came into the room with Ben. He grinned at Lucy and winked, then took a seat at the other end of the table, so every time she glanced up, she saw his face first.

Not half a minute later Ruby entered, slightly out of breath. "Oh, good, I'm not late. Carson's nephew fell off a horse. I wanted to make sure Brandon would be okay before I came."

"Great, everyone is here. Amelia, would you take notes on the meeting?" Lucy asked while Ruby took a chair between the pastor and Ben. "We have a lot to finalize tonight. We'll have one more meeting before the Easter-egg hunt this time next week. Will that be all right with everyone?"

Each member of the committee nodded.

"As y'all know, the Stillwater Ranch will be the location this year for the event. Lucy has filled me in on what has been planned so far, but I'd like to add some things to the festivities." Ben looked right at Lucy. "Instead of the children coming for an hour or so, why don't we make this several hours with more than just hunting for Easter eggs and a few age-appropriate games?"

Lucy groaned inwardly. "At this late date?"

"I thought we could add a couple of things like various races with eggs, an art tent and a reading circle. I saw on the internet the different activities they have at the White House at this time. The Easter Egg Roll is an annual event for kids from all over the United States." Ben looked at each member of the committee. "We have a large tent at the ranch. We have the art teacher from the elementary school in our congregation."

"Maybe next year—"

"Why wait?" Ben interrupted Lucy. "If I learned one thing, it's to seize the moment. One moment I was going to see Carson, the next I was lying on the ground unconscious. I didn't wake up for weeks. We don't know what's going to happen in the future, so why not make each day count? I'll do the extra work."

Stunned, Lucy searched for words to say. Too much was going on.

"I like it, Ben," Amelia said. "We already have the egg hunt, refreshments and a couple of games. The kids are already coming, and it would be fun to add a few more activities. If it's successful, we can think about doing even more next year."

"I'll set up the tent and recruit some teenagers to help with the arts and crafts. I suggested it today to the three girls that work after school at my ranch. They loved the idea. They thought they could get some of the teenage boys in the intern program to help with the races. We could have an egg roll like at the White House, racing with an egg in a spoon and an egg toss, especially for the older children." Ben scanned everyone's faces but Lucy's, as though he wasn't sure of her reaction.

Lucy was warming to the idea. She watched the excitement in Ben's expression, and it was contagious. He'd always played as hard as he worked, but this was different. This was about others. He wasn't thinking of fun for himself but for the children at the egg hunt. Had Ben really changed since the accident? Would it last? Or with all this extra work, would he burn himself out before summer? She didn't want to see that, either.

Pastor Mathers cleared his throat. "I don't see why we don't try Ben's idea, but we'll need to look at the funding."

"No problem. I'll give the money necessary for the supplies," Amelia said with a smile. "We've had so much tension in town the past six months that it would be nice to have a celebration like this for the children."

Lucy took in the faces of each member; the more she looked at Ben the more excited she became. His smile filled the whole conference room. In the past she'd seen glimpses of this new Ben, but he was shining bright right now. "Okay, we have a suggestion for expanding the Easter-egg hunt with three new activities— arts-and-crafts tent, storytelling area and egg races. Is anyone opposed to trying it this year?"

No one said a word.

"Then, it is decided. Ruby, you'll still be in charge of the refreshments, Amelia the egg hunt and now Ben the extra activities. We'll combine the games and races. I can help you since we only have ten days to get it in place." Even Ben had pulled her into the expanded egg hunt. "I can plan the arts-and-crafts activities and the races. Pastor Mathers, will you recruit readers for the storytelling part?"

"I'll volunteer to be one, and I have several others in mind, too."

"Good. Let's finish the rest of the business. I know we're all probably ready to have dinner." Lucy took the next twenty minutes going over the church's youth group running the different age egg hunts and manning the refreshment table, as well as where they could fit in with the expanded plan.

At the end the pastor rose first and skimmed the faces of the committee members. "I have to say I'm excited about the direction this is going. Our advertising is garnering a lot of interest even from the surrounding towns. I'm so glad we've opened it up this year to all children. Our community needs to remember how important love is in the midst of the tempers and accusations flying around. God is love, and I want to spread that word. Thank you for your help."

Amelia angled toward Lucy. "I'll send the notes to your email tomorrow. We need to get together soon. I'm going to catch Pastor Mathers about having Finn read to the children. They always love to see a Texas Ranger. See you."

As Lucy rose, Ben made his way to her. "How about grabbing dinner at Maggie's? We can discuss what we want to do in the art-and-crafts tent. I think I'll turn the races over to Maddy, Lynne and Christie to recruit some of their friends to help. I'm glad you're going to be there, too."

"Everyone will have to chip in to get it done. Why didn't you say something to me about your idea before you announced it?"

"Because you would look at the problems, not the possibilities. You're overworked and the uproar in the community has been stressful for you. I was in a coma a good part of it. So it's not the same for me."

As the rest of the committee filed out of the conference room, Lucy leaned back against the conference table, grasping its edge. "Where are all these ideas coming from? First the camp and now this."

"They've always been in the back of my mind, but I realized when I almost died that I couldn't wait until later to implement them. Later may never come. I talked with Pastor Mathers before the meeting. He likes the idea about having the Vacation Bible School at the Stillwater Ranch, so I'm going forward with it this summer."

"So your new motto is seize the moment?"

"Exactly," he said with a chuckle. "So how about dinner?"

Exhaustion still clung to her, but she couldn't say no to Ben. That adorable grin and twinkle in his eyes told her to seize the moment. "Yes. I'm hungry, and it beats my cooking for once."

"Good, because I don't have one artistic bone in this body. I'm gonna need your help. Maybe the girls should do the arts-and-crafts tent."

"Let's see who they recruit to help, then make the decision who will do what."

"See, you're perfect to run this committee. You know how to delegate."

Warmed by his compliment, Lucy left the church with Ben strolling next to her. The sunlight splashed in brilliant colors of red, orange and yellow across the sky. The air held a crispness as the end of the day neared while a bird chirped in a budding tree nearby. For this moment tranquillity ruled, and she relished it because she knew it wouldn't last.

Ben pulled out the chair at Maggie's Coffee Shop for Lucy, and instead of sitting across from her, he took the one kitty-corner from her.

Abigail handed them the menu and filled their water glasses. "It's nice to see you up and around so much, Ben. There were a lot of people praying you recovered."

He gave her a grin. "Thanks, Abigail. That's what I love about Little Horn. People care about their neighbors."

"Let me know when you're ready to order. Sheriff, I know you like chicken potpie, and that's our specialty tonight." Abigail turned and headed for the kitchen, her black ponytail swishing as she walked.

"Were you including Byron in that statement of neighbors caring?" Lucy closed her menu and set it to the side.

"He blusters a lot, but I do think he cares about the town, just not necessarily his relations."

"You're thinking about his cousin Mac. He was a proud man, and when Byron wouldn't help him, he fell apart one drink at a time and refused some people's attempt to help."

"Pride goeth before destruction. Proverbs has it right. As my relationship deteriorated with my father, I refused to make amends. I knew he was in pain from his back injury. When I was thrown from a bronco my last season on the rodeo circuit, I began to understand what he'd gone through. It took months for my back to heal. By the time I figured out how pain can change a person, my father had been dead a year."

"Personally I don't know why you would want to sit on a bronco just to be thrown off seconds later."

He chuckled. "It's the challenge. I could say personally I don't know why you would strap a gun to your waist and face down criminals."

"Someone has to keep the order."

Ben closed his menu and signaled for Abigail to take their order. "I'm just glad you're back in Little Horn. A city is much more dangerous than here."

"You sound like my father, but I needed to do that. I'm a better law-enforcement officer because of my years on the San Antonio police force. I told my father what was good for him should be good for me."

Abigail paused next to Ben with her pad and pen. "Ready?"

"Yes, I want the chicken potpie and a cup of decaf." Ben looked at Lucy.

"The same."

Abigail wrote down their orders. "Any dessert?"

"Pecan pie with a scoop of vanilla ice cream. How about you, Lucy?"

She shook her head. "A refill of decaf coffee will have to do."

"I'm with you on that, Sheriff. But if I'd lost a lot of weight while sleeping, I'd be ordering what Ben did and enjoy every second of eating the treats." Abigail smiled at him, took the menus and left.

This was the perfect chance for her to champion Abigail as a nanny or... She couldn't quite bring herself to think about Abigail as wife material, but that was what she'd thought last week. "She has a pretty smile. I'm surprised she's still single." Lucy drank her water, watching Ben over the rim of the glass.

"I imagine she hasn't found the right person. For the longest time she was the primary caretaker for her mother."

"But she died last summer. She's a hard worker, kind and loves children. She works in the nursery at church."

"That's right. She was playing with Cody when I picked him up last Sunday from the nursery." Ben took a big sip of his drink.

"You should ask her out. She'll make a man a good wife and—"

He nearly spewed his water, but instead ended up choking on it when it went down the wrong way.

Lucy pounded on his back. "Okay?"

He nodded while his eyes glistened with tears. Slowly he began drawing in deeper breaths. "What are you doing? This is the second person you've talked to me about going on a date with."

"I thought I would help as a friend. You said you needed a nanny or a wife. I was thinking of Abigail at least as a nanny. I can't answer for the other option. Only you."

"I can take care of that myself. If I were interested in her, it would be as a nanny. In fact, thanks for pointing out her work in the nursery. I think I'll talk to her. She would be perfect for that job. It certainly would take care of my immediate problem." Ben realized he'd toyed with trying to find a mother for Cody, but that couldn't be hurried. Lucy was right. Only he could make that decision, and for the first time in his life, he was thinking of it as an option for him. "Enough about me. Let's talk about the arts and crafts."

"I've got just the person to supervise the activities. Candace Quinn. She's a first-grade teacher, and the kids love her. I remember she is very talented with stuff like arts and crafts. You should ask her."

Ben eyed Lucy. What was she up to now? Although Candace might actually be the perfect person for the job. "I'm sure you know her better than I do."

"But this is your project. I'm only helping you, and I've been busy running down the leads. Remember the Robin Hoods, not to mention all the other things that happen in our county."

"Fine. I'll stop by the school tomorrow and see if she can. But just so you know it, I'm busy, too."

After Abigail set their chicken potpies in front of them, Lucy bowed her head and blessed the meal, then lifted her fork. "So Maddy, Christie and Lynne are going to help us in the tent?"

"That's what they said, while a few of their male friends in the intern program will probably do the races. That way it'll give you another opportunity to be around Maddy."

"I appreciate that, but I'm hoping the case will be closed by then."

"That would be nice. Life back to normal in Little Horn rather than neighbors eyeing neighbors with suspicion. It's clear the person has inside information. I've contacted a friend in Dallas, a private investigator. He'll start searching for Betsy in Texas, then move to the surrounding states. Maddy helped me with what Betsy likes and possible jobs she might apply for."

"If I can get enough on the McKay twins and they are the Robin Hoods, will you continue to look for Betsy?"

Ben hadn't thought that far ahead. Maddy had been excited when he'd asked for her help concerning Betsy. But would it be the best for Betsy? "I don't know.

Maybe. She fell through the cracks. We should have done more to help her, especially after her father died."

"But I can see why she left. A fresh start with no one judging who you are by your past and your family is appealing."

"And dealing with her cousins, especially Byron. I have a hard time doing that. I'm beginning to think I wasn't so bad off being in a coma. At least I didn't have to hear Byron's rants and raves like the rest of you."

"With money and power comes responsibility. Byron hasn't figured that out."

After a few bites of his chicken potpie, Ben washed it down with coffee, then said, "Maddy did tell me today she thought Gareth and Winston were upset about Betsy leaving town suddenly last year. Gareth told her he and his brother had been looking for their cousin. They wanted to help her even if their father didn't."

"A good motive for them to steal from Byron, but the other ranchers?"

"All part of the Lone Star Cowboy League, which wouldn't help Mac because he wasn't a member. Byron pushed that through. Technically he was right, but Carson is trying to change that rule. Not easy when Byron and his cronies are balking at it."

"Byron stands behind rules when it's convenient for him."

Hunger satisfied, Ben lounged back in his chair and sipped his coffee. It was nice discussing what was happening in Little Horn with Lucy. He cared about the town, and she did, too. Because he'd been in a coma, he could look at the situation from a more objective mind than the others.

Ben remembered what she said earlier. "So what leads are you running down tomorrow?"

"I'm driving to Austin. There's a jewelry store that sold the music box. Thankfully it's on this side of Austin on the outskirts."

"Why not send a deputy to see if Gareth purchased the music box?"

"I need a break. I'm leaving early, so I should be back early afternoon."

"I hope you'll let me know."

"I'll call you, and you can let me know if Candace will do the arts and crafts for the Easter-egg hunt." Lucy tilted her head to the left and looked toward the right, something Ben had figured out she did when she was thinking about what to do or say. "If she agrees, I think we should meet for dinner with her tomorrow, if she can, and then have a meeting with the teens on Saturday at your ranch."

"Where do you want to have dinner?" He loved seeing her work through a problem and come up with what to do.

"My house. Nothing fancy. Steaks, baked potatoes and salad."

"Are you going to have time for that with going to Austin? Why not come to my ranch for dinner tomorrow night?"

She fixed her gaze on him. "Because I don't want you to accuse me of trying to fix you two up."

"Is that what you're trying to do?"

She slid the last piece of her food into her mouth; again her head tilted to the left. "Okay, Candace would be a great wife and mother for some man. She's been here a few years and fits right in. Kids love her. But I suggested her because she's really good artistically. I did a presentation to her first-grade class about safety, and I saw firsthand all the creative projects her students have done."

"You don't need to do anything. I'm going to approach Abigail tomorrow about being Cody's nanny. If she accepts the job, then there isn't a problem." Even as he said those words, he couldn't dismiss the emptiness he felt, especially when he saw Grady and Chloe together. He wanted the best for his son, and he knew a loving mother could make a difference. But the only one he was even vaguely interested in was Lucy. There was something between them he couldn't describe, nor had he experienced it before. And she'd made it clear she wasn't a contender.

Smiling, Lucy relaxed back. "Well, then, I'm glad I pointed her out to you, and you can have the dinner with Candace and me at your house tomorrow."

Yep, he was definitely attracted to Lucy. She could hold her own with anyone—even Byron. She had dated before she left for San Antonio. Why didn't she go out now? Why didn't she want more in life than being the sheriff? What had happened in San Antonio?

The school secretary told Ben that Candace was in her classroom, eating lunch before her students returned. He paused in the doorway to room number twelve and peered inside. Candace had a sandwich in one hand while staring down at a paper on her desk. She was an attractive woman with short brown hair, a petite frame and large blue eyes.

He took a deep breath and knocked on the doorjamb. Candace glanced up and grinned. "What are you doing here, Ben? I don't think you need to worry just yet about your son and school."

Some of the tension siphoned from him as he headed toward the teacher at her desk. "From what I've heard, when he is ready, I hope he gets you as a first-grade teacher."

"He has a fifty-fifty chance, since there are only two of us. What can I do for you?" She put her sandwich down on a paper napkin.

"I know you don't have much time so I'll make this quick. As you probably know, our church is having the Easter-egg hunt next Saturday at my ranch. I wanted to do a little more for the kids and have suggested an arts-and-crafts tent."

"My class is excited about the event and would love doing something like that."

"Good. Would you be willing to come up with some projects they could do in a short time and be in charge of the tent? I already have some teenagers who want to help."

"I'd told my students I would be there, so why not? Sure, I can do it."

"Great. Lucy and I thought we could meet tonight at the ranch to discuss the event and make sure we have the right supplies. If tonight doesn't work, we can come up with another time."

"Tonight's fine. What time?"

"Six. We'll eat, then talk."

Candace stood and extended her hand, which he shook. "See you then. It'll be a good time to give Chloe and Grady their wedding gift."

"They should be there for dinner." As he left, he remembered their handshake. No sparks had flown when he'd touched her. Nothing. She was a nice lady—but she wasn't Lucy. That crept into his thoughts unexpectedly. His gait faltered momentarily.

Twenty minutes later he arrived at the ranch, checked in to make sure Cody was all right, then walked to the barn. His cell phone rang as he entered. Noting it was Lucy calling, he hurriedly answered it. "Tell me it's good news."

"It is. The staff identified Gareth as the teenager who bought the music box. Get this—for three hundred and fifty dollars, and the necklace was another one hundred and fifty. That's a lot of money for a sixteen-year-old who doesn't work. Byron is rich, but I checked with a source and discovered the boys only get an allowance. It would have taken Gareth months to save the money, not to mention the gifts Maddy received at Christmas from her secret admirer."

"I'm not surprised. Byron is stingy with his money."

"So where did the cash for the gifts come from?"

"Are you going to talk with the twins or Byron?"

"Not yet. I'd like another piece of evidence. What I have is circumstantial. The cattle thief the New Mexico State Police caught isn't involved in our case."

Ben slipped his cell phone into his pocket and went in search of Zed. He remembered being angry with his father, but he'd never considered stealing from the ranch, and certainly not from his neighbors.

Chapter Eight

"You may kiss the bride," Pastor Mathers announced to the small gathering Friday, not long after six.

Ben stood next to his brother, who wrapped his arms around Chloe and kissed his new wife. The whole time through the short ceremony, Ben had been happy for Grady. The smiles on the bride's and groom's faces touched a lonely place in Ben. He wanted that, but no one he'd dated all these years had come close to capturing his love. He wanted someone who would stick by him even through the bad times. He loved his mother, but she'd abandoned his dad when he was dealing with pain. There were always two sides of an issue, and until his coma, he hadn't seen his father's. Pain didn't make it okay to be grumpy and mean most of the time, but it did explain what had happened in their marriage.

When Grady and Chloe parted, their grins encompassed their whole faces. Ben couldn't help but do the same. His gaze latched on to Lucy's. In his eyes her beauty surpassed Chloe's. He didn't get that many chances to see her in a dress, but the pale green of her outfit made her eyes stand out.

She broke eye contact and hugged Chloe. "I'm so excited for you."

"Thanks." Chloe turned to Grandma Mamie and enveloped her in her embrace. "I appreciate all you've done to make me feel a part of the Stillwater family." Then she swept around and looked right at him. "I'm glad you have recovered. We didn't want to get married without you here."

Ben nodded. "I aim to please."

"So when are you going to get hitched?" Grady asked in the sanctuary.

"I was just waiting. You know how you like to be first, big brother." Ben clapped Grady on his back. "Enough of this. Let's go celebrate. Martha Rose, Eva and Grandma have been working for the past few days on this shindig."

Grady and Chloe led the wedding party out of the church. At Grady's car, he opened the door for Chloe. "We may just take the long way home."

Mamie stopped next to Ben. "No, you aren't. You have a lifetime with Chloe. You have guests waiting at the ranch to congratulate y'all."

Ben could tell by the barely contained grin that Grady had said that just to tease their grandmother. "If you don't show up, I'll eat your share, so don't worry, none of the food will go to waste. Grandma, you can ride with Lucy and me." He'd picked Lucy up earlier, insisting it was his duty to make sure the maid of honor got to the church on time.

"I'm going with Pastor Mathers. Someone has to keep him company on the drive."

As Grady and Chloe drove out of the parking lot, Ben turned to Lucy. "My chariot awaits." He swept his arm toward his truck, at least cleaned with no signs of the dust and dirt from the day before.

"I could have driven myself." Lucy strolled toward his vehicle.

"The least I could do for the wedding party is pick you up and take you home. Don't worry. This is not a date."

She looked at him over the hood of his truck. "I know, and I wasn't worried. More like preoccupied."

"Why?"

"Yesterday the Oklahoma State Police informed me they brought in an illegal cattle broker with ties to Texas. They're offering him a deal today to talk. I'm hoping he takes it and puts an end to the Robin Hoods."

"When will you know?"

"Sometime in the next couple of days."

"Then, we'll have to really celebrate. Of course, if it's Byron's twins, we all may be in for a long spring. It makes me feel sorry for those boys. Now that I'm a father, I'm aware of how important it is for me to set a good example for my son."

"We can both agree that Byron hasn't." Lucy climbed into the front passenger seat.

"For tonight, no thoughts of work. Chloe is so good for Grady. I'm getting used to him being around. I'm hoping they'll stay, and we can work together. There's so much I'd like to do."

"Are you sure you weren't plotting all these projects while in a coma?"

While he left Little Horn and drove in the direction of the ranch, he slid a glance to her. "I have a lot of time to make up for." Ben looked out the rearview mirror at Pastor Mathers following in his car. "You do know what Grandma is doing, right?"

Lucy peered over her shoulder. "Playing matchmaker."

"Yep."

"I'll just have to let her know we're only friends."

"Are we?"

He felt her eyes drilling into him but kept his attention on the highway before him.

"I thought we were friends. Has something happened?"

He pulled off the road onto the shoulder, switched off the engine, then angled toward her. "I think there is more, not less. What's between us feels nothing like it did in high school."

Lucy's eyes grew round.

Pastor Mathers slowed his car, and Ben rolled down his window at the same time Grandma did hers.

"Do you need help?" Mamie asked, a gleam of mischief barely contained by a straight face.

"We're fine. We'll be along in a minute."

"That's okay. I can take care of the guests at the ranch." She winked at him.

Ben barely contained his laughter at his grandmother's tactics. "We'll be there soon." When the pastor pulled away, Ben turned back to Lucy. "Can you deny something is different between us?"

"I think our friendship has grown recently, but I'm not interested in anything else."

"I'm not the same person."

She snapped her fingers as she said, "Just like that, you've changed."

"It happens. Look at the story of Paul."

"I can see you love Cody, but is he your new pet project? Will it last? For years you resisted putting down any roots, but now you want to?"

"My roots have always been here. Stillwater Ranch has expanded since I took over managing it. That wouldn't have happened without my being serious about my work."

"I know how you feel about your family ranch, but relationships with people are different. If you want one, you have to be willing to commit to it as much as you do to the ranch."

Again Ben wondered what had happened in San Antonio to make Lucy so wary and cynical. He wanted to ask but wasn't sure how. "I've committed to my son. I want to be the best dad I can be, and I know that won't always be easy to do. I've seen too many father/son relationships that fell apart. At least now I know it wasn't all my dad's fault. We both worked at tearing down the bond we once had."

She shifted around, so they faced each other. "That's it. Relationships take a lot of hard work. A person has to be willing to put the time and energy into it and not hightail it the first sign of trouble."

Like he usually had done in the past. "Did that happen to you?"

Half a minute passed, and Ben forgot to breathe as he waited for her to answer.

"Yes. I fell in love with an FBI agent I'd met while working. We dated for a year—the last six months exclusively—and had even been talking about getting married. But I discovered I wasn't the only woman he was seeing and spinning that story to. Jesse wasn't satisfied with one. He needed three in his life. He shuffled his time between us, but all that juggling caught up with him. When I discovered his other two, we met and learned he had spun the same tale for each of us. We confronted him, and I decided to leave San Antonio. After six years, I came back to Little Horn. I'm not a big-city gal."

"See, we have that in common. I can't imagine living in a big city. I don't even need to leave to know that." He reached and grasped her hands. "I'm sorry for what that guy did three years ago. I've always been up front with my intentions. The women I dated knew I wasn't looking for a serious relationship. The truth will always find a way to come out."

She leaned toward him and kissed his cheek. "We'd better get to the celebration before your grandmother comes back for us."

"Hardly. She's hoping we'll stay here," he said with a chuckle.

Ben started the truck and pulled out onto the highway. At least now he knew why she was leery of any relationship. If he was honest with himself, he couldn't blame her for feeling that way about him. For years, he'd tried his best to stay single with no obligations except to the ranch. Now he had to face the consequences of that behavior.

As the hour grew late, Lucy stood back from the crowd at Stillwater Ranch and sipped her punch while she watched the expressions on the guests' faces. Ben's house was big enough that it could accommodate more than fifty people at the wedding celebration. Chloe looked beautiful in her ivory-colored silk dress, and her face glowed, especially when she was with Grady.

I want that. I want to look at someone with love and

have it returned. I want a family. Those thoughts flitted through Lucy's mind as she took in the joy. How had Chloe let go of the fear Grady would end up like her first husband? Chloe had known Grady most of her life, but Lucy had first worked with Jesse, then dated him for months before she'd fallen in love with him. She'd thought she knew him well and that he would never cheat on her, like some of the people she'd worked with. Sure, Chloe had an unborn baby to think about, but still... *How do you know if it's forever?*

Amelia planted herself next to Lucy. "I'm so glad to see Chloe happily married. Grady will be a great dad for her baby. Remember when we used to talk about who was going to get married first? You were to supposed to marry before me, not be the last holdout."

"I've got three weeks before you walk down the aisle."

"And who are you pursuing?" Amelia asked with a chuckle.

"That is a problem. Just dodging Byron has taken all my extra time."

"Are you close to apprehending someone?"

Lucy turned toward her friend. "Yes, but until I have the evidence, I'm not accusing anyone. We've had enough people being accused without good evidence."

"I agree. Ruby's brother, Derek, was a good example of some people pushing for a solution without any proof. Speaking of that, where is Byron?"

"I don't think he was invited. Chloe told me she didn't want anything to spoil her day."

"Good for her, but that may make things dicey for Grady and Ben."

"What will be dicey?" Ben asked as he joined them.

"Not inviting Byron." Amelia waved to her fiancé,

Finn, who wove his way through the crush of people toward them.

"He'll have two Stillwaters to go through if he makes a ruckus about it. It's time we stand up to him. He's a bully. No wonder his sons have that reputation, too. He may have the largest ranch in this part of Texas, but he can't plow through everyone in his way."

Finn put his arm around Amelia's waist. "If you need help, I'm with you."

"I imagine the next Lone Star Cowboy League meeting will be interesting. I hope by then I'll know where Betsy is. I want to persuade her to return to Little Horn." Ben moved close to Lucy, goose bumps appearing on her arms.

"That won't set well with Byron." Amelia glanced at Finn. "We had a great time tonight. Thanks, Ben, for opening your home to us. I'm looking forward to next Saturday with the Easter-egg hunt and festivities."

"We're meeting with the teens tomorrow to work out the setup in the tent and the races. I have to say I'm getting excited." Ben shook Finn's hand and then he and Amelia walked off together.

"I'm glad Amelia found Finn. She's always giving to others. It's nice to see her happy. She deserves it." Lucy couldn't keep the wistful tone from her voice.

"And so do you." He clasped her hand and drew her away from the crowd. "Lately I've seen how hard you work, putting in long hours, and the thanks you get is Byron accusing you of not doing your job. Have you heard anything from the Oklahoma State Police yet?" Ben stepped in front of her, blocking her from the guests around them.

"No, but I'll let you know when I do. I want this settled, but if it's the McKay twins, I don't look forward to telling Byron."

"That's why I think you're right about getting the evidence first. Byron won't make it easy for you or anyone."

She needed to change the subject. She was so tired of thinking about the Robin Hoods case. It affected so many people in the county, especially around here. "I can't believe how Maddy managed to get Cody to go to bed. He was loving all the attention. I have a feeling you're gonna have your hands full with him."

Ben's expression brightened, his eyes twinkling. "Takes after his dad. A real charmer."

Laughing, she shook her head. "Incorrigible is more like it."

"Who me? Never. I'm a guy who goes with the flow."

Lucy cocked her head to the side and thought about how he'd been through the years. "Yeah, you're right. I have to admit it has been easy working with you the past few weeks, and the plans for the Easter-egg hunt are turning out to be much better. The kids have always enjoyed it every year, but this one will be special. I'm glad you woke up."

He placed his hand flat on the wall behind her and leaned close. "So am I. I feel as if I've been given a new life."

"When I returned to Little Horn three years ago, I felt like that." Normally when someone stepped into her personal space, she got defensive. So many suspects had over the course of her career, she'd become protective of that space. But Ben didn't make her feel like that. Maybe because she had known him for years and knew where he stood—or did she?

Carson approached and slapped Ben on the back.

"I've already told Grady good-night, but I wanted to tell you if you need help with the Easter-egg hunt, I'll pitch in. Ruby will be coming early, so I might as well."

"Sounds good," Ben said, moving next to Lucy, "but work on your timing next time."

Carson shifted his gaze to Lucy, then back to Ben. "Ah, so all the rumors are correct. Want to tell me anything?"

What rumors?

"Yeah, get lost." Ben chuckled.

Heat scored her face as though the sun had burned her skin. "I'll leave you two to work it out." She slipped between the two men and made her way toward Chloe who was talking to Amelia.

Lucy pulled the two women off to the side. "Do either of you know about the rumors going around town about Ben and me? And if so, why didn't you tell me?"

Chloe exchanged a look with Amelia, then said, "Do you mean the one about y'all dating?"

"But we're not."

"He brought you here tonight." Amelia pressed her lips together as if she was trying not to smile.

"I was Chloe's maid of honor. He was the best man. It seemed logical…" She'd let Ben steamroller her into coming with him, just like dinner the other night at Maggie's Coffee Shop. "Okay, I can see how some busybodies might get the idea we're dating, but I need you to set them straight. We're on a couple of committees together. That's all."

"Why should you care?" Amelia asked. "You and Ben have always been part of the rumor mill. When you two are together, sparks fly."

"They do not! Okay, maybe because he makes me exasperated at times."

"Yeah, sure." Chloe grinned.

Grady joined them, placing his arm around Chloe and bringing her close to his side. "I'm stealing my wife. We need to leave. We still have to drive to Austin."

"When will you be back from your honeymoon?" As Lucy stared at Grady, she saw Ben for a few seconds. It was disconcerting, especially in light of what people were saying about her and Ben.

"Tuesday. We're spending a few days away from Little Horn, but it isn't our official honeymoon. That'll come later when things settle down." Grady looked lovingly at Chloe.

"Let me know when that'll be." As if staking a claim to Lucy, Ben stopped beside her, so close their arms grazed each other.

"Do you have your bag packed?" Grady asked Chloe. She nodded. "Already in the car."

"Then, let's go."

Ben whistled and raised his arms. "Everyone, the bride and groom are leaving."

Cheers and clapping thundered through the room.

Grady took Chloe's hand and headed for the front door with everyone congratulating them again.

Ben took Lucy's hand. "Don't let the gossipmongers get to you. Half the stuff they spread around is wrong."

"Half? That doesn't change the fact we are the topic of conversations. Byron will find a way to use that against me. To him a sheriff is not allowed to have a life outside the job."

Ben glanced down at Lucy. "Is that why you work so hard?"

"Why do *you* work so hard?"

"Because I like to."

"That's my answer, too. I grew up knowing I would be a police officer. I don't just arrest people. I help them, too. That's fulfilling."

"C'mon. Wait till you see what Zed and the other ranch hands did to Grady's car." He tugged her toward the crowd walking outside to watch the couple leave.

Lucy broke out laughing when she saw the car in the glow of the porch lights. "It looks like a float in a parade." She took in all the streamers tied onto everything possible.

Grady spun about, his gaze zeroing in on Ben. "Just you wait."

Then Ben's brother helped Chloe into the front seat, rounded the hood and climbed in behind the steering wheel. Half a minute later, the multicolored car was heading for the highway, with two yards of empty cans bouncing around behind them, clanging together.

"I have a feeling he'll pull over soon and cut that rope with the cans," Ben murmured in her ear.

Chills zipped down her body. Tonight would fuel the gossipmongers, and there wasn't much she could do about it.

Shortly after Grady and Chloe left, the other guests began departing. Mamie stood at the door with Ben, saying goodbye to each one.

When the house was empty of guests, Lucy asked Ben's grandmother, "Can I help you clean up?"

"Don't worry about it. Maddy stayed after putting Cody to bed to help Martha Rose in the kitchen." Mamie swept her arm to indicate the living room. "This can wait until tomorrow. Go home. I don't know about you, but this has been a long day."

Lucy started to insist she could help when Ben placed his hand at the small of her back, nudging her toward him.

Outside as he walked toward his truck, he said, "I've learned not to argue with Grandma. If you stayed to clean, she would, too."

"I can come earlier tomorrow to help before we meet with the girls."

"No, I'll do a lot of it after she goes to bed."

"You do housework?"

When Ben sat behind the steering wheel, he finally answered, "I pitch in where needed, but I draw the line at cleaning windows."

Her laughter died when Lucy remembered Jesse not even taking his dishes to the sink after they ate, let alone helping to clean up after she fixed him dinner. "I'm impressed."

He threw her a glance as he pulled away from the house. "As I've said before, I aim to please."

"I'm not sure I can think of you as a peacemaker, but definitely a mischief maker."

"Who, me? No way."

"How about those times you teased me or tried to rile me in some way?"

"Okay, maybe a little, and I don't do my share of the chores around the house to make peace but to help. My grandmother and Martha Rose work hard to keep the house going. It's a big place. But I won't complain if someone takes over for me in that department."

"Are you hinting at turning around and going back so I can?"

With his eyebrows raised, he said, "Who, me?" then chuckled.

She playfully punched his upper arm. "It was a nice wedding. Small is good."

"Is that what you want?"

"I haven't really thought about it. I'm not serious about anyone. That probably needs to come first." And yet as she said that, she began to doubt the truth to those words. Ben was charming and attractive, but he also was a rogue. She didn't need that in her life. That was what had drawn her to Jesse and look where it got her.

"I thought all girls had their wedding planned by sixteen."

"Where did you get that idea?"

"Oh," he shrugged. "I don't know. Eva?"

Fifteen minutes later, he pulled into Lucy's driveway and started to get out of the truck.

"You don't have to walk me to the door. I've got my gun in my purse."

"You're kidding! At a wedding and dinner party!"

"I got in the habit of taking my weapon everywhere in San Antonio, and there were a couple of times I was glad I did."

"Any time while in Little Horn?" Ben exited the truck.

"Not yet, but it would be too late when the time came and I wasn't prepared."

He strolled beside her to the porch, but when she reached for her key, he clasped her arm and stopped her. Taking a few feet toward her, he stepped into her personal space. She remained where she was, her heartbeat accelerating, her throat going dry. With one of his large hands cupping the side of her face, he tilted it up. His lips hovered an inch from hers. Her breathing ceased—one, two, three seconds before he lay claim to her mouth, covering it with his.

Her knees went weak, and she grasped his shoulders as his hand slid through her hair. She'd been kissed before, but nothing like this.

When he pulled away a few inches, he rested his forehead against hers and cradled her face in both hands. "I couldn't resist. You are beautiful, caring. You deserve happiness."

She couldn't think of anything to say. All she could focus on was the movement of his mouth as he talked, the warmth of his hands against her skin, the woodsy-scented aftershave teasing her nose.

"I'd better let you go to sleep. We have a long day of planning tomorrow. See you at ten." Ben backed away. "But I'm not leaving until you're safely inside."

She held up her purse. "Remember the gun."

"Don't care." He pointed to the floor of the porch. "Not moving until you go inside."

She fumbled for her keys in her purse, her fingers brushing against her gun. Hurriedly she let herself into her house, hearing through the wood, "Good night, Lucy." The words penetrated her defensive wall around her heart, but more than that, his kiss had left her changed—uncertain.

Ben stood out on his front porch, the day promising to be a gorgeous one. In the seventies and not a cloud in the sky. But what really brightened his day was that Lucy was coming. He glanced at his watch. In the next few minutes.

He should be exhausted. He'd slept very little last night. There was something about their kiss that had left him different. He'd done it on an impulse, but the sensations it had created in him had taken him by surprise. All he could think about was kissing her again.

Her sheriff's SUV turned into the ranch entrance and headed toward him. As he watched, his pulse sped up, and a smile graced his lips. But even more, he looked forward to seeing her. She wasn't like other women he'd known. She was special.

When she parked in the front, he descended the steps and handed her a fresh cup of coffee he'd brought for her. "Good morning. The girls are cleaning the stalls. They'll come to the house when the guys show up."

"Who?"

"Gareth, Rob and Kent."

"Gareth is part of the intern program?"

"No, but Maddy asked him. I couldn't say no to it." He offered his hand. "C'mon in. Grandma Mamie hoped you would join her in the living room before the teenagers come up to the house to talk about the Easter-egg hunt."

"She did? Why?"

"Beats me. I thought I would go to the barn and hurry them along. But I think she's in a matchmaking mode. Just a warning."

"Benjamin Stillwater, don't you go—" The ring of Lucy's cell phone cut her words off.

She quickly answered it and turned her back to Ben. After listening to the person on the other end, she said, "I'll be there Monday morning. This is great news." When she pivoted toward him, excitement glowed on her face. "That was the Oklahoma State Police. Mark Ballard accepted the deal, and he is willing to talk about who he had as clients. He has ties to this area."

Chapter Nine

A weight seemed to lift from Lucy's shoulders as she faced Ben to tell him about the break in the case. "I'll drive to Lawton, Oklahoma, on Monday to get his statement. This may be what I've been looking for. If Ballard can ID Gareth and Winston, then I can arrest them for stealing cattle at the very least."

"Who is this Mark Ballard?" Ben sipped his coffee and headed for his front porch.

"Apparently a legit cattle broker who does illegal deals on the side. From what the Oklahoma State Police said he has some associates in this part of Texas. They had been keeping an eye on him until they had enough evidence to arrest him. They want to shut him down, but they also want the cattle rustlers selling to him, so that's why the authorities are offering him a deal. While I'm there, I'll see if he has bought any cattle from others in the county, although I think the most recent rustling has been by the Robin Hoods."

"Interesting. I wonder how the Robin Hoods knew about him."

"That will be a question I'll ask them when I finally

get to interview them. I remember this time last year one of Byron's ranch hands stole five cattle from him. Maybe the twins overheard something. Thankfully we caught the guy before he could sell them. I have a feeling both Gareth and Winston know a lot of what goes on around here, especially at their father's ranch."

"Having lived under a heavy-handed tyrant, I feel sorry for the boys."

Lucy mounted the steps to the porch. "But you didn't steal from others."

"I had Grandma Mamie to rein me in. I often wonder what I would have done without her. She has kept this family together and been a great example of how you should live. I don't think Byron's wife would stand up to him. My grandmother did with Dad when she thought she should."

Lucy's heart broke as she listened to Ben talk about his relationship with his father. She cherished hers with her dad. "So you think we should give the boys a break?"

"I didn't say that. Grandma never intervened when I deserved a consequence from my actions. If Gareth and Winston did it, they should pay, but as juveniles. I know some will want the book thrown at them because of Byron. He isn't a loved man. But that shouldn't color the decision against Gareth and Winston either way."

"I thought the stealing split the town down the middle, between the ones who benefited from the Robin Hoods and the ones who didn't. This may be worse." The scent of coffee enticed her finally to take a long drink. "This is delicious. Did you make it?"

"Not if I don't have to. My coffee is never like Mamie's."

After another sip, Lucy said, "Ultimately the charges will be up to the DA."

"You can't tell me you don't have input with him."

"Yes. What do you think is fair?"

"Tried in juvenile court. Maybe juvenile detention until eighteen, then some kind of probation at least until they are twenty-one. They need counseling. They need ways to channel their anger, because if they stole from their father, they are two angry teens who need help to see the right path."

The fervent tone of Ben's voice made Lucy wonder if he was partially speaking from experience. Had he turned his anger into playing recklessly and having fun? "You aren't Gareth and Winston" slipped out of her mouth uncensored.

His eyes grew round, his mouth dropped open. "I wasn't talking about me."

"Are you sure you weren't thinking about your teenage years?"

He stared off to the side, his forehead furrowing. When he looked back at her, whatever he'd been wrestling with had been resolved. "Maybe I was. I had some intense feelings concerning my dad. Most of the time I thought he hated me, so I hated him. But now I see I was wrong. It wasn't hate I felt for him but anger. He was hurting physically and emotionally and lashed out at the people closest to him. Grady left. I didn't, so I got the brunt of it."

"Maybe your father needed counseling to deal with the pain."

"Probably. But that is behind me. I'm not letting that influence me now. It did for too many years." He pivoted and opened the front door as though he was signaling the topic of conversation was off-limits. "Cody is walking along the furniture more each day. Wait till you see him."

When Lucy entered the living room, Cody stood at the couch and sidestepped down its length. She went to Mamie and gave her a hug. "Has he exhausted you yet?"

"Give him another hour. I asked Maddy to help me after church tomorrow. Too bad she isn't older. She would be a perfect nanny." Mamie sank against the cushion. "When are the kids going to be here?"

Ben checked his watch before he bent down to pick Cody up. "Fifteen minutes or so. If you have anything to do, Grandma, please do. I'll watch Cody, even during the meeting."

"If you're sure. There's always something to do around here. When will you go to the barn?" Mamie pushed herself to her feet, her movement slower than usual.

No doubt, the wedding preparations on top of an eight-month-old baby in the house were taking its toll on Mamie.

"I have a new horse being delivered today. I want to be there for her arrival. Her foals will bring in some good money for us. I need to make sure she settles in all right. For a mare she is high-strung. It'll be at two."

"Although Cody will be napping most likely at that time, I'm gonna call the ladies at church and tell them I can't make Bible study today."

"No, Mamie. You should go. I can watch Cody while Ben is dealing with his new horse," Lucy offered.

Ben's grandmother shook her head. "I can't ask you to hang around that long."

"I don't mind. It's probably only going to be an hour

or so after the teens leave." Lucy wrapped her arms around the older woman. "You go. Have fun and enjoy yourself. We'll take care of things here."

When Mamie pulled back, a light brightened her eyes, and the tired lines around them didn't seem as deep. "Thank you, child."

As his grandmother left the living room, Ben came to her side, still holding Cody. "I can wake up my son and take him to the barn or have Maddy come up and look after him while I have to be gone. You don't have to do it."

"I know. I want to. Being with Cody reminds me of all the good things in life, and as a police officer, that's a nice feeling to remember." She stroked Cody's back as the baby started to wiggle in his daddy's arms.

Ben's son stopped his restless movements and looked at her. Cody held his arms out and leaned toward her.

Ben passed his baby to Lucy. "He likes you. He doesn't do that to everyone."

"I'm glad. It'll make it easier if he wakes up and sees me this afternoon."

The bell rang and Ben strolled toward the front door to answer it. Lucy cuddled Cody to her because she knew when the teens came into the living room, he'd be curious about them and want to check them out. His scent of baby powder and lotion stirred a dream she'd locked away when Jesse betrayed her. She'd wanted children.

"Look who's here. Cody, my little man, did you sleep well last night?" Maddy took the baby from Lucy and hugged him. "He's wonderful to watch," she continued to say to Lynne and Christie.

Ben came into the living room with Gareth, Kent

and Rob right behind him. Gareth's gaze sought Maddy, and as they sat to start the meeting, he rarely took his eyes off her.

After everyone was settled and Cody was showing them how he could walk holding on to a piece of furniture or their hand, Lucy knew she needed to find a way to talk to Gareth without seeming as if it was part of her job.

Ninety minutes later, Ben put his pad down. "I think we've covered everything about next Saturday. If each one of you can recruit another teen to help, we should have enough helpers with the arts-and-crafts tent and the races. Any questions?"

"Are we using hard-boiled eggs in the races?" Gareth sat cross-legged on the floor and tried to persuade Cody to come to him.

"Yes for the younger kids, but for the older ones the eggs will be raw. It makes it more fun." Ben watched as his son, at the end of the couch with one hand on the cushion, assessed Gareth and the distance to him. Cody released his hand, wobbled, then grabbed onto the sofa.

Sitting next to Ben, Lucy nudged his leg and pointed to his son. "It won't be long. He wants to go so badly."

"Yeah, I know." To the group Ben said, "We'll need you here an hour before the Easter-egg hunt starts. I'll have the tent set up, but there will be some last-minute things to do. Okay?"

Everyone responded with a yes or a nod.

Grandma Mamie stepped into the living room. "We have refreshments in the kitchen. I hope y'all stay and enjoy them. Nothing much. Just some pizza, Cokes and chocolate-chip cookies."

His grandmother knew what people enjoyed eating.

As the teenagers followed Grandma to the kitchen, Ben grabbed Cody and trailed after the group. He came up behind Lucy and whispered, "Are you going to talk to Gareth?"

"Only with the group. I'm gonna ask you about Betsy and see where it leads the conversation."

After the teens and Lucy filled their plates with pizza and cookies, they sat in the kitchen at the large table that held eight people and dug in.

Mamie took Cody. "I'll feed him and put him down while you eat."

Ben dished up some food and joined the rest, taking the last place. "I have another project I hope y'all can help me with." When they looked at him, he continued, "The Little Horn sign has been recovered and been returned to where it belongs, but the area around it is weedy and overgrown. I'd like to have the students in the intern program take it on as a project. I thought I would bring it up at the Lone Star Cowboy League meeting, but in the meantime, this afternoon after my mare is delivered, I'm going to the sign with my interns and whoever else wants to. We can at least mow the weeds and grass, then if any of you want, we could finish planting some flowers and shrubs tomorrow."

Maddy grinned. "I love that idea. I'm in for tomorrow, too."

"I can't. We're going to see my grandfather in the nursing home in Austin after church," Lynne said.

"I can." Gareth picked up a slice of pepperoni pizza. "And I'll get Winston to help."

Ben slid a glance toward Lucy. "How about you?"

"Sounds great."

"I'll help today and tomorrow," Rob said, quickly followed by Christie.

Kent frowned. "Sorry, I can't either day, but it's about time we got our sign back. I think our rival school took it. Why would the Robin Hoods do that and then bring it back?"

"We checked into that when it happened during football seasons. If someone at Blue Creek High School did, they have kept it awfully quiet. Same with the other schools we have a big rivalry with." Lucy took a swallow of her drink. "That reminds me, Ben, have you had any success in finding Betsy?"

"You're looking for my cousin?" Gareth asked, his eyebrows raised.

"Yes. I want to make sure she's all right. Do you know where she might be, Gareth? Or any of you?" Ben shifted his gaze from one teen to the next, ending with Gareth. "Maybe we can help her even from afar if she needs it. She left so suddenly."

Sitting next to Gareth, Maddy turned toward him. "Didn't you tell me you and your brother tried to find her?"

His grip on his fork tightened, his knuckles whitening. "We tried. She disappeared," Gareth said, then under his breath muttered, "Thanks to my dad."

Ben wasn't sure exactly what he heard, but Lucy sat across from the teen and might have heard it clearer. "I'm glad my brother has returned to Little Horn. Family is special. It takes them being gone sometimes for us to appreciate them in our lives." As he said that, Ben realized he meant every word. It didn't make any difference what kind of relationship or problems he and

Grady had had in the past. It was what they did from here on out.

Maddy stared at her empty plate. "Sometimes it takes you losing them to—" she paused, swiping her hand across her eyes, keeping her head down as she finished "—realize how important they are to you."

Gareth touched her arm, then took her hand, his jaw-line sharp as though he was wrestling with himself about saying something.

Using her napkin, Maddy dabbed her eyes. "Sorry to get all down. This is the month my parents died in a car crash." She raised her head. "But the Derrings are good foster parents."

Uncomfortable with the silence, Ben grabbed the plate of cookies and took one. "Anyone else want dessert? I know our cook makes the best in the county."

Rob took one and passed it to Kent. "I totally agree."

Lynne asked the group about the spring dance coming up. Who was going? The girls began chattering about it while the boys remained quiet, but Gareth didn't let go of Maddy's hand.

Later when Ben walked the teenagers to the door and thanked them, he watched Gareth stroll with Maddy toward the barn, off from the others. The young man slid his arm around her shoulder. If he was one of the Robin Hoods, he hated to think what kind of uproar would occur when the town found out. He felt for the twins. He sensed smoldering anger barely held in check under the surface.

"I'm more convinced than ever he and Winston are the Robin Hoods." Lucy came up behind him and stood in the doorway with Ben.

"I'm afraid you're right."

"You don't sound happy the problem plaguing us for months will finally be over soon."

Ben faced Lucy. "I was much like Gareth when I was his age."

"No, you weren't. He and his brother often bully when they don't get their way. Or so I've heard. No one will come forward against them. You weren't like that."

"I used the rodeo activities I did to get rid of my anger toward my father. That helped me, but I still did things I'm not proud of. I see the potential in Gareth. He really cares for Maddy in spite of what his father would say if he knew. He's here helping with the Easter-egg hunt and the town sign."

"Because Maddy asked him."

"But he got into the planning like everyone else. I could tell he enjoyed himself."

Lucy clasped his arms and gazed at him with a softness in her eyes. "This is why you're good working with kids. I'm glad you're thinking of expanding what you already do."

Her words washed over him and lifted his spirits more than winning the championship at the rodeo. "Thank you. That means a lot to me."

He wanted to kiss her. Awareness he was standing in the doorway with a partial view of the barn didn't deter him. Lifting her chin, he looked into her beautiful eyes that sparkled, then bent his head toward hers. Their lips touched, a gentle kiss that quickly evolved into a deep one that made Ben realize he would never think of Lucy as only a friend. In that moment their relationship changed.

When he drew back to look at her, her face glowed,

much like he felt inside. The moment hung between them, neither saying a word.

Until a cry resounded through the house at the same time a truck hauling a horse trailer came toward the barn.

Lucy glanced outside, then said, "I'll get Cody. You go see to your horse."

"They're early."

"That just means we can go take care of the sign early." Lucy hurried toward the back of the house where Grandma Mamie had put Cody down to sleep.

Lucy had been trying to set Ben up with others when she was the one he was interested in. She was caring, someone he could share himself with, and whenever he saw her with children, she was a natural with them. He started for the barn, whistling the song "The Yellow Rose of Texas."

When Lucy arrived at the location of the town sign off the highway, it looked as if she was the last one to come. Gareth, Winston and Rob were unloading the back of Ben's and their trucks while Maddy, Christie and Ben were putting up a border around the sign, leaving an area of six feet square to plant bushes and flowers.

Lucy parked on the shoulder behind the pickup and approached Ben, who was digging a place for the border while the girls set up the interlocking stone pieces. "Sorry, I'm late. I had to go into the station and take care of a problem."

Ben stopped and smiled. "I thought Sunday was your day off."

"In my dreams. Remember, 24/7. A rancher in Blue

Creek reported some cattle missing, but as I was driving toward his place, he found them in the field one over. Apparently when he was searching, they were sitting down under a tree and a small raise in the land blocked his view."

Ben's gaze skimmed down her length. "You didn't even get a chance to change."

Lucy still had on the clothes she had worn to church, a blue dress and flats. "Nowadays when I hear cattle are missing, I go right away." Off to her side, she noticed Gareth laying the bag of river rocks by the border near her, his attention drifting to Ben and her when she'd mentioned that cattle were gone. "I thought by the time I went home and changed, you all would be almost finished."

"Tell you what. While we finish the border, why don't you arrange where we should plant the bushes and flowers?"

"I've got some boots in my trunk." Lucy traipsed to her Mustang, retrieved her boots and returned ready to do what she could. "Who donated the plants?"

"Carson and me."

"Our dad took care of the rocks, and Lynne's dad bought the edging for the border," Winston said as he put down the last sack. "So where do you want us to dig a hole for these?" He gestured toward the bushes.

"The ones that grow taller ought to go in first." Gareth grabbed one bucket with a shrub. "I think this Texas purple sage should go near the sign. Its flowers through the summer will add color and allow the sign to stand out."

"Have you done landscaping before?" Lucy asked.

"Yes, at the ranch."

Surprised the boy had, Lucy decided to work with Gareth laying out the plants where they would go. Then they all stepped back to take a look. "I like this. Gareth, you have a good eye."

"I'm glad *you* appreciate it."

The way the teenage boy stressed the word *you* made her wonder who hadn't appreciated his work. "I sure do. A pretty garden makes a drab place look good."

"Tell that to my dad," Gareth mumbled, snatched up a shovel and started digging the first hole.

When the border was completed, the girls planted the flowers. Ben stepped back to watch the five teens work. "We should be through soon."

"I wish I could have done more. In fact, Gareth is the one who really arranged everything." She lowered her voice and asked, "Byron really donated the river rocks?"

"Yeah, surprised me when Gareth told me yesterday. They brought the rocks in their truck and were waiting for me to come. If we need more, Gareth said he would bring more."

Lucy turned her back to the group and whispered, "Do you think they have regretted what they did—that is, if they are the Robin Hoods?"

"Possibly. I hope you'll call me after you meet with Ballard tomorrow. Will you arrest them when you get back or wait?"

"It'll depend on the time. If not, the next day after school. I don't want to make a scene at school."

"I understand. If you poke the grizzly, it gets madder."

"No, that's not it. I don't think anything I do will make Byron happy. You're rubbing off on me. When

I look at them from your perspective, I see them differently."

"Nothing is black-and-white." Still holding his shovel, Ben glanced beyond Lucy. "Can I help you, Winston?"

"Yeah, Gareth wanted to make sure if you like the placing of the holly bushes or if they should come out more."

Lucy turned toward the teen and noticed the progress made. "Maybe half a foot at most. We'll probably have to trim the shrubs every spring. It looks really nice. We should have done this a long time ago."

"I guess our break time is over." Ben moved toward the bushes still in buckets off to the side and grabbed one to plant.

Lucy remembered a towel she had in the backseat of her Mustang and retrieved it. Using it to kneel on, she helped Maddy and Christie finish putting the flowers in the ground.

An hour later the garden was finished with the last bag of river rocks dumped and spread out. The group stood back to see how it looked from a distance.

"Beautiful, even without all the flowers blooming yet." Holding his hand, Maddy stood next to Gareth, who smiled from ear to ear.

"Yeah, I agree," Gareth said, looking at Maddy as though the rest of them weren't even there.

Winston poked his brother in the ribs. "That's Dad coming."

Lucy peered at the truck barreling down the highway. She wished she had her radar gun to clock him, especially when Byron came to a screeching halt, slammed out of his vehicle and marched toward them.

Now what? Lucy had had about enough with Byron. She stepped toward him.

He bypassed her and halted in front of his twin sons. "I didn't give you permission to take the river rocks out of the shed."

"I left a note telling you." Winston backed away a few paces while his brother stayed still.

"Yeah, I know. Why do you think I'm here?"

Gareth squared his shoulders and fisted his hands. "You want them back? It's for the town."

Red-faced, Byron looked at the garden and finally realized everyone was staring at him and his sons. "Just because you left a note you were taking them doesn't make it all right."

"We'll pay for them." Winston stepped next to Gareth. "We thought you would want to donate something like Lynne's dad, Mr. Stillwater and Mr. Thorn did." The expression on Winston's face challenged his dad to disagree.

Again Byron skimmed his gaze over everyone in the group, coming to rest on Maddy. A tic jerked in his cheek, and he narrowed his eyes on Gareth. "Time for you two to come home. The rocks can stay. Follow me in your truck." Then he stomped toward his vehicle.

The twins exchanged glances, then Winston mumbled to the group, "Sorry about that."

Heads down, they trudged to their pickup.

Ben jogged to them, and Winston rolled down the window. "Thanks for your help today and yesterday."

After the boys nodded, Gareth drove off, throwing a look at Maddy as he left.

Lucy took in a deep, calming breath. The twins had been wrong not to ask their father face-to-face, but her heart went out to the pair. Their relationship reminded her of what Ben had gone through with his dad. Byron had a strong personality that needed to dominate the people around him.

She shifted toward Maddy to see if she was all right and glimpsed her swiping her hand across her cheeks. Christie had her arm around Maddy and was speaking to her in a low tone.

When Ben returned with deep lines of concern in his expression, he said, "This is a good start. Now all I have to do is come up with a maintenance plan for the garden. If any of you want to help, please let me know."

"There's a horticulture class at the high school. Maybe during the school year they might want to take this on as a project."

"Great suggestion, Rob. I'll talk with the teacher this week. The most important thing is the sign is back and looking good as people drive into Little Horn. Thanks for your help."

"Rob, I'll drive you home since Winston and Gareth had to leave," Christie said as she and Maddy headed for her Chevy.

When the teens left, Ben stood in front of Lucy, releasing a long breath. "That was tense."

"How are you?"

"I'm fine…" He shook his head and said, "That's not exactly right. It brought back memories of my own father and me, especially those last years in high school. Byron explodes at them, letting his anger go while those boys have to keep it buried inside them. It's like a pressure cooker. Something is going to give. I've been there with that kind of anger."

She'd had such a good childhood with supportive

parents. Ben's situation, as well as the twins', reminded her that not all kids did. No wonder he wanted to work with young people. The more she was around him, the more she respected him. Ben could have turned out so different. "I'm going to leave before dawn tomorrow for Lawton. I want to be back in time to arrest Gareth and Winston in the evening. I don't want to give them time to start robbing again."

"How about tonight?"

"I'm going to have a deputy keep an eye on their ranch. With that hill that overlooks Byron's property and his house, hopefully the deputy can alert me if the twins go anywhere."

"Now we just have to wait until tomorrow to see if the case is finally solved and Little Horn can return to normal." She was hopeful, but then she would no longer have any reason to spend time with Ben. And that thought bothered her more than it should have.

Chapter Ten

Hoping to find the lunch crowd gone, Ben parked near Maggie's Coffee Shop at one thirty on Monday and started to climb from his truck when his cell phone rang. He quickly answered when he saw it was Lucy calling.

"Good news?" he asked as he spied Byron leaving the restaurant.

"Yes, for the case, but not for the McKay family."

"So Gareth and Winston are the Robin Hoods. It makes sense knowing what's going on with them. When will you be back in Little Horn?"

"I'm on the road now. I'll probably be back in three hours."

"Would you be upset if I paid Byron a visit right before you come? I think his boys will need some support. I won't if you say no."

"What pretext are you going over to see him about?"

"Smooth over what happened yesterday."

"I can do this myself, but I agree about Gareth and Winston having some support if needed. This isn't going to be easy, but it will be nice to have an end to this case."

Ben watched the twins' father drive away. "And maybe Byron will need it, too. I remember before you came yesterday that Winston mentioned his mother was visiting her sister in Houston for a few days."

"I didn't know that. I'll give you another call when I arrive in town. Talk to you later."

When Ben disconnected with Lucy, he didn't move from the front seat. He stared out the windshield, trying to figure out what was going on with him. With Lucy.

Although the situation wouldn't be a good one, he was looking forward to seeing her even briefly this evening. This wasn't like him.

A knock on his side window jerked him out of his thoughts, all centered on the sheriff. Ben nodded at Carson and finally climbed from his truck. "What are you doing in town?"

"Lucy called me to tell me what has developed in the Robin Hoods case. I understand she also told you."

"This is going to cause some problems in Little Horn."

Carson's laugh held no humor. "You think? We have our monthly meeting this week of the Lone Star Cowboy League. I'm scrapping my agenda. I'm sure the only thing the members will want to discuss will be what to do with Winston and Gareth. I want to make sure you're going to be there. You're not ready to lock the boys up and throw away the key like a good part of the town will want, especially with Byron's behavior about this situation. I can't even image Ruby's reaction. Positive her brother was the cattle rustler, Byron wanted to string up Derek when all this started."

"How are you going to break it to her?"

"Delicately." Carson pointed toward the restaurant. "Are you going inside?"

"Yeah, for a late lunch and because I need to see Abigail."

"Abigail? Is something going on? I've been in Austin a few days and everything falls apart around here."

"I'm going to see if Abigail is interested in being Cody's nanny."

"Don't let Maggie know."

Ben chuckled. "Are you going inside?"

"I wasn't, but I am now. I'm curious to see what Abigail says to the offer."

Ben made his way toward the coffee shop. "So do I. I'd better not hear any snickers coming from you."

The thinning lunch crowd allowed Ben to sit at a table in the back where he and Carson could have a quiet conversation and Maggie wouldn't hear him ask Abigail about the nanny position.

Abigail took their orders of chicken-fried steak, mashed potatoes and green beans, and Carson waited until she was out of earshot before asking, "When are you going to ask her?"

"Give me time. I have to think of the best intro. I want her to take the offer seriously and accept."

"Not take you seriously? Never."

"You mock me. Watch out. I might get my feelings hurt and be absent at the Lone Star Cowboy meeting. You'll have to deal with Byron all by yourself."

Carson tossed back his head and laughed. "Good thing we're such good friends or I would think you're serious."

"Oh, no. I'm never serious." Ben grinned, having missed this give-and-take with his childhood friend.

If anyone knew what he'd gone through growing up, it was Carson, who had a difficult father, too. But his dad had come from love, whereas Ben wasn't so sure his father had loved him. "How's life with Ruby treating you? I go to sleep for a while and wake up to find you're a man in love."

After Abigail served them their lunches, Carson answered, "Ruby and I wasted so many years. We should have gotten married years ago, but my father never told me Ruby didn't accept the check he wrote to her to leave Little Horn without me."

Ben whistled. "Maybe what your father did tops mine."

"It isn't a contest, Ben. We both tried to please men who couldn't be pleased. I never thought I wanted to be a father, but with my nephew, Brandon, around, I've discovered I'm not such a bad dad. He's spending more time with my sister now, though, so I think by the start of school next fall she'll have full-time custody."

"And how do you feel about that?" Ben cut his chicken-fried steak and took a bite.

"I have mixed feelings. But my sister has a job she likes with the veterinarian. She really seems to be trying to be more responsible and a good mother when she's with Brandon. My nephew is responding to her, too. How about you and fatherhood?"

A well of emotions rose into his throat. Ben swallowed several times before answering. "I never thought I wanted to be a father, either, but Cody has changed my life in the past six weeks. I can't imagine not having him."

"Have you thought of finding a wife?"

After savoring some of his chicken-fried steak, Ben asked, "Why? Do you have anyone in mind?"

"I think you have someone in mind. Lucy."

"Those rumors going around about us are just that, rumors. We aren't really dating."

"Would you like to be?"

"Yes" was on the tip of Ben's tongue. Then he began thinking of all the reasons it wasn't a good option. "I need a mother for Cody. Lucy is married to her job and loves it."

"I'm not asking what Lucy wants. What do you want?"

"I don't know."

Carson sipped his water, assessing Ben over the rim of his glass. "That's a first. In the past you would have quickly answered, 'Having fun with no ties to anyone.'"

"That's the past. I have a son now that I have to consider." What if his interest in Lucy had more to do with Cody needing a mother than his falling in love? When he did commit to someone or something—like the ranch—it was totally. His family had fallen apart when his mother left them. He never wanted that for his son.

Ben looked beyond Carson and signaled for Abigail as she finished up with a customer.

When she approached, she placed their bills on the table. "Did you need anything else?"

Ben took a gulp of his ice water and asked, "You do a wonderful job with Cody in the church nursery. Would you consider working full-time as a nanny for Cody?"

Stunned, Abigail stared at him, opened her mouth, then snapped it closed.

Ben pushed a chair out for her to sit.

When the waitress sank into it, she finally said, "I don't know what to say. I never thought about doing that."

After Ben stated what he expected of a nanny and how much he would pay her, he waited as Abigail processed the information.

Finally she panned the coffee shop, then said, "I need some time to think about it."

Ben removed his business card and scribbled his cell phone number on the back. "Call me."

She pocketed the card and rose. "I'll let you know by the end of the week." Then she scurried across the restaurant and disappeared into the kitchen.

"I've rarely seen Abigail speechless. She'd be a good choice as a nanny. She's worked at the church nursery since she was a teenager." Carson placed his money on top of his bill. "I need to be heading home."

"So do I." Ben followed suit, paying for his lunch, then standing.

As Ben drove in the direction of Stillwater Ranch, he thought of his son being held by a woman, and it wasn't Abigail. He remembered Lucy on Saturday rocking Cody because he was fussy when he woke up early from his nap. The peaceful look on her face had snatched Ben's breath.

With a warrant tucked into her pocket, Lucy pulled up to Byron McKay's huge mansion and parked behind Ben's truck. She had several deputies on standby in case Byron became difficult, but she wanted to keep this as low-key as possible. She knew the next hour or two would be rough, but seeing Ben's vehicle eased some of the tension gripping her.

On the porch, she rang the bell, then glanced around her at the sun setting, brilliant oranges and reds streaking across the blue sky. Beautiful. She wished she had time to appreciate it.

When the door swung open, Byron seemed to fill the whole entrance. A scowl darkened his features as he took in her uniform and the sheriff's SUV behind her, then her expression. "Is something wrong? Has there been another robbery?"

"No, I'm here to talk to your sons. I have some questions concerning the thefts and gifts."

"What in the world would Gareth and Winston know about them?" Byron's voice rose several decibels.

"I'd like all of us to sit down and talk. We can do it here or at the sheriff's office." Lucy peeked over the man's shoulder and spied Ben at the entrance to the living room and the twins on the second-floor landing, staring down at them.

"Are you arresting them? You're crazy if you think they would steal from me. Now I know we need a new sheriff." Byron remained in the doorway.

She'd had enough of his bluster. Straightening, she looked him in the eye. "You have a choice. We get to the bottom of this here or at my office. If they don't have anything to do with it, then no one else needs to know."

Byron gestured toward Ben. "He'll know."

Ben moved toward Byron. "I don't spread rumors. If Gareth and Winston are innocent as you say, then that is it."

Byron glanced from Lucy to Ben before snagging his sons' attention. "Come down here. I want this taken care of now and never brought up again. And, Ben, you stay. I want you to know the truth, too. My sons would never steal, especially from me. They have everything they want. Why would they need to?"

Gareth and Winston descended the staircase. A gray tinge colored Gareth's face while Winston's expression was neutral.

Too bad the twins were under eighteen. She would love to talk to them without their father.

When they were settled in the living room with Ben standing by the entrance, Lucy sat in a chair across from the couch where Gareth and Winston were. Byron hovered at the end of the sofa, opening and closing his hands.

"Gareth, where did you get the money to purchase a silver music box, necklace and iPod?" Lucy thought she would start with the gifts to Maddy.

Gareth didn't reply for a long moment until Byron snorted and said, "What's that got to do with the cattle rustling? If you don't have more than that, leave."

"Gareth?" Lucy ignored Byron and kept her focus on the twins.

"Dad bought me my iPod, and I don't have a music box or necklace," Gareth finally mumbled, his gaze lowering.

"This is ridiculous—"

Lucy cut off Byron, saying, "I know you purchased the music box and necklace at a jewelry store in Austin."

Gareth hunched his shoulders.

"Even if he did, it has nothing to do with the case." Byron stepped closer to Gareth, and the sixteen-year-old stiffened.

Although she didn't see Ben, Lucy was aware of his presence. "When the Derrings received special presents at Christmas, Maddy also did and continued to after that. At that time it appeared the gifts came from the Robin Hoods. That was the consensus and why the robbers were given the name of Robin Hood. I started trying to find where the gifts were coming from."

"This still doesn't explain why my boys would do something like that. Steal from the rich to give to the poor? No way."

"But the piece of evidence that clearly identifies your sons as the thieves is Mark Ballard."

"Mark Ballard? Who is he?" Byron's voice lowered to a menacing hiss by the last question.

Winston dropped his head, twisting his hands in his lap.

"They sold cattle to him over months. He works out of Oklahoma and was brought in for selling stolen cows. He ID'd Gareth's and Winston's photos as someone he dealt with handling cattle and equipment they brought him."

"You're falsifying evidence. You're mad at me because I'm going to make sure you aren't the sheriff next year. In fact, when I'm through with you, you won't be next month. Where's the motive?"

"Your sons are upset at how Betsy and Mac McKay were treated last year. They needed help, and you wouldn't give them any. Mac's drinking led to his death, and Betsy left town months before she graduated from high school because of what happened. They were family, and you turned them away." Lucy directed her gaze to Gareth, who stared at her. "Isn't that right, Gareth? You and your brother were close to them."

"Mac was the cause of his own problems. He—"

With tears streaming down his cheeks, Gareth surged to his feet and glared at his father. "You are the reason he died. He had someone steal his cattle and some equipment and you wouldn't help him. He was more a father to me than you were. He always asked how we were doing. He listened to us when we had a problem. He'd try to help us." Gareth's face grew redder as he shouted. "Betsy is our cousin, and you let her leave town. You wouldn't even help her when her father died. You're a mean man, and I hate you."

Gareth rushed from the room and slammed out the front door.

Ben turned, heading after the teen. "I'll go get him."

Byron looked at Ben leaving and moved his mouth up and down, but no words came out of him. Lucy had never seen Byron so stunned or speechless.

He sank onto the couch next to Winston, his son's head still down. "Is that why you did it?" Byron finally asked the remaining twin.

Winston's Adam's apple bobbed up and down.

"Is it?" Byron said in a more demanding voice.

"Yes. There were a lot of people around here that needed help. You've got everything you need. They didn't. Mac was family."

Byron's gaze fell on Lucy. "I'm calling my lawyer. Not another word."

She nodded, then talked on her cell phone to one of the deputies waiting for her call. "We're ready."

When she disconnected, Winston looked at her with a pale face and huge eyes. "Ready for what?" His voice shook as he continued to twist his hands together.

"I have a warrant to search the ranch."

"But the cattle are gone."

"It still has to be done."

"Winston, I said not another word," Byron said as he reentered the living room.

"She's got a warrant to search the ranch."

Lucy withdrew the piece of paper and offered it to Byron.

He snatched it from her hand and scanned it. Rage mottled his face. "You'll regret this."

"Regret doing my job? I don't think the other ranchers will feel that way." She'd tried to make it as easy as possible for the twins' sakes, but Byron was determined to go down fighting. When she got to the sheriff's office, she would call Pastor Mathers. Maybe he would be able to give Byron the peace and guidance he needed.

Ben spied a dark figure disappear into the McKay's barn and hurried his pace. He could remember having that kind of anger buried deep inside him at Gareth's age. He should have been able to turn to Grady, but for some reason they'd pulled further apart. If he had had someone to talk to, maybe he wouldn't have chosen the reckless path he had. Instead, he'd kept it bottled up inside him and rebelled any way he could. He understood where the twins were coming from and hoped he could reach Gareth before he did something else destructive.

When Ben entered the dimly lit barn, he paused to see if he could hear any movement. Other than the rustling of a horse in a stall to his left, it was quiet. "Gareth, running from your problem won't change your situation. I'd like to talk to you. I've been where you are—angry with your father, wanting to lash out. Please let me help you."

A door opened to the tack room to the right and Gareth stood in the entrance. "No one can help me."

"I can listen to what you have to say. I'm discovering the more I talk about what's going on inside me the more I'm beginning to understand myself and my motives."

"You didn't steal from others."

"No, but I was wild. All I wanted for a while was just to have a good time, which meant drinking and being with women." Ben slowly covered the distance between them. "You know, I really wasn't having that much fun because so many times it was useless and meaningless. I just knew it would make my dad angry."

"What changed? Your dad dying?"

Ben shook his head. "No, I still did it after he died because I was still angry at him. But slowly as I became involved in running my ranch I began to replace that destructive behavior with something that had purpose. Ultimately my accident last year is what was the final epiphany for me. I woke up to discover I was responsible for my own son. I want to be the best example of a dad I can be. I don't want what happened between me and my father to happen between Cody and me."

"All my dad wants is his way. He doesn't care what Winston and me want or think. When we came home yesterday from helping to put up the sign, Dad yelled at us for half an hour, then ended with telling me I was not to see Maddy. She wasn't the type of girlfriend for a McKay. Now she's gonna hate me for what I did."

"I can't answer for what Maddy will do, but I know she cares about you."

"We're going to jail, aren't we?"

"You'll be arrested. What comes after that is up to the court. But running away won't change the situation, only make it worse. Face what you did and learn from it. I'll be here for you."

Gareth inhaled a deep breath, then exhaled it slowly.

"Are you ready to go back to your house?"

Gareth trudged toward the exit. "You really mean what you said? You'll be here for me?"

"Yes, and Winston. Y'all aren't alone." In that moment Ben realized he'd never been alone because the Lord was always with him. He also had Mamie, Cody and Grady…and now Lucy. But would she still be there now that the case was over?

Chapter Eleven

As she glimpsed Ben heading for her table at Maggie's Coffee Shop Wednesday evening, Lucy smiled. The gesture seemed alien, since the past two days all she'd been dealing with was the Robin Hoods case and the fallout from arresting Winston and Gareth. She didn't look forward to the meeting tonight of the Lone Star Cowboy League. Carson wanted her there to let the members know what was going on with the case. A lot of rumors were flying around town and tempers were high.

Abigail stopped Ben and said something to him. When he resumed his trek toward her, a frown furrowed his forehead.

"What's wrong?" she asked as he sat next to her.

"I asked Abigail to be Cody's nanny. She just told me no. After thinking about it and praying, she decided no. She likes her job here and doesn't see herself as a full-time nanny."

"I'm sorry to hear that. She would be good. You'll find someone. In the meantime, you'll have Chloe and

Maddy to help. That gives you some more time to find the perfect solution."

After Abigail took their dinner orders, Lucy checked her watch. An hour, and then no telling what would happen.

"You're thinking about the meeting tonight."

"It's that obvious?"

He touched her forehead with his fingers, running them back and forth as though that would erase the lines and stress of the past months. "Byron has been pretty silent in the past twenty-four hours."

"Maybe Pastor Mathers's visit helped him."

"I'm not sure I see him changing anytime soon."

But from what she had seen, Ben had—or was the transformation temporary? "Why do you say that?"

"I went to see Gareth and Winston this morning, and Byron refused to let me talk to them. When I left, I glanced up at the second floor and saw one of the twins standing at the window. I believe Gareth, but I'm not sure. He's hurting, and he needs someone to talk to."

"Pastor Mathers?" With tempers flared, Ben was a voice of reason, and she appreciated that with all she was dealing with.

"I hope Byron will let him talk to the boys. I went to see our pastor before coming here. He's going to be at the meeting tonight, too."

"A calm voice in the midst of the angry ones."

"I pray people will listen."

Abigail set their dinners in front of them along with their bill. "I understand some people who aren't members are going to the meeting tonight."

Lucy nodded. "Carson opened it up to the public, but

members and myself are the only ones allowed to talk." She slid a glance at Ben. "And perhaps Pastor Mathers."

"I have to work or I'd be there. Not sure many people will be here tonight. But in the past couple of days that's all anyone is talking about. They can't believe Gareth and Winston stole the cattle and equipment, nor that they gave gifts to others."

When the waitress left, Ben frowned. "I think the boys care more for the townspeople than they realize. They could have sold the items and kept the money for themselves. They didn't. You said one of your deputies found a duffel bag with a lot of money in it, right? And a note addressed to Betsy said the money was rightly hers and that it came from Byron McKay's ranch."

"It still doesn't make it right."

"I didn't say it was. I'm just trying to look at it from all angles."

"This from the guy who used to think things were either black or white."

Ben picked up a piece of fried chicken. "I'm discovering nothing in life is that clear."

"But the law is."

"Not really, because judges and juries are human and don't always see it as clear-cut as the law is stated." He pointed to her chef salad. "You can have some of my fried chicken if that doesn't fill you up."

She laughed. "At the rate you're going you're going to be back to your preaccident weight. Then you won't get to flaunt all the high-calorie food in front of me."

"Even before the accident, I could pretty much eat what I wanted."

She harrumphed. "Your color has come back, too."

"Working more outside at the ranch. Spring is my favorite time of year."

"Mine, too."

"Ah, I knew we would eventually have something in common."

"We do besides that. We both care about Little Horn and the people." That was one of Ben's most endearing qualities. "Are you going to speak tonight?"

"Maybe. We'll see how it goes. What are you going to recommend?"

"I'm still waffling, but what you've said makes sense. Ultimately it will be the judge and DA, though, who make the decision."

"Not a jury?"

"I do want them to be tried as juveniles. I want to see them have counseling as part of their sentence."

"Because you don't think Byron would take them to a counselor?"

"I don't know, but I do know they need to have guidance and ways to handle their anger." Lucy stabbed her fork into her salad, her stomach churning at the thought of the evening before her.

"Carson started to cancel the Lone Star Cowboy meeting tonight. He wanted to give the town some time to process what happened. I talked him out of it."

Lucy lifted her palm to his forehead to feel his skin. "Has the hot sun baked your brain?"

"Not talking it over in a place where there is some kind of order and decorum doesn't mean feelings will go away. Like Gareth's and Winston's anger at their father, it will fester until someone explodes."

She studied his handsome face. "How did you get to be so wise?"

"When I was lying in the hospital bed after I woke up, I had a lot of time to think about life. I started thinking about the kind of world I want my son to grow up in. I grew up with a lot of anger in me, but also there was anger in my father. I know I don't want that for Cody."

She prayed this Ben stayed around, but she'd seen many people profess to have changed and not, especially in her line of work.

Wall-to-wall people crammed into the meeting hall of the Lone Star Cowboy League's Little Horn chapter. Ben stood in the rear with Lucy, so near he could feel the tension pouring off her as heated conversations filled the room. She constantly scanned the crowd while two of her deputies stationed in other strategic places did the same.

As Carson called the meeting to order and ran through a few items, restlessness took hold of many surrounding Ben. Carson repeatedly called for order before he finally brought up the topic all the people were waiting for.

Ben leaned close to Lucy and whispered, "If you need any help, just say the word. I feel any second a war will erupt."

"Exactly. I should have had some of my off-duty deputies here, too."

"Did you noticed the ranchers stolen from are sitting on one side of the room while the ones who received gifts on the other?"

"Yep. With a big red line down the middle."

Ben clasped Lucy's hand near him while Carson said, "For the past six months we've been dealing with thefts of animals and equipment. It has caused numerous problems in this community. I have invited Sheriff Benson here to explain about the apprehension of the thieves and what will be done with the suspects. She is the only one who will talk right now, so remember that."

Lucy squeezed Ben's hand, then released it and strode toward the front of the room. She walked with authority and assurance, as though she'd been the sheriff for a long time. The more he was with her the more he realized she was an incredible woman.

Lucy took the microphone that Carson handed her and paused while she took in the townspeople all staring at her. The silence in the hall hung for a long moment before she said, "On Monday night I arrested Gareth and Winston McKay for cattle rustling and robbery. Charges will be filed in juvenile court tomorrow morning, and they will go before Judge Nelson."

Some in the crowd jumped to their feet. "Juvenile court! They'll get a slap on the wrist and be back out in no time to terrorize us," Paul Martelli, one of the prosperous ranchers stolen from, shouted from the left side of the room.

Ben observed Byron seated next to Carson give the man a withering look, but that didn't stop another rancher who'd been hit to jump to his feet. "We need to make a statement that cattle rustlers are *not* tolerated here."

Dan Culter rose. "Yeah, I was robbed. I have enough to worry about."

Carson struck his gavel against the table several times but more joined in, some of the ranchers who benefited from the gifts trying to calm the irate ones.

Mr. Donner, one of the struggling ranchers, put his hand between his lips and blew a loud whistle. "I believe the sheriff has the floor, so sit down, act like the gentlemen you're supposed to be and listen."

A few grumbled, but the room grew quiet.

"One of the stipulations the DA is asking for is restitution for the ones robbed. The gifts I have confiscated will be sold, and the money will go into the fund. The method of raising the rest of the money needed will be decided by the court. We will need everyone affected to fill out a report of what was stolen and the value." Lucy went on to go over what had led to the arrest. "We are a community who has cared for our own for years. Don't let this cause a rift among you." She passed the microphone back to Carson, then moved off to the side but stayed in front.

Pastor Mathers walked down the middle aisle and said to Carson, "May I speak?"

Carson nodded.

The pastor, without the benefit of the microphone, swung around and faced the audience. "I'm not going to give a sermon tonight, but I'm going to challenge each one of you to forgive the McKay twins. That is what our Lord wants. That doesn't mean they won't be held accountable for their actions, but that isn't in your hands. The court will decide. But you can decide to show the teenagers grace. Only you."

Then the pastor retraced his steps and stood by the door in the back as though he was in church and going to greet everyone as they left.

Mr. Wentworth called out, "Byron, why haven't you spoken? You certainly had enough to say these past months about the case. Everyone has heard it."

"Yeah, more than once," Derek Donovan, one of the guys accused unjustly of being the thief, added when Mr. Wentworth sat down.

Byron yanked the microphone from Carson's hand

and surged to his feet, his large bulk towering over everyone on the small stage at the front where the board sat. He panned the audience, his glare intimidating. "You have convicted my sons without the benefit of a trial. They have not been found guilty yet." His face reddened as he spat out the last sentence.

Worried the man might have a heart attack, Ben pushed off the back wall, his breath held.

Byron opened his mouth but the sound of a cell phone ringing from his pocket cut into rumblings rippling through the crowd. He retrieved the phone, turned away and answered it, speaking in a low voice.

All cell phones except the sheriff's were supposed to be silenced until the meeting was over, but it didn't surprise Ben that Byron didn't follow the rules. He thought he was outside them.

Suddenly Byron jerked to attention. The whole room heard him say, "Be right there." When he swung around, the color had been leeched from his face. He charged for the side exit near the stage.

Lucy stepped in his path and said something to Byron. Ben hurried toward them. Something was wrong. By the time he reached Lucy, Byron had slammed out of the room.

"What happened?" Ben asked Lucy.

"Gareth overdosed on sleeping pills. At least that's what Byron's wife said. His son has been taken to the hospital."

"Let's go. They need help." From Byron's performance and continual denial of what his sons had done, it was obvious he wasn't dealing with the situation, which probably meant the boys weren't, either.

"I'll tell Carson. Let Pastor Mathers know and meet me at my SUV."

Although others wanted to know what was going on, Ben made a beeline for the pastor, told him and quickly left before he was detained. He'd feared something bad would happen because the McKays were a dysfunctional family, much like what he'd had as a teenager.

It took Lucy five minutes to get to the hospital. When they arrived, Ben hopped out before she even turned off the engine and headed for the sliding glass doors of the small emergency room. He should have said more to Gareth. Maybe this wouldn't have happened.

Byron stood outside a room, gesturing and talking in a loud voice. "How long will that take?"

The doctor answered in a low tone so Ben couldn't hear what was said.

"He'll be all right after you pump his stomach?" Byron was in the man's face as though that would heal Gareth.

Lucy joined Ben, and they approached Byron as the ER doctor said, surprisingly patient, "Your wife is in there. She requested you stay outside. The room is small. I'll keep you informed."

"You tell Eleanor to come out here and explain to me why I have to stay out here."

The doctor entered the room and closed the door.

Byron started forward. Both Ben and Lucy hurried toward the man. Byron had made a scene over lesser issues. Ben stood in the man's path while Lucy grasped his arm.

"Byron, give the doctor time to work on Gareth. Can you tell me what happened?" Lucy's voice held such a soothing tone that Byron actually stopped and looked at her.

"What are you doing here? This isn't any of your business. Haven't you done enough?" Byron shook her hand off his arm. "You've made a mistake. My sons didn't do anything they said they did. They wouldn't steal from me."

Ben took a step toward the man. "We're only trying to help. I know you're upset and angry—"

"You don't know what I'm feeling. Did you hear my so-called friends talking about throwing the books at my sons?"

"What did you want them to do?" Ben asked, moving even closer to Byron.

"Give me time to fix this. My sons didn't know what they were saying. They are mad at me because of Mac."

Lucy came up beside Ben. "Besides the fact Gareth and Winston admitted what they did, there are other pieces of evidence, some found on your property during the search. There was a duffel bag with a letter to Betsy, telling her the money in it was for her."

Byron's gaze drilled into Lucy. "I'm going to challenge the search in court."

"Don't forget about Mark Ballard. He ties the boys to the cattle rustling."

"In order to get a better deal, he is accusing them. My lawyer can challenge that, too."

Ben glanced around and noticed people watching them. "Let's go where it's more private."

"They need to know my sons are innocent," Byron yelled.

Ben caught sight of Winston standing in the entrance to the waiting room. Myriad emotions flittered across the teen's face from surprise to anger to embarrassment. Ben headed to the sixteen-year-old, hoping that Byron would follow once he saw his son. "Let's go in here, Winston."

"Why's he here making a scene? He's the reason all this is happening. Gareth could be dying. I couldn't wake him up. I..." Tears shone in the boy's eyes as he glanced toward the room where the doctor was treating his twin. He whirled around and ducked back into the empty waiting area.

Ben entered right behind the teen.

Wet tracks ran down the teen's face, and he scrubbed his knuckles across his cheeks. "Everything has to be his way no matter what. Well, guess what? This won't be. We're glad everyone knows, and *he* can't change the fact we're guilty. That's eating him up."

"Quit saying you've done it," Byron bellowed from the doorway.

Winston's eyes narrowed on his father. "No, I'm not. It's the truth."

"I don't have sons that are criminals. I—"

Winston charged his father. "Listen to yourself. It's always about you. I this. I that. Do you ever care what Gareth and me think or want?"

Byron started toward his son.

Ben quickly stepped between father and son. "This is not the time or place for this conversation." Ben stared into the large man's eyes until he finally backed into the hallway.

Byron glanced around, red invading his face, not from anger but embarrassment. He started to say something, but didn't. Instead, he strode toward the exit to the building.

"I'll go after him," Ben said to Lucy, then in a low voice added, "Winston is hurting. Stay with him."

"I will. Pastor Mathers went into the room where Gareth is." She took hold of his arm and for a few seconds peered at him. "Thanks for being here. This is a mess."

"I'll see what I can do for Byron, but I never could talk to my dad."

"You're not the same person."

Lucy's words stayed with him as Ben hurried outside to find Byron. The crisp air felt good as he panned the parking lot looking for Byron's truck. That was when Ben saw the man pacing by his vehicle, the security light illuminating him.

God, I need You to tell me what to say. I can't do this without You. Ben leaned on Byron's pickup, giving the man a chance to walk off some of his anger.

Finally Byron halted in front of Ben. "Have you come to gloat?"

"No. There's nothing to gloat about. I hope I can help you."

"Help me? Why? What do you want from me?"

"Nothing. I'm here for you."

Byron scowled, his eyebrows slashing down. "No one is here for me. All people ever want is something from me. Usually money. Don't get me wrong. I like being wealthy and have worked hard for my money. But I'm not an ATM."

"With wealth comes responsibility to the people around you."

"My daddy told me to be careful with my money or people will suck me dry. I'm just trying to show my boys the same way my father showed me."

"By being the town bully, trying to strong-arm everyone to do it your way."

Byron sucked in a deep breath. "You have no right—"

"I'm only pointing out what is happening. You think by denying the truth about Gareth and Winston it will go away. That the townspeople will let them walk and you can go back to the same way things have always been."

Byron's mouth dropped open, his eyes round. "No one has ever dared say that to me."

Ben pushed himself off the back fender. "Then, it's time. In recent months I have had to face my past... shortcomings. Maybe it's time for you, too."

"I can't accept my sons are criminals. I brought them up better than that."

"You can continue to spout off that your boys are innocent, but they have stepped up and admitted their guilt. Winston told me earlier he and Gareth are glad they did. If your sons are ready to face the consequences of their actions, don't you think you should be there to support them rather than embarrass them?"

"Embarrass them? I'm trying to save them from themselves."

"Is the point to save them so they think they can get away with anything? That your money will buy them out of trouble? What kind of example is that?"

His eyes piercing Ben, Byron curled his hand into a fist.

"Go ahead. Hit me if you want. But I warn you, I'll strike back." Ben noticed Pastor Mathers approaching. "Quit thinking about yourself and think about your family. When you grow old and look back on your life, what will you have to show for yourself? Sons who want nothing to do with you? People who are scared of you? That's how my father died. Lonely and unhappy. He couldn't take his money with him, and neither can you."

Pastor Mathers joined them. "Good evening. Ben,

Lucy is inside waiting for you. She'll drive you back to your truck."

"Thanks," Ben murmured, hoping his words helped Byron deal with the truth. Unlike his father, his wasn't physical but emotional. It appeared Byron raised his sons as he had been raised. That made Ben even more determined to be a good example for Cody.

As he started for the entrance, Ben overheard the pastor saying, "Byron, I came to tell you Gareth is being moved to a room for overnight observation. He's in transient right now but will be in room 124. I thought you and I could pray for his recovery."

The sight of Lucy at the emergency room sliding doors lifted Ben's spirits after the intense few hours.

She smiled. "I was afraid I would find you two battling it out."

"We were, with words. Are you able to leave?" A strong urge to hold his son inundated Ben.

"Yes, I'm coming back tomorrow morning, not as the sheriff but a friend. Gareth will be evaluated before he leaves the hospital." Lucy strolled toward the sheriff's SUV.

Inside her vehicle Ben sighed, exhaustion suddenly blanketing him. "I feel as though I've worked for the past twenty-four hours."

"I'm praying for peace for Little Horn." Lucy left the hospital parking lot.

"And that people can put this behind them, especially at the Easter-egg hunt this weekend."

"What time do you need me on Saturday?"

"Eight. I'll have a mug of Mamie's coffee waiting for you."

"Ah, what an incentive for me, but do you think that's

early enough? The hunt starts at ten and a lot of kids show up early." She pulled up to the side of his truck and angled toward him. "Thanks for all your help with the twins. I think that outburst in the waiting room actually helped Winston."

"What about their arraignment tomorrow morning? There's no way Gareth will be strong enough to be there."

"I talked with Eleanor, and she's going to call their lawyer and ask for it to be postponed until Friday. I can't imagine the DA not agreeing, but I'll be at his office first thing in the morning to make sure."

In the dim shadows of her vehicle, Ben wanted to pull her across the seat and kiss her. Instead, he gazed at her as though this was the first time he'd really seen her. She cared for this town and its people. She was the right person to be the sheriff.

When he didn't move to leave, she asked, "Is there something else?"

"Yes."

He took her hand and gently tugged her toward him, his fingers delving into her hair to cup the back of her head. His lips grazed hers once, twice before settling on hers and surrendering to the sweetness of the kiss. When she pulled back, their gazes linked across the small space between them.

"See you Saturday," Ben said in a thick voice, then slipped from the front seat and paused as Lucy drove away. After the Easter-egg hunt there wouldn't be any reason for them to see each other. His shoulders sagged at the thought. Somehow he would have to put Lucy out of his mind in the months to come and concentrate on Cody and finding a good nanny for him.

Chapter Twelve

Lucy reached to ring the doorbell at the Stillwater Ranch, but the door swung open before she had a chance. Ben stood in the entry with a mug in his hand, steam wafting upward.

"I just poured this for you." He pushed open the screen to let her inside and passed her coffee to her, then retrieved his on the hallway table.

"I noticed the tent has been set up."

"Zed, Grady and I did it yesterday afternoon and set up the tables and chairs for the arts-and-crafts station. I figured since it wasn't supposed to be windy we could get that done beforehand and give ourselves a few minutes to enjoy our coffee. Did you have any breakfast?"

"I got up later than I planned."

He smiled and took her hand, starting for the back part of the house. "Good. Grandma is making one last batch of Texas-size French toast, and I haven't had a chance to eat, either. I was up late with Cody, and if Mamie hadn't awakened me this morning, I might not be up now. My son gets to sleep in."

"I'm jealous. Why was he up late last night? His tooth?"

As Ben entered the kitchen, he shrugged. "I don't know. He has that tooth, and I don't see any others coming in. Maybe it was because he had a long nap later than usual yesterday. At the Easter-egg hunt, I'm going to wear him out so he takes one on time today."

Listening to Ben, Lucy realized how well suited the role of dad was to him. When he talked about his son, he beamed. He was a natural like her father. "I've got some good news. Dad and Mom are coming home this week for a month before heading back out on the road."

"That's great. I know you've been wanting them to for some time."

"Normally I don't like surprises, but when they called last night, I loved hearing that."

"When was the last time they came?"

"Christmas, but only for a short time, then they headed for Florida and warmer weather. I never thought of my parents as snowbirds." The scent of fried bacon, coffee and French toast stirred her appetite.

"What's this about snowbirds?" Mamie asked as she took the French toast out of the pan and brought it to the table.

"My parents. I was telling Ben they are coming home next Tuesday."

"It'll be nice to see your parents again. You need to bring them out to the ranch one evening for dinner. How about Thursday?" Mamie walked back to the counter and picked up a platter of bacon and set it in the middle of the table.

"They'll enjoy it. They always do when they come

out here. Mom raves about your cooking." Lucy sprinkled powdered sugar over her French toast.

"Where are Grady and Chloe?" Ben asked, then took a bite of his thick French toast dripping in maple syrup and butter.

"Already down at the barn setting up the race area." Mamie headed for the door. "I'm bringing Cody down to the egg hunt. I've heard him fussing around upstairs in his bed. And don't worry about the dishes. Martha Rose will be back soon to take care of them. She delivered some treats for the kids setting up this morning."

Even with only powdered sugar, the breakfast was delicious and the coffee perfect. "I could get spoiled eating here, or rather I'd probably add pounds in no time."

"Not with all you do. You're rarely in your office."

"I should wear one of those counters that keep track of your steps."

"Easily ten thousand steps for you."

"You're right. Pass me the maple syrup." She poured some on the last half of her French toast.

"We'd better hurry. This expanded Easter-egg hunt was my idea. I don't want my brother thinking I'm slacking on the job."

"How are you two doing?"

"Actually good. He enjoys the cattle management, and I like the training and handling of the horses. I'm wanting to expand where we raise broncos for the rodeo circuit. I think diversifying will be good for the ranch. When beef prices are down, hopefully the other areas we are in will be doing good."

"And you've got connections with the rodeo world." Lucy finished her last bite and washed it down with lukewarm coffee.

"Yeah. It's nice to have those years come in useful for the ranch."

"Do you miss riding in the rodeo?"

"No. It was fine for a few years, but my life is here. If it hadn't been for my precarious relationship with my father, I probably wouldn't have pursued the rodeo circuit in the first place. I have more than enough to keep me busy here." Ben shoved his chair back and rose. "Ready?"

"Yep, but I'm grabbing another cup of coffee to take with me."

Ben refilled her mug and his, then made his way toward the front entrance. The sound of Cody crying rang through the house. He glanced upstairs. "I know Grandma is with him, but something might be wrong. I'll be right back."

"Take your time if you need to. I'll go down to the barn and start working on the arts-and-crafts tent. I'll make sure your brother knows you are seeing to Cody, not twiddling your thumbs."

"It won't be long before he'll be in the same place."

Lucy left out the front door, paused on the large porch and took a deep breath, the air perfumed with the honeysuckle in the flower beds along the house. No doubt one of Mamie's touches. She descended the stairs and headed for the barn, a spring to her step. The Robin Hoods case was solved, and her county could get back to business as usual. She prayed Pastor Mathers's words Wednesday night would help heal the tension that the area had been under for six months.

As she neared the tent setup, she pushed the thought of work from her mind. Ben had it right. This was for the children and nothing was going to spoil it.

Until she entered the tent and saw Maddy with Christie, crying.

* * *

Ben rushed into Cody's room and found Grandma Mamie rocking him while he bawled. "What's wrong?"

"He felt hot, and I took his temperature. It's a hundred and one. He's stuffed up and has been rubbing his ears. I know Tyler and Eva are coming. I think Tyler should check him out. He might have an ear infection."

"I'll call him. What can I do?" Listening to Cody crying broke his heart and made him feel helpless.

"Nothing. You used to get them when you were young. If it's an ear infection, Tyler will write a prescription for him."

"But he has a fever."

"This won't be the last time he does. It's part of growing up. I gave him baby Tylenol."

"I'll take him while you call Tyler." He needed to hold his son, make sure that Cody knew he was here for him.

He took his son from his grandmother's arms, then sat in the rocking chair when she left to phone Tyler. Cody looked up at his face, tears in his eyes. The sight tore at Ben's composure. "Son, we're getting help for you."

Cody rubbed the left side of his head against Ben's shoulder, his crying easing into whimpers. Ben rocked him and hummed a new country-and-western tune he'd heard on the radio the other day. Slowly his son nodded off, and by the time Mamie had returned Ben had risen to put Cody to bed.

"I'm amazed at how he's taken to you." His grandmother peeked into the crib.

Ben moved to the hallway and said in a low voice, "When is Tyler coming?"

"He and Eva were already on their way. He has his

medical bag with him, so he'll come up to the house when they get here."

"Good. Let me know if I need to drive into town and get a prescription for Cody."

"Eva already said she would. You need to be at the barn. This is your shindig."

"But I shouldn't leave him."

"Why not? I raised your father, you and Grady. I think I can handle Cody. I looked out the window and everything is proceeding as planned but you know how that can change." She waved him away. "Go now. The kids will arrive in an hour and a half."

Ben hesitated.

"You aren't abandoning your child."

"I've got my cell with me. Call if Cody gets worse."

"I will."

He walked away slowly, not sure if he could immerse himself in the Easter-egg hunt when Cody wasn't feeling well. No one was better than Grandma when a child was sick. By the time he'd neared the tent, he'd convinced himself he was doing the right thing.

When he entered, the area was empty except for Maddy and Lucy, sitting at a table in the corner. The teenage girl's back was to him, but the look of concern on Lucy's face urged him forward.

"What's wrong?" he asked as he approached.

Maddy twisted about, her eyes red, but Lucy was the one to say, "Two of the girls made some catty remarks in front of Maddy about Gareth stealing to give her gifts."

"But he didn't. Gareth used his own money to buy those gifts. He told me when he called me."

"When did you talk to him?" Ben sat across from Lucy.

"This morning before I left the house to come here.

He wanted me to tell you he's sorry about not being able to help today. His father won't let him."

Ben recalled Wednesday evening when the teen had overdosed on sleeping pills. "In this case with all that has happened this week, that's probably a good decision."

"That's what I told him. He needs to consider what's best for him. He didn't mean to take all those pills. He hadn't been able to sleep, and he kept taking them."

"What did you say to the girls?"

"That Gareth needed our prayers, not condemnation."

"I hope they listen." Hopefully time would heal the wounds the teenagers' actions had caused.

Lucy glanced toward the entrance into the tent. "Candace is here. We need to finish setting up. Maddy, can you have Christie and Lynne return to help?"

"Sure."

"I wonder if Byron knows that Gareth is calling Maddy," Ben murmured as the girl left.

"Yes, he does. In fact, she is going to dinner at his house after church tomorrow."

"She is? Byron agreed to that?"

"According to Gareth, he suggested it. She's a bit intimidated by the invitation, but she wants to support Gareth. She has a gift. She looks at the best in everyone."

"We need more like her in Little Horn."

Grady stuck his head into the tent. "Since Gareth and Winston aren't coming, I need some help with the races. I've mowed the field, but there are some holes we need to fill in. I don't want a kid breaking his leg."

"I'm coming." Ben looked back at Lucy, said, "I'll see you around," then winked at her.

* * *

Over two hundred children ran around looking for Easter eggs in three separate areas. In the barn, the babies to three-year-olds were in a special place to look for their treats, with Chloe and Amelia supervising. Lucy watched over the four-to seven-year-olds while she spied Ben and Grady with the kids eight to twelve.

"Remember, when your basket is full, you need to stop hunting for the eggs," Lucy called out in the front yard as she walked around seeing where any hidden goodies still were, then helping the youngest to find them.

Eva joined her. "Sorry I was late. I had to run to town for a prescription for Cody."

"He's sick?"

"Ben didn't tell you? He has an ear infection."

"No, but we've only seen each other from afar, except when he first came out. Maddy was having a problem, and we dealt with that. Then everything got crazy." Lucy studied Eva a few seconds. When she saw Tyler and Eva together, she was reminded what a good marriage was like. Her parents had it. As a young girl, she'd yearned for one like theirs. "Something is different lately, Eva."

"Am I that obvious?"

Lucy nodded.

"I'm not sure if you've heard or not, but Tyler and I are looking into adopting a child. It will take a while, but the idea of having a baby thrills us."

Lucy hugged her friend. "I hadn't. That's great. You'll make a wonderful mother. I saw how good you were with Cody."

"I don't want too many people knowing since it's a long process."

"I'll pray for you two. You and Tyler will make good parents."

Eva beamed and shifted her attention to the young ones still hunting eggs. "The children are having so much fun."

"What I like is once they have a full basket they can go do something else with the other activities."

"Ben knows how to throw a party."

"Yes, he's good with kids." Lucy scanned the area for Ben. No wonder he'd looked troubled when he'd first come in the tent.

"Both Ben and Grady were always good to me when I followed them around growing up. Ben has a way with children."

"Will Cody be all right?"

"Yes. Maybe a little fussier than usual, but the medicine should work soon. It's handy to have a doctor around. We were on the way when Aunt Mamie called. Tyler always takes his medical bag with him, so we just kept coming."

"I guess that's why I haven't seen Mamie with Cody. I was hoping to hold him."

"Why don't you go relieve her for a while? I know she was looking forward to seeing the children."

"Are you okay by yourself?"

"You were. See all the moms and dads hanging around taking pictures? I'll recruit one of them if I need someone."

Lucy started for the house. "Where are they?"

"They're upstairs in Cody's room."

As she walked toward the house, Lucy smiled at

the news from Eva. She hurried her pace because she wanted to hold Ben's son. When she did, she felt as if she'd come home. Probably not what she should feel, but the baby was so adorable and trusting. She could get lost in his big brown eyes with those long dark lashes. They reminded her of Cody's father. The vision of Ben with his son in her mind sped her heartbeat.

Inside, she mounted the staircase two at a time. When she entered his room, Mamie finished changing his diaper, then glanced back at her.

"He's been fed, had another short nap and his medicine seems to be working." Mamie picked Cody up and turned toward Lucy. "How's the egg hunt going?"

"The kids are having a great time."

"I'm glad. Ben was worried that y'all couldn't pull it off so quickly."

"May I hold him?" Lucy held out her arms, and Ben's grandmother passed the baby to her.

"Is that why you're here?" A twinkle brightened Mamie's eyes.

"Yes, he's adorable, but don't get any ideas. I actually came to let you go to the egg hunt for a while."

"Sure, Lucy. You keep telling yourself that. You'd be a terrific mom like your own."

"Ben and I are not dating. We've been spending time together because of the case and the Easter-egg hunt. That's all."

One of Mamie's eyebrows rose. "I won't be long. You'll be needed in the arts-and-crafts tent after refreshments are served." She strolled toward the hallway. "I appreciate your giving me a break. It'll be nice when everything is settled with a nanny or…" Her voice trailed off as she moved farther away.

Lucy held Cody out and in front of her. "Your great-grandma will have you fixed up with a girl before you know it, but if you're anything like your daddy, you'll run. So, big boy, what do you want to do?"

He flung his body from side to side.

"Are you telling me you want down?"

He gurgled and answered with gibberish.

"Okay." She scanned the room. "Let's go downstairs, where it looks like most of your toys are."

She cuddled Cody against her and headed for the stairs. His sweet baby scent stirred yearning in her heart.

Ben searched the kids swarming the refreshment table with various teenagers trying to keep order as they served the snacks and punch. Where was Lucy? In fifteen minutes the children would be ready to rotate through the different activity stations.

Then his gaze zeroed in on his grandmother. Who was with Cody? Was he asleep? He headed for Grandma. "How's Cody doing?"

"Great. Lucy relieved me for a while. I thought I would bring Cody outside to enjoy a few minutes of fun. I see you set up a little petting zoo for the young ones. When did you do that?"

"Last night I started thinking the babies and toddlers might not do the crafts or races, and I don't know how long they would listen to a story. But animals seem to enthrall them, so I had a few ranchers bring some and set up a small pen in the barn. Ruby brought a pony so a parent can walk around holding a young one on its back."

His grandmother looked him up and down. "Where

was this side of Ben Stillwater hiding? That's a great suggestion to entertain the ones under two or three. Don't be surprised if you have some four-and five-year-olds in the pen, too."

"I'm going to get Cody. Are you staying?"

"Yes, this is where the action is."

Ben strolled toward the house. When he stepped inside the entry hall, he heard giggles coming from the living room. At the entrance he stopped and watched Lucy.

Her arms out in front of her, she said, "You can do it. You walked along the furniture like a pro. Grab my hand."

Cody smiled, scooted to the end of the couch and studied Lucy's fingers only a couple of feet away. His son took one step toward her. Then letting go of the cushion edge, he walked toward her until he realized he wasn't holding Lucy or the sofa. His eyes widened, and he plopped down on his bottom.

Lucy scooped him off the floor. "You did it, Cody. Two steps by yourself." She twirled him around, his giggles filling the air. Then Lucy saw Ben. Her face flushed, she brought Cody down next to her chest. "How long have you been there?"

"Long enough to see my son's first steps." Ben's heart swelled at the sight of Cody in Lucy's arms as though he belonged there.

"We were playing with his ball and he was so close to going and getting it once that I thought I'd encourage him."

"I can see in his eyes he wants to badly. I came up to get y'all. Mamie sent me. She wants Cody to see the petting pen."

"He'll love it. Where is she?"

"Near the arts-and-crafts tent." When she started to give him Cody, he shook his head. "He likes you holding him."

"And I like holding him."

As they made their way to the Easter-egg hunt, Cody played with Lucy's gold stud in her right ear, trying to figure out how it got there. Ben was ready to intervene if he pulled on her ear, but soon his fascination turned to all the children and adults at the ranch.

"He's so curious. Reminds me of you." Lucy looked sideways at Ben.

"Yeah, I got into a lot of trouble because of my curiosity."

"Are you going to be in the tent or at the field where the races are?"

"In here. Grady thought Chloe should help him in case a girl has a problem, but I'm not sure how much help I'll be. I never color within the lines."

"Whereas, I would get upset if I went out of the lines."

"And yet, you and I get along. Amazing."

Lucy stopped near Mamie, and she took Cody. "What's amazing?"

"My son. I saw him take a couple of steps by himself today."

Mamie grinned. "He did! He must have wanted something a lot."

Ben's eyes gleamed. "Yes, he did. Lucy."

"Ah, I see. Good taste, Cody," Mamie said to his son.

"Okay, you two, if you're trying to make me blush, you are succeeding. I'm going inside to see what Candace wants me to help with."

"I'll join, Lucy. I see a herd of kids coming this way."

For the next hour Ben was so busy going from one child to the next that when the Easter-egg hunt was over, he was surprised. He peered at Lucy across the room, the sunlight slanting in through the entry and pooling about her. She'd suggested several women for him to date who would make a good mother for Cody, but she was the one her son responded to. And he knew she did to his son. But that wasn't the main reason he'd rejected all those other women.

In that moment Ben realized he'd fallen in love with Lucy—at least this was what he thought the deep ache for her coupled with the need to be with her all the time was. In his twenty-eight years, he'd never allowed himself to care that much about a woman. He could say this had sneaked up on him, but not really. This past month had been surreal—flying by but at the same time crawling by. When he was with her, he couldn't believe how fast their time together passed, but then when he wasn't, all he thought about was seeing her again.

But where did he stand with her? Did she still think of him as the old Ben, never dating a woman for long? His gut tightened. He'd always been the one to walk away, not the other way around.

Later that evening Lucy finally plopped into a cushioned chair on the back porch at the Stillwater Ranch. "The dishes and kitchen are clean, and my legs hurt from being on my feet so much today. Where's Ben and Grady?"

Chloe sat in the lounger and propped her legs up. "At the barn, checking to make sure everything was returned to its former place. Ben forgot to take down the pen for petting animals, so he and Grady went to do it."

"Did Cody go down all right?"

"Yeah, and Mamie went to bed right after she put Cody in his crib. Today was a good one but tiring. My feet are swollen. Which has happened a few times since being pregnant." Chloe leaned back and sighed. "I may never move from this spot."

"I know what you mean, but I've got to drive home soon. I thought I would wait until Ben got back and say good-night to him." Lucy stared at her lap for a long moment, then asked, "Do you think Ben has changed since we were teenagers?"

"Yes, he's about two inches taller and twenty more pounds, all muscles. Well, he was before the coma, but his weight is returning. I've enjoyed working with him on his physical therapy. He didn't give me grief like Grady did at first."

"Grady's leg is so much better. He hardly limps anymore."

"That's because I insisted he do his therapy. Men can be so stubborn at times."

"I'm glad to hear Ben is cooperating with you."

"The old Ben might not have. He never took many things seriously. But he does now."

Yes, she'd noticed that, especially his son, but would it last? As a police officer she'd seen many people confess to be changed, but the first trouble they got into they reverted to their old ways.

"What's wrong?"

Lucy shook her head. "Just thinking back to when we were teenagers. I realized I had a crush on Ben in high school for a time, then he broke a friend's heart when he stopped dating her."

"Linda?"

"Yes. Within days he was dating another girl, who lasted about two months."

"And this is an issue, why?"

Lucy shrugged. "I care about him. In fact, my feelings concerning him scare me."

"You just care? That's all?"

"We're friends. Scratch that. We're more, but I can't go through another bad relationship. I thought I knew Jesse so well, and I didn't. Before we started seeing each other, Jesse had been a womanizer who convinced me he wasn't that person anymore."

"Like Ben?"

Lucy nodded. "How can I ever really trust him?"

"Good question, and I don't have an answer."

"How did you with Grady? Your ex was a cad."

"I prayed and turned it over to the Lord because I think it's impossible to know everything about a person. You have to decide what you want in life and how much you'll risk to have it."

Male voices coming from the kitchen drew Lucy's gaze to the window. "Grady and Ben are back."

"If you need to talk, I'm always here," Chloe said hurriedly as the back door opened and the men joined them. She glanced up at Grady and held her hand out. "You're just in time to help me up from this chair. I'm ready for bed. Mamie has the right idea."

Grady tugged Chloe to her feet. "Sounds good to me. Good night, Lucy, Ben."

Ben slipped in the chair beside Lucy. "Now I'm positive everything has been taken care of. Tomorrow will be a day of rest, one I need."

"I'm with you on that. This week has been long and difficult. But other than those two girls saying something to Maddy, I didn't hear anyone talking about Gareth and Winston. Did you?"

"No, but then children were around and some people might get riled and cause a scene. So glad they didn't." Ben leaned his head against the back cushion and stared at the ceiling.

"I have only one more thing to do involving this case. Find Betsy. You said something about the Dallas/Fort Worth area."

"Yeah, the private detective I hired is running down some leads. He established she was there last fall, but she isn't in the apartment he had an address for."

"Next week I can try again to see what I can discover. I was spread so thin that I really didn't have the time to put much effort into the search. I'll feel better at least contacting her and making sure she's all right." She needed to go, but once she sat down she didn't want to get up; it was as though weariness glued her to the seat.

"I'll be talking with the private investigator in the next day or two, and when he's got a solid lead, I'm going to the Dallas/Fort Worth area and assist in the search. I won't feel right until this is resolved. We didn't do right by her. I'm hoping Betsy will come back to Little Horn."

"With Byron here? I'm not sure she will."

"Maybe Byron will learn from this and change. Maddy is going over there for dinner tomorrow after the Easter service. I never thought that would happen."

"Do you think he can change?"

"I don't know. Time will tell, but I think he got scared when Gareth took the sleeping pills. Maybe it'll be enough for Byron to see his high-handedness was driving his sons away from him."

"Yeah, but you know the old saying you can lead a horse to water, but you can't make him drink it."

"With anything, the motivation has to be there for it to truly work. We still need to go out and celebrate the case being solved. How about Monday night before your parents come into town?"

"A date?" She needed him to clarify what he thought this relationship between them was. Friends? More?

"It's time for us to admit what's going on between us isn't just being friends. At least for me." He scooted his chair around so he could see her and clasped her hands. "I love you, Lucy. When you were trying to fix me up with other ladies in town, no one interested me but you. You are who I need."

He loves me. Is it really love? Panic raced through her, and she tugged her hands free and rose, sidling away. "Do you know what love is? You spent most of your life avoiding it. Now you want a mother for Cody and you see how much I care about your son, but marriage is so much more than that."

He pushed to his feet. "I know marriage is."

"I worked hard to become sheriff, and I don't want to give it up." Lucy backed away. "I like helping the people of this county."

"I know how hard you work, and I haven't asked you to quit your job. I'm not even talking about marriage. I'm talking about loving you."

"I've always been here. Why now all of a sudden?" She wouldn't risk her heart again. Jesse had been a reformed playboy who talked a good game, then cheated on her. "This has come out of the blue." She spun around and started for the back door to grab her purse and leave before she gave in and believed he could change that much.

He followed.

She held up her hand. "I can let myself out. In fact, I prefer to."

After yanking the door open, she fled inside, relieved that he didn't come in with her. As she headed toward her Mustang, she realized she'd thrown every excuse at him but the one that frightened her enough to walk away from a man she was falling in love with when she knew she shouldn't. She wanted a total commitment from the man, and she didn't think Ben could change that much.

Chapter Thirteen

Ben sat at the kitchen table, sipping his coffee. He hadn't slept more than an hour last night after talking with Lucy. Maybe he deserved her rejection. How many times had he walked away when a woman started getting serious?

He lifted his mug in a toast. "Touché."

"Who are you talking to?" Grandma Mamie asked as she came into the kitchen and looked around. Her forehead's wrinkles deepened. "No one?" She picked up the coffeepot. "It's empty. How long have you been up?"

"A few hours. I finally got tired of staring at the ceiling in my bedroom and came down here."

Mamie shot him a quizzical look, then went to work preparing another pot full of coffee. While it was brewing, she moved to the table and sat across from Ben. "So what had you up all night? Lucy?"

"How did you know?"

"It's your hangdog look. What happened after I went to bed?"

"I told her I loved her, and she got out of here so fast you would think a wildfire was after her."

In spite of the seriousness, Mamie grinned. "That doesn't sound like our sheriff. I know she has feelings for you. Anyone who sees you two together sees it."

"Well, tell her that. She didn't get the memo."

"Tell me what you said and her reply."

As though he had the scene from the night before memorized, he repeated all the reasons she gave him that it wouldn't work between them.

Mamie held up her forefinger. "Number one, you did spend your youth running from any kind of commitment."

"Okay, I admit I did. I knew I wouldn't be a good husband, not while I held such anger toward Dad in my heart. But that doesn't mean I can't change my mind."

"Okay, let's say you've changed. How can she be sure?"

"Because I've never given my word and not meant it. When I dated those women, they knew up front I wasn't looking for a long-term relationship."

"Two, what about her job? How do you feel about a wife working?"

"That's why I'm looking for a nanny. I recognize we need help here with Cody, and Chloe's baby due in a couple of months. And I have already set up something for the summer."

"But Maddy will go back to school in the fall. I wish I could do it all," Mamie said with a sigh, "but I know my limits. I'm seventy-eight and don't have the energy I used to when you boys were growing up."

"I know. Lucy is good at her job. If she wants to work, I don't want to stand in her way. All that would cause would be resentment."

"Like your mother toward my son."

"Let's face it, that was why she left. She wanted more than being a mother and wife."

"Did you bother talking it out with Lucy? There are solutions. I helped raised y'all, and we could hire a good nanny for Cody and Chloe's child. It's not as if we wouldn't be around to make sure the nanny does a good job. What's nice about your job is you can be flexible. Lucy as sheriff wouldn't be able to as much as you. Her hours can be unconventional. That might be what concerns her. I think there's more to it, though, than her job."

"What?"

"Could it have to do with why she came back to town three years ago? I know from her mother she'd been dating someone seriously, then suddenly it was over and Lucy left the San Antonio Police Department."

"She told me about the guy she dated for a year. At the time they were talking marriage, he was seeing two other women."

Grandma Mamie pressed her lips together into a hard, thin line. "That can definitely make a person gunshy. Did she tell you she didn't love you? Was that one of the reasons?"

Ben thought back to the conversation, remembering an almost scared expression on Lucy's face, and shook his head. "You're right. That might be it. Maybe it wouldn't work in the long run if she sees that other guy every time she sees me. Look at how long I've been dealing with my relationship with Dad. He influenced me a lot in my youth."

"He was an unhappy man that took his anger out on the ones he loved. It's not right, but unlike the McKay twins, who let their feelings toward their father cause them to make some bad decisions, we have to make the best of what's given to us. Talk to Lucy. What do you have to lose? You have a lot to gain if you love her."

"Thanks for helping me. You are a wise woman." Ben walked to the counter, refilled his mug and poured coffee for his grandmother, then returned to the table and gave it to her. "I'm going riding. I have some decisions to make and this is a good time to work some things out. It's quiet and nothing beats a sunrise around here."

Ben kissed Mamie's cheek, then left out the back door, nursing his coffee as he ambled toward the barn. He spied Thunder in a paddock close by, his black coat shining in the sun as the rays spread outward from the horizon. Pausing, he rotated slowly, taking in his ranch. What if he was wrong and he hadn't changed enough for Lucy? He only wanted to be married once.

Lucy hung up the phone after talking with the DA about the Robin Hoods case, pleased everyone was on board with the boys being tried in juvenile court. She liked Judge Nelson. He could be reasonable and creative. Gareth and Winston would pay for their crimes but at the same time get help. And she might not have considered the teenage boys' side of what had happened if it hadn't been for Ben.

When he'd said he loved her on Saturday night, she'd been stunned because she remembered once right after graduation Ben declaring he would never marry. It was too restrictive. He'd been adamant, citing what had happened to his parents' marriage. His mother had come back for graduation, then left immediately, and Lucy wondered if that was the reason for his statement.

That was ten years ago.

She'd changed in that time. Had Ben changed enough?

A movement in the main part of the sheriff's station drew her attention. Her dad was here and talking to the dispatcher. One of her deputies came in and joined their conversation.

Her parents had arrived the night before. And she needed their distraction, or all she would think about was Ben. The days since she had seen him at church on Easter had been the longest ones. She'd even caught herself earlier before her parents showed up wanting to call Ben or go out to see him at the Stillwater Ranch, but when she finally had called and Chloe answered, she'd discovered Ben had left that morning and would be gone all day. Chloe hadn't been sure when he would be coming back.

Was he leaving for good? She didn't think so because Little Horn had always been his home, but she couldn't shake the doubt completely away.

Her dad stuck his head through the opened doorway. "Ready to go to lunch at Maggie's? I sure miss her good food."

"Is Mom coming?"

"Nope, she's visiting with some friends, then stopping by Olivia Barlow's ranch. She was so happy to see Olivia has a man in her life now. You know how your mother frets over others in need, and Olivia certainly had been in need with her triplet boys."

"Clint Daniels will make a wonderful father for those boys." Lucy rose and headed out of the sheriff's station with her father. "I forgot to eat breakfast again, so I'm hungry."

"Good. Alice noticed that this morning and made me promise to make sure you ate a big lunch. I told her not to worry. You're doing just fine but that won't stop her. According to her, she won't stop worrying about you until she's dead."

"A mother's job is never done."

"And neither is a father's." Her dad pulled open the door to Maggie's and gestured for Lucy to go first.

After Abigail showed them to a table and took their orders, Lucy decided to approach the subject of the Robin Hoods case with her dad before he brought it up. "As I'm sure you know, the cattle rustlers were finally caught last week."

"Yes, a good job at tracking down the evidences."

"But it took me months to solve the case."

"That happens sometimes. Cattle rustlers can be hard to catch. Often they work in an area, then move on before they are caught. In the twins' case their robberies had to do with settling a score in their minds, not making money."

"I heard this morning Byron has started paying back the ranchers who the boys stole from. Carson came by the station this morning and told me after Byron paid him a visit with Gareth and Winston."

"The twins won't have to be responsible for paying it back?"

"What was so surprising about the visit is Carson said that Byron will require his sons to pay him back every cent, but he wanted the ranchers paid immediately."

Her dad grinned. "Well, I'll be. Never thought I would see something like that. He usually won't admit he's wrong."

"I don't know if he's done that, but when Gareth took the sleeping pills, I think Byron realized going around town insisting his sons were innocent wasn't going to work because they were insisting the opposite."

Abigail put their lunches before them, topped off their coffee, then left as more customers kept coming into the café.

After he said a blessing, her dad sipped his drink. "Some things don't change. Maggie makes the best cup of coffee in this part of Texas."

"So who have you seen already this morning?" Lucy asked, then took a bite of her hamburger.

"I went over to pay Iva a visit. I hated to hear her health was failing, but she seemed to be in great spirits."

"Ruby's grandmother is like Ben's. Wise with a lot of gumption."

Her father chuckled. "So true. And I'm glad we're going to the Stillwater Ranch tomorrow night for dinner because I want to make sure I see Mamie, too, while I'm here."

"I might not go."

He put his fork down and peered at Lucy. "Why not? She called your mom this morning and said the invitation was for all of us."

"I know. I forgot to tell you all last night."

"That's not like you. I was good friends with her son and she is one I always see when I visit."

Lucy stared at her half-eaten hamburger, no longer hungry. Her stomach clenched like a fist at the thought of going and Ben not being there.

"Are the rumors true about you and Ben seeing each other?"

Lucy yanked her head up. "Who told you that?" She hadn't said anything to her parents about the time she and Ben had been together the past month because she didn't know what to make of it. Her mother would have her married off to him before she got off the phone because she wanted grandchildren.

"Iva. Then when I asked Carson, he told me y'all had been working on the Robin Hoods case together as well as the annual Easter-egg hunt. He implied something was going on."

One look at her father and Lucy did what she always had done growing up—confided in him. "Yes. It didn't start out that way. We just began spending more and more time together. What do you think of Ben?"

"My opinion isn't the important one."

Lucy told her dad about Ben's son and how he was trying to change. "He takes his father role very seriously, which has surprised me."

"Why? He's always cared about others, sometimes when other people didn't."

She thought of Ben with Gareth and even Winston, especially when some of the townsfolk had wanted to railroad the twins.

"I know Ben's daddy wasn't the best example, but there was a time when he wasn't so angry at the world before his back injury and his wife leaving him. Some get stronger under ordeals, but Ben's father wasn't one of them. He even tested my friendship at times."

"I've seen people say they are changing, but they never do. Do you think Ben could? He said when he came out of the coma he knew he couldn't continue going through life like he was."

"And you don't believe him, or is it something else?"

"I don't know. He told me the other night he loved me, but I've always thought Ben didn't want to be in a long-term relationship. When growing up, he certainly avoided them. He might have the record for dating the most women in the county."

"Nope. I did. Before I met your mom, I didn't want to get married. I thought the worst thing that could happen to me was to be tied down. But that all changed when your mom came along." He patted her hand between them. "So tell me the real reason you don't want to fall in love."

As her father said the last sentence, Lucy realized she'd already fallen in love with Ben. Every time she'd seen him with Cody her feelings had deepened, but when they kissed, he'd sealed it. She twisted her napkin in her lap, balling it in her fist. "I'm afraid to believe he's changed. I can't risk going through the same thing that happened with Jesse. When I first met Jesse a year before we started dating, he always had a different woman on his arm. He loved flirting. As we were getting serious, I believed him when he told me I was the only one for him. Before he'd just been looking for something casual, but now he knew what he wanted— me. Later I discovered he'd been lying to me even then. I felt like such a fool. It got to the point I didn't want to stay and get all those pitying looks."

"I'm glad you came home, and I'm figuring Ben is, too. Why do you take risks in your job but can't in your personal life?"

"It's different."

"How?"

"I won't get hurt as much."

"I remember when you got beat up taking a chance on the job. I have a feeling that hurt quite a bit."

"Not the same."

"Isn't it? Remember what God said about waiting for

perfect conditions? Nothing will get done. That's not you. You are a doer. I hope you'll reconsider going to the Stillwater Ranch tomorrow evening."

She couldn't get what her father said to her at lunch out of her mind the rest of the day. It wasn't like her not to face a problem head-on and deal with it. She would go tomorrow evening and hope that Ben was there. They needed to talk.

Ben slanted a glance at Betsy sitting in the front seat of his truck. After going to a short list of places the private investigator had given him in the Dallas/Fort Worth area, he'd finally found her at a church's day care. He might have messed up his chance with Lucy, but at least he'd been able to find Betsy. He'd hated being away from Little Horn and Cody, even for a short time, but it had been worth it when he'd seen the surprise on Betsy's face when she spied him.

"We're almost to Little Horn," Ben said as he passed the welcome sign, remembering his time with Lucy beautifying the bed around the sign. He didn't want it to be over with them. Would he be able to convince her he was a changed man?

"Do you think my cousin will let me see Gareth and Winston?" Betsy swung her attention to Ben, her long ponytail swishing around.

Her hair reminded Ben of Byron's strawberry blond, but that was where the similarity ended with her cousin. When Ben had approached Betsy yesterday at the church where she worked in the day care, he'd spent time watching the eighteen-year-old with the children and made a decision right then and there. "Gareth likes Maddy, and Byron invited her to dinner after church last Sunday. Maddy told me it went well, so yes, I think Byron will let you see the twins." He hoped. But if Byron didn't, he and his family would be there for Betsy.

"Maddy had a crush on Gareth before I left Little Horn. I'm sure this whole situation has been very upsetting to her."

"If you're going to take care of my son, I'd like you to stay at my ranch. We have a big house. But you don't have to. I thought that would help you save some money for your college tuition. I'm still going to see if the Lone Star Cowboy League can give you a scholarship like Tyler had. We can always use good teachers at our school." He was going to make it a priority to start a scholarship fund to go to one youth each year, maybe even talk Byron into helping.

"I've loved working with the kids. Cody sounds adorable."

"He is. He took his first few steps over the weekend, so it won't be long before he's all over the house." Ben turned into the gate at the Stillwater Ranch. "No one knows where I went. I wanted to surprise everyone."

"I never thought anyone in town would be looking for me. My cousin didn't make me feel welcomed at his ranch nor in Little Horn. I had to put distance between us. Six months ago I couldn't have returned. It was too painful."

"Byron is only one person. A lot of people were concerned where you disappeared to." Ben parked next to a SUV, probably Lucy's parents'.

Would she be here, too? He hoped so. They needed to talk. Saturday he hadn't made himself clear. His old life held no appeal to him.

"Ready, Betsy?"

"Who's here?" She pointed toward the SUV.

"The Bensons. They are back for a month and staying with Lucy."

"Is she here, too?"

"I don't know. She was invited, but her job can interfere with her plans." But more likely, the reason would be that he'd told her he loved her.

Betsy carried a duffel bag toward the front porch while Ben grabbed her two pieces of luggage where she packed all her worldly possessions. When he opened the door, the sound of voices came from the living room. He put her suitcases down and gestured her to stay until he went inside.

The first and really only person he saw when he stepped through the entrance was Lucy. Her eyes lit up, and she smiled.

"Where have you been? I was getting worried," Grandma Mamie said, pulling his attention to her.

"I went to the Dallas/Fort Worth area and came back with a surprise. I have it with me now."

Betsy came into the room and stood next to him. "Ben convinced me to return to Little Horn." Her gaze took in the grinning faces but stopped at Maddy's. Tears filled both girls' eyes.

Maddy leaped to her feet and hugged Betsy, both of them now crying. "Thank You, Lord, for bringing Betsy home."

Again drawn to Lucy, Ben looked at her and her eyes were glistening, too, as well as her mom's, Chloe's and Mamie's. There was a spot next to Lucy on the couch, and he took the seat.

She turned toward him. "You found her. Things are definitely looking up. Is she staying?"

"Yep. I gave her a job. She's going to be Cody's new nanny. She belongs here."

"What about Byron?"

"She's family. It's his loss if he doesn't acknowledge that. With the twins probably going to the juvenile detention facility in Austin soon, Betsy and his wife will be all the family he has here." Ben scanned the people in his living room. At the moment Lucy's mother held Cody, but he wiggled, ready to be put down.

Lucy's mother set him on the floor by her feet. Cody crawled to Ben, then pulled himself up to stand next to his legs with his arms raised up.

Ben bent forward and gathered his son into his arms. "Did you miss me, little man?"

Cody reached out, grabbing for Ben's face while jabbering.

"I think he did," Lucy said.

The question Ben really wanted to ask was "Did you miss me, Lucy?" But he would have to bide his time.

Lucy put the last plate in the dishwasher and closed the lid. "Finally we're done."

"You didn't have to help me. You're a guest." Chloe wiped down the counter by the sink. "But I'm glad you did. You've been awfully quiet tonight. Something bothering you? Perhaps connected to Ben? At church on Sunday you two didn't even talk."

"He told me he loved me Saturday night."

"And what did you say?"

"I panicked. I've been under fire before and when he said the L word all I could think about were the reasons he didn't really."

One of Chloe's eyebrows arched. "Oh, and why do you think that?"

"In the past, when has Ben ever been serious about a woman?"

"Never, but there is always a first time." Chloe lounged against the counter, studying Lucy. "You two talked a little earlier."

"Only pleasantries."

"What do you want?"

"I need to make him understand about why I reacted like I did. When we departed on Saturday, Ben was clearly upset."

"That's because I've never told a woman I loved her except my mom and grandmother." Ben leaned against the doorjamb, his arms folded over his chest.

"I think that's my cue to leave." Chloe hurried around Ben and left them alone.

Silence electrified the air.

Ben shoved away from the door, closed it and crossed to Lucy. "So why did you react as if I asked you to drink a vial of poison?"

"You took me by surprise."

"When I said I loved you?"

She nodded, her throat jammed with emotions she'd been wrestling with for the past few days.

"I meant what I said. It wasn't a spur-of-the-moment thing. I've never felt like this before. I've certainly never been in love."

"Are you sure? Maybe what you're feeling is gratitude?"

"For what? Nope. While I was looking for Betsy, all I thought about was you. Somehow I had to make you understand I'm not going back to the man I was. I want to spend the rest of my life with you, but I'll go as slow as you want. If I have to prove to you I mean what I say, I will. One day I'll wear you down."

"I told you about Jesse dating two other women when we were supposed to be exclusive. What I didn't say was that he'd had a reputation for being a ladies' man, and I believed him when he told me he wasn't that guy any longer. That I was the one for him. The only one."

Ben closed the space between them. "And you were afraid I would be just like him?"

"You used to be like that. You dated a woman for a while, then moved on, never really committing to a relationship."

"The key words are *used to be*. God gave me a wake-up call, and I listened. In all the years you've known me, have I ever gone back on my word?"

"No." His nearness revved her heartbeat, making her mouth go dry.

He pulled her against him and locked his hands behind her back. "I don't ever want to let you go. I want to marry you, and *when* we do, you'll decide what you want to do as far as your job. I'll be here to support your decision. That's why I went to find Betsy. Maddy reminded me she used to babysit for extra money and loved working with children. I wanted to give her a good reason to return to Little Horn. She's going to work and go to the nearby community college in the evening."

She remembered what her father had said about taking a risk. She'd never been a coward before, and she wasn't going to start now. She wound her arms around him. "I love you, Ben. But even more than that. I trust you."

Ben smiled and bent his head toward hers. When he kissed her, she knew she'd made the right decision. Every part of her responded to him as though he was the only other person in the world—and he was for her.

Epilogue

After the wedding party's photos were taken in the church, Lucy entered her reception in the hall with her husband next to her. Dressed in her mother's gown of beaded satin, she had never felt as feminine as she did right now.

Ben paused in the entrance, squeezing her hand. "I didn't realize so many people were here."

"It looks like the whole town."

"You are the sheriff."

When he smiled at her, it warmed her from head to toe. "And you are the president of the Lone Star Cowboy League."

"Never thought I would do something like that, but with Carson gone a lot for his job with the state, it makes sense."

"Just so long as Byron didn't get the position. I'd much prefer working with you in the future." Lucy searched the huge crowd in the large church hall and saw the man under discussion. "He's mellowed some in six months."

"Yeah, wonders never cease. He even told Betsy she

could go with him and his wife to see Gareth and Winston next weekend at the juvenile detention center. Are you ready to mingle with our guests, Mrs. Stillwater?"

Goose bumps raced up her arms when he said her new name. "I see Grady waving to us."

As Ben threaded his way through the townspeople, Amelia snagged Lucy's attention. When she neared her friend, Amelia hugged her and whispered, "I'm thrilled for you. You seemed to float down the aisle."

Lucy laughed. "I hardly remember walking into church, let alone down the aisle. Everyone was a blur except Ben."

"I know what you mean. I was so glad Finn and I had a lot of pictures taken to recall what happened at my own wedding."

When they continued their way through the crowd, guests kept delaying Ben and her. By the time they reached Grady and Chloe, Cody had fallen asleep in his uncle's arms.

"I tried to keep him up until you got here, but he's worn-out. Our Emma conked out halfway through the wedding, according to Grandma. Betsy is going to drive them back to the ranch and put them down for the night. Maddy is going with her to help. Since you two are leaving on your honeymoon after the reception, I thought you might want to say good-night to Cody."

Ben took Cody and nestled him in the crook of his arm. "I'll carry him to the car."

Lucy kissed the little boy's forehead. "I know we'll only be gone a week, but I'm going to miss him and Emma."

"And when you get back, I'll be having my grand opening of the physical therapy clinic." Chloe beamed, her gaze trapped by Grady's. "I'm waiting until you all are back. Without Grady's and Ben's help, the clinic wouldn't have been possible."

"We know firsthand how good you are as a physical therapist," Ben said, Chloe's second-biggest champion, having completely regained his mobility from the mild stroke caused by his head injury.

While Ben started for the exit, Grady pushed the stroller next to his brother. Grady said something to Ben, and they both laughed.

Carson and Ruby joined Lucy and Chloe. "I wasn't sure those two would ever mend their relationship."

Chloe turned toward the couple. "It's hard for them to stay mad at each other when Cody is like a big brother to his baby cousin and won't let anything bad happen to Emma."

Lucy saw Eva and waved at her. "Did you hear Eva and Tyler got a call about a baby up for adoption?"

"Yep. Once Mamie found out, it was probably all over Little Horn within twenty-four hours," Carson said with a laugh.

Ben returned, saw Clint and went to him. After he said something to Olivia's husband, who strode to the exit, Ben headed straight for Carson. "I thought I'd let you know Brandon and Olivia's triplets are in the big elm by the parking lot. I think one of the triplets is stuck up in the tree. Grady is trying to get them down. I told him I would find you and Clint."

In less than five minutes most of the wedding party and guests were outside, trying to figure out how to get Noah down from the very top of the elm. Grady had made it halfway up the tree but had to stop and try to coax him down with words. It wasn't working. Noah clung to the thin branch he had managed to perch himself on. Clint was under the elm, helping down Noah's two brothers, Levi and Caleb. Brandon was the last one to hop from the tree, Carson bear-hugging his nephew.

Lucy saw Olivia's face lose its color and quickly said to Ben, "Do you have your cell phone on you?"

"Yes." He drew it out of his pocket.

She called the volunteer fire department, and Larry promised to be right there with the hook and ladder truck. When she hung up, she looked at Ben.

"And that's why you're the sheriff. You know what to do in an emergency. I hope we don't have to rescue Grady, too."

Twenty minutes later, everyone, including Grady, was out of the elm, as sounds of the cheering crowd filled the air. The kids at the reception were swarming all over the hook and ladder while Larry showed them what it did.

As the crowd slowly headed back inside, Ben grabbed Lucy. "I love you, Mrs. Stillwater. You saved the day."

Blushing, she put her arms around his neck, tugged his head toward her and gave him a kiss that held all the emotions she felt toward this man. Six months ago she'd made the right choice that she knew she would never regret.

* * * * *

IF YOU ENJOYED THIS BOOK
WE THINK YOU WILL ALSO LOVE

LOVE INSPIRED
INSPIRATIONAL ROMANCE

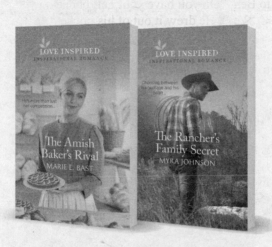

Uplifting stories of faith, forgiveness and hope.

Fall in love with stories where faith helps
guide you through life's challenges, and discover
the promise of a new beginning.

6 NEW BOOKS AVAILABLE EVERY MONTH!

*When Susannah Peachy returns to her grandfather's
potato farm to help out after her grandmother is injured,
she's not ready to face Peter Lambright—the Amish
bachelor who broke her heart. But she doesn't know his
true reason for ending things…and it could make all the
difference for their future.*

Read on for a sneak peek at
An Unexpected Amish Harvest *by Carrie Lighte.*

"Time to get back to work," Marshall ordered, and the other men pushed their chairs back and started filing out the door.

"But, *Groossdaadi*, Peter's not done with his pie yet," Susannah pointed out. "And that's practically the main course of this meal."

Marshall glowered, but as he put his hat on, he told Peter, "We'll be in the north field."

"I'll be right out," Peter said, shoveling another bite into his mouth and triggering a coughing spasm.

"Take your time," Lydia told him once Marshall exited the house. "Sweet things are meant to be savored."

Susannah was still seated beside him and Peter thought he noticed her shake her head at her stepgrandmother, but maybe he'd imagined it. "This does taste *gut*," he agreed.

"*Jah*. But it's not as gut as the pies your *mamm* used to make," Susannah commented. "I mean, I really appreciate that Almeda made pies for us. But your *mamm*'s were extraordinarily *appenditlich*. Especially her *blohbier* pies."

"*Jah*. I remember that time you traded me your entire lunch for a second piece of her pie." Peter hadn't considered what he was disclosing until Susannah knocked her knee against his beneath the table. It was too late. Lydia's ears had already perked up.

"When was that?" she asked.

"It was on a *Sunndaag* last summer when some of us went on a picnic after *kurrich*," Susannah immediately said. Which was true, although "some of us" really meant "the two of us." Peter and Susannah had never picnicked with anyone else when they were courting; Sundays had been the only chance they had to be alone. Dorcas, the only person they'd told about their courtship, had frequently dropped off Susannah at the gorge, where Peter would be waiting for her.

"Ah, that's right. You and Dorcas loved going out to the gorge on *Sunndaag*," Lydia recalled. "I didn't realize you'd gone with a group."

Susannah started coughing into her napkin. Or was she trying not to laugh? Peter couldn't tell. *How could I have been so* dumm *as to blurt out something like that?* he lamented.

After Lydia excused herself, Peter mumbled quietly to Susannah, "Sorry about that. It just slipped out."

"It's okay. Sometimes things spring to my mind, too, and I say them without really thinking them through."

It felt strange to be sitting side by side with her, with no one else on the other side of the table. No one else in the room. It reminded Peter of when they'd sit on a rock by the creek in the gorge, dangling their feet into the water and chatting as they ate their sandwiches. And instead of pushing the romantic memory from his mind, Peter deliberately indulged it, lingering over his pie even though he knew Marshall would have something to say about his delay when he returned to the fields.

Susannah didn't seem in any hurry to get up, either. She was silent while he whittled his pie down to the last two bites. Then she asked, "How is your *mamm*? At the frolic, someone mentioned she's been…under the weather."

I'm sure they did, Peter thought, and instantly the nostalgic connection he felt with Susannah was replaced by insecurity about whatever rumors she'd heard about his mother. Peter could bear it if Marshall thought ill of him, but he didn't want Susannah to think his mother was lazy. "She's okay," he said and abruptly stood up, even as he was scooping the last bite of pie into his mouth. "I'd better get going or your *groossdaddi* won't let me take any more lunch breaks after this."

He'd only been half joking about Marshall, but Susannah replied, "Don't worry. Lydia would never let that happen." Standing, she caught his eye and added, "And neither would I."

Peering into her earnest golden-brown eyes, Peter was overcome with affection. *"Denki,"* he said and then forced himself to leave the house while his legs could still carry him out to the fields.

Don't miss
An Unexpected Amish Harvest *by Carrie Lighte,*
available September 2021 wherever
Love Inspired books and ebooks are sold.

LoveInspired.com

LOVE INSPIRED

INSPIRATIONAL ROMANCE

UPLIFTING STORIES OF FAITH, FORGIVENESS AND HOPE.

———————

Join our social communities to connect with other readers who share your love!

Sign up for the Love Inspired newsletter at **LoveInspired.com** to be the first to find out about upcoming titles, special promotions and exclusive content.

———————

CONNECT WITH US AT:

f Facebook.com/LoveInspiredBooks

🐦 Twitter.com/LoveInspiredBks

Facebook.com/groups/HarlequinConnection

HARLEQUIN

Heartfelt or thrilling, passionate or uplifting—Harlequin is more than just happily-ever-after.

With twelve different series to choose from and new books available every month, you are sure to find stories that will move you, uplift you, inspire and delight you.

Get 4 FREE REWARDS!

We'll send you 2 FREE Books plus 2 FREE Mystery Gifts.

Love Inspired books feature uplifting stories where faith helps guide you through life's challenges and discover the promise of a new beginning.

FREE Value Over $20